WISH WRECKED

Cover: Sarah Penney

Editors: Kourtney Spak & Jessica Julien @ Desert Ink Editorial

Formatting: Jessica Julien @ Desert Ink Editorial

ISBNs: 979-8-9923453-0-8 (Paperback); 979-8-9923453-1-5 (eBook)

First edition 2025

For all the persevering and patient new authors who helped me realize that I can be the genie who makes my wishes come true.

CONTENTS

Chapter 1

DOT

Dot needed a win.

Her bad days were getting out of control lately, and today was proving to be especially crummy.

"You had to know this was coming."

And it was even a Friday.

"I can promise you, Howie, I didn't. I think we're great together!"

She tried to sound calm, not like she really felt—clawing desperately at the ground while slowly sliding over a cliff.

She and Howie were supposed to be together forever. He was supposed to be the person who would pull her from her dreary existence into a comfortable life of love and laughter.

Howie ran a hand through his sandy hair. He did not look convinced. "I can see how *you* might feel that way. Sometimes I feel like you're expecting me to pull you from your dreary existence into a comfortable life."

"Of love and laughter," Dot finished quietly.

"So you get it?"

"Not really."

She could see the frustration pooling behind his eyes. It was a familiar sight.

"It takes two to have a good life together. I'm the only one putting in the effort. I've had to nag you for months to get your passport so we can travel together, and you haven't even gotten your picture taken! That's the easy part!"

Dot looked down at her Pad Thai. "The lady at Walgreens looked busy. I didn't want to inconvenience her."

"It's her job, Dot."

She shoved a forkful of noodles into her mouth to keep from crying, noting how Howie still held his chopsticks perfectly even though he hadn't touched his food.

"I can't be responsible for both our happiness," he said, chopsticks waving through the air. "That's not how relationships work. You can't even stop eating to look at me when I talk. Even in the breakup, I'm doing all the work."

She swallowed. The noodles were sitting sourly in her stomach. Part of her considered fighting, but a bigger part of her wanted to run and hide. That was the part that usually won out. "I don't hold you responsible for my happiness," she said. "I just...sometimes I need a little push to get out of my comfort zone, you know? You're good at pushing me. I *need* you."

Howie dragged a hand down his face. "Do you even hear yourself?"

She frowned, not sure why that wasn't a good argument. He should be flattered.

"Do you even care about what *I* need?" he asked.

She squinted, searching her brain for a suitable answer. Was this a trick question? He was the most stable and successful person she knew. What could a boyishly handsome nurse anesthetist with a house and a cute dog named Barney possibly need? He had it all.

Her stomach churned. It wasn't a trick question. She had none of those things. She relied on him for everything. If he did need anything, she knew she had almost nothing to offer.

"Love?" she said, flicking her eyes to his face, then back to her plate. "You need love. And I...love you."

"Listen, I know you've had it rough," he said, ignoring her declaration. "But that's not unique to you. You've always used your bad luck as an excuse for your lack of trying. And I'm over it. I'm sorry."

She closed her eyes. That was it. Love was her last card. She had nothing left to play.

The battle was over. The end had come.

"...we have some happy memories to take away from our time together, at least..."

Why was she surprised? Okay, she wasn't *that* surprised.

"...and I really do wish you the best. With everything."

Par for the course, really. She was lucky he stayed around as long as he did.

"Hello? Are you even listening?"

She stared at the wall behind him, disassociating to save herself. There was a pretty drawing of the Great Wall of China, even though the restaurant was called *Thai Noodle House II.*

Howie sighed. "I'm...gonna go. I've said what I needed to. Take care. I really do mean that."

Then, he got up and left. Dot slumped back in the booth.

She braced herself for the tears, but none came. She was dejected and upset, sure. But at the moment, those feelings were no match for the cloak of numbness she used to protect herself from the more unpleasant emotions. Her eyes remained fixed on the drawing on the wall for a few more seconds, then she turned back to her noodles. After a moment, she flagged down someone to bring her a box for Howie's uneaten meal. It was already paid for, and she wasn't about to leave free food behind.

The numbness of the breakup lasted a few days. Dot was in between jobs (again) so there wasn't anyone to get angry at her for wasting away the hours rewatching her comfort movies of choice (all eight Harry Potter films) or eating only microwave mac 'n' cheese (when she remembered to eat). There was still time until her landlord came asking about the rent. She'd have nothing to give him, but he'd take pity on her. Hopefully. Maybe.

The tears came eventually, too. They always did, like an annoying relative who wouldn't tell you *when* they were coming, just that they were coming. Then they'd show up in the middle of the night, expecting immediate accommodation. Or, in Dot's case, a Tuesday morning, where they were set into motion by a film that autoplayed on whatever streaming service she had left on. It was about a family torn apart by a tsunami who then found each other in the end against all odds.

A tsunami would have been an easier end to her relationship. Then at least she would know exactly what to blame and why.

Once the tears started, they didn't seem to stop. Her eyes became perpetually puffy, and her nose perpetually leaky. This was her state when her landlord arrived to collect her rent a few days after it was due.

"Holy..." Jorge said when she opened the door. The thin, balding man wrinkled his gray mustache as he took in the mess before him. Along with her feelings and mental welfare, Dot had also become indifferent to both hygiene and cleanliness over the past few weeks. Jorge's stupefied expression made her realize the depth of her decline. Empty mac 'n' cheese containers and tissues littered the floor. Soiled dishes covered the coffee table. Dirty clothes had accumulated in discarded piles as far as the eye could see, which, to be fair, was not far. She lived in a single-wide, after all.

In the middle of it all stood Dot, wrapped in a plush blanket.

"Howie broke up with me," she said, her voice raspy.

Jorge's face fell. "Oh, no. I thought he was really good for you."

"Me too." More tears. Jorge's eyes darted nervously around the room.

"Hey, you paid on time last month, so I'll give you a break today. But next month you will have to pay double the normal amount, do you understand?" He spoke slowly and gently, like she was an upset child and he was explaining that he wasn't going to make her clean her room today.

She blew her nose on her blanket. "Thank you, Jorge."

Jorge was probably too soft to be a landlord. His wife Yasmin, however, was going to have a fit when he came home without the rent. But that was a problem for future Dot. Most problems were.

"You might want to clean up a little, though," he said. "In case Yasmin wants to stop by. I'll tell her you're having a bad time, but you know how she is."

"Okay." Dot sniffled.

He nodded and gave her one last worried glance, then backed out the door, clearly anxious to get away. She didn't blame him, but she also didn't want him to linger.

The next morning—well, a quarter past noon—Dot woke to pounding on her front door.

She already knew who had come knocking.

Yasmin.

Dot peeled herself from her bed, cringing when she caught a whiff of her stale body odor, and slowly plodded to the front door. The blanket around her shoulders dragged behind her, stirring up the collection of discarded trash that lay in her path.

"*Hijole*!" Yasmin said when she laid eyes on her tenant. The stout woman carried a big black trash bag and wore rubber cleaning gloves. Her black hair, sprinkled with a few gray strands, was tied back with a bandana. Her disgusted grimace became more defined when she looked into the house. With palpable agitation, she pushed past Dot and shook out her bag, shoving handfuls of anything within reach inside.

"What are you doing?" Dot asked with very little feeling.

Yasmin stopped her purging to glower. "What does it look like, *chica*? I am cleaning up. You didn't pay your rent this month, so I can do whatever I want."

Dot wondered if she should argue with the woman, but seeing her clean up the overwhelming mess triggered a spark of relief.

"Okay." She turned back towards her room.

"Oh, no! You are not going back to bed. You are bringing me your laundry and then taking a shower."

Dot sighed drearily. Couldn't Yasmin do her thing while she laid in bed and watched old sitcoms on her phone? But Yasmin could get mean, and so far she hadn't pressed for the rent. The idea of doing anything exhausted her, but she decided it would be best to obey the fiery little woman.

She was overdue for a shower anyway.

In the bathroom, Dot stared at her reflection, trying to make sense of what she was seeing. Sure, she had showered a time or two since the breakup, but that had been during her numb phase. During those first few days, nothing had sunk in yet. She then entered a phase of deep depression, constantly crying and deliberately avoiding mirrors, knowing she wouldn't like what she saw.

She should have waited to look until after the shower.

Her long, dirty (both in color and in condition) blonde hair sat in a lopsided tangle on top of her head; a few greasy tendrils hung around her face. Dead blue eyes, underlined by dark circles, stared back at her. Her lips were chewed and raw, and her cheeks had sunken in a bit, certainly not as rosy as they had once been.

The unrecognizable image in the bathroom mirror rattled her. It wasn't like she was expecting to see a stone-cold fox—that had never been her—but she had always found her appearance pleasantly unassuming. What she saw was neither pleasant nor unassuming. She smoothed her eyebrows down.

The person staring back at her was not cute.

As she stood under the hot shower, shaving her fuzzy legs and washing the week of grime from her hair, she decided it was time to move forward.

Yasmin yelled through the door that she would be back soon with groceries, and Dot wondered if she heard her correctly. This was a side of the woman she had never experienced. Yasmin had only ever been the bad cop to Jorge's pushover cop; a mean, hardened, typically dislikable landlady. Why was she suddenly being so...nice-ish? The woman's concern was concerning.

A little while later, Dot's reflection had improved greatly, though it still had a long way to go before she looked like herself. Truthfully, she'd been trying to look like herself for years now, whatever that was. She'd know it when she saw it.

Dressed in actual clothes (all her pajamas were in the laundry) she shuffled into her newly cleaned living room and dropped onto her saggy couch. The single-wide only had four rooms—bedroom, bathroom, and kitchen being the other three—so she didn't have to shuffle far, and Yasmin didn't have too great a space to clean.

Yasmin had already swept the linoleum floor, vacuumed the ragged rugs, and drawn the dusty blinds. She even lit a Cucumber Melon candle that had been gathering dust on the end table for years. Amazing how a little polishing could make such a difference in a room and a person. And less clutter seemed to allow for productive thinking for the first time in months, like how maybe she should seriously look for a job.

A month earlier, she had quit her first waitressing job. It hadn't taken her long to decide that she didn't have the brain for juggling as much information as some of the more seasoned members of the wait staff. It was like they were *trying* to make her look bad by not carrying around a notepad. On top of that, she always ended up with the most demanding, impatient customers, which seemed unfair, especially for someone who had hit their limit for unfairness long ago.

Howie didn't like her working there anyway, so she took her time looking for another job more worthy of him and his desires for her, which could be pretty lofty at times. It's possible she had used that as a personal excuse for not looking as hard. She could get by for a little while with having a boyfriend who paid for anything she asked him to. Now that she thought about it, that definitely could have been a factor in the whole being dumped situation.

Obviously, things had changed.

She had considered interviewing at Target before Howie had implored her to set her sights higher. Now that she didn't have to worry about that, Target sounded great. Maybe she could work in the back unloading trucks so she wouldn't have to talk to people.

Yasmin entered, carrying several bags of groceries, as Dot filled out the online application on her phone.

"*Gracias a Dios*, you're clean!" she said, hefting the bags towards the kitchen. "Come help me put these away."

Dot obeyed, following Yasmin through the kitchen doorway. Silently, the two of them emptied the bags. With each item Dot put away, she became more aware of what she was seeing, and her face twisted in confusion. Fruits and vegetables, chicken breasts and rice—these were things she hadn't bought in months. But what had she expected Yasmin to buy? For some reason, not this. Not healthy, quality food that cost more than the generic brands.

"Why…" she choked. She had hoped the crying days were behind her, but the clean cupboards and empty sink along with this *actual* food stocking her bare refrigerator—all thanks to the meanest person she knew—overloaded her emotions and her eyes flooded with tears.

Yasmin sighed heavily. She stood half a foot shorter than Dot—who was average height—but she carried herself like a Mexican wrestler: angry and confident, disdain for everything in her path. Just having Yasmin's eyes directly on her freaked Dot out.

But the landlady didn't yell, or rip into her with criticism or accusations, or pile-drive her. She only stared, frowning.

"You are a frustrating tenant," she finally said. "I tried to convince Jorge to evict you once, and I would have tried again, but when he told me what he saw here yesterday...I am not good at saying '*oh, I'm so sorry you got dumped,*' but I am good at getting things done. You're not. So, I'll help you get some things done, but next month you're on your own. You get a job, pay your rent, and clean your house or you're out! Do you understand?"

Dot wiped her face on her sleeve and nodded with a whimper.

The landlady returned the nod, turning back to the groceries. "In all my years, I have never met a person as miserable as you. It's about time you do something about that, *chica*."

Chapter 2

DOT

The universe was making Dot suspicious.

The landlady-to-the-rescue incident was nice, yes, and unexpected. And let's not forget appreciated. But that didn't mean Dot assumed she had a new best friend. Or even that Yasmin had chilled out as a person, or that life in general would be easy from here on out. She knew her landlady enough to classify her random act of kindness as just that: random. And she knew life enough to know that for every positive, a negative wasn't far behind. Nothing good could exist without something bad coming along to overshadow it. At least not in her experience.

After securing an interview at Target with disturbing ease *and* finding that the cost had gone down on her anxiety meds, she was on edge. Consecutive fortunate occurrences. Ominous indeed. Something really bad must be on the horizon. Maybe something worse than being abruptly kicked out of the most stable relationship of her life.

There had been times before when she had erroneously concluded that she had reached rock bottom, but now, after twenty-five years of raw life experience, she knew the hole could always go deeper.

Three days into the "Move Forward" phase of her break-up, she headed to her interview at Target, knowing that if it went well, it might just put her more on edge.

"So you've lived in Tallahassee your whole life? Me too. Where in the city did you grow up?"

To Dot, the worst part about getting a job was the interview. It was especially awful if the interviewer tried to make small talk. But she couldn't deny she needed this. And despite her stalky build and subtle mullet, Mary, the interviewer, was surprisingly friendly. That was a good sign.

"Um...Fuller Park."

Mary frowned. "I thought that was a retirement community?"

Dot tried not to squirm in her seat. She hated explaining this to people.

"It is. My grandma raised me. She got special permission for me to live there."

"Wow. That must have been an interesting childhood."

"Yeah." Dot did not love delving into her personal history with anyone. A potential employer least of all.

"Does your grandma still live there?"

Now the squirming was becoming more difficult to suppress. "Uh...no." She laughed nervously. *Why did you laugh?* "She died during the pandemic."

Mary sighed sympathetically as her shoulders dropped. "From Covid?"

Dot nodded.

"I'm so sorry to hear that."

Even though she had mourned plenty over the four years since her grandma's death, she still felt a slight sting at the corners of her eyes. These reactions tended to be involuntary sometimes, unfortunately. She stared unblinkingly at Mary until the sensation passed, hoping that her eyes weren't turning red or watering too excessively.

"Thank you," she finally said.

Mary turned back to the application. "You've worked retail before, I see. Starting when you were in high school. Made manager pretty quickly at Birkin's Books. Didn't those all close down?"

"Yeah. A casualty of the pandemic."

"That pandemic did a number on you, didn't it?"

What Dot almost said, but thankfully didn't, was that the pandemic was just a nail in the coffin. Grandma's coffin, literally, but also the coffin of Dot's adult life, which had been pretty much dead on arrival. She also didn't offer the reason she went to work during high school and made manager as quickly as she did. If Mary really thought about it, she might ask.

Fuller Park was not a cheap place to live, but thanks to the small fortune Grandpa left behind, Grandma had the means to live there...right up until an internet scammer bled her dry during Dot's senior year of high school. Dot missed her high school graduation because they had to move that day. Grandma hadn't been the same after that. One of their old neighbors helped Dot get the job at the bookstore, and soon after, the manager position, only because he knew how dire their situation was. Dot did nothing to earn the promotion, but she had everything to do with eventually being demoted from it. She silently willed Mary not to ask anything else about her former employment. Dot didn't like talking about it. She didn't even like knowing about it.

Mary looked up from the application. "How are you with people?"

Awkward? Heavily judged? "Good. I...don't mind people."

Lies.

"Great! I think we can find a position for you." She smiled. "I'll be in touch by the end of the day."

Dot tried not to appear suspicious. This was good news, of course—great news. Which is exactly why it worried her. Getting a job had never been this easy. This was yet another sign that something truly devastating was about to happen. Maybe her car would finally explode. Or she'd finally get evicted. Or her heart would just stop, although would that really be the worst thing?

Until the big, terrible thing was revealed, there was nothing she could do about it. Her only option was to accept the position and earn a paycheck until the inevitable lightning strike.

She stood and shook Mary's hand, plastering on her best fake smile. "Thank you so much. I look forward to hearing from you."

Mary stuck to her word and called later that day to offer Dot a position in customer service. Blech. But it was a job. At least at a place like Target, they'd take back anything with or without a receipt. Though, to be perfectly honest, she was the type of person to go against company policy to avoid a confrontation. She would happily empty her register to an unhappy customer if it would make them go far away from her.

Getting the first and only job she had applied and interviewed for was another unnatural stroke of luck, but it was progress nonetheless.

"Okay. I've got a job, a clean house, and I don't have to worry about rent for a few weeks...I'm taking care of myself. Like an adult."

Mindlessly scrolling through social media, she lay on her couch, liking the content of strangers who didn't know or care who she was.

"Now I'm just...alone."

Another side effect of growing up in a retirement community and making friends with the elderly folks meant now they were all either dead or senile. Her classmates in school had never been more than acquaintances. No one wanted to hang out with the kid who crocheted and smelled like old people.

Before the scamming incident, she had started to come out of her awkward phase. Some of the nerdier boys were noticing her, and she had started hanging out with some of the only slightly weird girls, but once everything imploded at home, she dedicated her free time working with authorities to get Grandma's money back. And when the investigation led nowhere, Dot was forced to focus on finding a job and somewhere to live. No time for socializing.

Now, as an adult, every friend she'd made had been Howie's friend first. She wasn't the type of person to reach out, anyway. And to be fair, if someone reached out to her, she'd probably say she was fine. Not that they would. She couldn't imagine that anyone else in the world ever had Dot on their mind.

Her phone vibrated in her hands. She read the caller's name off the screen and groaned.

There was *one* person who called her up now and then. Not someone she particularly liked talking to, but...she was family.

"Yes, Diane? What do you need?" Dot answered warily.

"What kind of greeting is that for your mother? If I had ever called your grandma by her first name, she would've smacked me!"

Dot had no energy to hide the impatience in her voice. "I'm not worried about being smacked when you're not even in the same state."

"Why do you think I only call when I need something? I wanted to check in. See how you're doing."

"Mmhmm." Dot put the phone on speaker and placed it on her chest. She knew her mother's patterns as well as she knew her own. Diane could never cut to the chase. A hearty appetizer of forced small talk always preceded the overcooked meat of the conversation.

"How's life? Are you doing anything fun this weekend?"

"Fine and no."

"Hey, what if I came out for a visit? Would you help me out with a plane ticket? I'd pay you back by doing your laundry."

Dot laughed harshly. That was a lie.

"Mom, I don't have a job right now. I can't even pay my rent."

Silence. Then, "Could you put it on a card? It would earn you some miles."

"I don't need miles."

"I'd be happy to use them for you," Diane said with a laugh, even though they both knew it wasn't a joke.

"I really can't afford it, Mom. But if you found your own way out here, sure, we could hang out." Dot knew the attempt was futile, but she didn't see the harm in subtly inviting her mother to *be* a mother whenever she had the chance. The subtle invitations had been ignored for twenty-four years now, ever since Diane had decided that getting pregnant young had unfairly robbed her of her youth. Apparently, she still hadn't "found herself" in all the time that she'd been looking.

"If I came down there, I would have to make time for my old girlfriends, too. Plus, I'd have Brendan with me."

"Funny how you were the first to mention coming for a visit, then added a disclaimer so I wouldn't assume it would be to see me," Dot countered. "And I thought your boyfriend's name was Connor?"

"Oh, no. Connor was over months ago. And don't make this about you. If you had friends, you'd feel obligated to make time for them, too."

This conversation was getting less interesting by the second.

"Then it's a big fat shame that neither of us has any money or time. Bummer. Okay, bye." Dot ended the call.

The phone immediately buzzed again. She silenced it.

"That actually went...well," she said to herself proudly. Calls with her mother weren't usually that succinct. "I should tell Howie...oh."

Howie had always encouraged her to be more forthright with Diane.

"I know she's your mother, but you don't have to be nice to her," he had lectured. "You've got to let her know when you're done listening. I'm not sure why you listen at all. Your mother is toxic."

Hanging up on her mom suddenly didn't feel as empowering as she thought it would feel a minute ago. Could she really afford to shut out the one person in the world who thought about her spontaneously? Even if it was in more of a doormat sort of way?

People were confusing. The person she thought she could always rely on was gone, and the person she knew she couldn't would probably never leave her alone.

The sheets on her bed still smelled clean, even days after Yasmin had washed them for her. It hardly ever crossed Dot's mind to wash her sheets. She was still learning to take care of herself. Grandma never had much of a chance to help her transition into adult independence, and Howie eliminated the need for her to figure it out for herself.

Though she tried to stop herself from thinking about it, she remembered meeting Howie near the end of the pandemic, after she had buried Grandma (with very little help from her mother) and moved into the single-wide. It was a modern day meet-cute. The only reliable job available to her in that unstable era was delivering takeout to quarantining citizens, and Howie became one of her regular customers. For close to a year, she left burritos and hamburgers on his porch, waving to him from a safe distance each time he cracked the door to retrieve his food, affording them both the human connection they were missing. When the pandemic calmed down and things opened up, she stuck with making food deliveries. She wasn't ready to give up on the weird social-distancing connection they had forged. Then one day, when the Mexican restaurant that he had ordered from was out of the soda he wanted, she texted him to ask for an alternative. He responded by saying he'd be okay if she could replace the drink with a date.

Her complacency had been what drove him away, she knew that now. Two years was a long time for a good thing to last, and she got comfortable being taken care of—though didn't he deserve some of the blame for enabling her dependency? He had the audacity to complain about doing all the work in the relationship when it was kind of his fault for being such a control freak.

A tear slid down her cheek and formed a wet spot on her pillowcase. The bottom line here: she'd had a good thing, and it was she who had blown it, not the universe.

In an effort to ease her mind, she forced herself to admit it was probably for the best. Maybe she had loved him, but it was a very practical sort of love. Maybe it wasn't even love at all, but convenience. Whatever it was, it was done, and she was on her own. Like she was always destined to be.

It would do no good to waste another brain cell on Howie. She wiped away the wet streak the tear had left on her cheek and resolved it would be the last one. It was time to prepare herself for the next terrible thing that was inevitably coming. If only she had some idea of what that would be.

After a successful first day of training at Target, Dot's suspicions were beginning to lessen. Maybe things *were* looking up. Like, for real. If that were true, she deserved to celebrate. To treat herself, she stopped at a convenience store to buy a cookie and a scratch-off lottery ticket, just to test her theory. She almost choked on the cookie as she sat in her car and scratched away the silver coating to reveal a twenty-dollar payout.

Should I go to Vegas?

It was odd to feel so lighthearted for once, so on a whim, she turned into her old neighborhood on her way home, to reflect on a time when she was too young to realize that life sucked. Seeing the homes where her elderly friends once lived generated a nice boost of dopamine. In them, she had learned how to bake and crochet and answer in the form of a question.

The corner of her lip turned up into a small smile as she approached the modest home she and Grandma used to occupy. She slowed down. A garage sale was set up out front. Memories of garage-sale-hopping on Saturday mornings with Grandma (and getting free loot because the old folks thought she was cute) filled her thoughts. She had twenty dollars to burn. Why not relive a happy memory? She pulled over and parked.

"Hi, there!" A chipper, snowy-haired old lady waved from a camping chair in the driveway, folding the grocery store flyer she was reading and placing it in her lap. "Looking for anything in particular?"

Dot looked over the cluttered driveway.

"Hi, no. Just browsing. My grandma used to live in this house."

"Is that right? Well, welcome back. What's your grandma's name?"

"Dorothy Dudley," Dot answered.

"Hmm, I don't think I knew her," the lady said. "But I only moved in this year. Are you named after her? Is Dot short for Dorothy?" She gestured towards the nametag still pinned to Dot's red top.

"Yeah, actually." Dot unpinned her tag and shoved it in her pocket. "You mind if I look around?"

"Sure, sure," the lady said. "You might find it interesting where I got all this stuff."

What is: One of those hoarder-enabling bin stores?

Dot knew a thing or two about people from the older generations.

"It's from a castle!" the lady declared without giving Dot time to respond.

She smiled politely. "Nice."

"My cousin lived in a castle in Ireland. He died and his kids didn't want any of his junk—their words, not mine. I told 'em I'd love to look through some of it if they wanted to send it across the pond. His daughter didn't want to, but then she sent me a few boxes once I agreed to cover shipping. Why let anything from a castle go to waste?"

Maintaining her polite smile, Dot turned her attention to a table that held a variety of vases, dishes, and glassware. Nothing looked particularly old, merely tacky. She picked up a tall, gaudy metal cup—a goblet covered in jewels.

But upon closer inspection, the gems on the rim were plastic, glued on in an uneven pattern. She didn't want to dampen the old lady's spirits, but clearly, her cousin's family kept the valuable stuff for themselves.

Dot placed the goblet back on the table, next to a mottled green glass bottle—not anything she'd normally pay much attention to, but for some reason, her eyes lingered on it. Its rounded shape, narrow neck, and crusted-over interior gave it an unassuming, almost forgotten, kind of prettiness. It looked like the kind of bottle people might put messages in and throw into the ocean. She picked it up, noticing the brown cork stuffed into the top, and peered closely to see if anything was inside.

"The top on that is stuck tight," the lady pointed out, watching from her camping chair. "But there's something in there. I can't tell what it is. Glass is all foggy and gunked up, but it's too heavy to be empty. I figured maybe someone else might want to try and get it open."

Dot tested the weight. It did feel like there *could* be something inside. Maybe an old treasure map, but more likely a clod of dirt. She placed it back on the table.

She perused a minute longer, but saw nothing she was willing to part with twenty dollars over. Just to be sure, she took one last scan of the tables.

Her eyes stopped again on the bottle. Did it just...?

She glanced at the old lady who was once again lost in a list of BOGOs.

Dot turned back to the bottle and narrowed her eyes.

It fell over.

She flinched. She thought she had seen it wobbling, but how? And why? Curiously, she picked it up and examined the bottom. Flat. It had no business being unsteady.

Maybe there's some kind of creature trapped inside, like in those Mexican jumping beans.

She shook it. Whatever was in there didn't move when she rattled it.

She set it back on the table gingerly.

"You seem interested in that bottle." When Dot looked up, the old lady stood directly beside her.

"I'm really not. It fell over. I was just standing it back up."

"How about you take it? Free of charge."

Dot took a step back and frowned. "Oh, no thanks. I'm good."

The lady leaned forward, hovering in her personal space.

"Do you believe in ghosts?" she whispered.

Dot laughed nervously. Not because of the ghost question, but because of the uncomfortable proximity of the woman.

"I think this bottle might be haunted. It has a strange air about it. You'd be doing me a favor by taking it off my hands." The old lady inched closer as Dot took another step away. Why would she want a haunted bottle? But she'd do almost anything to get this woman out of her face.

"Why not just throw it away?" she asked in a last-ditch attempt.

The old lady blinked as if that was the dumbest idea she'd ever heard. "It's from a *castle*. It might be invaluable. I could be doing *you* a huge favor."

A peculiar prickle rippled across the back of Dot's neck, and she wasn't sure why.

"Okay, fine." She snatched the bottle from the table. "I'm late for...something. Thank you. For this."

The old lady smiled, clearly pleased with her salesmanship. "Thanks for stopping by!"

Dot gave a nod and a wave, walking quickly towards her car before getting inside.

With the door closed, she took a second to quietly analyze the bottle in her hands. "Another free piece of junk from a yard sale. I guess I still got it."

The prickling along her neck returned as she ran her fingers along the smooth green glass.

"Haunted? No way...but maybe there's something..."

She took one more look at the bottle and laughed.

"I watch too many movies."

She tossed it into the passenger seat and started the car. Time to head home. She had to work tomorrow.

Chapter 3

DOT

Two entire weeks went by at her new job with no incidents or accidents, and Dot's paranoia was reaching brink-of-insanity levels. Her list of positive happenings was lengthening; not only had work gone well, but she had already gotten a raise and made a friend. As much as she wanted to accept that maybe life was finally throwing her a bone, with every positive occurrence, the word *omen* seemed to echo in the back of her mind.

It was scary to admit, but the Moving Forward phase was proving successful. When she had gotten her first paycheck deposited, the balance in her bank account felt like being healthy again after a long illness.

But maybe she was only in remission.

So she downplayed her so-called luck. The raise wasn't *that* much. She was probably misquoted the starting pay and so they had to make an adjustment. And Skye, the friend—a tall, bubbly, brown-skinned beauty a few years older—was her trainer, and proximity could sometimes give off the illusion of friendship. Skye had a chatty, extroverted personality, too, and anyone who could effortlessly fill the awkward silences that Dot generated was certainly a friend under her definition.

Winding down on a slow Tuesday night shift, Skye was, as usual, making offhanded observations during a lull.

"The things people return are so random, right? I mean, just today, there's been hand lotion, a set of cutlery, a kettlebell, and then that dude returned a candy bar because he didn't realize it contained nuts. Consumerism is bonkers. There are so many things that people think they need when they really don't."

Dot nodded. She wasn't a fan of small talk, but she liked Skye enough to attempt taking part in the conversation.

"So true. I went to a garage sale a couple weeks ago and all of it was junk. The woman was adamant people would buy it because it came from some castle in Ireland." Hopefully that didn't sound too much like she was pandering, even though she was.

"Oh yeah? That's cool. Did you buy anything?"

"No. But she practically forced an old bottle on me for free."

Skye crinkled her nose. "That's so weird. Why a bottle? Is it decorative or something?"

With every question, Dot slightly regretted jumping into the conversation. "Um...maybe. It looks old, but like, ordinary old. Not valuable old. The woman said she thinks it's haunted." She snort-laughed accidentally, then tried to cover it with a loud throat clearing.

But Skye wasn't laughing. Instead, she became very serious.

"Haunted? Are you saying you casually accepted some old lady's demon artifact? Girl, I hope you threw it away."

Dot scratched her head. "I think it's still in my car."

"Oh, no," Skye said in a way that made Dot wonder if she had done something very wrong. "Are you sure it hasn't moved itself into your house? You should really check on that. Or maybe your car is haunted now. Have you noticed if anything feels...*off* when you're driving around?"

"No. No ghost would want to haunt my car. Between the talking to myself and the off-key singing, I'd probably end up haunting *it*." Dot chuckled at herself, silently relieved when it didn't include any involuntary snorts.

Skye laughed loudly, too, and Dot felt a pleasing warmth at the reaction.

Am I funny now?

"Okay, well...if it's not haunted, and it came from a castle, was there at least anything cool inside?"

"I haven't tried to open it yet. I actually forgot all about it until now. The lady seemed to think something's in there, but she couldn't get the cork off. And the inside of the glass is all calcified and foggy. I can't tell if she's right."

Skye shrugged and looked at the clock. "It's almost closing time. Let's go back by the dumpsters after work and bust that thing open."

The suggestion caught Dot off guard. It may have been a small request, but it had been years since she had been invited to do anything with a coworker outside of work. The last time was an invitation to help someone move, and free labor probably didn't count as hanging out. Not that she even went.

"Yeah, okay." She smiled.

A little less than an hour later, Dot found herself behind the building next to the dumpsters with Skye, bottle in hand.

"What do you think will be inside? We have to make a guess before we break it," Skye insisted.

"Um." Dot tried to think of something exciting. "A one-hundred-dollar bill."

"Girl, aim higher!" Skye laughed. "I'm guessing it's an old love letter, written by a sailor stuck on a desert island to his sweetheart. Only it never made it to her and they both died, sad and alone."

"That's...specific," Dot said.

"It's realistic. So you're sticking with the hundred dollars?"

Dot fidgeted under the pressure. "Fine, I'll change it to...a thousand dollars."

Skye side-eyed her. "Way to be creative. Okay. Let's smash it."

Taking a deep breath (though she wasn't sure why), Dot flung the bottle hard towards the pavement. It made a loud *clink* upon impact, then bounced high into the air, landed, then rolled several yards away, completely intact.

They watched as it came to a stop. Skye frowned. "Are you sure it's glass?"

Dot ran to pick it up, examining it carefully. There wasn't so much as a scuff anywhere on it. She brought it back to Skye and handed it off to her.

"You try."

Without hesitation, Skye took the bottle by the neck and whacked it hard against the side of the dumpster.

Bongggg. The metal of the dumpster reverberated, but the bottle remained unscathed in Skye's fist.

She directed a questioning glare at it...then dropped into a squat, beating it against the pavement recklessly.

In the streetlight, Dot saw particles of dust flying off the asphalt, but the bottle itself stayed intact.

Skye stood up, holding the bottle close to her face. "You're right, it's too foggy to see, but there's gotta be something in there. And this thing ain't breaking, so it's probably something valuable. Or gross. Ugh, what if it's like a dried-up cow liver?"

"Maybe the old lady was right," Dot said.

"You mean about it being haunted? I don't know. It's just a bottle. I'm not getting any creepy vibes, you know?"

Dot took the bottle and placed it upright on the pavement, then backed away. "I thought I saw it moving on its own at the garage sale," she mentioned.

"Wait, what?" Skye stepped backed, too, further than Dot. "Why didn't you lead with that?"

Why didn't she?

The unbreakableness of the bottle was giving her second thoughts. "I figured it must be the wind or something. But...it wasn't really windy that day, now that I think about it."

The two of them stared silently at the bottle. After a tense minute, Dot moved to pick it up, but before she reached it, it wobbled ever so slightly.

"Nope!" Skye shouted, throwing her arms in the air. "Good night!"

It was enough for Dot that Skye had seen it, too. It was nice to know she wasn't crazy. "Maybe there's another way to get it open."

Skye had said it herself: there were no creepy vibes here. But there was *a* vibe, one that Dot could only describe as magnetic. Something that ignited her curiosity rather than her fear.

"I know you're not about to try and release whatever demon is living in there!" Skye said, pointing a finger. "I know I said no creepy vibes, but that was before the thing went Annabelle on us."

The bottle wobbled again, more noticeably than the first time.

Skye turned and began walking away. "Okay," she yelled over her shoulder. "I'm going home. Byieee!"

Still curious, but not wanting to disregard her friend, Dot retrieved the bottle and followed Skye to their parked cars.

Skye glanced over her shoulder and stopped. "Are you seriously taking it home? Or are you going to do the smart thing and throw it off a cliff?"

"I wanna know what's inside," Dot said honestly. "Aren't you *more* curious now?"

Skye resumed walking, her pace quickening until she reached her car. She pulled the door open and slid into the seat. "You go ahead and find out what's inside that thing, but don't come crying to me when a poltergeist starts breaking your dishes in the middle of the night!"

"My dishes are all made of plastic," Dot answered as she watched Skye close her door and drive off. Hopefully, this piece of paranormal garbage hadn't stunted the growth of their budding friendship.

She looked down at the bottle in her hand. Her intuition hadn't exactly been spot-on in the past, but the more she handled it, the more desperate she became to open it. Maybe it was boredom. Maybe she just needed proof that whatever was inside wasn't as mystical as she was building it up to be.

She scoffed at the thought. It was silly to think the contents of an old bottle would be anything more than disappointing. Too many good things had been happening lately, and it clouded her judgment. Still...she'd try another way to get it open. What did she have to lose? Besides a poltergeist-free house, which, realistically, might help with her loneliness.

Once home, she quickly changed into flannel shorts and her favorite oversized Orlando t-shirt that she'd found at a thrift store. This task required comfortable attire, as most worthwhile tasks did.

With the bottle on her kitchen counter, she rummaged through her drawers until she found what she was looking for: a corkscrew. With one hand on the bottle, she stabbed the point into the cork and began to twist.

"What the...?" The pointed end wasn't digging in like it should; it scraped across the surface of the cork as if it, too, was made of metal. With more force, she stabbed it again, bending the tip of her corkscrew.

"How old is this thing?" she asked herself. "Is this a petrified cork?"

For good measure, she began whacking it against any hard surface, but nothing was more solid than the pavement they had tried earlier.

I need one of those hydraulic presses that I've seen on the internet.

But she had no idea where to get one of those, and no one to ask. Frustrated, she took the bottle and plopped herself on the couch.

"Maybe I should call Howie..."

Hearing the words out loud instantly changed her mind. She was finally doing fine without him. Better than ever, however discomforting that was. He always nagged her to do things herself anyway, so that's how she would open this bottle: On her own. She was as capable as anyone else.

As if in response, the bottle shuddered in her hands. At least she thought it had...maybe it was just her own hands trembling. Regardless, her resolve to know what was inside deepened.

She peered around the room, scanning it for another idea, when her eyes fell on the candle on her end table.

It gave her a thought.

The tiny flicker of the candle would take years to do anything to the cork, let alone the bottle. But she did have an oven, and maybe heat was the key.

She would melt this mother down.

Back in the kitchen, she cranked her oven up to five hundred degrees, the highest it would go, and tossed the bottle inside. Once the room started filling with residual heat and the scent of burning dust, she grabbed an oven mitt.

She grunted in irritation to find that the bottle wasn't even smoking. Maybe it wasn't hot enough. Although she couldn't know for sure; she had never paid much attention in her science classes. At the very least, maybe it had been enough to loosen the cork. With her mitted hand, she took the bottle by the neck and, once again, whacked it as hard as she could against the counter.

Nothing.

"This is ridiculous," she mumbled, surveying every inch of the bottle carefully. What was her obsession with this piece of junk? Is this what her life had come to? Spending her evenings doing made-up science experiments with something that belonged in her recycling bin?

Maybe she deserved to be alone.

But then something caught her eye that made her self-criticism cease mid-thought.

A letter.

No, *a lot* of letters. Written in a curly script. Words, maybe. Small, black, and etched into the glass so smoothly it was like they were screen-printed on. And they were fading as the bottle cooled.

"Ha!" She didn't know what a bunch of hidden letters on the outside could do to open it, but they might hint at what was inside. Leaving the bottle on the counter, she retrieved a lighter, a pad of sticky notes, and a pen. She flicked the lighter on, running the flame up and down one side of the bottle.

Methodically, she heated the glass, searching for and then writing down the tiny letters. Each side seemed to have a spiral of them, making it difficult to tell if they were actual words or a stream of nonsense. After almost a half hour, she was quite certain she had found and copied every letter onto the sticky notes now stuck across her countertop.

"What language is that?" she wondered out loud. Then her brain began to pick out words. "Holy...that's English!"

She rearranged her sticky notes, half understanding and half still struggling to make sense of it. Finally, she had it arranged into something of a poem.

ICOMMANDYOUTOOPEN

MYVOICEISTHEKEY

IAMYOURMASTER

GRANTMEMYTHREE

"Let's see if I can figure out what all this says. I...comm...and—command," she read, slowly disconnecting the words from one another. "You...too...pen—open!"

The words on one side of the bottle lit up.

With a shriek, she dropped it, watching it bounce and clatter across the linoleum floor until it rolled to a stop.

"Okay, that did something." Her eyes remained fixed on the totally ordinary-looking-but-possibly-legitimately-haunted bottle on the floor. She stepped towards it and gently kicked it over with her foot to confirm what she had seen. The circle of letters continued to glow gold. After a minute, the letters had faded until it was just a plain old glass bottle again.

She realized then that she was shivering, but not from fear. There was fear there for sure, but the shivering came from a morbid curiosity built of dread and excitement—the only thing stopping her from personally tossing it into a landfill.

What if this is the terrible thing the universe has been building up to?

The thought almost convinced her to let it be. But then another came.

Or maybe I've been looking at it all wrong. What if the universe has been building up to something good?

Either way, she needed to know.

"No creepy vibes." Exhaling a deep breath to hype herself up, she gingerly lifted the bottle back to the counter. "Okay. Time to say the magic words."

She organized her sticky notes beside the bottle and swallowed before she spoke.

"I command you to open..."

Her eyes darted to the bottle. The letters flashed gold again. She turned it a quarter of the way, simultaneously reading and watching as she continued.

"...my voice is the key..."

More etchings lit up. Her voice was starting to shake.

"...I am your master..."

The third spiral began to glow. She rotated the bottle to the final side.

"...grant me myth ree. Myth ree? Oh...*my three*. Wait, grant me my three? Does that mean...?"

Before her brain could fully interpret the implication, the final letters began to shimmer, and the bottle vibrated against the counter. She reached to steady it, but her nervous hands knocked it to the floor. This time, it didn't clatter around, it landed upright, and with a burst of sparkling gold light, the cork exploded from the opening.

Dot stumbled backwards into the living room. The light pouring from the kitchen was almost blinding, but she forced away her natural sense of cowardice and kept her sights on the bottle, holding her hand up to shield her eyes. Then the bottle was no longer visible, though she could still hear the glass rattle against the linoleum. When the light finally became too much, she turned her face away. As the golden light reached its peak, the lights in her house blinked off and everything went dark.

This can't be what I think it is.

She climbed to her feet, trying to get her bearings as her eyes moved around wildly. Then, as suddenly as the lights had gone out, they blinked back on.

She spun her head towards the kitchen and screamed.

Amid the fading gold sparkles lingering in the air, a youngish, *very shirtless,* man stared back at her wearing a matching look of surprise. He dropped to the floor in the kitchen doorway, landing on his hands and knees, touching his face to the ground. Almost like he was...bowing?

She scrambled to the coffee table and grabbed her phone, looked at it, then turned back to the prostrating intruder.

"Can I text 911 or do I have to actually talk to someone?" she cried urgently to no one in particular.

"My...lady," the man said, peeking up at her before lowering his face back towards the ground. "I am your humble servant. Your voice has called me forward, and it is my honor to grant you three wishes."

Dot's phone clattered to the ground. "You have got to be kidding me," she whispered.

"What is your first wish, so that I may have the pleasure of making it so?" The guy peeked up again. Dot noted that his only clothes were a pair of puffy purple pants.

"Like Aladdin," she breathed.

"Aladdin? Really?" She heard the guy mutter.

"Are you seriously a...or am I just...?"

Her mouth hung open as the man eased into a kneeling position, giving Dot her first real look at him. She quickly memorized his features in case she needed to recount them to the police later: a pleasant sandy skin tone. Cheerful brown eyes. Perfectly tousled dark, wavy hair. Neatly trimmed beard. A polite smile. She tried not to let her eyes fall below his neck, but she couldn't help it.

A toned chest that is not unpleasing to the eyes.

She cleared her throat to refocus herself. He didn't look dangerous, but dangerous people never did.

"Do you, perhaps, have a husband or brother or father you'd like to transfer my services to? Unless...I guess gender roles don't work the same anymore, do they?

Wow, a lot has changed." He climbed to his feet and placed his hands on his hips. His chest muscles sharpened.

Dot blinked.

Did I just summon a hot, sexist genie?

She shook her head. *No, he isn't a genie. Genies aren't real. Everything that has happened tonight is not real. Either he's insane or I am.*

He looked around when she didn't answer. "The twenty-first century, huh? The land of Florida. That's new. And look at this modern architecture. It's very..." He rubbed his fingers against his beard thoughtfully. "Well, it's simpler than I expected. Very low ceilings. Still lovely, though. To you, I'm sure."

"Y-you're a genie?" she finally sputtered.

He turned his attention back to her and bent at the waist in a shallow bow. "I see my reputation precedes me. I *am* a genie. *Your* genie. And it would be my pleasure to grant you three wishes. What is your first wish?"

Dot glanced around. "I don't have a wish ready yet! I'm still processing"—she waved a hand towards him—"this."

The man straightened, standing a few inches taller than her. "Maybe this will help speed up the processing," he said.

Her shoulders dropped. "Maybe what?"

"Look at me...up here, yep, just like that."

He snapped his fingers. Around her, the interior of her house faded away.

Then they were standing outside. Not just outside, but somewhere else entirely.

Like a dead weight, Dot's jaw dropped, almost pulling the rest of her with it. Her eyes were sending signals to her brain, signals that made no sense. Rotating slowly, she studied the lush, green landscape around her. She stood on a grassy hillside overlooking an endless ocean. The wind whipped her long hair around her face; she could taste the salty air.

"Is this real?" she breathed, but her words sounded small, absorbed by the space around her. Tentatively, she kneeled down and ran her hand over the soft grass beneath her feet. She dug her fingers into it, until they pressed into the soil it grew from—real, crumbly, earth-scented soil. She rose back to her feet and turned, taking a few slow steps towards the ocean. She was close to a cliff, and she could hear the crashing of the waves against the rocks below her.

She glanced back at the genie. He watched her from a few feet away, arms crossed, an orange sunrise at his back, framing him like some sort of god in ridiculous puffy pants. An exuberant grin took up most of his face.

As beautiful as the landscape was, it was hard not to stare at him.

He raised his hand and snapped his fingers again, and in a blink, they were back in her single-wide, him still standing in the entrance to the kitchen, her facing him from her drab living room.

She brought her hand up to her eyes to gawk at the soil on her fingertips.

Her odd streak of luck continued in that instant. She chanced to be standing in the perfect spot so that when she fainted, she hit the sofa instead of the floor.

Chapter 4

RAJI

The twenty-first century.

How had it been so long? Raji's infinite knowledge was still absorbing all the updates—there were so many! Practically everything had changed since his last venture outside the bottle, which he now understood had been six hundred and twelve years ago.

Six hundred and twelve years. "The longest stretch so far. Someone must've hidden the bottle well," he murmured, momentarily dazed with all the information streaming into his head.

Thankfully, his new master had passed out (not an uncommon reaction) and he had some time to orient himself in this drastically different world.

He approached the woman laying askew and unconscious on the sofa.

He had been summoned by many women over the centuries, but unless they were of noble status, they had all handed him off to whatever male figure governed their existence. His updated knowledge revealed that a lot had changed for the fairer sex in six hundred years, more than had changed in the previous two thousand combined. Many women were now afforded more rights than either of the two female masters he had served in the past. One had been a princess in seventh-century China and the other the wife of a pharaoh in fourth-century Egypt. Both turned out to be just as greedy and corruptible as the majority of his male masters, so this latest master also being a woman didn't rule out the possibility that she too could turn out to be a huge jerk, noble status or not.

Though according to the incoming data his magic supplied, a young woman in northern Florida was unlikely to be considered nobility in any sense of the word.

He leaned over her to get a better look. Though mature in appearance, she still looked younger than him, physiologically speaking. She reminded him of the fair-skinned maidens in old English tales. Lovely straw-colored hair splayed about her head like a halo, her pink lips had fallen open, and though the upper one stuck to her top teeth, it struck him that she was certainly beautiful enough to be a princess. Any of the kings and princes he had served in the past might gladly take her as a concubine at the very least.

Out of respect, he made a valiant effort to avoid letting his gaze stray lower than her neck, but he couldn't help himself. Her baggy gray top had billowed up when she fell, revealing a petite belly button and the soft, inverted curves of her exposed waist. A quick look, and then he carefully pulled her shirt back into place. He shouldn't stare at his new master, even if she was unconscious.

She seemed a little high-strung, he recalled as his eyes drifted down her long, unnaturally smooth legs.

She didn't look like a jerk. But jerks never did.

The power of infinite knowledge filled in all the blanks about cultural, linguistic, and geographical information relevant to his new master; the more specific details—family, trade, social status, certain temper triggers, strange fetishes, etcetera—remained unknown. He usually discovered that stuff through trial and error or simply by observation, but in this case, he might be able to glean some of that knowledge by taking some time to look around.

First, however, he needed to celebrate.

A triumphant smile formed on his lips as he stood up. "I am *out*!" he whisper-yelled.

With one more glance at his new master, he made for the front door.

Outside, the night was alive with new sounds. Insects, animals, but also all the new-fangled machinery. Engines and sirens and the hum of streetlights. He sucked in a breath of fresh oxygen. It didn't smell...great. He looked over the wooden rail of the rickety porch. A bin filled with what he presumed to be waste sat in the shadows below, accompanied by the sound of buzzing. His knowledge informed him that even though conditions nowadays were more hygienic than ever, the amount of garbage was also at a record high. No time period was perfect. At least not one he'd been in.

He stepped off the porch, running his hand along the top of the automobile in the driveway. Maybe his master would let him take a ride. This world was oozing with new opportunities, even for him. What an exhilarating time to be released.

In the dark, he noted the thick foliage surrounding his master's little abode. Florida appeared to be wonderfully green and fertile. That would be nice, since most of his outings had been spent in desert climates.

"I'm back!" he yelled loudly into the night sky with a giggle. It felt good to use his voice, to move his limbs, and to *see* signs of life around him. It might be a much different Earth than it had been the last time he was on it, but it was the same Earth he had been born on. The same Earth his family had lived on all those centuries ago, before...certain events. With his master incapacitated, he could take a second to honor that.

A slightly unpleasant sensation tugged on his stomach as he walked out into the street, a reminder of the invisible cosmic leash tethering him to his master. He ignored it, knowing he wouldn't be straying far.

Driveways and parked automobiles lined the paved road in either direction, illuminated by the electric lights on poles that hung over the street. How amazing to be able to see so clearly in the dead of night. He stepped back into his master's small, sparsely grassed lawn as a pair of headlights approached. A car passed by, which he observed with delight.

Back inside, he paused to check on his master, contemplating covering her with a blanket before he began his self-guided tour. Outside, the air had been warm, but inside it felt different, chilled. The effects of an *air conditioner*. He could think of a few previous masters who would have enjoyed one of those.

In fact, this tiny house was full of things past masters would have gladly spent a wish on—a television, a refrigerator, an alarm clock. This place came equipped with more conveniences than some of the more extravagant palaces he had brought to pass. Did the people in this century realize they were surrounded by technology that had once been considered magic?

With a wave of his hand, a blanket appeared out of thin air, floating down until it settled over his master's body. Her eyes remained closed, but just to be safe, he placed a hand on the side of her head and magically helped her brain fall into a more restful sleep. Not a long one; he couldn't make her stay out longer than the equivalent of an afternoon nap without her permission.

"Time to explore," he told himself. "For the benefit of the master."

As she slept, Raji spent the time he had matching objects to the information flooding his brain, testing mechanisms and inspecting inner workings. At the same time, he hoped to dig up some ideas about what to expect from this master, in terms of both temperament and wishes. He didn't find much, but what he did find was interesting.

The home included only one bedroom with one bed. It was a bed large enough for two, but the one toothbrush, the one car, and the one size of clothing suggested his new master lived alone. In every culture in which he'd ever served a master, a woman of her age and physical appeal would be married and probably raising a couple of kids by now. But there was almost no sign that she had a family of any kind.

Only a single, dusty photo, prominently centered atop the dresser in the bedroom, alluded to a relationship of some kind with another human. It featured an elderly lady and a blue-eyed child with the same haircut. A child that looked an awful lot like the snoring woman on the sofa. They were both dressed in black robes, posing dramatically in front of a statue of a dragon on a stone building. If that child was, in fact, his master, then the elderly woman in the photo was likely dead by now, or close to it.

A familiar ache caused his heart to constrict. If his master had lost someone, that might explain why she lived here alone. Sometimes loss made people bitter, difficult, and not fun to be around. He knew this from personal experience. In the early days of his geniehood, when he had foolishly tried to fight his unwarranted fate, allowing his grief to take control had always bred pain—sometimes self-inflicted, sometimes inflicted by impatient masters.

He knew what it felt like to be lonely. That didn't necessarily mean she would care, though. In his experience, once his masters understood his value, the last thing on their mind was commiserating with him.

At the end of his thorough inspection of the dwelling, he ended up in the kitchen. Naturally. There were so many things he missed when he was dormant in the void. Company being number one, but there was a close second.

Food.

There were many things about his situation that were miserable and unfair, but possibly the most unbearable was the constant hunger. He could eat and eat and never be satiated. So if there was an opportunity to partake, he partook. Food wasn't required for his survival, as it had been when he was mortal, but there were many things people didn't need that they still craved. He had indulged many masters with things of the sort, which is how he rationalized taking a little snack for himself.

The master's kitchen—aside from all the technology—didn't measure up to any of the grand kitchens he'd been in (or created). There didn't seem to be a pantry at all, or a wine cellar. Only a few closed cupboards, which Raji opened quietly. A shelf of colorful boxes caught his eye. He paused for a moment, then reached for one.

As he brought the box down from its perch, a painful stab bloomed in his chest. Not emotional pain, but physical, though not caused by any outside force. This was pain tailor-made to deter a disobedient servant. A security system installed by his makers almost three thousand years ago. Their sadistic wiring forced him to feel pain when he disobeyed his masters or misused his magic outside of a wish. In this case, the punishment came because he didn't ask before touching his master's stuff.

Over the course of almost three thousand years, Raji had trained himself to withstand small doses of the pain in order to sneak himself these tiny, harmless indulgences. If the box held anything truly valuable, he'd be hurting much worse than the minor centralized sting he was currently feeling. He could manage a small bowl of the stuff.

Cereal. Generally eaten for breakfast. Cheap, but popular. Available in many varieties. Served with milk. The type he selected was made with real cocoa, the box proclaimed, an ingredient which once upon a time had been rare and expensive, but now was a common ingredient in cheap food.

The twenty-first century was wild.

Once he prepared his cereal, he stepped back into the living room. Sunlight began to creep through the window; a soft ray of it illuminated his now drooling master, bathing her in an almost ethereal light. For a moment, he stood transfixed.

He shook his head and turned his attention to the food in his hands. Just because the world was different, that didn't mean anything would change for him. All signs pointed to this being another rags-to-riches, underprivileged-to-snob-bishly-entitled situation, which was fine. He'd choose that over serving a criminal, a sorcerer, or a royal any day.

Still, before he dug into the cereal, his gaze flickered towards his master. Since he wasn't prohibited from hoping, he silently hoped she would be a decent master, a kind one, easy to work with, slow to reach selfishness, maybe even appreciative. He had these hopes with every job, but in this completely transformed world, staring at this mysterious new category of master, he inexplicably wanted it more than ever. But, of course, he'd keep his expectations low.

She began to stir, so he slunk back to the kitchen doorway, not wanting to cause her any alarm before she was completely conscious.

The break had been nice, but it looked like it was time to get to work.

Chapter 5

RAJI

His master sat up, rubbing her head and wiping the spittle off her chin with her sleeve. Noticing the bottle on the coffee table, she reached for it.

"It must've been full of hallucinogenic gas or something," she muttered, holding it up to her eye to look inside.

"No, it was me. I was inside," Raji said, leaning against the kitchen doorframe.

She yelped and sprung to her feet, holding the bottle in front of her like a weapon.

"Who are you and what do you want?" she demanded.

The skeptical response was not uncommon, only a little exhausting. But he wouldn't let it annoy him. He was a professional. Professionals didn't get exasperated. They remained collected, unaffected, and approachable. Magically, he put a little sparkle in his eyes. It tended to put masters at ease.

"You know what I am. You said it yourself." He shoved a spoonful of cereal into his mouth, unable to keep his eyes from rolling back as he chewed. He did not expect cheap food to have so much flavor. "Food has gotten so much better."

"No," she retorted. "No. Genies aren't real! And if they were, they wouldn't...eat cereal and speak perfect English."

He swallowed his mouthful. "Aren't I doing both of those things?"

Her eyes swept down his body. "But...you're not blue and...floaty."

With a history spanning millennia, misconceptions and embellishments were bound to spread, even more so as the master-count increased. But where modern filmmakers had gotten the blue and floaty idea, he wasn't sure.

"Not to seem disrespectful, but have you ever met an actual genie before now?" He scooped up another spoonful, noticing that her eyes tracked the utensil as he lifted it. "Oh, is it alright if I eat this? I haven't eaten in six hundred years," he asked, shoving the spoon into his mouth.

"Huh?" she said. He would count that as an affirmative response. He chewed slowly as he watched his master slump her shoulders and drop the bottle on the floor. "This is so...I don't even know what this is."

He pointed his spoon at her. "Let me help you: it's good! You are a very lucky woman. I hope you're looking forward to making some wishes, because I'm looking forward to granting them. I've only served two other female masters, and they were...well, they were mean. Maybe you're mean, too, I haven't really—"

She held up her hand. "Could you be quiet for a second? Please. So I can...assess."

Reality check. A spike of pain hit him in the chest. He swirled the hand holding the cereal bowl, and it vanished into thin air.

He stood at attention, head lowered. "As you wish, Master."

She blinked. "Master? No...no, my name is Dot. Sorry. I'm really not trying to be rude."

An apology? Raji sifted through his infinite knowledge. Yes, American culture emphasized common courtesy. Even towards unexpected strangers in one's home, apparently. This might be a tricky custom to adapt to, considering their dynamic. "You don't have to apologize, Master Dot. I am your servant. I'm here to do whatever you wish."

"This is weird," she said after a long pause. Keeping his eyes lowered, he watched her bare feet pace the floor. "Do you have a name or something?"

His stare traveled from her feet to her legs. He didn't need infinite knowledge to know it was inappropriate to let his eyes move as slowly as they did, but, like indoor plumbing, a woman's exposed legs were a new and interesting development since the last time he'd been out of the bottle. "I'm Raji, but don't let that stop you from calling me anything you want." He placed his hands together and bowed.

"Could you quit it with the bowing?" she asked. "Sorry, it's...adding to the weirdness of what's going on...um, Raji. Ugh, the fact that you do have a name somehow makes it even more weird."

He straightened and began to bow again, but abruptly stopped and returned to his upright position. That would be a tough habit to break, but it was the will of his master, who now had a name. Dot.

Without being able to stoop into a bow, he suddenly didn't know where to look. As the servant, he definitely shouldn't point them at hers. Should he? Then he realized she was having the same dilemma. Dot looked everywhere but at him.

Perhaps he was making her uncomfortable. He could explain to her again that she could transfer his services, but he decided against it. He settled his eyes on her face.

The way she chewed on her lips, averted her gaze away, showed she was undoubtedly nervous. It was probably pointless to feel sympathetic to someone whose dreams were about to come true, but the urge to put this poor, frightened woman at ease was suddenly overwhelming.

"Master Dot, I promise I mean you no harm. I understand it's hard to believe, but I am what I say I am. I am here only to serve you."

"Then...explain this to me," she finally said, lowering herself onto the sofa with trembling knees. "Like, where you came from and how all this works, so I can tell if it's some kind of elaborate prank."

Be respectful. Be approachable. Pile on the praise.

"I would love to answer your questions, Master Dot. May I sit?"

She didn't answer, but scooted to one end of the couch to make room. Raji took that as a yes.

"Thank you." Fighting against another bow, he moved towards the sofa, maintaining a friendly smile as he sat. He pulled both his legs up to sit cross-legged, facing her. Her head turned as her wide eyes followed him, apprehensive as she gripped the arm of the sofa.

"To answer your questions, I came from that bottle there on the floor, and I'm here to grant three of your deepest, most longed-for wishes."

Her eyes narrowed. "And before I passed out...was that real? Did you *teleport* me somewhere?"

He nodded. "I like to give my masters a small preview of my power. It's not uncommon for people to distrust my reality. I'm able to do a little magic outside of granting wishes to prove myself, but to see the extent of my power, a wish is required. That was Scotland, by the way. Where my last master lived."

Dot's attention shifted to her hand. He watched as she studied the dirt beneath her fingernails. "The bottle came from a castle in Ireland," she said.

"I don't know how my vessel gets from one place to another. Or to an entirely different continent. This place hadn't even been touched by the Europeans last time I was here."

She dropped her hand. "How do you know all of this?"

"Infinite knowledge. It's part of the gig." He tapped his skull lightly. "To put it in terms someone from the twenty-first century might understand: as soon as you released me, my brain began an instant download of your culture, language, history, geography, even your popular slang. It's kind of a bussin' skill. It guarantees that I always slay, no cap."

A deep crease appeared on her forehead.

"Too cringe?" he asked.

"I feel like this is a joke," she said, then her face fell. "Except...I can't think of anyone who would go to these lengths to prank me. I don't have any close friends or bitter enemies, depressingly enough."

A telling statement.

"Okay, there's just one more thing I have to do to make sure..." She leaned towards him with an outstretched hand. He knew exactly what she was implying. It wasn't anything out of the ordinary. He held out his arms.

Avoiding his eyes, she gently gripped his forearm, her touch moving upwards. She patted his cheek and stroked his beard. Then she lowered a hand to his chest and pressed it lightly over his ever-beating heart.

That's when her eyes met his. She turned her head and yanked her hand away.

The whole process hadn't felt as unpleasant as it had in the past when male masters with giant hands or sickeningly long fingernails had needed the same physical reassurance of his existence. Dot's hands were soft and gentle; it was not a way he was used to being touched. A pang of disappointment washed over him when she pulled away, a feeling which he quickly dismissed.

"Okay, so you're real." She chuckled awkwardly, folding her arms against herself.

Her eyes flicked back up to his.

"So you can seriously grant wishes? *My* wishes?" She bit her lip to cover a slight curl at the corner of her mouth, but he noticed it. It was her first smile since meeting him.

"I can." He grinned.

"And I get three?"

"No more, no less."

"And I don't have to share them or pay taxes on them?" A sparkle blossomed in her blue eyes—an authentic one—and her timid smile grew.

"Uh, no. No sharing or taxes. As long as you specify that."

Uncrossing her arms, she ran both her hands through her hair, resting them on the top of her head. "And I can wish for anything I want?" She leaned against the back of the sofa, staring starry-eyed into space.

"Well..." Raji shrugged.

Her grin deflated. "Oh. There are rules, aren't there?" she asked, letting her arms drop back to her sides.

"There have to be some boundaries, or things could get out of control very fast."

"Are they the movie ones? Like no killing, no raising from the dead, and no...you know, making people fall in love."

He squinted curiously; did he detect some heartache in her voice? "You are partly correct. I am forbidden from doing any of those things, but they fall under the umbrella of more general rules."

"Which are?"

She wanted to know the rules—all the rules. A strong start for a master who hadn't believed he was real until a few minutes ago.

Raji relaxed and rested his elbows on his thighs. He was used to rigid submissive movements, but as long as she wasn't demanding he grovel, he wouldn't grovel.

"Number one: I have no power to directly overrule another person's free will or right to live. I can influence or compel or plant ideas, but there is never a guarantee that other people will do what you wish them to do. Therefore I can't make people fall in love. Number two: I don't have the power to change the past. Which is why I can't raise anyone from the dead. What's done is done. Number three: I do not have the power to elevate any of my masters from mortality to immortality; I can't turn you into a god or a genie. And finally, my limit is always three wishes. Don't try to think of loopholes to wish for more. It won't work."

Dot listened attentively. "Wow. Okay. Is that everything?"

There was one more restriction. But...it was nothing she would wish for. So he nodded firmly, ignoring the flare in his chest. "That's all. But if you wish for something that I can't give you, I'll let you know." He rubbed his hands together, anxious to move on. "So. Have you decided on your first wish yet?"

Her expression changed. And not to one of unabashed exhilaration. No, Master Dot's mouth drooped, her eyes glazed, her brow furrowed, her head swayed, her breathing deepened—

She was panicking. *Panicking.* Though he'd seen masters panic plenty of times, he hadn't seen it before the first wish was made. It usually came when a wish was wasted. One where things didn't turn out as expected, or placed the wisher in an undesirable situation, or came at an unexpectedly high cost.

Panic often led to rash decisions. Despite his usual lack of caring, it was hard not to worry about this master. She was looking abnormally distressed.

"Did I say something wrong?" He placed a hand on her knee.

Her eyes zeroed in on it. The ebbing pain in his chest suddenly intensified and he pulled his hand away.

She didn't like that.

"I just need a minute," she choked, sucking in and releasing one breath after another.

He moved off the couch to give her space to lie down, which she did, hugging a throw pillow to her chest. Patiently, he waited. After a moment, she noticed his concerned expression.

"No. No, you didn't do anything wrong," she said as her breathing calmed. "It's just...these are big decisions and I'm not great at big decisions. It's stupid, I know, but I would kind of prefer it if this wasn't happening."

He noticed a trace of fear in her eyes. Interesting.

"That's not stupid," he assured, lowering himself to the floor. "Usually, the magnitude of such good luck doesn't hit people until after they've made their first wish. But some get it right away. This measure of good fortune is a startling blow for people who have only ever known misfortune."

She turned her head and locked her eyes on his, as if his words resonated. "Yes, magnitude is a good word. I am feeling the magnitude. This is...this is magnitudinous."

He offered his most comforting smile. "I may be the one granting the wishes, but sometimes, in the dark void my conscious exists in between masters, I think about what I would wish for if I was the master instead of the servant. It's overwhelming just thinking about it."

"Thanks, that's super helpful," she said dryly.

"I'm only saying that it's good to recognize the weight of such a gift before you can waste it. There isn't a deadline as far as I know. Take your time. Think about it."

A warmth replaced the fear in her eyes, then her eyebrows drew together. "A dark void? That sucks."

Another reality check. He hadn't meant to turn her attention to him. He quickly smiled and waved it off. "It's fine. I'm *designed* to be your servant. Don't let me distract you from this chance of a lifetime."

He smiled as reassuringly as he could. She frowned back at him, but it wasn't a panicked frown. It was more resigned. It appeared he'd eased her concerns successfully. It was nice how well they were already getting along.

She pulled herself up to a sitting position, brushing the throw pillow to the side. "So...do you just hang out in your bottle while I think about my wishes?"

Raji's smile disappeared. The thought of returning to his bottle after six hundred years was not one that appealed to him, especially when he had access to a century like this one.

He knew he might regret it, but he made a split-second decision to do something he knew he should never, ever do.

Lie.

"Oh...uh. Well, you see, I don't go back into the bottle until my work here is done. But I'll be useful. I'm your servant, after all. I can fetch you things, care for your livestock, fan you with palm leaves—those are just a few examples of how I've been utilized in the past."

As she grimaced, another blow struck his chest. This one made his eyes begin to water. He held his breath to keep from whimpering.

"Really?" she asked with clear disappointment. "I mean...I don't have anywhere for you to sleep. I have this couch, but it's not great."

Raji emptied his lungs with a rapid burst of laughter that made Dot jump. "Oh, I don't sleep. I mean, I don't need to, but I can if you desire it. I also don't need to eat, and I don't urinate or defecate—"

"Okay! Great. You're low maintenance. I get it. Thank you."

The pain subsided a little.

She's warming up to the idea.

"That's good, actually. I'm not great at taking care of things. I can barely take care of myself." She smiled uneasily.

Raji rubbed his chest as the pain lessened. He was getting away with it. "But that's part of *my* job. I'm here to take care of *you*. I would never expect you to worry about me. That's ridiculous!" He chuckled and scratched the back of his neck absently.

"Oh," she said. "I guess that's fine, then."

Her eyes narrowed into slits. Then, with a shake of her head, she checked her wrist, though he didn't see a watch on it. "Well, I've got work soon, so I guess you can just...stay here and do the dishes or whatever."

"I can come with you!" he said. "I can help you with your tasks."

"Oh, no. Let's not do that." She grimaced again. He pretended not to notice.

"Alright. I can stay here. What's your trade? Do you work nearby?"

"My trade? Oh, I work customer service at the Target about ten miles away."

His infinite knowledge provided him with several possibilities regarding what "the Target" might be. No matter what she meant, he'd have to come along if it was that far. "I'm sorry, Master Dot. I'm cosmically bound to you. I can't be too far away or else I'll bounce back to you. But I have a lot of experience making myself inconspicuous. I can stay out of your way."

He watched her consider his words. Maybe his relief at escaping banishment had been premature, because her expression looked sour.

"Fine," she finally said. "But after I get ready, we're gonna go over *my* rules."

"I live to follow your rules, Master Dot."

"Good. First rule: no Master. Just Dot."

She disappeared into her bedroom, closing the door behind her. The rattle of the doorknob suggested the turn of a lock.

No doubt this would be a memorable experience.

Chapter 6

DOT

In all her twenty-five years, Dot hadn't lived with a single person besides her grandmother. She and Howie had never moved in together; neither of them ever really got to where they were willing to give up their own space.

Now here she was, suddenly forced to share her home with someone for the first time since Grandma because she got curious about a dumb, old bottle.

This shouldn't be happening to me.

So much had been thrust upon her in such a short period of time that she was struggling to focus. As she looked down, she groaned, realizing she was squeezing lotion onto her toothbrush.

Before hopping in the shower, she double-checked that the door was locked. She still hadn't entirely ruled out the possibility that this was some perverted scheme.

Why don't I kick him out? Why don't I call the cops?

Those would be the logical things to do, but would a pervert really go to such lengths? The man had teleported her halfway across the world. He made a bowl of cereal disappear before her eyes. Either this was a real genie, or her mind had finally gone and the vivid hallucinations had started. Admittedly, a genie was much better than a clown with a knife, which is what her elderly neighbor, Enid, started seeing when she started to lose it.

When she was cleaned up and dressed in her red shirt and jeans, she returned to the living room, half-hoping the genie would no longer be there, only to discover him engrossed in an old People magazine he must have found under her coffee table. She felt bad about not having much for him to do, but he *had* mentioned living for centuries in a void of nothingness. Surely he knew how to entertain himself.

"So...when I'm at work," she said. He shut the magazine and stood at attention. She didn't love when he did that. "Okay...um, when I'm at work, how am I supposed to explain the exotic shirtless man hanging around the store? I've barely started this job. I don't want to mess it up."

"You could wish for a different job. What's your dream job?"

The question caught her off guard. She had never had the luxury of pursuing any job besides the quick and easy ones. Several options crossed her mind, yet none felt like they'd be her *dream*. A CEO? Too much responsibility. A doctor? She couldn't trust herself with peoples' lives. An actress? Too many eyes on her. She settled on evasiveness. "I'll think about that, but I'll focus on the job I already have for now."

"Does my attire bother you?" he asked with pointed eye contact.

She didn't want to make him feel self-conscious, but... "A little. But not because you don't look good! Your body is very nice...I mean, not nice, it's healthy. And nice. You look nice and healthy. It's just your pants...thing—"

"They call them genie pants now. Isn't that funny? When I first put them on they were just called pants. Not the legacy I expected to leave, but—"

"Cool." Watching him admire his pants felt wrong. "That's...neat, but it's not normal to only wear pants. I mean, some guys do. The good-looking ones. Not that you're good-looking! I mean, not that you're *not* good-looking. I...listen, I work in a public place, okay?"

The weight of the silence that followed almost broke her. Her cheeks burned with the fire of a thousand suns. When she noticed an amused smile playing at the corner of his mouth, the heat intensified, forcing her to bury her face in her hands.

"I am so sorry. I don't know how to talk sometimes," she said into her palms.

"Don't apologize. My aim is to ensure your comfort. Is this better?"

Dot raised her eyes. His outfit had changed. Now he wore slim jeans and a dark t-shirt, one that didn't do much to divert her attention away from his chest. Coupled with his messy waves and dark facial hair, he suddenly looked more like a modern young adult than she did. Not the kind that were prevalent along the Florida panhandle, but she didn't know if he could do anything about that.

"Oh," she said a little too emphatically. "Is all this...real?"

"Yes. As long as something isn't of significant value, I can conjure it outside of a wish."

She barely heard him. She was too busy trying not to look like she was checking him out while she checked him out. The puffy pants hadn't done him justice. "This is good. You look...decent." She backed up a few steps, anxious to move on before her cheeks turned pink again. "If you have to be nearby, I want you to blend in, and this blends. I mean, could you imagine if I had to explain you to anyone?"

"I could explain myself for you."

"Please don't. That sounds even more stressful. I barely believe this is happening right now, so there's no way I'm ready to try convincing anyone else it is."

He followed her to her car. No one had ever been as impressed with her old Altima as he was. After opening and closing the door a few times, he settled into the passenger seat and messed around with the seat belt, buckling and unbuckling it while watching it closely. She didn't know what to make of his curiosity. Were this a movie, she'd find it amusing, but seeing how this was real life, she wondered how long she should let him mess with things before telling him to please stop.

Once they were on the road, he reclined his seat all the way back. "This is the best century so far," he said. "I can't believe regular people have this kind of stuff."

She kept the stereo on as they drove to deter him from talking to her, casting him a hesitant glance as he bobbed his head to Lady Gaga. As the type of person who always opted for the self-checkout and hung up if a real person answered when she called a customer service line, she knew it would take time to relax around him. She wondered how, in this day and age, the system hadn't been updated to one that didn't require a middleman. A cosmically bound genie didn't seem necessary for the process.

And now I'm taking this strange man to work. I've lost all common sense.

Once they arrived, she dropped him off at the front entrance, then parked in the employee section of the lot. It was a relief to be rid of him for the first time since the previous night. Her instructions to him were simple: he could spend her shift browsing but not touching, buying, or breaking. His ability to call forth knowledge should help him know how to do that normally, but Dot still felt a little uneasy about sending him off on his own.

After entering through the employee entrance and stowing her bag in a locker, Dot made her way to the Customer Service counter and greeted Skye, then began surveying the small section of the store she could see.

"You alright?" Skye asked. "You seem skittish."

Dot relaxed her shoulders and forced a yawn, hoping it would make her look less on edge. "No, I'm fine."

"It has something to do with that bottle, doesn't it? Tell me you chucked that thing off a bridge."

"I can take the next customer!" Dot yelled to the queuing shoppers.

"Girl, I hope you know a good priest," Skye muttered.

An hour passed with a steady flow of customers, but between the refunds and exchanges she saw no sign of Raji. Another hour passed just the same.

During a break in customers, Skye continued her questioning. "You kept it, didn't you? You're obsessed with that relic of the devil."

"It's not a relic of the devil."

"Did you get it open?"

"No," she lied.

"But you're gonna keep it until you do, aren't you? The way some people take their own life in their hands, I swear."

"It was probably just the wind moving it last night."

Skye stared skeptically. "You can keep blaming the wind, but we both know there was no wind."

A customer approached Skye's register. Dot took advantage of the distraction and searched the faces of the visible passersby.

"Who are you looking for?" Skye asked. So much for her being distracted. The customer was still there, glancing at Dot curiously while Skye began the return.

"Me?" Dot looked behind her.

"Yes, you. Are you expecting someone? You keep looking around like you've got a stalker." Skye lowered her voice. "Do you have a stalker?"

Both Skye and the customer stared at Dot curiously.

"No! Not that I know of."

"I had a stalker once," the customer interjected.

Skye narrowed her eyes at Dot. She didn't seem convinced.

After close to four hours, it was time for Skye's break. Dot's would come after. Naturally, once alone, a long line formed and Dot was left to handle it by herself.

After a few easy customer interactions, a disgruntled-looking middle-aged woman arrived at the counter, her impatient frown evident before Dot could even greet her. That was never a good sign.

The woman dropped a box on the counter. An expensive gaming console.

"I want to exchange this," the woman snapped.

Dot held in a sigh and examined the box. "Does the item still work?" she asked robotically.

"No, it doesn't work! Hasn't worked since I bought it."

"Are all the parts here?" She pulled the console out of the already open box.

"What does it matter? The piece of junk doesn't work."

Dot took a deep breath. She could feel her pulse quickening.

How do I always end up with these customers?

Regardless of the answer, as the only employee available—and because she was new—she needed to remain calm.

"It's just we can't take returns on partial items."

The woman scoffed loudly. "Partial items? Are you accusing me of being dishonest? The important part is there if you'd open your eyes."

Calm.

Dot placed the console on the counter and checked inside the box. There were definitely no cords, but there also weren't any controllers. Which meant she was forced to ask the customer more questions. "Ma'am, did the item come with controllers?"

"It was supposed to come with controllers, but it didn't. I told you, it's a piece of junk! You people should check for these things before you put them on the shelves so you're not wasting peoples' time like you're wasting mine right now!" The woman's grating whine was increasing in volume. The other people in line went quiet as they started to pay attention.

Dot concentrated all her energy on remaining composed, but the effort made her dizzy. She didn't want to snap back at the woman in front of all these people, and she didn't want to cry at work when she was still getting to know her coworkers.

"I want to exchange this for one that actually works, and I don't have a lot of time, so quit standing there and staring at me like an idiot!"

The queuing customers began to murmur amongst themselves. Dot scanned the area for a manager, but got distracted when she noticed an overly attractive middle eastern man step into her line. The genie. She quickly looked away. Was he here hoping she would use a wish to get out of this? A vision of the woman falling from the sky into the middle of the Atlantic flashed through her head. As tempting as that was, it would still be a waste of a wish. She had handled her mother's manipulation attempts alone, and she could handle this alone, too. Although a manager would be nice.

Regrettably, she didn't spot one. "Ma'am, I'm only trying to help you by making sure you have everything in order for an exchange. If you say it didn't come with controllers, fine. I'll still exchange it. But I will need you to go back to the electronics department and get the product you'd like to exchange this for and bring it up." Dot gave herself an imaginary pat on the back for getting that many words out without letting her voice quiver.

But deep down, she feared nothing she said would be good enough.

The woman's face turned a deep red. "You're kidding, right? Isn't that *your* job? I come in here, a loyal customer, I might add, and a minimum-wage cashier is asking me to do *her* job? Where is your manager? I demand to speak to someone who will show me some respect!"

"Is there a problem here?" Mary appeared behind her. The relief that swept over Dot made her knees wobble.

"Yes, there's a problem! I'm trying to do an exchange and your employee is trying to get me to do her job! I'm not walking all the way to the back of the store to get another one of these. I have arthritis!"

Dot glanced at her manager, who nodded reassuringly and gave her a discreet apologetic frown as she lifted her walkie-talkie to her mouth. "Jeff, could you track down a product for me and bring it to Customer Service? Fast?"

The walkie-talkie crackled and Jeff's voice answered. "Yep, what's the product?"

While Mary and Jeff got on the same page, Dot took another look towards Raji. Intently, he watched the still-fuming customer, who grumbled to herself as she waited for Mary.

"We'll have the item up here in just a moment," Mary said.

"Good, and I want this girl seriously reprimanded for the way she treated me." The woman jabbed a finger towards Dot. "She's trying to make me out like I don't know what I'm talking about. She has no right to do that to a customer."

Dot couldn't help it; she rolled her eyes. And she wasn't restrained about it.

"See that! What a little—"

Jeff appeared with a new console.

"I'll need to see your original card to complete the exchange," Mary said, obviously just as anxious to get this woman out of the store. Dot noticed a few people in line were now holding up their phones to record the spectacle. *Great.* Now she would be humiliated all over social media for eternity. But unlike Raji and his pants, this was not far off from the legacy she expected to leave behind.

The woman dug into her purse with overstated irritation. "I have never had to jump through so many hoops to make an exchange!" She slapped a credit card on the counter and shot Dot a scathing glare. Dot looked away. Once this woman was gone, she knew Mary wouldn't blame her for any of it, but at this point, it was little consolation. The woman would leave having gotten what she wanted and Dot would be left with the embarrassment of being yelled at and ridiculed in front of a growing crowd of onlookers *and* her boss. Her eyes began to sting. She fought back the tears, and as she did, she caught Raji's eye. He was mouthing something to her.

"*What?*" she mouthed back.

"*Look in the box.*" He gestured downwards, and Dot quickly understood his meaning. She looked down at the counter, picked up the box for the faulty game console, and looked inside.

The woman noticed. "Your employee's attempting to steal!" she yelled at Mary.

Mary looked sideways at Dot from where she was punching numbers into the register. Dot ignored them both and reached inside the box. Her hand landed on a folded piece of paper stuck to the side. She pulled it out and unfolded it.

"What is that?" The woman immediately tried to snatch the paper away, but Dot stepped back so that she only came away with a handful of air. "I don't know what that is!"

It took a moment for Dot to make sense of what she was seeing, but once she did, the oncoming tears dried up. She glanced at Raji—who winked—and handed the paper to Mary.

"What? What is that?" the woman said.

Dot spoke before Mary could; she wanted the joy of having the words come out of her mouth. "It's a packing invoice," Dot said, finally daring to look the mean woman in the eye.

Mary's expression turned cold. "Ma'am, the name of the recipient on this invoice matches the name on your card. You didn't buy this here, did you?"

Dot peeked over Mary's shoulder. "According to this, the product was purchased from a foreign website and look at the description. It says *used*."

The onlookers gasped. The woman's eyes bulged.

Dot began cramming the old console back into the box while Mary yanked the new one off the counter before the woman could grab it.

"Here you go," Dot said, pushing the box towards the woman.

"No—that's not—how did that? I thought I—"

"I can take the next customer!" Dot yelled.

The crowd applauded, parting as the woman clung to her cheap game console and darted towards the closest exit. But the automatic doors didn't open. Realizing it too late, she plowed into the glass and fell over backwards. The crowd oohed. A man attempted to help her up, but the woman swatted him off as she struggled to her feet. Finally, the doors opened and she disappeared.

By then, even Mary was chuckling. And Dot couldn't help smiling. She had *never* experienced a public win like that before. It felt...good. *Really* good.

"What did I miss?" Skye appeared behind them, sipping on a soda.

"Dot, go ahead on break. I'll help Skye with these customers," Mary said. "I'm sorry about that...person. Unfortunately, people like her come with the territory."

Dot glanced towards Raji, who had stepped out of the line and casually flipped through a sales flyer nearby.

"I'll...go this way," she explained, though neither Skye nor Mary were paying her any attention. She headed towards Raji and grabbed him by the arm as she passed, pulling him into the empty greeting card aisle.

"That was you, wasn't it?" she asked quietly, releasing his arm as they came to a stop.

"I'm a genie," he said matter-of-factly.

"Yeah, you've mentioned that, but I didn't wish for anything."

He shrugged. "I told you. I have a little magic allowance between wishes."

Dot crossed her arms. "Okay, how did you know she was trying to con me? Your infinite brain covers that stuff?"

"Actually, no. I didn't know she was conning you. But I knew she was causing you distress. Before this, I was browsing the electronics section, checking out all this twenty-first century tech. Morgan, the gentleman who works that department—"

"You talked to someone? You didn't tell him you were with me, did you?"

Raji raised his hands calmly. "I was only doing as you asked and acting like a run-of-the-mill, indecisive customer. I didn't mention your name."

"I guess that's fine, then." She looked around to make sure they were still alone.

"Anyway, Morgan told me this tech is accessible to everyone, which is amazing, but also that you have to be careful about where you buy it if you're using the internet. So...I merely planted evidence that the nice lady got a used product off of an untrustworthy seller and tried to switch it with a new one, which is probably the truth, let's be honest. The internet says it's a common con. Have you seen the internet? I guess these days infinite knowledge isn't as magical as it used to be."

"Yes, I've *seen* the internet. And that was...kind of diabolical of you," she said with reluctant approval. "I mean, it would've made no difference to the company if we had gone through with the exchange, but it was nice to put someone like that in her place in front of a crowd. I'm normally the one looking stupid."

"Yeah. She was a total Karen." He rolled his eyes.

A laugh escaped her, taking her by surprise. She raised her hand to punch him playfully, then wondered if that would be weird, so she redirected and scratched her nose instead. "Maybe it won't be so bad having you around, after all."

"I live to serve my master." He smiled. Then frowned. He suddenly looked like he was enduring an inner struggle of some kind; his expression switched from gracious, to nervous, to pained.

"Are you okay?"

"I...this is the first culture I've been in where bowing isn't a thing and it's sort of a hard habit to break. I'm not sure how else to illustrate my contrition."

"You really don't need to worry about that..." The bowing was strange, no question, but at the moment she *was* feeling like a boss. "...but if it makes you feel better, you can bow a little. But this is the last time, okay?"

"Absolutely!" He placed his hands together and bent forward as an old man stepped into the aisle.

Dot quickly patted Raji on the shoulder. "Okay, that's good."

He rose, oblivious to the shopper's sidelong look.

"Thank you. For helping me. I really appreciate it." She smiled, and it was genuine. This morning, she had struggled to see how having a genie was a good thing (or a real thing), and she still wasn't entirely convinced, but her tightened muscles had relaxed a bit. "Okay. Well, I have a thirty-minute break. You do whatever you've been doing. I'm going to sit in my car and eat a Lunchable."

He looked like he was about to say something, but changed his mind. Despite proving himself, she still wasn't eager to hang out with him if she didn't have to. His lack of objection was another point in his favor.

He was catching on swimmingly.

Chapter 7

Dot

Skye was waiting to hear all about the now-legendary victory over the unpleasant woman when Dot returned to start the second half of her shift. Between customers, she recounted the tale, unable to hold back a proud grin at the plot twist.

She kept looking, but she didn't see Raji again before closing time. Even then, she waited around nervously for an employee to find him lurking in some aisle, but no one did. He also wasn't waiting in the parking lot as she walked to her car.

"Hmm," she said to herself, taking one more look around. "Well, I'm not his babysitter."

She opened her car door and slid into her seat.

"Hello!" he said from the passenger seat. She jumped.

"I don't like not knowing when or where you're going to show up," she said once she had settled. "Maybe let me know next time."

"Absolutely. Have you thought about that first wish?"

Dot threw her head back and groaned. "This again? You said there was no time limit. And I've been at work for the past eight hours."

"Yeah, but how are you not thinking about what you're gonna wish for?"

Dot rubbed her temple. His enthusiasm was fine, just a bit much. She liked to allow herself the space to be cranky and tired after a long shift.

"I haven't eaten much today. I might stop and get something if that's okay."

Raji frowned. "Don't ask for my approval. If you want to do it, then I want you to do it."

"Sorry." She started the engine and pulled out of the empty lot.

"And...what's the apology for?"

Maybe it wasn't his excitement that was a little much. Maybe it was the constant questions. She shrugged. "I don't know. Sorry for asking, I guess."

He didn't respond. She glanced at him to find his head tilted in confusion. Lady Gaga had started playing loudly again, but Raji looked like he wanted to say something. She clicked off the stereo.

"Have you ever been the master of anything before?" he asked. "You almost behaved like a servant to that woman today, even though you knew more about what you were doing than she did."

The comment rankled her. It sounded like something Howie would say.

"The customer is always right."

"That's false. That woman was clearly wrong."

Dot laughed wryly. "Can you not criticize me for how I do my job?"

From the corner of her eye, she thought she saw his mouth twist in offense. Whether or not she was imagining it, she immediately felt guilty.

"I'm sorry. That was rude. I'm just...hangry." She looked over at him. His head was bent forward again, his eyes directed downward.

"You can say whatever you want to me, and you never need to apologize. I'm the servant, you're the master. I only meant to say that it's important that you come to terms with that. But I see that you're getting it. Please forgive me for sounding critical. I won't do it again."

An awkward tension—Dot's specialty—settled inside the car.

Way to be mean, she chided herself.

She was so not a people person.

A neon OPEN sign on a burger restaurant caught her eye, and she pulled in. Maybe she could ease the tension with food. "Do you want a cheeseburger?"

"Dot, I don't mean any disrespect, but I get the feeling that you may have some financial difficulties. I don't need to eat, so don't feel obligated to spend any of your money on me."

She still couldn't see his face. It remained lowered into the shadows. Was he really offended? Or was he just being...professional? Reading people was not her strongest skill.

"Think of it as a thank-you gift for what you did today," she said, approaching the drive-thru. "Cheeseburgers are good. And cheap. You need to try one. I *command* it."

He didn't argue with her, and the cashier had already come on to the speaker to take her order, so he didn't have much of a chance to. After receiving their food, she pulled into an empty parking spot beneath a streetlight, tossing a wrapped cheeseburger to Raji.

"Give me your honest opinion," she said.

Watch him hate it, she thought, discreetly watching him as she began to unwrap her cheeseburger.

When he moaned loudly, she smiled with relief. "No wonder everyone is rounder in the twenty-first century!" he said with a full mouth. "Thank you so much!"

Another imaginary pat on the back. Food was the universal peacemaker. Her crankiness began to dissipate. "This is poor people food. If I had money, I could *really* show you good food."

She glanced over to see him wearing an *I know how to fix that* smirk, though his mouth was filled with cheeseburger.

"Yeah, I know. Money is definitely something I'm considering for one of the wishes."

Raji nodded contently and returned to chewing his food.

"But there are so many ways to get money. Do I wish for a lump sum? Or some sort of steady income? Should I wish for a job? But where's the fun in wishing for a job?"

"You said the word *fun*," he pointed out. "I love fun wishes." He took another large bite, already halfway through his burger. As the food entered his mouth, his eyes widened. He quickly swallowed. "But my idea of fun and yours may be different, and you should wish for what's fun for you."

"Did you even chew that bite?" She frowned.

"What? Oh, no," he laughed lightly. "I swallowed it whole. But don't worry, I'm not going to choke."

She lifted her eyebrows. "Oh, that's right. You're invincible."

"Immortal," he corrected.

"What's that like? Have you always been immortal? Like, have you always been a genie, or were you normal once and something happened to you?"

Instead of answering, he quickly shoved the last chunk of burger into his mouth. This time he chewed slowly, then pointed to his mouth and shrugged.

When he finally swallowed, he seemed to shrink a little under her continued stare.

"Don't worry about all that," he said. "You were talking about possible wishes, weren't you?"

She wondered if she should pursue this line of questioning further. Judging by his deflection, he had an answer, he just didn't want to share it with her.

Let the guy do his job. Don't pry. You hate when people pry.

She could go back to the wish topic for his comfort, she decided. But she made a mental note to further investigate his origin later.

"Okay...so if I go with a well-paying job, do I need to wish for an education first?"

He laughed, and she thought she noticed a touch of relief in his tone. "No. Wishes can bypass all that stuff. But knowledge is a very popular wish." He licked some mustard off his lip. "Knowledge is power, and power is the *most* popular wish."

"I don't want power," Dot said. "I hate being in charge of stuff. Being the manager when I worked at the bookstore was the most stressful job I've ever had. People always wanted me for stuff."

"Power over others and power over yourself are two different things."

"That's...that's a good point." She took a nibble of her hamburger and leaned back. "Then maybe I need to think of a job that empowers me, but where I don't have to be responsible for anyone else. And it has to pay well...hey!" She turned in her seat to face him. "What if I invented my own job and salary? Like getting paid to travel the world and stay in expensive resorts? Or watch movies and eat takeout?" That was a tantalizing thought.

"You could do that," he said. "But inventing things in wishes can be risky. If it's something no one has ever done, there can be side effects you may not foresee." He adjusted himself so that he was facing her more directly. "Case in point, I had a master once who wished for a unicorn-bear hybrid as a pet for his daughter. He figured he'd be famous for having the only specimen. He thought he was getting two wishes for the price of one. But the unicorn part by itself was a disaster. The horn was constantly catching on things or knocking things over. Almost impaled the daughter. Then to combine that with a bear? He specified the bear part be the fur and the paws, so that it would be cuddly. A unicorn is already part horse, and horses are jumpy. Every time its horn caught on something, it got spooked, and the paws went wild. It's a miracle nobody died. I mean, besides a few of the servants that worked in the stables. It eventually had to be put down."

"Oh my gosh," Dot said. "Okay. I won't make up something."

He cleared his throat loudly. "Hold on. Please understand that I'm not trying to influence your wishes. Your wishes are yours. It isn't my intention to talk you out of anything. If I'm overstepping, feel free to tell me to shut up."

"No, don't shut up. That was helpful." *If a little disturbing.*

The story did give her an idea, though. "You know, you make a good point. Not about the unicorn bear, but about your experience. Who better than a genie to give me advice about what to wish for? You've seen it all, right? You know what works and what doesn't." She popped the last bite of her burger into her mouth.

He frowned. "That's...kind of you to say, but your wishes should be all about what *you* want. Not anyone else. Especially not me. I don't want you to feel like I'm telling you what to wish for."

Dot laughed, and a piece of lettuce flew from her mouth, splatting against the steering wheel. She flicked it off, hoping Raji hadn't seen. "Are you kidding? I have no idea what to wish for. I'm the worst decision-maker of all time!"

Again, he gave her a puzzled look. Somehow, everything she said seemed to confuse him.

"What?" she asked, reflexively wiping her chin.

He rolled back into the seat. "You seem to be an adequate decision-maker. Don't you think you're judging yourself too harshly?"

She scoffed, amused at the ignorance of someone who claimed to know every-thing. "No. I'm not judging myself too harshly, believe me." Her post-work irritability was kicking in, and she felt the never-helpful urge to overexplain. "You just met me, so let me tell you a little about myself: I'm average. Below average, but not so much that I'm the lovable underdog or anything. I have no marketable skills, I have no close friends or family, I have no redeeming qualities. I'm dull and depressing and anxious and too cautious and so intimidated by big decisions that I avoid them at all costs. I'm afraid that if I put effort into anything, I'll ruin it, because I always have. I am literally the last person on earth who can handle three wishes. I already know I'm gonna do it all wrong. If anything, you're not judging me harshly enough."

Raji listened patiently, even though she was sure that no one wanted to hear all that. Sheepishly, she looked down at the empty cheeseburger wrapper in her hands. "I'm also awkward and I overshare. Sorry. I didn't mean to dump all that on you."

When she looked up, her eyes stumbled onto his.

For a moment she forgot he was a genie, and she felt...*tingly* with his deep brown eyes on her like that. They were pretty eyes. And it felt like they were looking at her in a way no one else ever had, as silly as that sounded. Like he truly wanted to understand where she was coming from. This must be what people mean when they say they feel *seen*.

She wasn't sure she liked feeling seen, though, especially by this guy, so she turned away and pretended to be very interested in wadding up the cheeseburger wrapper.

"If you're afraid, then you can transfer my services to someone else before you make the wishes. Because I can't tell you what to wish for."

She flinched. Maybe it was because it felt like they had just shared a moment, but she expected him to say something more profound and inspirational. Or at least argue that she was wrong. Her jaw tightened. "I'm not afraid. I'm just cautious. Like I said." She tossed the wrapper into a cup holder. "I should get home. I mean, *we* should. Not that it's your home..."

She sighed and started the car. Late nights had the tendency to make her talk too much. It could have been that the darkness made it feel like she was speaking into nothingness, or her brain was too tired to keep her thoughts in her head where they belonged. Either way, it had been a day since she released this ancient, all-powerful being and her diarrhea of the mouth was already lessening his opinion of her.

Poor, poor Dot.

But she decided she didn't need or want a mythical creature's sympathy, no matter how pretty he was. What she needed was to get these wishes made so she could go back to being newly independent, eternally pathetic, Dot.

Dot awoke the next morning, mortified to find herself thinking about Raji's eyes. He was possibly thousands of years older than her, which meant staring into his eyes the night before while he stared back was actually kind of creepy.

Don't make things more awkward than they already are! she reminded herself.

Sadly, it wasn't the first time this had been her morning affirmation.

Today she didn't have to work. That meant she could focus on her first wish and get this surreal freakshow on the road. It would also mean being stuck alone with Raji all day. She wasn't sure how to feel about that.

Hypnotic brown eyes aside, his valuable wisdom from last night solidified her resolve to seek his help with her wishes, regardless of his protests. On her own, she would surely fumble the opportunity. As much as remotely-made-wishes appealed to her, she now saw the genius in having the three-wish plan come with a personal consultant.

She got out of bed and approached her closed door. Though it was already late morning, there were no sounds coming from the living room. No snoring, rustling, or muttering. It was a little unnerving.

She cracked her bedroom door open and peeked out.

"I'm right here." Raji suddenly appeared in front of her, standing *right there* as she opened her door. She squealed.

"I wanted to make sure you knew where I was as soon as you opened the door so I didn't scare you again."

"You did great," she said dryly, holding a hand against her pounding chest. "I wasn't startled at all."

"What's on the agenda today? A wish, I hope."

Dot skirted past him into the living room and flopped onto the couch.

"Maybe," she answered. "But if you want to grant a wish, I was serious about what I said. I need you to coach me."

He frowned. Just as she suspected, he wasn't as into the idea as she was. "I told you I can't tell you what to wish for. I don't know you like you know yourself. And frankly, it's not in your best interest to care what I think."

"What's that supposed to mean?" Why couldn't he ever answer with a simple yes or no? "I'm not asking you to *tell* me, I'm asking you to *help* me. Isn't that why you're here?"

He didn't respond, which made her feel bad. And a little stupid. She grabbed her phone from the end table and pretended to be busy on it, mindlessly tapping in and out of her social media apps. After a sufficient amount of time, she peeked at Raji.

He had changed clothes sometime between last night and this morning. Today he wore a white T-shirt and a pair of gray sweatpants. She looked down at her pajamas. She wore her Orlando T-shirt and a pair of black sweatpants.

Does this guy not know how to think for himself?

His hands were in his pockets, and his shoulders sagged as he stared at the ground. Had she made *him* feel bad? Was she completely sure he *had* feelings?

She dismissed the question. Best not to get hung up on that kind of thing. Though he looked—and felt—like a regular human being, he was far from it. He was magic and eternal. She was the exact opposite of both those things—ordinary and expendable. Attempting to relate to him would be like attempting to relate to the British monarchy.

He cleared his throat. "Okay. I'll help you."

"You will?" She smiled as she tucked her phone away. "Uh, okay. I'll grab some paper."

A few minutes later, the two of them were sitting across from one another at Dot's small kitchen table; a pen and notebook lay before her. Both she and Raji were finishing a hearty bowl of Frosted Flakes, though Raji was on bowl number two. The silence in which they sat and ate may have been the first comfortable silence of this looney partnership so far. They both liked food. So that made one thing she could relate to him about.

"I once had a master wish for a thousand pounds of sugar," he said. "Now poor people are eating it for breakfast—no offense."

"None taken," she said, setting her empty bowl on the table.

"Let me take care of that for you." He swirled his wrist, and both of their empty bowls disappeared. She heard a *clink* in her cupboard. "Your dishes are now clean and put away." He smiled proudly.

The disappearing and yanking things out of thin air still hurt her brain.

"Thanks..." she said, electing to disregard the mind-bending magic. She picked up her pen. "Nice pajamas, by the way."

He glanced down at himself. "Thank you. When you changed last night, I suddenly became better dressed than my master, which is never a good look on a servant. I could've gone back to the genie pants, but you didn't seem to like those."

She scoffed like it was an accusation. "It's not that I didn't *like* them," she tried to explain, fidgeting under his concentrated attention. "It's just...you...didn't have a shirt."

"I understand." He nodded sensitively. "So, what would you like to know first about making wishes?"

She breathed a silent sigh of relief at his well-timed changing of the subject.

His chair wobbled as he leaned towards her, and the table tipped slightly as he used it to steady himself.

"Sorry," she apologized, noticing the wobbles. "The set was free, so I can't complain."

"If I've learned anything from previous masters, it's that you can complain about anything you want." He placed both hands on the table and wobbled it some more, experimentally. "What do you say to a change of scenery for this exercise?"

Dot only had to take a quick glimpse of her kitchen before answering. "I say yes."

"Do you have any requests, or do I have permission to surprise you?"

"What about somewhere cozy? I like cozy. But no people."

He nodded and began rubbing his beard in thought. Then he held a finger in the air with a grin. "I think I know a place."

Chapter 8

RAJI

Almost all Raji's wish-granting escapades had taken place in warm climates, especially for the first thousand years when his vessel had mainly stayed in China, India, or Northern Africa. Florida in the spring was at least green, but still pretty warm. It would be nice to go somewhere cozy.

Despite the still-developing relationship with his master and the ease of travel compared to the previous millennia, he got the feeling that maybe Dot hadn't gotten out much.

He still wasn't quite sure what to make of her. She could be polite one minute, then irritated the next. Closed off, then suddenly very open. Excited about her incredible luck but then overwhelmed by it. Last night she even seemed to suggest she was undeserving of having her dreams come true. This morning though, she seemed ready to get the ball rolling.

While the change of pace was interesting, it was also a bit disconcerting. Which is why he agreed to give her the input she was asking for. Although there was no reason he couldn't, doing so required revisiting past experiences—something he usually avoided. There weren't a ton of fond memories there. And the fond ones were the most painful to think about.

But he wanted to do his job and do it well. It was the only satisfaction he got out of life. Yes, she was an odd master, but something about that excited him. Over-enthusiastic masters he had dealt with on many occasions. Impatient masters, even more often. An uncomfortable, self-deprecating master is something he truly never expected. It was a new challenge, and new challenges revitalized the little bit of his life that he had control over.

With a snap of his fingers, the kitchen vanished.

The sound of her gasp thrilled him; her eyes lit up as she took in the room that now surrounded them, a room at least four times larger than her kitchen, outfitted with sleek, timber walls, a tall, vaulted ceiling, and an impressive stone fireplace taking up an entire corner.

Then she turned, and her mouth widened in synchronization with her pupils. What appeared to be a wall was actually floor-to-ceiling glass revealing a sweeping landscape of massive snow-capped mountains duplicating for miles until they faded into the gray sky.

He leaned forward on the robust, not-wobbly wooden table centered against the window where they now sat. He watched as she reverently flattened her palm against the glass, still captivated by the view.

"Where are we?" she breathed.

"The Rocky Mountains." His genie heart leaped at his success. Reluctantly, he peeled his eyes away from her and took in the view himself. It made him a little breathless, too. "Wow," he murmured.

"I know, right?" She stood and began looking around. A big, fluffy sofa dominated the room's center, draped with equally cozy blankets facing the blazing fireplace. From the way she both smiled and gaped when her eyes landed on it, he knew his servant foresight was developing correctly.

"There aren't any doors," she observed.

"Did you want to go outside? I can make a door."

She stared back out at the infinite blanket of snow and shook her head.

"So this is technically a preview, like the other night?" She flopped onto the sofa, pulling a blanket on top of her.

"Yes. You paid attention."

"But how can you do something like this if I didn't wish for it?"

"This is all temporary. This structure didn't exist before we got here and it will cease to exist when we leave in a few hours, which is the most these previews can last."

"And you said it's been how long since you last granted a wish?"

He stood and wandered towards her. "About six hundred years."

"How did no one find you for so long?"

He gripped the sofa behind her, admiring his handiwork. "I have no idea. When I'm not someone's servant, I am nothing and nowhere, a consciousness existing in an empty void. And my vessel has changed, too. At first it was a ring that a master simply had to put on to summon me, then it was the infamous lamp which required a rub. The last time I served a sorcerer, he had a lot of enemies, so he changed it to the bottle. He couldn't seal it indefinitely, thankfully, but he did make releasing me a lot more work. It really cut back on business." They were getting off track. "So is this an acceptable place to brainstorm?"

"Absolutely." Dot adjusted the blanket so that only her face was visible. "Except..." She wrinkled her nose doubtfully. "You probably can't bring us any food, can you?"

He wasn't going to say anything, so he was glad that she did.

He waved a hand towards the table. Next to her notebook and pen that joined them on their journey from her kitchen, two steaming mugs of hot cocoa and an open box of doughnuts materialized. She giggled and raced back to the table, pulling her blanket with her. Raji followed with his hands in his pockets as he quietly observed her reactions.

Wrapping the blanket around her body like a bath towel, she parked herself in a chair and reached for a doughnut. When she looked around for a place to put it, a small plate appeared in front of her.

"Now you're showing off," she said, placing her doughnut on the plate and licking the glaze off her fingers through a delighted grin.

Impressing a new master could be hit-or-miss, and up until now he hadn't been able to peg Dot as the barely impressed type or the easy-to-please type. A doughnut on a plate was a pittance compared to what he could do within a real wish, so her excitement over it implied that this had the potential to be an exceptionally gratifying gig.

The pleased smile on his face apparently gave away his thoughts. "I think you like being a genie," she said, ripping off a chunk of her doughnut.

He fought against responding honestly. The satisfaction that came from doing well at the only thing he could do didn't really count as *liking* it. But if it appeared that way to her, it was best to let her believe it. He shrugged. "It has its merits."

"Last night you said fun wishes are the best kind. Tell me what wish has been the most fun for you to grant—and don't say unicorn bear."

"Oh, no, *that* was terrifying." He lowered himself onto the chair across from her. "It's hard to answer that question. Most masters are looking for instant gratification, so oftentimes granting a wish is basically just me waving my arm around. A fun wish allows for a little creativity. And if it's received well..."

He paused, his smile fading. It wouldn't be prudent to share any further information. But when he glanced at her, she was listening, fully engrossed. It managed to sway him to bypass the normal barriers. His mouth kept moving.

"There was a master I had who was obsessed with this beautiful young woman," he began. "He threw a tantrum when he found out I couldn't make her fall in love with him, and for her sake, I was glad I couldn't. This guy was...well, in today's terminology, he was gross. In more ways than one. Much older than her, questionable motives, no teeth and bad hygiene—even for the time period, which was around seventh century China."

Dot nearly choked on her doughnut. "Seventh century? As in, over a thousand years ago?"

"Yes, as in over a thousand years ago." He laughed, realizing that a thousand years to Dot must seem like an impossible length of time. "The young woman was the daughter of a well-known man in the city, and her father wanted someone richer and more reputable than my master for his daughter to wed. It wasn't an unreasonable goal. She was gorgeous enough to marry any man she wanted. But she was kind of picky."

Across the table, Dot had ceased eating. She rested her chin on her fist and leaned in.

"She and her father wanted nothing to do with my master, but he was so obsessed with her, he used up all three wishes to woo her. For the first one, he wished for a garden of exotic flowers, and he had a bouquet delivered to her every day for a month. When that didn't send her running into his arms, he realized he had to go bigger. He wished for an ornate palace filled with expensive spices and perfumes and gowns—all of it tailored to her tastes. He thought it would lure her away from her own home."

"Did it?"

He shook his head. "No. She let me show her around, but even that couldn't make her agree to marry my master." He paused. He had started the story without thinking about how it ended. Though it was unintentionally abrupt, he had to stop there.

He scratched his beard and leaned back in his chair. "Anyway, those wishes have always ranked among my favorite to grant, but again, I should remind you how not-about-me and only about-you your wishes should be focused."

He took a sip of his cocoa and tried to ignore the deep frown growing on Dot's face.

"What about the third wish?" she asked. "You can't leave me hanging like that."

He waved his hand dismissively. "The first two were the fun ones. It only gets less fun from there. A lot more boring, to be honest. Now, you said you were thinking about something in the financial sphere for your first wish?"

Her eyebrows dipped. "I still want to know what happened. For research purposes."

"I really don't think the rest of the story—"

"Raji. Don't make me play the boss-lady card."

She certainly catches on quickly.

He placed his mug on the table. "You're sure you want to know?"

Her head bobbed up and down. He sighed.

"Fine. For the final wish, the master *tried* to wish for her parents to die, but obviously I couldn't grant that one."

Her eyes widened. "Are you for real?"

"Unfortunately, yes. But it gets worse. When that wish was denied, he wished for poverty and disease to come upon her entire family, to the point that her parents would beg him to take their daughter in marriage."

Her jaw dropped. "No way. Did it work? Please tell me it didn't work."

"It worked." He turned to the window and stared at it blankly. "She married him, and I went back into the lamp. I wasn't released again for another thirty or forty years, in a whole different part of China. I never saw either one of them again."

The memory still hurt a little. He remembered when it had hurt a lot. In those early days, when he had clung so desperately to his mortal past, life had been full of pain. It tainted every miniscule moment of happiness that his miserable fate afforded him. All these years later, he had learned to accept the hard truth about his job: it wasn't about him. He was made only to satiate the selfish whims of whatever master summoned him, good or bad.

"Sheesh. As a genie, I guess you wouldn't get much closure in those kinds of situations. I hope karma destroyed that guy."

Raji raised his eyebrows. "You believe in karma?"

"I mean..." She shrugged. "I like the idea of it, but if it's real, I must have done some terrible things."

Raji cocked his head introspectively. "I think I agree with you—about liking the idea of karma—but it stops there. In my line of work, I haven't seen a lot of evidence that good things happen to good people. For some reason, it's usually the worst of humanity that ends up with their very own genie."

Her expression fell into one of unmistakable hurt, and a jolt of pain erupted in his chest.

"I don't mean you, though!" he quickly backtracked. "I don't know anything about you, so I can't judge you. I can't judge any master until after the wishes—not that I'm *planning* on judging you...wow, I am so sorry." He offered his most penitent smile. "We've established you don't like bowing, but what are your feelings about me lying on the ground and begging for forgiveness?"

Her expression softened, and the pain ebbed quickly. She didn't seem to think he was serious. "No, that's not necessary." She swirled her mug and peered into her cocoa. "My mouth gets away from me sometimes, too."

Inadvertently offending masters wasn't anything new for him, but her instant forgiveness was. He rubbed his suddenly pain-free chest with subdued bewilderment.

"And I think I see what made those two wishes fun for you," Dot said, a sly look in her eyes as she shifted them back towards him. "You liked the woman. Didn't you?"

This was precisely why he never should have said anything. "No." He laughed nervously. "I don't *like* people. That's not—"

"Who delivered her flowers for a month? Did the master go, or did he send you?"

"I did it, but—"

"And you customized that palace for her and gave her the tour."

"The master wanted to be waiting at the end so he could propose."

Dot raised her chin proudly.

This didn't seem like safe territory.

"Fine. If I wasn't a genie, I might have liked her," he said, cringing at his own words.

Being cosmically bound to a master each time he was out of the bottle didn't allow Raji much of a personal life—a deliberate design, obviously—but he had plenty of daydreams. And he didn't share those with his masters. The one time he had...the consequences of doing so had only led to a stronger determination to keep his feelings to himself. Somehow, though, Dot had made him slip.

She picked up her notepad and pen and angled it towards her as she scribbled something down.

"What are you writing?"

"Don't worry about it," she said.

When she noticed his worried expression, she put down the notepad, flipping it so he couldn't see. "I actually think it's sweet. Very sad, but sweet too." She cleared her throat, running her finger around the rim of her mug. "So genies can have crushes, huh? That's interesting. Were you involved in any other forbidden love affairs in the last few thousand years? Any other ladies who caught your eye?"

His eyes followed the motion of her finger and stayed on it as she raised it to brush a honey-colored lock behind her ear. This question wasn't a hard one to shut down. Not even an interesting, pretty, relentlessly curious master could convince him to answer that. Not out loud, anyway.

I'm still human, he could have said.

But he didn't. "It's a personal rule of mine not to talk about myself," he finally answered. "Not that there's anything to say. I have one purpose, and that is to grant your wishes. There is nothing else outside of that."

I've been in the bottle too long. That's why I keep taking a mile of conversation every time she gives me an inch.

He could feel her stare as he redirected his attention to the window. It would be so nice to have a friendly, normal conversation with a regular person—and she seemed like the perfect candidate—but that wasn't why he was here.

"Okay," she said. "But I have old wounds, too. We all do. I won't force you to tell me about them if you don't want to. We can keep this professional. But..."

Old wounds. If she only knew. "But what?" He turned back to her.

"But the master-servant language is weird. I released you from your bottle, I get that, but I don't want to treat you like my servant, and I really don't want you to treat me like I'm your overlord. It feels a little icky."

He stared, then nodded curtly. "Alright. You're the master. I'll behave however you'd like me to."

She snorted and drew out an eye roll. "Didn't you hear me? I don't want to be constantly referred to as your master. The way you talk about masters—they all sound awful. I don't want to be lumped in with those guys." She wiggled her shoulders. "I'm cool, you know. I'm a cool..." She stopped herself. "How about you think of me as your client?"

All the unnatural twenty-first century body language distracted him for a second. With amusement. "Okay. Yes. Client."

"And you're like...a wish agent."

Raji frowned. "An agent and a servant are two different—"

"Nope, that's what it is. That is our relationship." She gestured from herself to him. "Client and agent. That would make me feel a lot better. And it will remind us that all of this is a professional transaction. I don't like talking about myself either. We have that in common. I get it."

He straightened his lips and nodded. "Alright."

"Agents are experts at getting their clients a good deal, right?" She picked up the pen. "So help me get the most out of my contract."

He let a bit of twinkle return to his eyes as his mouth turned up into a careful smile. "You're very magnanimous, Dot."

"I...don't know what that is. Is it like magnitudinous?"

His smile became a little less careful. "It means you're a very considerate client."

A pair of matching dimples materialized on either side of her mouth. "I'm really not, but I'll take the compliment so we can move on," she said, her cheeks flushing pink.

It was kind of cute.

But a diplomatic master, treating him as an equal and insisting he see himself as one—that was also cute. The twenty-first century was starting out pleasant enough, as was Dot, but over thousands of years of servitude, there had always been one thing that remained consistent: people were selfish. And here in the most materialistic era the world had ever seen, there was no reason to believe anything had changed. Once the wishes began, Dot's focus would gradually turn inward and Raji wouldn't bat an eyelash. It was how these things always went, with one exception he could think of.

Across the table, Dot sipped her cocoa, her gaze once again fixed on the breathtaking scene outside, a humble smile on her lips. Though her ego would kick in eventually, he wasn't completely disappointed with who she was now, pre-corruption. That would at least be something nice to think back on once this job was over.

Chapter 9

DOT

The sky outside the window of their little retreat in the Rockies never changed from a soft gray the whole day, so when Raji alerted her that it was getting late (in Florida time), Dot was genuinely surprised. Even a little sad.

But her notebook was now filled with notes and ideas, as well as a few doodles of genies coming out of lamps and bottles. Overall, she had close to ten pages of possible wishes. The problem was, there wasn't one that felt like a sure choice.

Raji had kindly recounted a few less personal experiences (riveting nonetheless) that helped her know what *not* to wish for. Exotic animals, invisibility, flying, and mind-reading all proved to produce more problems than they solved, and trying to find loopholes to make people fall in love was practically guaranteed to backfire. Also, wishing for objects that could get lost or stolen, like jewels or gold, didn't seem like a great idea for someone like Dot who was constantly leaving her debit card at various drive-thru windows.

That's to say nothing of the type of wishes Raji had granted most frequently with the worst results: wishes that endowed greedy people with oppressive powers. His power-hungry masters seemed to think that simply being hired was all it took to be a successful leader, but inexperienced rulers made easy targets for seasoned conquerors. The amount of people who used a wish to get on a throne made Dot want to revisit her high school history class and figure out which incompetent ancient kings might have been clients of his.

On the other hand, there were a lot of wish categories that piqued her interest. Financial security, definitely. Easy living wishes. Even revenge wishes sounded fun. One of Dot's favorite stories of the day was of a boy in India living under the rule of a cunning, cruel, and oppressive Maharaja who had his father arrested and killed for stealing food to feed his family. After getting a hold of Raji's lamp, the ruthless kid wished that the Maharaja would be subjected to unending public humiliation, forever branding him as an incompetent fool. The Maharaja's downfall came when his greatest supporters fled under the weight of their secondhand embarrassment. The boy became king, and...well, got conquered soon after. Still, the story intrigued Dot, but maybe only because the satisfaction of the Target lady incident was still fresh in her mind.

Her impression of Raji was also taking better shape. In their two days together, there had undoubtedly been some weird, uncomfortable moments—both of them clearly having some history they weren't too keen on talking about—but having a predetermined topic had helped the conversation flow easily, especially coupled with doughnuts and cocoa. If he hadn't insisted on it, she would have never suspected this guy of being a thousands-of-years-old genie. He was more like a stunning male embodiment of Siri. It was hard to believe that if other people knew he existed, they might even commit murder to be in her shoes—which according to Raji was the only way someone could steal a genie already in use. Another good reason not to try to explain his existence to anyone else.

How did *she* get to be one of the few throughout history to find him?

Am I better than everyone?

The two of them sat on the overstuffed sofa, both wrapped in separate blankets, an empty box of doughnuts at their feet.

"Ready to go?" Raji asked.

"No." Dot turned her head to take in the incredible landscape one last time. "But we should."

He poked a hand from beneath his blanket and snapped his fingers.

They returned to her single-wide, settling into the gloom of her depressing living room. Their blankets had evaporated, and an annoyingly situated streetlight outside spilled some of its light through a window so that they could see one another.

"I hope I was helpful," he said.

"Of course you were helpful! You reduced my wish-making anxiety to a manageable level. Although after hearing about some of your past clients, I almost feel like I should let you make the wishes." She laughed, meaning it as a joke, but Raji suddenly became very serious.

He stared gravely. "No, Dot. I'm here to grant *your* wishes, not mine. I don't make wishes. I make them come true."

The air in the room became heavy, and she had to stop herself before she responded dismissively.

"Okay. I just meant...thank you," she explained. "You could easily let me waste my wishes on stupid things. It wouldn't matter to you anyway, and then you could be on your way."

His expression softened. "It's not every century that I get a client who cares to include me in the process. Sharing my experiences is a chance to show my appreciation."

In the glow of the streetlight, he offered her a tiny half-smile. She still had so many questions, and not all of them were about the wishes. There was more to Raji than making stuff that people wanted appear out of thin air, that had become clear over the course of the day. She wanted to know more about *him*, but she didn't want to make him uncomfortable again after he had put up with her so patiently.

"Well, thank you for humoring me. People dream about finding a genie in a bottle, but I don't think anyone understands the pressure that comes with it."

"Lucky for you, you do. Maybe it will make your wishes more meaningful. Not like some clients I've had who shout out the first vague thing that pops into their heads. Like, 'I wish to be rich!' or 'I wish I had a different wife!'" he mocked.

She giggled. "Or, 'I wish for a—'"

Raji's eyes widened and his hand flew to her mouth where he pressed his fingers firmly against her lips. Her stomach lurched when she realized what she had almost done.

For a moment, they only stared at one another, horrified. Then his eyes fell down to his fingers, and he slowly pulled his hand away.

"You just saved me from wishing for a unicorn bear!" she gasped. It would have been the wish disaster she expected herself to inflict. But he had stopped her. In that moment, her mind officially changed: she was very grateful that he was here and not hanging out in his bottle.

He blinked, then laughed in a relieved sort of way. She smiled awkwardly and chewed on her lip. It tasted like doughnut glaze.

"Dottie, I don't know how I'd live with myself for eternity if I granted that idiotic wish twice!"

The nickname caught her off guard, and she froze. Many people had used it before, but she never liked it. Her mother only used it when she was fed up with her ("Dottie, it's unbecoming to complain!") and Howie used it when he was lecturing her like a disappointed dad ("Dottie, what have I told you about putting plastic in the microwave?"). She guessed she didn't give off the impression of having such a casual nickname to others. It sounded forced when anyone tried, and they quickly reverted back to the curt, easy-to-get-out-and-over-with 'Dot'.

But from Raji, the nickname fell from his lips so naturally that it sounded convincing. Like it was a happy thing. She wanted to hear him say it again.

He frowned when he noticed her pensive expression. "Did I say something wrong?"

"No. You...you called me Dottie. No one really calls me that. But it's okay. I don't mind if *you* do." She explained it like it wasn't a big deal, and it wasn't. It definitely wasn't.

He smiled.

Dot's pulse quickened. It was a nice smile. It went fantastically with his eyes.

Her brain went out of focus for a moment and all she could think about was *not* looking at his mouth. In the process, she realized how good he smelled. Like warm sand and some exotic spice she couldn't quite place.

Get it together. He's an ancient mythological creature. Remember how much it annoys you when humans date outside their species in popular fiction?

Like an internal alarm system, her stomach ruined the moment (or salvaged it) by emitting a long, low animalistic grumble.

"I should have summoned you a proper meal," he said with a frown.

She had eaten almost a dozen doughnuts, but she was starving, and relieved for the excuse to stand and get away. "I'll just heat up a frozen burrito before bed. Do you want one?" she asked with forced casualty.

"As much as I like trying all this twenty-first century cuisine, I worry that I'm unnecessarily eating all your food."

"It's fine." She headed to the kitchen and flipped on a light. "Frozen burritos are cheap. They're all I ate when I was a kid, unless one of my friends invited me over for dinner. I lived with my grandma who wasn't much of a cook, unless you count Jello salad as cooking. That woman could make a mean Jello."

She fished the burritos from the back of her iced-over freezer as Raji entered the kitchen behind her.

"Did you have a lot of friends growing up?"

She chuckled. "I did, but not the kind you'd think. Grandma and I lived in a retirement community. Normally, they don't let kids live there, but my grandma had a way of attracting pity. All the old people loved me, and I loved most of them. There were some grumpy ones, but for the most part, they were so much kinder and easier to be around than the kids at school, and less judgmental, if you can believe it."

"So you and your grandma were...are close?" Raji took a seat at the wobbly table.

"Were." It hit her that she was talking about herself without stressing over what he would think. And the conversation was coming easily. "I complain about my life a lot, but after my parents...dispersed...it's a good thing I still had her. She was very kind." She dropped a burrito on a plate and placed it in the microwave. "Too kind, maybe. She was ruined by a stupid internet scammer. My senior year of high school, an African Prince sunk his claws into her and I didn't find out until she had been sending him money for months. All of our money, basically. The guy had promised her a *ten-million-dollar* return! It still makes me sick to think about it. Because of that guy, we ended up so...poor..."

Her words trailed off as she stared at the rotating burrito through the microwave's grease-splattered window. Thoughts formed in her brain. Thoughts of money. Family. Revenge. Her mind flashed back to the day before, when the con-artist customer had been publicly exposed. Watching that lady walk out of the store having failed her crooked deed—Dot had never felt so good.

"Is something wrong? Is your burrito okay?" Raji asked.

As the microwave beeped, an idea started clicking into place. She grinned.

"I think I have an idea for my first wish."

The First Wish

Chapter 10

DOT

Dot barely slept that night. She couldn't. The prospect of having something she wanted come to pass was finally registering. Leaving Raji to her old magazines, she shut herself in her room and spent most of the night writing out different iterations of her wish. The wording had to be perfect to ensure she got the absolute most out of it. People were always saying to be careful what you wish for, and she wanted to take that warning seriously.

The wish checked many of her boxes. Financial increase. Avenging a loved one. Humiliating a terrible person. And one more.

She flipped back to the beginning of her notebook and looked at the first note she had written down the day before, though she wasn't sure if she spelled his name right.

Make sure Rahgee is having fun.

This should check that box, too. It had tickled her the way his eyes lit up when he talked about his favorite wish grantings. She wanted her wishes to invoke that kind of reaction, too.

The light of dawn shimmered between the cracks in her blinds as she lay on her stomach across her bed, turning back to the page where her final draft was written.

"Whatcha writin'?"

After her body shot several inches off the mattress, she rolled to the side to see Raji leaning against her dresser, arms folded. She did not like that he could show up in her room unannounced. He was cute, but he was still a strange man squatting in her house.

He winced. "I'm sorry! I shouldn't have popped in. But you can't say that you have an idea for your wish and then shut yourself in your room all night. I can create suspense, but I don't handle it well."

Too anxious and excited to chide him, she sat up and offered him the notebook. "What do you think of this wording?"

Raji looked surprised by the question, but he took it and sat on the edge of her bed. She tensed slightly as she tried to read his expression.

"The wording is specific, very thought out. But I'd still have a lot of flexibility here, not that that matters. This is a very good wish."

She balled her fist in quiet victory as he tossed the notebook back to her, raising his eyebrows up and down with a smile. "You ready to say it out loud? That's all it takes. Just look me in the eye and tell me your wish."

"What? Now?" As expected, the crippling doubts arrived. She bit her lip. "I don't know. Does it need more detail? Do you think it's stupid? Will it be dangerous? Maybe I should think about it a little longer."

He scoffed lightly. "Dottie, give me your hand."

The sound of that nickname on her eardrums in his voice was like a sitcom slap to her spiraling worries. He reached towards her. She straightened, then hesitantly slipped her hand into his. He gripped it firmly, not breaking eye contact.

"I promise I will do my best to make sure this wish is granted safely and successfully. When you speak the wish, I will know what you mean and I will deliver. It's part of the magic."

Her mouth felt dry, and her hand began to sweat, but when he spoke, it somehow eased her anxieties.

"I know you've only just met me," he went on. "But trust me. *This* is what I live for. Or at least it's what I'm alive for."

"Okay," was all she could manage to respond.

With a satisfied nod, he dropped her hand and jumped to his feet. Her trembling fingers gripped her notebook as she slid to the edge of the bed. Ignoring her rapid heartbeat, she silently reread the words one more time.

Is this really gonna work?

There was only one way to find out.

She looked at Raji. He nodded again, and she took a deep breath.

"I wish..."

His brown eyes gleamed with anticipation. They were the push she needed. In one breath, she let the words spill out.

"I wish to receive ten million U.S. dollars by scamming the scammers that scammed my grandma...which I get to keep for myself...and that I will not have to pay taxes on."

The genie clapped his hands together. "Great one to start with. Love a good revenge wish!" His irises flashed purple and he dropped to one knee, bowing low before her, but she didn't care to stop him right now. "Dot, my client: your wish is my command."

She clamped her eyes shut and waited.

After a second, she realized that she didn't know what she expected to happen. She opened one eye, then the other. Raji was on his feet, beaming proudly.

"Did it work?" she asked.

"You tell me."

She frowned and looked around, not sure what she was supposed to be looking for.

Then, on her nightstand, her phone dinged with an email notification. She reached for it reflexively.

One unread email had appeared with the subject line: Please help, not a scam!

A surge of what she could only describe as confidence rushed through her body. It wasn't something she felt often. Or ever.

"I need my laptop!" she cried. Raji bit his lower lip and fist pumped the air.

They moved to the kitchen, where her laptop sat on the table. Not where she left it, but she didn't question it. There was an itch she could only scratch by reading this email. She sat down and opened it, going straight to her inbox.

Dorothy Dudley,

I hope this lettr finds you well. I am writing to extend a very special invitation to you that could change yur live forever and make you a reel hero

as you may be aware, africa is a country of immens wealth and prosperity, and I am proud to say that I am a prince in this great nation.

recntly my brother stole $500,000 in priceless jewels from my family and fled to America.

America police will not arrest him, so he must be brouht back to africa. I believe that with your help we can have justis here inafrica and return the money he stol. I would like to award you $100,000 for your help you may use this reward to start a business invest property or simply enjoy a simple life of welth,

if you are interested in joining me in the name of justis, please reply to this email and I will tell you the way you can help.

I look forward to hearing from you
devotedly, Prince of Africa

Raji chuckled as he read it over her shoulder.

"This can't be real," Dot said. But words began flooding her mind.

She knew how to respond.

She hit *reply* and began to type, and the words flowed from her fingers.

Dear Prince,

I am glad you reached out. My father is the CEO of a large, rich, successful tech company looking to expand in Africa. The African people have been so kind to him. Can you please tell me how I can help?

Dorothy

She hit *send*. "I have never typed a reply faster in my life."

"Wishes can endow you with certain skills."

"Like lying?" she asked.

"It's despicable, I know, but it can also be kind of fun."

She stared at the so-far unchanged screen. "Now what? Do I just wait?"

"This isn't exactly an instant wish, but I think things should move relatively quickly."

Doubt was creeping in again at the mention of the word 'should.' But it was too late now.

"Trust me," he said, as if reading her thoughts. "I've got it under control. So. Dot is short for Dorothy, huh?"

"Fittingly, I shared that name with my grandma. My mom got pregnant with me out of wedlock and she thought naming me after her mother would soften Grandma's shock and disappointment. She was Dorothy, I was Dot, er, but like I said, Dottie's fine, too," she stammered.

Thankfully, her phone dinged with a new notification. Another unread email with the same subject line as before popped up in her inbox.

Dear Dorothy,
I must pay a private investigator. He will not take international credit cards. Follow these instructions carefully.

The rest of the email detailed how to send a wire transfer for the amount of three-thousand dollars. Dot quickly responded.

Are you sure you don't need more? I can send more.

She kept glancing at Raji. He kept watching her eagerly.
The reply came almost immediately.

If this is true I will call. tell me your phone number where I can reach you.

"Aw, I have to talk to someone on the phone?" she complained.

"You don't have to. Not to this guy. You don't have to give out your personal number either." Raji nodded towards the table. "Just follow your instincts and you'll be fine."

A smartphone—not hers—lay on the table beside her computer.

She started a return email, and as she typed out the phone number, a string of digits appeared. Magically. She glanced again at Raji who winked, then she added one more line.

Can we text instead? I don't want anyone to overhear.

Email sent. Soon after, the phone on the table buzzed. She picked it up to read the text that had appeared on the screen.

"That escalated quickly," she said. "He's asking for a wire transfer of ten thousand now. I think I've got him hooked."

She responded in the affirmative, and then, as if on autopilot, she sent another text.

> Can I give you the money in person? I've always wanted to meet a real prince.

She panicked. *Why would I ask him that?*

> No. must be wire transfer

> Wire transfers always feel like scams

> This is not a scam!

Raji tried to stifle a snort.

> Then where can I bring the money? I'd love to meet you and take you to lunch.

> Is this a Catfish?

> No.

> Send pic

Dot angled the phone and took a selfie. She looked at it and blinked. In the image, she looked much hotter, in a fake sort of way. "Holy...what filter is this?"

"It's exclusive. Go with it," Raji said.

She sent the photo. A reply came swiftly.

> I must talk to advisors

"This is incredible! He's doing everything I say!" she squealed. Then frowned. "But how is this going to escalate to ten million dollars? We'd have to be going back and forth like this for months."

The magic phone rang. The number calling wasn't the same number as the one texting. Her anxiety threatened to flare.

"Don't worry, you'll know what to say," Raji said gently.

His support was helping. The line between magic and reality was blurred, yet every time Raji spoke or caught her eye, it refilled her resolve to act rather than to think. Taking a deep breath, she accepted the call, putting the audio on speaker.

"Hello?" Dot said timidly.

"Good morning, ma'am," said a stern female voice. "My name is Agent Lydia Daines. I'm with the FBI. We've had an alert on a phone number that is currently texting *this* telephone number. We have reason to believe you are the target of a scam."

"You mean the prince? But he seems so genuine." Dot almost laughed out loud as the words left her mouth. Raji came around the table and sat in the wobbly chair across from her. At some point, he had conjured himself a bag of popcorn.

There was a faint sigh on the other end. "Yes, ma'am, that is their goal. This is highly unorthodox, but would you mind keeping him engaged so that we can get a trace on the cell phone and gather some more information? The last thing we want is for this guy to ditch or turn off the phone. The likelihood that we would be investigating a suspicious phone number at the same time it's being used for a scam is nothing short of a miracle, and I can't blow this chance. All you have to do is keep texting, but I would advise you not to give out any personal information. Uh, except...what is your name, ma'am?"

Dot felt a little sweaty, but she introduced herself and took down the agent's phone number and email before hanging up.

"Is this all still part of the wish?" she asked Raji.

"You could have asked for ten million straight-up," Raji shrugged. "But you didn't. And that's a good move, because it's less fun that way. And it messes with inflation."

"I hate talking on the phone and I hate strangers," she pouted.

"As long as the wish is still unfolding, you'll be okay. You also chose a wish that helps you face your fears! So smart."

She scowled at him, though she blushed slightly at the compliment. "I'm doing a lot of work for this wish."

"*You* wanted to scam the scammers," he pointed out, leaning back and tossing a piece of popcorn into his mouth. "You never specified you wanted me to do it, or how you wanted it done. But trust me, your wish is in the granting process. I have everything under control. It'll be an adventure you'll never forget."

Despite her moment of doubt, when the phone buzzed a second later, she picked it up to read the text.

"He'll meet me!" she exclaimed. Her frown returned. "In California."

She knew she should call the FBI agent back. Incredibly, she felt no fear as she dialed, only urgency.

"This is Agent Daines," said the same stern woman's voice across the speakerphone.

"Hi, Agent Daines, this is Dorothy Dudley." Dot's latest inclination surprised her. "We just spoke. About the scammer?"

"Yes. Miss Dudley, is there a problem? We're still working on the trace."

Dot cleared her throat. She looked at Raji, who nodded encouragingly.

"Agent Daines, I'm going to be honest with you. I knowingly replied to this scammer for the purpose of...messing with him. I was not duped, as I may have led you to believe."

There was silence on the other line. "That is a very dangerous game, Miss Dudley." Dot felt the tiniest surge of panic at the reprimand. Surely Raji wouldn't allow her to get in trouble with the FBI. Right?

"Miss Dudley," Agent Daines suddenly continued. "I can't divulge much over the phone, but we have reason to believe the individual scamming you—or trying to—is the leader of a large ring of internet defrauders. We've been trying to bust him for years, and due to a stroke of incredible luck, the specific phone number that contacted you only a few minutes ago, happened to be on a special list—a list that contains thousands of phone numbers, mind you—and one of my agents coincidentally decided to monitor the messages of the one you are in contact with at the exact moment a scam was being arranged. Though I would normally advise against engaging with a suspected criminal, we can't pass up this opportunity. If you can keep him hooked, you will be helping us a great deal with our investigation."

Dot blinked, astounded at the revelation. "If it helps you take down an entire ring of scammers, I'm happy to help."

"That's good to hear, Miss Dudley. It's always appreciated when a civilian is willing to cooperate. Thank you."

"You're welcome..." Across the table Raji mouthed the word *California*. "Wait! I got a text from the guy. I convinced him to meet me so I could give him cash in person."

"How in the world...?" Agent Daines's voice trailed off in disbelief. "Alright! We got the cell tower where the messages are originating from!"

"Is it near San Francisco? Because that's where he wants to meet."

"Yes! Wow. This is a huge break for my investigation. I have no idea how you got him to agree to this so quickly, but tell him yes. See if you can make it happen tomorrow or the day after. My team will get you a flight out today."

"A *flight*? Where am I going?" Dot tried not to stutter. Part of her was aghast and panicked about this plot twist, but another part of her remained cool and confident.

It was a fascinating experience.

"We'll need you in San Francisco, Miss Dudley. Assuming you can keep in contact with the scammer."

"Chyeah!" Dot answered stupidly.

"Great, watch your phone for a boarding pass."

"Okay. Thank you—wait! Can I have two boarding passes? So I can bring a..." Raji watched her with amused anticipation. "...friend?"

"As long as it's someone you trust. I'll have an agent contact you soon with flight information," said Agent Daines hurriedly. "Thank you for your cooperation, Miss Dudley. I will see you in California."

The call ended.

"What is happening right now?" Dot said after a beat of silence.

"I told you it was gonna be fun." Raji grinned.

"You made this a whole thing! Couldn't I have just...I don't know, asked the guy for ten million dollars under a false name? Wouldn't that count as scamming?"

Raji swirled his popcorn bag away and leaned forward, the table teetering as he did. "Dottie, I have to think logically about these things, especially when it involves other people. I can't *force* anyone else to do anything they wouldn't normally do, but I can create a scenario where they feel *compelled* to do something they wouldn't normally do. Would someone just hand over ten million dollars? No. They have to be compelled. And I know how to do that. Don't worry, all the players here are playing along beautifully. It will all work out in your favor."

His answer strangely made sense, but it failed to comfort her completely. She suddenly remembered the scammer waiting for her response and grabbed the phone.

> I can be there as soon as tomorrow.

> I would prefer it if you came alone.

> It is hard to know who to trust these days.

Was this guy seriously worried about *trust*?

"Ugh. Cry me a river." Dot rolled her eyes. "You're right, I'm ready to waste this guy."

> Deal

Then her phone and computer were silent. A smile worked its way across her lips.

"How do you feel?" Raji asked.

"I actually feel okay. Maybe even a little excited."

Raji's genie authenticity had been proven. Never—*never*—would she have been able to do all of that on her own. She never said the right words. She never persuaded anyone to do anything. She never agreed to meet an internet stranger in person on the other side of the country—though that was something she wasn't particularly ashamed of. And the best part was, she still felt like herself, just cooler.

She checked her watch. "I guess I need to text my boss to tell her I won't be in today. Or tomorrow."

A cheeky grin spread across Raji's face. "Or ever again."

Chapter 11

RAJI

"When you woke up this morning, did it ever cross your mind that you'd be on the other side of the country by the end of the day?"

Raji was eating pretzels next to Dot in their first-class seats, compliments of the FBI. The captain had just announced they were beginning their final descent into San Francisco International Airport and she was moments away from the next step of Raji's plan. Dot had spent half of the six-hour flight freaking out about being on an airplane for the first time (sometimes excitedly, sometimes anxiously), and the other half sleeping. Now she was awake and staring out the window at the Pacific Ocean, and Raji was trying not to stare at her.

The granting process could be very thrilling, depending on the wish, and when he had seen Dot's, it had taken a lot of willpower not to pick her up and spin her around gleefully. It checked so many of his boxes. Potential for adventure. Immersive in twenty-first century elements. Taking down a bad guy. And he had enough creative liberty to make it fun. For both of them. Of course, he knew she didn't make this wish for him, but she might as well have.

So far she had handled everything like a pro, but now, during this break in the action, he worried she might be having second thoughts, which for her were more like a recurrence of her first thoughts. In fact, it seemed to take her quite a few rounds of thoughts to convince herself to do anything.

As if on cue, she turned to Raji, her face strained with trepidation. "Is there still a chance something could go wrong? Or that I could mess everything up?"

"Your wish will play out as expected. You don't have to do anything but go with the flow and trust your instincts."

She leaned back in her seat. "This airplane is more comfortable than my bed," she said with a sigh. "Can I just stay here?"

"There's still a lot to do, and you've gotta be the one to do it," he replied. "Don't get too comfortable."

And neither will I.

Having a master like Dot had led to experiencing a new dynamic. She was unsure, nervous, and reluctant to trust herself, and so she turned to him—a lot—for reassurance or direction. Still, it probably wasn't great to make it seem like he was the boss. But it was still early enough to keep him from worrying about that too much.

She'll get accustomed to being in charge soon enough, and then I'll slink into the background like I always do.

The danger in this dynamic was that he didn't mind reassuring her. It made him feel acknowledged and appreciated, like he was a teammate, not a lackey. That rarely happened when hard-headed, self-important people were the wishmakers. He wanted to enjoy this experience as much as he could, but there was a line he was toeing that he had to be careful not to cross. Not after what happened last time.

She turned her head towards him, her brow furrowed. "Do you ever get nervous granting wishes with so many moving parts?"

He munched on another pretzel. "To tell you the truth, it's rare that I put this much detail into the granting process. But...I like you."

He watched her cheeks redden.

But it was a reasonable thing to say.

"You don't have to blush, Dottie," he said, and her hands flew to her cheeks. "If you met any of my previous masters—sorry, *clients*—you'd agree that compared to them, you're *likable*. I'm not trying to make you uncomfortable. I'm being honest. Complimenting you."

He'd magicked himself into slacks and a button-down shirt, something appropriate enough to meet the FBI in, and a touch more refined than his typical style. Within the bounds of a wish, he had a lot more leeway in his magic usage, and he liked to take advantage of that as much as he could get away with.

Dot got a minor makeover, too. She wore her hair down, lightly curled and falling over her shoulders instead of in her signature messy clump atop her head. After browsing some pictures from the internet, she had settled for a breezy blue button-up blouse with a pair of high-waisted black pants. Until now, he never would have guessed pants would do anything for a woman's figure, but after seeing them on Dot, he had been relieved once they boarded the plane. It was six hours that he would be free from the temptation to stare.

"Wish-granting has brought out another side of you," she remarked.

"It's what I do, Dottie. Everyone shines when they're in their element. I'm making dreams come true in the twenty-first century. What more could I ask for?"

There were many, many things he could ask for. Just nothing he would ever get.

"Has granting wishes always been your job?" she asked a little too nonchalantly.

"Irrelevant," he said, tossing another pretzel into his mouth. Maybe she thought she could catch him off guard in a good mood, but he was more vigilant than ever.

"I told you stuff about my past; it's only fair that you tell me something about yours."

"I've told you a ton about my past. So has popular media. Ever seen *Kazaam*? *Three Thousand Years of Longing*?"

"So those are more accurate than *Aladdin*?"

"Just the parts where the genie grants wishes. But that is the extent of my life story. Though I'm sure no one would mind if I looked like Idris Elba."

"I definitely wouldn't," she said, releasing a low sigh.

He would ignore those implications for the benefit of his ego.

"But you've gotta have an origin story," she continued. "Is it really that complicated? Were you like, born from a shooting star or something?"

The relentlessness of her attempts to get him to talk about his past was the only thing about Dot that he could do without right now. It was another reason he couldn't let himself get comfortable. She wanted to talk about his *past* past. And he couldn't—wouldn't—tell her. He already liked her too much, and that would soon change now that the wishes were underway. In the early days, he thought he could be friends with his masters, but that almost never panned out. Though he'd go along with her updated labels, he would do well not to forget that she was his master, not his client. Certainly not his buddy.

He wadded up the empty pretzel wrapper and shoved it into the seat-back pocket. Then he picked up the in-flight magazine and began to flip through the pages.

"Are you blatantly ignoring me?"

He looked up, hoping she caught the plea in his expression. "Listen. My origin story, assuming I have one, has nothing to do with you or your wishes. Can we please focus on the wish at hand?"

She reached over and snatched the magazine out of his hands, cramming it back into the seat-back pocket. "I know we agreed on a client-agent relationship, but a lot of clients appreciate knowing how their agent came to be an agent. It's not wrong for me to be a little curious about how you got here. Give me *something*, man."

Relentless.

He took a second to consider, scratching his beard and shooting her a side-glance. He was in a quandary. He was constrained to fulfill the will of his master, so if her will was for him to tell her about his personal life, he had to comply somehow.

She was staring the same way she always did when he spoke. With genuine interest. It both flattered and irritated him. Reluctantly, he submitted. "No. I haven't always been a genie. I was born to two regular human parents, like everyone else."

Her eyes lit up like he had added fuel to a very dangerous fire. "Okay, that wasn't so hard, was it?" she said.

He already regretted it.

"No, but..."

"But what?"

He shrugged tensely. "It stirred up more questions, didn't it? So it probably isn't going to satisfy you and you'll keep badgering me until I tell you more, when it has never done myself or any of my masters any good to get attached."

Dot flinched. A stab of pain hit him in the chest so sharply it made him recoil into his chair, closing his eyes as he waited for it to pass.

His tone had gotten terse. Being terse with a master was a no-no.

It's for your own good! he wanted to tell her. But if he did, she would want to know why. And then he'd spill more and more until...he couldn't assume exactly what would happen, but it was better to be safe than sorry.

"I'm not trying to...*get attached*..." she said. He could hear the uncertainty in her voice. Maybe that wasn't the greatest choice of words.

He took a deep, even breath and released it along with the brunt of the pain. He opened his eyes and forced a smile. "I think we're about to land."

Within seconds, the airplane shuddered as the landing gear connected with the ground. Raji was relieved at the interruption, but he feared she wasn't going to let up on the questions. She would probe again when she got the chance and he needed to be ready. Even as the plane slowed, though she gripped the armrest with white knuckles, her eyes lingered on him, glinting with such sharpness he might have spilled his guts if she pressed him again in that moment.

She had seemed harmless at first, but it was becoming evident that this woman had a strange and scary effect on him.

By the time the plane reached the gate, however, her interest in him had become replaced by the subtle signs of panic. Her breathing became rapid, and she closed her eyes as she attempted to slow it. Raji experimentally placed a hand on her knee—partly to reassure her, but also as a sort of peace offering—wondering if it would cause the same reaction it had the other night.

No pain.

The flight attendant opened the door at the front of the plane. Then Dot moved her hand on top of his, and his breath hitched unexpectedly. When a loud *ding* triggered the echo of unbuckling seat belts, her fingers squeezed his. Reflexively, he squeezed back. Her eyes blinked open as the apprehension drained from her face.

That was a kind of power he didn't even know he had.

"You got this." He smiled. She nodded and quickly removed her hand to unbuckle her own seat belt.

They were met by a large man in a black suit and sunglasses holding up a "Dudley" sign almost as soon as they disembarked.

"No way. I get a sign?" Dot muttered under her breath. "How is he allowed up to the gate without a ticket?"

"The federal government probably has some special permissions," Raji responded quietly beside her.

"I'll need to see some identification," the man said when Dot introduced them. She and Raji presented their IDs. Raji had conjured himself a passport under the name of Roger J. Rajington. It had earned him a confused glance from Dot when they had gone through airport security.

"That can't be your real name," she'd said.

"Anything can be anybody's real name," he'd answered with a wink.

The man ushered them through the airport to an employees-only side door that led down a long, windowless corridor. It eventually opened to a service road where a black town car was parked at the curb. Their escort opened the back door and waved them inside.

"Miss Dudley! It's a pleasure to meet you in person. Thank you for coming. And you, Mr. Rajington." A serious-looking woman with straight red hair and pointed features greeted them from the passenger seat. Even sitting, Raji could tell she was tall by the way her head rose higher than the headrest. The man in black took the driver's seat and started the engine.

"I'm Agent Lydia Daines," the woman continued. "This is Agent Jones, he's with our San Francisco branch." She gestured to the driver.

"Nice to meet you," Dot said politely.

"May I see your cell phone?"

"Uh, yeah." She pulled out her wish phone and showed Agent Daines the text thread. Before they left Florida, Raji assured her there was no need to bring her real phone. The success of this wish scenario would work best if she was fully present.

Daines took the device as Agent Jones pulled away from the airport. She studied it, then gave it back to Dot.

"He wants to meet late, and this address is in a dubious part of the city. I'll send one of my guys with you."

Raji settled into his seat and watched as Dot adapted beautifully to her improved instincts.

"No. He wanted to meet me specifically. Alone," she argued (with a federal officer, no less). "You're not gonna get anything if I don't show up by myself."

"I don't think that's a good idea, Miss Dudley. Just let us handle it."

"With all due respect, Agent Daines"—Dot shot Raji a surprised glance as she spoke—"this guy has been pretty easy for me to persuade. If you're looking for names, IP numbers, or hideouts, I'm confident I can get that information out of him. If someone else is with me, he'll get spooked. It could risk your entire investigation."

Agent Daines was wearing sunglasses, but her raised eyebrows made it obvious she was struggling to make sense of the rando in the backseat who had inexplicably given the FBI a miraculous break in their investigation. Part of the fun of these kinds of wishes was observing the side players who had no idea that he was the director and his master was the star.

Daines turned away. Dot looked at Raji and mouthed, "*IP numbers?*"

He shrugged.

"Miss Dudley," Agent Daines said, facing forward. "There is a lot of information we are rightfully withholding from you. All of that is classified, but be aware this isn't some socially inept virgin photoshopping himself into Star Wars movies in his mother's basement."

Dot gave Raji a confused frown. "Is that usually who it is?"

Agent Daines ignored her. "We believe the man who is communicating with you has ties to something much bigger."

"I can handle it," Dot said. "I'll ask him to switch the meeting place to somewhere public if that makes you feel better."

Agent Daines sighed. "Miss Dudley, is there any particular reason you're so bent on *messing* with this dangerous criminal?"

The determination on his master's face intensified. "My grandmother was scammed out of everything by one of these guys. This is about good old-fashioned revenge."

"Well, you sure hit the jackpot when you chose this guy," Agent Daines said quietly. "I'll talk it over with the rest of my team. I can see why the suspect is eating out of your hand. You're very persuasive, Miss Dudley."

Dot glanced at Raji. He guessed she'd never heard anyone call her persuasive before now. That wasn't completely magic, though. That's power she already had; she had persuaded him to say many things he had never said to anyone else and had never planned to say. In fact, she might be surprised to know that she already possessed most of the right instincts for this wish. The magic only relaxed her anxiety enough to use them. If she knew that, it could do a lot for her personal life.

But it's not always that easy.

There were reasons that Dot lived alone. There were reasons she had no obvious family. There were reasons that realizing her heart's deepest wishes unnerved her. And there were reasons why she didn't feel like she should be in control of things, even though she was perfectly capable.

Everyone had their reasons.

Maybe she would divulge them in time, but most likely, once she had this money, she will have forgotten all about them.

For that reason, he wouldn't get hung up on it, or on her, or on anything else besides granting the living hell out of this wish.

Chapter 12

DOT

The FBI had set up operations in a suite at a classy hotel close to the airport. Classy might've been an understatement. To Dot, it was positively grand.

She and Raji were escorted to their own double-queen room, where two FBI agents stood guard, one just inside the door, and one on the balcony, even though they were on the ninth floor. The presence of the agents made it impossible to pass the time asking Raji about his over-the-top wish-granting or the odd outburst he'd had on the plane. But she wouldn't know what to say about that anyway.

Attached, he had said. Surely he didn't mean to her. Or worse, maybe he thought *she* was getting attached to *him*. That was a terrifying possibility.

She didn't want to overthink it, but he didn't know how neurotic she could be in social situations. She read into everything. It's how she maintained such hearty levels of self-doubt.

So, the two of them remained mostly silent. After almost an hour, the sky began to darken, and Dot paced the room impatiently, anxious to keep the wish moving so that she didn't have time to feel apprehensive, while Raji picked at the last of her room-service dessert. Finally, Agent Lydia Daines marched into the room.

"Alright, Miss Dudley, you may send a message to the suspect asking him to meet you at this restaurant tomorrow night." She handed her a slip of paper. "If he accepts, we'll send you in alone. If not, I'm pulling you out altogether and sending one of my agents instead."

With a nod, Dot read a slip of paper in one hand while typing a message with the other.

> I just sent you the address of a great restaurant. Let's make that our meeting place so I can buy you dinner.

She sent it, then waited silently. Agent Daines no longer wore her sunglasses, so when she stared Dot down, there was no mistaking that she was *staring Dot down*. Daines crossed her arms. Dot smiled awkwardly. Raji dropped a spoon on the metal tray and a loud *CLANG!* reverberated throughout the room.

"Sorry!" he said.

Agent Daines did not react. Her stoicism would have greatly intimidated Dot if the wish wasn't automatically keeping her confidence up.

The phone buzzed. Agent Daines raised her eyebrows impatiently as Dot lifted the screen to her eyes.

> I will meet you there instead. Bring the money. Same time.

She silently celebrated. Of course this would go her way. She briefly contemplated the irony that in this case "her way" meant meeting a dangerous criminal face-to-face and somehow convincing him to give her ten million dollars.

"You win, Miss Dudley," Agent Daines said. "We'll brief you on the plan in the morning. For now, you and Mr. Rajington should get a good night's sleep. Someone will come to get you at nine a.m., sharp. We'll keep a man outside your room should you need anything."

"Absolutely, thank you. We'll be ready."

"And Miss Dudley," the tall woman added. "You may feel compelled to run. Please don't. You've gotten yourself in too deep at this point."

"Oh, you don't have to worry about that," Dot answered with more bravado than she would ever dare to use with law enforcement in any other circumstances. "I plan to see this through straight to the end."

Dot assumed she wouldn't be able to sleep that night, but then the time difference caught up to her and she hit the pillow like a brick. She woke the next morning to find Raji sitting on the other bed, eating a bowl of cereal despite the feast on the room service tray between them. Croissants, fruit parfaits, sausage, bacon, eggs, coffee, and orange juice. "Paid for by our new friends at the FBI." He smirked.

"They sent it up?"

"No, I ordered it and put it on the room. But they're paying for the room, right?"

"Then why the cereal?" She quickly smoothed her hair and tried to tell if she had morning breath just by using her sense of taste.

"The variety, Dot. How am I going to try it all if I don't eat it every day?"

After a quick shower, she promptly devoured a healthy amount of the delicious spread. Raji ate whatever she left behind, maybe adhering to some rule of genie etiquette, and they both looked up, mouths full, when the same agent who had met them at the airport let himself in. It was exactly nine a.m.

Instead of being taken to the suite where operations had been set up, they were escorted to one of the hotel conference rooms and left to wait.

"How come nobody cares that you're tagging along everywhere?" Dot asked. "From everyone else's perspective, you're not doing anything."

"When a wish-granting is active, I can make my presence seem...negligible. Sometimes I need to be present, so I can make sure things unfold correctly, but I don't want anyone to make a fuss about me. I can go invisible if you like. A lot of my previous clients preferred that."

Sometimes she wondered if Raji was implying that she should be treating him worse. "I can't believe all your previous clients were as terrible as you say. Aladdin was real, right? Wasn't he nice?"

His lip curled down at the mention of the name. "The guy the story of Aladdin is based on started out fine, but once I turned him into a prince, he became a pompous brat. I can say that because he's not my client anymore." Raji looked suspiciously at Dot. "By the way, I know you're probing. Aladdin is my most famous client—shockingly—but he has nothing to do with my *origin story*."

Dot sighed. She'd keep trying.

"Oh, I almost forgot. Kidding, I never forget." He reached over and tapped her on the head. A very long and specific number formed in her mind. "That'll come in handy later."

"It better," she said, rubbing her skull.

The door swung open and Agent Daines strode in, a dossier tucked under one arm, her dark suit and red hair as smooth and straight as her disposition. Two unfamiliar male agents stepped in behind her, and one of them closed the door.

"Good morning, Miss Dudley, Mr. Rajington. Let's walk you through what you'll be doing and who you'll be up against, shall we?"

"Absolutely," Dot said, settling into her wish persona by sitting upright and inhaling a deep breath.

Agent Daines plastered a photo of a pale, weaselly man on the wall with a crooked frown and uncaring eyes. His blond hair already graying even though he didn't look older than forty. There was a series of small, dotted scars across one side of his face, like he had gotten too close to an explosion and received a cheek-full of shrapnel.

"This is Avros Orlov. We suspect he is the scammer you've been communicating with. The phone number he is using has been tied back to him before, so it is odd that he used it again. Lucky for us, though."

"Yes. Very lucky," Dot agreed, glancing at Raji.

Agent Daines continued. "By himself, he's not much more than a sniveling henchman, probably started the scamming business for fun or notoriety among his criminal peers. However, the bigger picture is that he is the youngest of eight sons born to Russian crime boss Ivan Orlov. Orlov runs a very extensive and illegal operation of trafficking drugs and weapons into the U.S., but because he's based in Russia, we can't touch the bastard. We can, however, nab Avros, who we believe has been hiding in the U.S. for a few months now, possibly trying to start his own crime syndicate, or a U.S. based branch of his father's business."

Dot felt more and more lost as the agent spoke. "I thought he was just a scam artist?"

"That seems to be his desired field, perhaps his hobby, but he is much more than that, Miss Dudley."

Dot took a deep breath. Was this part of the plan? She glanced again at Raji and caught a glimpse of his brown eyes, sending her another dose of magical reassurance. She turned back to Daines. She couldn't let this new information shake her confidence.

"Okay...what do you want me to do?"

"We want information, like you said, Miss Dudley. This guy undoubtedly knows some family secrets that the bureau and our colleagues overseas would be eager to get their hands on."

It was difficult not to waver. This was a big ask for someone as unremarkable and insignificant as Dot.

But underneath the table, Raji's hand squeezed her knee, so she nodded. "What's the plan?"

Dot spent the afternoon absorbing way more information than she would have ever been able to remember without magical aid. It included additional background on Avros and his family, and a briefing of the FBI's plan for her impending meeting with him.

The bigger part of her instruction, however, had to do with hypothetical situations: what to do if Avros pulls a gun on her, or if it isn't Avros that shows up, or if he's wearing a bomb. The regular, anxious part of her personality constantly struggled against the empowered, confident part that had been bestowed with the wish. A wave of self-capability eventually washed away every moment of doubt and fear, but that didn't mean the doubt and fear didn't poke their heads above water as often as they could.

Late that afternoon, Agent Daines offered her a break after the information dump she had endured. To ensure their safety, the agent had explained that the break needed to be taken in their hotel room. There were too many risks that came with going out and exploring the city. Normally that might bum her out, but she had a bone to pick with a certain bottle-dweller.

As soon as the door was closed, Dot turned on the genie. "Raji! How is this granting my wish?"

He had the audacity to seem surprised at the outburst. "What? You're doing great. Just have fun with it!"

"You think going out with an international criminal and persuading him to let me in on his illicit family secrets while I'm secretly working with the FBI is *fun* for me?"

He frowned. "You're losing sight of what's happening here. This will all lead to you getting ten million dollars from this guy."

"How is this even the same guy who scammed my grandma? Didn't my wish specifically say that I wanted to scam *that* guy?"

He looked offended, though judging by his facial contortions, he was trying not to.

Maybe he didn't understand the dangers of the twenty-first century. Maybe he didn't understand that if you screwed people like this guy over, they would find you and kill you. She had seen enough true crime specials to know there are people you just don't mess with.

"I know all of this seems crazy to you, but the fact that a crime lord's son scammed your grandma is, unfortunately, a random coincidence if you can believe it. So, in order to scam him, we have no choice but to work around that fact, which I am doing with carefully orchestrated occurrences disguised as happenstance. It's all a part of the process."

"Well, it's...stressful. I don't even know if I want the ten million anymore." She flung herself onto the bed and buried her face in the stack of pillows.

"Dottie," he pleaded. "You already wished it. Maybe you wouldn't have if you knew who you were scamming, but you can't do anything about that now. It's happening. The best thing about it is that you can't mess it up, no matter how hard you try. If you want to swindle this guy, trust your instincts. You have the right ones to get through this." She felt the bed shudder as he sat down. "Not just get through it. You're gonna come out on top. Remember, you're not doing this alone."

She slowly rolled onto her back, convincing herself to listen to him. Like Daines had said, she was in too deep. What choice did she have?

His expression softened as he caught her eye. "Maybe this isn't a great time to tell you this, but I'm not going to be able to make my presence irrelevant to someone as paranoid as Avros. You'll be meeting him on your own, or so it will seem. But I want to make sure you know that even if you can't see me, I'm around, pulling strings and manipulating space and time for *you*. Some of my past masters trusted me enough to remember that. Like the one who wished to fight and subdue a tiger with his bare hands in front of his entire village."

"Huh?" she said, slightly intrigued.

"I wasn't there fighting beside him," he continued. "And there was probably some doubt in his mind when I gave the tiger the upper hand a few times to make it seem believable. But he followed through and the tiger was subdued, as he wished. Could he have tapped out when those doubts came into his mind? Yeah, though he'd still have to fight a tiger another day. It was his choice, like going through with this now is your choice. No matter what you do, it's inevitable that your wish will come true, but you'll only prolong it and complicate it by not trusting me."

She stared at the ceiling. He must have laced his voice with magic, because she could feel her anxiety calming. "How often have you had to recalculate a wish that your master self-sabotaged?"

"A few. And it really throws a damper on my whole process."

Dot grunted her acknowledgement. She was a pro at self-sabotaging. And it was because she tended to back out of things when they got hard. Howie used to love rubbing that in her face. Various jobs, saving for a better house, getting her passport, a book club—like ticker tape, all these examples of self-imposed failure streamed through her brain. Maybe it was a good thing she was locked into this one. Although it didn't seem fair to compare refusing to read a regency romance with conning the Russian Mafia out of millions of dollars.

Raji's tone lightened. "What else do I have to say to help you feel better? This is exciting! Don't you feel like you're in a movie?"

"This does not feel like a movie. It's much too real."

Raji climbed on the bed and laid parallel to Dot, leaning on his elbow to face her. She tried not to look at him, but his unwavering stare drew her eyes to his. It really annoyed her.

"It's *okay*," he said. "It'll only take a few more hours. Then the wish will be complete. Try to enjoy it. Please. You seem like the type of person who could use an adventure. One where *you* are the hero."

He presented her with a smile, which was worth ten million dollars in and of itself, and she drew in a breath. Those deep brown eyes were homed in on her, and she was too tired to resist them. Although now, after spending more time with him, the list of things she liked about his face was lengthening. His voluminous hair was all dark and wavy and probably buttery soft. His beard nicely accentuated his cheekbones. And for being thousands of years old, he had spectacular teeth.

As much as her stubborn, overthinking brain fought it, she felt another wave of that magic confidence sweeping in. "If it's just a few more hours...then okay. I'll man up."

What was it about him that kept driving her forward? Howie always struggled getting her to do what he wanted her to. So did her mother. Neither of them inspired her to have the kind of trust in herself that Raji did. The expected answer would be magic. But even if that were true, she didn't want to minimize the role the wish-granter himself was playing in all this, although she couldn't quite pinpoint what it was. Confident coach? Unruffled business partner? Faithful friend? Emotional support...guy? Whatever it was, surely he wasn't contracted to do anything for her but grant her wishes. All this unrestrained encouragement couldn't be part of the package. Could it?

If it was, he deserved a raise.

Chapter 13

DOT

Outside the French restaurant, Dot hesitated. It was the thought of Raji's steady confidence in the hotel room that finally pushed her forward. Though she hoped that because she hadn't wished to scam the scammer in front of an entire village, Raji wouldn't feel the need to give Avros the upper hand at any point. But Raji was turning out to be unpredictable with his wish execution.

She adjusted the sleek black designer bag on her shoulder. It easily held the ten thousand dollars in cash, an amount of money that surprisingly didn't require a large briefcase packed full like she originally pictured. The tight red cocktail dress she'd been given to wear, with its low-cut, rhinestone-studded neckline, drew even her attention to her cleavage. After adding some heels, slicking her hair into a sleek ponytail, and piling on an exclusive filter's worth of make-up, Daines and her team had pushed Dot out into the San Francisco night to meet her date. She understood they needed her to look like a frivolous heiress, but she had never been dressed like this in her life. What if she couldn't act natural?

No. I will not *be self-conscious Dot tonight*, she reminded herself. Tonight she was Wish Dot. And Wish Dot was turning heads like normal Dot never could.

"I'm meeting a prince here. Has he arrived?" Dot asked the hostess, careful to continue her charade of obliviousness.

"Ah, yes. The...*prince*...has reserved a private room for you. Right this way."

A private room? Doesn't that defeat the purpose of a public meeting? she wondered.

Trust me. Raji's words echoed in her mind.

"Stay calm. We'll get an undercover agent in there to keep an eye on you," Agent Daines added.

How many people were in her head?

Then she remembered the earpiece in her earring, and the pinhole camera hidden in the rhinestones on the front of her dress. This wasn't just a date with a criminal, this was a legitimate FBI operation. So many moving parts.

The hostess showed her to a dimly lit room, aglow with the light of a tall candle on a single table flanked by two chairs—both empty.

"The prince will join you momentarily," the hostess said, pulling out a chair and gesturing for Dot to sit. She did her best to discreetly pan the room with her chest before settling in. The hostess exited.

There was no menu on the table, she noted with a frown. She had been low-key looking forward to seeing the food options (and prices) at this kind of establishment. There were, however, a lot of forks.

"Are we still doing this as a society?" she muttered. "Do different forks really help people feel better about themselves?"

Her phone buzzed, and she dug it out of her bag. A text message from Prince Scumbag (as she had saved him in the contacts) appeared.

> I saw you come in. You are beautiful. But maybe you will not want to see me.

"Aw, crap," Dot muttered.

> Why wouldn't I want to see you?

> Because I am not an African Prince. I am a prince of a different kind.

> I still want to see you.

A moment passed without a response, and Dot sighed. Raji better follow through. She was doing her part, that should make it easier for him to do his.

"Hullo," said a voice with a heavy Russian accent.

She turned in her seat. The greasy guy from Agent Daines's photo stood in the doorway. Though the dim light obscured many of the unpleasant details of his face, it was him, cleaned up in a crisp cream suit with polished brown loafers. His hands were in his pockets as he puffed his chest out like a gorilla.

This is it. Follow your instincts.

"Who are you? Really?" she said in a mystified voice.

"My name is Avros. As you can see, I am no African Prince, and I am sorry to have deceived such a lovely woman."

"Why did you lie to me?" Now she tried to sound hurt.

Avros walked around the table and took the seat across from her. She suppressed a grimace at his over-greased, graying blond hair, his yellowing teeth, and his excessively lip-balmed lips which he smashed against the back of her hand.

"I had to be sure I could trust you." He slid his fingers down hers. "Did you bring the money?"

She withdrew the stuffed envelope from her bag. Avros snatched it, peeked inside, then casually tucked it inside his jacket. He returned his attention to Dot, leering intently. "When I saw your picture, I wanted to meet you very much."

"I wanted to meet you, too, Avros." She said his name so breathily, bile began to rise up in her throat.

He smiled with satisfaction. "Wonderful," he said, pronouncing the 'w' as a soft 'v.' "I am so pleased to be dining with such a beautiful woman."

There was a soft crackle in her ear. "You're doing great," Raji's voice said.

It momentarily caught her off guard.

"Don't be caught off guard. Given our earlier conversation, I thought it'd be less stressful for you to hear my voice in your head instead of Agent Business McBusiness Lady's. Keep doing what you're doing. I'll let you know if she gives you any specific directions. Oh, and I don't know if you've picked up on it yet, but I think Avros might be into you."

Dot could practically hear the wink in his voice. She couldn't decide if it was a good thing or a bad thing to have Raji be the one chattering in her ear.

Across the table, Avros went on. "The waiters already have our order. I have chosen for you a special meal. My *father*"—Dot noticed he said the word with disdain—"and the owner are old friends."

The thick haze of his heavy cologne made her stifle a cough. Her personal objective here wasn't exactly clear, but her FBI objective was to get him to spill as much information as she could. So that's where she would start.

"Avros, tell me why you're in trouble. I want to help if I can." She reached across the table and stroked his hand.

Ew. Was she being seductive? But it was instinctual. She knew it would put the guy at ease, but she silently prayed that's as much touching as she'd have to do for those ten million dollars.

His eyes widened slightly. "First, tell me why you want to see me? Did you feel connection when we spoke, as I did?"

"Oh, yeah," she said, struggling against the questionable instincts Raji had inflicted upon her. "I felt like you really needed me. I knew I had to respond."

"I was in very dark place, Dorothy. I am sorry for tricking you. You see, I have eight brothers, and my father is a very rich man, with many businesses, some very dangerous."

She nodded understandingly.

"On the day we began with the email and then the texting, my father had chosen one of my idiot brothers to be in charge of something *I* should be in charge of."

"I'm so sorry to hear that," she said. "I really am."

"Daines is about to wet her pants, she's so excited. She wants you to keep him talking," Raji's voice said.

"I wanted to kill my brother!" Avros slammed his fist on the table. Then he relaxed his shoulders, waving in a waiter who filled their wineglasses and promptly exited. "But instead, I try to distract myself with thing I do for fun. The only thing I am good at."

"What's that?" she asked.

He frowned pensively. "I...chat on internet."

"Mmm." She nodded. "You are good at that."

"I think, maybe I...get some help, and prove to my father I can do things better than my brother!"

"Is that why you said your brother stole jewels? Was that code for him taking something valuable from you?"

Avros stared blankly for a moment.

"In your email," she said, amazed at how well she was keeping up the charade. "You said..."

Understanding dawned on Avros. "Oh, *da*! Yes. That was all...code words. I don't want to give too much information, you see?"

"Well, I am so glad you reached out, even if you weren't completely honest. You're more handsome than I expected."

I better win an Oscar for this, she thought.

He chuckled lightly. "You are very flattering woman." He gently moved his hand closer to hers and started playing with her fingers. Dot forced a smile so hard her eyes began to water.

"Avros, let's run away together." She tried not to throw up as the words came out of her mouth, though she knew they were the right words to say. "What else are you doing tonight? Let's go to France! Right now!"

The Russian's jaw dropped. "Forgive me, but this I am not used to. Usually I have to *make* beautiful woman come to me. Compared to my brothers, I am not too handsome or charming or smart. They think I am only good at...chatting on internet."

"They're wrong about everything but the chatting." She fluttered her eyelashes. Was Raji's plan for her to flirt her way into getting the money? The thought exhausted her. She was already approaching her limit.

As though in response to her thoughts, Raji urged her on. "You're right there, Dottie. Don't give up!"

"But I cannot leave now," Avros went on. "I am on an important errand for my father. I must do something for him tonight."

Dot rolled her eyes. "I hate that he takes advantage of you and won't even give you any real responsibility."

The Russian's eyes darkened sinisterly. "But this is why my luck has changed, Dorothy. First, I meet you, and now my father gives me opportunity to close very important and dangerous deal. If I do good job, I get more power than *any* of my brothers!"

"I'm so happy to hear that!" The next question she wanted to ask would be an important one. She hoped he liked her enough to answer. "What's the deal?"

His eyes narrowed.

"Avros, you can trust me."

"You've got Daines panting over here," Raji said.

Avros smiled, then reached into his suit pocket and removed his phone. He tapped the screen a few times, then turned it so she could see. Casually, she adjusted her chest so that the pinhole camera picked up the image on the screen, which showed an array of very illegal looking firearms. He swiped. More weapons. He swiped again. Still more appeared.

She looked up to see Avros watching her, an evil look of pride plastered across his vile, pockmarked face.

"This is sale my father arranged. He sent them from Russia. None of my brothers want to do it. They are nervous around Americans."

A sale. The conversation was getting interesting. "How much is your father getting for these?" she asked.

Avros leaned in very close.

"Ten million dollars!" he whispered, his pupils dancing.

Dot's heart began to pound. It had been pounding all along, but now it rattled like a jackhammer. This was it. She could see the light at the end of the tunnel. "Where are you meeting them? How far?"

Avros frowned, leaning back and tucking his phone away, and she silently kicked herself for revealing her eagerness so quickly.

"Be patient, I promise, you're almost done," Raji said.

Two waiters came in and placed a bowl of something that looked like regurgitated cherry licorice before each of them.

Avros clapped his hands together in delight. "Ah, the borscht! I made special request."

Dot's smile had to be the most unconvincing one yet, but he didn't seem to notice. She wondered if he was really this stupid or if his judgment was just clouded by her wish.

He tucked his napkin into his shirt like a bib. This seemed like his normal amount of judgment.

Once the waiters had left, Dot asked again, more coolly than before. "Is this deal happening soon enough that I can meet up with you later? Somewhere...nearby?"

Borscht dribbled down his chin as he furrowed his brow in thought.

"Do not worry about that. This information is too dangerous for such a lovely woman. But!" He caught her eye and leaned over his bowl, his lips red from the soup. "I mean it when I say we have connection. If you feel the same, Dorothy, if you really care for me, I change the time of deal and we leave tonight. There is a pier near where I meet my father's buyers. You will wait for me there?"

Dot swirled her spoon in her borscht. Pink chunks floated to the surface. Between that and Avros's face, she was having trouble finding a pleasant place for her eyes to land. "I will. Could you write down the address? Or text it to me?"

Avros leaned back. "*Da.*" He dabbed his chin with his napkin and brought out his phone again, tapping away at the screen. His eyes flicked from her to his phone. Was that suspicion in his eyes? No. He was considering something. "How well you know this city?"

"Not well," she said truthfully.

Avros grunted and laid his phone on the table. "Do not write it down; you must memorize it."

She picked up the phone and held it low in front of her, letting it linger at chest level in view of the camera.

"Okay. But I'm not very good at memorization, so I'll need to look at this for a second. Could you get me another soup?" she asked. "There's a hair in mine."

Avros's face turned as red as the borscht. He picked up her bowl. "Whoever is responsible will be fired, my Dorothy!" He began shouting in Russian until a waiter appeared.

On the screen she found a note written in a memo app, an address in large, bold letters. But at the bottom of the screen, she could see that the note continued. Impulsively, she moved her thumb to scroll down. There was a second address in the same memo with the heading *LOCATION OF DEAL*.

This guy is the world's dumbest criminal.

Something compelled her to swipe to the side, and she didn't ignore it. A second note appeared. This one was written completely in Russian, but as she scrolled further, she held in a startled gasp as her brain began to perceive what the words said.

They were instructions.

```
Meet the buyers.
Let them inspect the merchandise.
Get the payment before handing over the goods.
```

`Transfer money to this account.`

A long series of digits followed. Even though it was in a completely different language, her mind lingered on a single word.

Schet. Account.

Dot quietly sucked in a breath as she realized what she needed to do.

As Avros tore into the poor waiter, she held the phone high and out of view of the camera on her chest while she erased the number and replaced it with the one Raji had zapped into her brain that morning. Then she swiped back to the previous note and slid the phone across the table.

Raji's voice sang in her ear. "My wish senses know all, and they're telling me you made the switch. I knew you could do this, Dottie!"

The praise almost made her blush, but she willed herself to stay composed. With a satisfied smile, Avros tucked his phone into his pocket as the waiter scurried back to the kitchen.

"I'll meet you there, Avros." She reached for his hand, hopefully for the final time, and gripped it. "And I'll wait forever if I have to. But first go close this deal so that you can finally show your father that you are a better, braver man than your brothers."

"They are idiots!" he agreed. A wicked grin spread across his face. "My Dorothy. You have made me very happy man!"

She winced as he pulled her arm towards him so hard she almost flew across the table.

His voice lowered. "Promise I will see you again tonight." She shuddered as a wave of beet breath hit her face. "Now that we have met, it is better for you if you do not break my heart."

It almost sounded like a threat. For the first time since meeting Avros, he was scaring her. He may be a buffoon, but he was a buffoon capable of terrible things.

But she wouldn't give herself away. "I promise."

Hopefully he didn't notice the tremor in her voice.

Chapter 14

RAJI

Raji waited in the backseat of the car that had arrived for Dot. Deciding they had gotten enough information, Daines initiated Dot's extraction, sending an agent into the restaurant to flash his badge at the hostess. Word got back to Avros in less than a minute and, over the earpiece, they listened as he apologized quickly and excused himself. Agent Jones confirmed the Russian had exited out the back, entering his own getaway car, presumably headed to the location of the arms exchange. After dispatching a tail, the mountain of an agent had driven around to pick up Raji and Daines from the nearby surveillance van. All three of them applauded as Dot slid into the vehicle next to Raji.

"Miss Dudley, that was quite a show," Daines said. "You got us some extremely valuable information. We're getting teams to both of the locations listed in his phone as we speak. In my line of work, you assume the most successful criminals are also the smartest. Orlov proved that assumption can be very, very false."

"Thanks for all the support over the earpiece," Dot said, addressing Daines but shooting Raji a sly smile. He bowed his head graciously. "So, what's next?" she asked. "Do you need me to be there when this deal goes down?"

"You've done more than enough, Miss Dudley. I think you've earned a break."

Raji nodded in agreement, and he heard Dot breathe an unmistakable sigh of relief.

Back at the hotel, Dot received another round of applause upon entering the suite being used as operation headquarters. One female agent—Agent Akins (Raji liked to learn the names of every person who unwittingly assisted him in wish granting)—even threw an FBI jacket around Dot's shoulders. As the tech guys—Agents Ford and Grady—extracted her earpiece and camera, Raji stood by the door and watched with satisfaction.

Was any master ever so radiantly happy after a wish as Dot was right now? The money wasn't even in her hands yet, but to her, the wish was granted. That spoke to what kind of soul this woman had. He noted how she smiled kindly at Agent Grady, how she blushed when Agent Bellingham came and patted her on the back, how she shook Daines's hand proudly and firmly.

Maybe he had assumed wrong. Maybe she wouldn't turn out like other masters. It surprised him to realize that he really hoped that she wouldn't.

Then she laughed at something Agent Ford said and revealed her matching dimples. Raji let his gaze linger on them, then he let his gaze dip a little more, following the curves of her figure in the red dress. Captivated with such a combination of beauty and happiness, the vice he kept on his thoughts slackened and he imagined what it might be like to spend time with her not as her genie, but as a man. How things might go if she had gone to that restaurant to meet *him* instead of Avros, flirted playfully with *him*, uttered *his* name seductively—but genuinely, not as part of some ploy.

He shook his head. *What am I doing?*

It was only the rush of an exciting wish granted successfully that incited such thoughts. It wasn't wrong for him to imagine himself living a different life—he did it all the time—but it was alarming to find Dot at the center of his fantasizing. He did like her. Very much. She was nice. Pretty. Different in an interesting way. But none of that should matter. Yet, the more time they spent together, the more he noticed that she made him feel things—human things that he wished his creators had prohibited him from feeling so that he wouldn't have to deal with this kind of situation.

After Daines assured them the FBI would handle Avros, they were excused to their hotel room for the night. Dot closed the door and threw her arms around Raji. He hesitated before squeezing her back, discreetly inhaling the citrusy scent of her hair. She let go quickly, but it was enough to get Raji's mind swirling with more impossible fantasies.

"I'm so pumped up on adrenaline right now! I just swindled a professional criminal in front of the FBI!" She pulled out her hair tie and he watched her hair fall around her shoulders.

"Yeah, you did great, Dottie. You were incredible."

She rested her hands on her waist and smiled. "So, what now? That number you gave me is a bank account. Who's?"

"Yours." Happy for the distraction, he reached into the purse she had dropped on the floor to pull out her phone. After tapping the screen a few times, he turned it around to show her. It displayed the balance of a bank account in her name. The account number matched the one she had typed into Avros's phone, though right now the balance sat at zero.

"I've never heard of that bank," she said. "Is there one in Tallahassee?"

Raji laughed. "No, it's Swiss. Secure and tax-exempt. Once Avros makes the deal and transfers the payment—which the feds will allow so that they can pin the buyers with the charge—the money will go into this account instead of the one Avros's father wanted it in. It'll be easy for him to blame his son's incompetence for the failed transfer."

"Is this *dirty money*?" she whispered.

"It's money criminals pass around between each other, in a never-ending cycle of illegal sales. You get to stop that cycle. Put it to honest use, however dishonestly you acquired it."

"Is there a way to scam someone honestly? Who cares? Revenge feels amazing!" She looked up at the ceiling. "I got him for you, Grandma!"

She laughed at herself, then bit her lip, drawing Raji's eyes to her mouth.

She noticed, and her smile faded as her eyes widened.

A palpable tension settled in the silence. Good or bad, he wasn't sure. But...if he was doing anything against her will, he'd feel the pain in his chest. All he felt now was his thundering pulse, which was probably worse.

"You were right," she finally said. "This was fun. Thrilling in a way I've never experienced. You really do know what you're doing. Thank you."

Her gratitude caught him off guard—though he already was. "I thought you might appreciate an adventure." He held her gaze, wishing he could tap into their cosmic bond to read her thoughts. He wasn't sure if she felt uneasy or was being coy.

Obviously, uneasy was the preferred option. Maybe. He actually wasn't sure.

She adjusted the strap of her dress, but he was determined not to let it draw his stare like the lip-biting had. He barely succeeded.

"I should change," she finally said. "Although it was kind of nice to feel so pretty for once."

He scoffed blithely. "You've always been pretty." He said it honestly, as a fact, not as a pick-up line.

Regardless of the delivery, it had a clear effect on her. She pressed her lips together as she took in a breath.

"You're probably required to say that to your clients," she said.

"No, I'm actually not," he clarified. "I've never said it to any client before now."

"Really?" She flinched. He both loved and hated how every compliment seemed to surprise her. She cleared her throat loudly. "I'm...going to change and head down to the pool. To...decompress."

Only then did Raji realize that he'd been stepping closer to her throughout what he now recognized as a highly inappropriate interaction with his boss. He took several steps backwards and reluctantly pulled his eyes away from her. "Yeah. That's a good plan. Go for it."

She vanished into the bathroom, the door shutting before he finished speaking.

He slapped a hand to his forehead and groaned. "For that, I deserve every ounce of punishment I get," he muttered.

Shifting his hand to the center of his chest, he waited.

But nothing happened.

Raji stepped into the hallway with a heavy sigh. Through the bathroom door, he had asked Dot if it would be okay for him to go listen in on the bust while she went for her swim, then tried not to feel hurt at her rapid and enthusiastic response: "Yes! Go! Stay as long as you'd like!"

He berated himself as he walked down the hall.

I'm only feeling this way because I was in the bottle too long. Because she's an attractive female master. Because she put her trust in me and absolutely nailed that wish without becoming a terrible person. Because my makers found a way to torture me for finding any personal enjoyment in my job.

His cloaking magic allowed him to enter the operations suite unnoticed, save for a few mechanical nods from various agents. No one would care that he was in here.

Agent Lydia Daines had left to oversee the greatest arrest of her career, but Ford and Grady had a couple of monitors set up to watch the whole ordeal. Raji sat in a corner nearby where he could get a good view.

Silence filled the two still screens, one showing a dark alley, and the other an equally dark pier. Apparently, they were still waiting for the deal to go down.

Then something happened. Something very odd.

His wish magic began to fade.

It wasn't an unfamiliar feeling. In fact, it was something he fully expected to happen tonight. Just not right now.

It meant Dot's wish had been granted. The money had been transferred to her secret Swiss account and his master was officially a multi-millionaire thanks to the Russian Mafia.

Yet, the FBI agents continued to watch the monitors with extreme focus.

"Excuse me." Raji leaned forward, addressing Agent Ford, who jumped. With the wish granted, his inconspicuousness would be wearing off, too.

"Mr. Rajington. I didn't see you come in. You really shouldn't be here. We're in the middle of a bust."

"It didn't already happen?" he asked.

"Well...no. Our team is in position; we're just waiting."

But it *had* already happened. It must have.

Understanding dawned on Raji. Avros must have given Dot, and by extension the FBI, a bogus address.

The deal had been made elsewhere.

I guess that's fine...

But it wasn't fine. This isn't what he planned.

He recalled a master he'd had who wished to find stolen family treasure, hidden somewhere deep in the Egyptian desert. To fulfill his master's wish, Raji presented him with a map. The journey was filled with many obstacles and dangers, and Raji ensured his master's safety along the way. But when his master finally uncovered the treasure in a hidden cave, Raji's wish magic turned off—as it does once a wish is fulfilled—leaving him powerless to detect or stop the booby-trap rigged to go off once the treasure was removed. Raji could only stand by and watch his master take a dozen arrows to the face. The wish had only been to find the treasure, not take it home.

At the time, it hadn't been particularly upsetting—that guy had a weird obsession with Raji's feet—but it reminded him that just because a wish was granted, that didn't mean his master was free of danger. Sometimes a wish could lead to unexpected peril that Raji couldn't anticipate.

He thought he had prepared for that, though. Why else would he involve the FBI? He needed Avros behind bars. Otherwise, he might hunt Dot down once he figured out he had been duped...

"Crap," Raji muttered.

He relaxed a little when he realized there was no pull on his cosmic tether. It meant Dot was close, probably still at the pool. He needed to get down there, but it would cause an uproar if he finger-snapped himself from here. He'd have to do it from the hallway.

As Raji made his way towards the door, he made a rash decision.

The wish-granting power may be shutting down, but it would take a few minutes to turn off completely. He could keep grasping at it and force it, the way one might force themselves to do something that required every ounce of strength and willpower they had, like lifting a car, or completing a triathlon without training. Neither task was impossible, but both were very, very hard to do and could result in a lot of pain. He needed to search time and space to locate Avros and his buyers and get that information to the FBI immediately, and he could only do it with intense effort. And because using that kind of power outside of a wish was against the rules, it would hurt. Badly.

Pulling the door closed behind him, he stepped into the hallway. But when he raised his hand for the finger-snap, a massive hand grabbed his, twisting it forcefully behind his back.

Another fun little quirk his sadistic makers endowed him with was the capability to feel limitless amounts of physical pain without the relief of passing out or dying. If he wasn't immortal, the bones in his wrist might have been pulverized by the force they were currently under. Raji managed to turn his head amidst the searing pain to get a look at his assailant.

"You!" he cried.

"Me," Agent Jones answered, grabbing Raji by the front of his shirt and picking him up off the floor.

So the biggest, strongest, scariest member of the team was a double agent. That didn't seem fair. But when had life ever been fair to Raji?

With his other hand, he tried to finger-snap as the behemoth man dragged him down the hallway and flung him into a maintenance closet. But things were happening too fast. Jones had shut himself in the closet with Raji and was now—very violently—tying Raji's hands behind his back. A plastic bag was pulled over his head, followed by the sound of duct tape being stripped off the roll. Jones began wrapping it around Raji's neck, sealing the bag in place.

With a final forceful kick to Raji's stomach, which caused him to fly against a shelf of cleaning solutions and topple to the ground, the double agent left, locking the door behind him.

"That was unexpected," Raji sputtered after regaining some strength amidst the pain. He sucked the plastic into his mouth as he gulped for air—he wouldn't actually suffocate, but the sensation of suffocating wasn't exactly pleasant.

He could still feel the magic slipping away; it wasn't completely gone yet. Now seemed as good a time as any to break the rules.

Especially since now he could feel Dot getting farther and farther away.

Chapter 15

DOT

Knowing she'd be staying in a hotel, Dot made sure to pack a bathing suit. As a child, whenever she and her grandma traveled—always within the state of Florida—Dot spent as much time as she was allowed swimming in the hotel pool. It was the highlight of every vacation she'd ever known. So taking a dip felt like a fitting way to celebrate avenging the generous woman who raised her when she had every excuse not to.

It had come as a relief when Raji had offered to hang out in the operations room. After being pushed together almost every minute for four days now, she suspected he might be trying to give her some time alone, which she welcomed. She also wondered if it had anything to do with their mildly flirtatious exchange in the hotel room a few moments earlier. There was no way he was seriously *interested* in her. Was that even possible? She still wasn't completely sure what he was, or if they were even compatible species. It also didn't seem like his job was conducive to dating. Which meant she had to be right: it must be a requirement for him to flatter her and make her feel smart and beautiful and funny and pleasant.

No wonder he needed a break.

As usual, she was the one making it weird by getting a dry mouth and a fluttering heartbeat every time his deep brown eyes found her, eyes which were probably magically engineered to incite those kinds of reactions.

She forced those thoughts aside as she approached the edge of the outdoor pool. She liked thinking about Raji, but it was a nice night, and luckily for her there were no other guests to interrupt her solitude. She needed to take advantage. There was something peaceful about night swimming, especially after a long day of espionage, and she deserved to soak in her triumph. Triumph for her was almost nonexistent until now.

Looking down at her reflection in the water, she paused, surprisingly filled with pride. She achieved some pretty impressive things in just a couple of days. Things she never dreamt she could be capable of. For once, her image projected happiness and health. The thought brought a small smile to her lips as she dove in.

As she stroked her way across the pool, her mind wandered to the ten million dollars currently making their way to her fancy Swiss bank account. She had chosen the amount because it had been the amount her grandma had been fooled to expect, but now that it was practically hers, it felt like way too much money. What would she do with it all? Definitely pay Jorge and Yasmin all the backlogged rent she owed them. And pay off her credit card debt. But then what? A house, but nothing too high maintenance. A car that wouldn't break down every five seconds. What about an education? She'd never had the chance to even consider that before. She would also research charities. It would be nice to use criminal money to help other people.

As much as she had enjoyed being a rich heiress tonight—minus the ogling of a slimy criminal—at no point did she feel like she was doing anything other than playing a role. Hopefully being a millionaire wouldn't make her feel like she had to become that person. For the first time in a long time, she kind of liked who she was right now.

Raji said he liked her, too. Well, he said she was likable.

And don't forget pretty. Even underwater she couldn't help blushing at the memory.

Her fingers brushed the edge of the pool, signaling that she had reached the other side. As she resurfaced, a strange and random thought popped into her head. At the restaurant, Avros had mentioned the owner was a friend of his father. But hadn't the FBI chosen that location? And how did the waiter know Russian if the restaurant was French? She'd have to ask Raji about that later.

As she lifted herself out of the water, a pair of large, strong hands wrapped around her arms and yanked her the rest of the way. Before she could react, duct tape covered her mouth, a bag went over her head, and her arms were bound. The stranger—a male, as evidenced by his size and the deep grunting sounds he emitted—lifted her over his shoulder and carried her away. After a short distance, she felt herself being thrown into a vehicle. The doors slammed and the engine started.

Is this seriously not over?

It didn't take long to get wherever they were going. The hotel was near the airport, so close that she could hear the distinct sound of jet turbines passing overhead. Surely that's where she was being taken. What if she got transferred to a plane? Would Raji be on it?

Don't panic. It has to be part of the plan.

The car stopped. She was, yet again, aggressively picked up and carried a short distance. A door opened, then slammed behind them. She winced as she was dropped onto a solid cement floor. Then a familiar voice cut through the silence.

"My Dorothy."

The bag was yanked from her head. Avros stood before her, a sickly smile on his crooked lips.

A frantic look around revealed a large, empty space with a high, curved ceiling. A closed airplane hangar. The only light came from a fixture directly above Dot. Avros stood at the light's edge, holding a handgun at his side.

There was one other person present: a big man with a tiny head. Dot felt her stomach drop. She recognized him immediately, though until now, she had only seen him with sunglasses on.

Agent Jones smirked as he reached into his suit jacket and flashed his own handgun.

"The FBI, Dorothy? Why do you do this to me? We had connection!" Avros waved the gun around as he spoke and she flinched each time the barrel was directed at her. Had this been why Raji had let her wander off alone? Was this yet another scenario that needed to play out in order for her wish to be granted? If it was, then Raji was probably already here, winking from the shadows. The thought made her angry. The rest of the wish had almost been fun. This was too far.

"I knew all along, Dorothy. I knew they wanted you to spy on me. And I was going to use you to trick them. But when I see how beautiful, I still hope you would choose me."

She tried to listen to her instincts, but nothing clear was coming in. What was her objective now? More seduction? Begging for her life?

"You hypnotize me like siren. I really believe you feel something for me, even when Boris tried to warn me. He offered to kill you! But I decide to give you little test, and…" He rubbed his forehead with the hand that held his gun. "You fail."

This guy was in no state to be handling a weapon.

"You showed my address to FBI pigs with your teeny tiny camera! You broke my heart! I told you not to break my heart!"

Her body trembled as his volume increased. She closed her eyes for a brief second. Focusing as hard as she could, she pushed aside the anxious, frightened Dot and drew forth the part that Raji had put there, the Dot who didn't mind being rude, or direct, or reckless. Fearless Dot. The only part of her fake persona she actually liked.

With determination, she pulled herself up to kneel, a struggle with bound hands and wet skin.

Avros narrowed his eyes and stepped forward, dropping into a squat so that their eyes were level.

"What, you think you can escape? You are in strange city. Nobody knows where you are, not red hair policewoman, not even your little bodyguard. Yes, I know about him. I have bad news." He jutted his lower lip and shrugged. "Boris killed him."

The words almost shook her. Almost. But there were factors at play that Avros didn't know about, things he would never dream of. Raji *couldn't* die. And as much as he believed he did, Avros did not have the upper hand. Not for real. Not before her wish was granted.

Raji is not dead. He's pulling all the strings right now.

That knowledge was the push she needed to get magically enhanced Dot back in complete control. Avros wouldn't have the satisfaction of witnessing her needless panic.

As Avros cracked one more crooked grin, she furrowed her brow, then lunged at him like a dog on a chain. She toppled onto her side, but her threat had the effect she wanted. The Russian fell on his backside, then scrambled to his feet and recoiled. She had scared him.

"American women are *crazy*!" he yelped, brushing off his suit, his face a boiling red. "I have more bad news for you!" he barked from a safer distance as she painfully struggled back onto her knees. "But good news for me. You think you are good at tricking people, but I am the best! The address you showed your little friends? Decoy! There will be no one to arrest. They will walk away empty-handed! Boo-hoo! But *I* will not. You will come to Russia with me and I will decide whether to kill you, torture you—or worse, turn you over to my father. It would have been better for you to come willingly, but no matter what, you are coming with me. You are *mine* now."

He laughed, displaying a mouth full of teeth the color of old socks. Training his gun on Dot, he looked at his two-faced thug. "Boris! See if Nikolai is bringing plane over!"

An idea formulated in Dot's brain.

This has to be the right thing to do, because it goes against all my typical instincts.

But she had to wait for the exact right moment—the moment when Boris stepped out and Avros still had his back to her.

No hesitating.

She pulled one leg up in front of her and used it to propel the rest of her body forward, slamming into Avros's knees, knocking him to the ground. She shuddered and blinked at the sound of gunshots, praying none would find her as he pulled the trigger wildly mid-fall. When he hit the ground, she leveraged herself against his heaped body and staggered to her feet faster than she expected.

She kicked the gun far away, then planted another hard kick in Avros's face, reveling in the satisfying crunch of her foot connecting with his nose. Frantically searching for some way to escape or hide, she limped quickly into the shadows. Raji sure was taking his time.

The door that Boris had disappeared behind burst open and the traitor ran back in, gun poised in front of him. Dot stooped down in the far opposite corner of the hanger between a shelf and a wall, hoping the brute didn't think to turn on the lights.

Upon seeing his boss writhing in pain and bleeding from his nose, Boris began scanning the hangar slowly. After a second, he paused, then shifted his attention towards the ground, a satisfied grin appearing on his face.

If her mouth wasn't taped, Dot would have cursed.

Still wet from the pool, she had left dark footprints on the concrete leading from the center of the light towards her hiding place. In the split second she had, she knew she couldn't get herself up and out of there fast enough with her hands tied.

Fearless Dot evaporated. Now all she felt was intense, disorienting fear. She would die exactly as she expected. Scared and alone.

Boris lifted his gun, aiming into the darkness towards her, and pulled the trigger.

Chapter 16

DOT

Dot's eyes squeezed shut as the sound of gunshots echoed across the hangar.

But instead of the sting of bullets, she felt a warm body press against hers and heard the distinct snapping of fingers near her ear.

The air changed. An air conditioner's soft hum replaced the ringing of the hangar. Against her back, the metal wall became upholstery. The pressure of a body against hers remained, now accompanied by a loud moan.

Dot opened one eye to find herself face to face with Raji, who winced, obviously in pain. Her other eye shot open, and she tried to speak, but could only emit a series of frantic muffled noises.

Amid whatever agony he was feeling, Raji lifted a hand and placed it against her mouth. When he removed it, the duct tape had vanished. He rolled off her, allowing her to get a better look around. They were back in the hotel room, lying on one of the beds.

Her attention turned to Raji; his face was still twisted into a pained expression and his movements were stiff.

"Raji! Were you shot?"

"Yeah, but I won't die," he grunted. "It'll just hurt for a little while. Really, really bad."

"My hands are still tied!"

He slid a hand behind her back and tugged on the cord. When it fell away, she rolled towards him, placing a sympathetic hand on his face.

"What can I do?"

Slowly, Raji's eyes opened until they were looking into hers, they dipped, then returned to their starting position. "This is helping."

Dot frowned...and then realized what he meant. His arm remained behind her back. Her body, clothed in only a damp bathing suit, leaned against his. One of her hands rested on his cheek and the other had fallen onto his chest. Their faces were only inches apart.

She took in a long, slow breath.

Then pushed him off the bed.

"Ow!" he yelled. "I only meant it felt nice!"

"Couldn't you warn me about stuff like this? Give me an itinerary of how my wishes will play out so I'm not blindsided when I'm kidnapped? Or maybe just take the whole production value in general down a notch. Or two. Or eight!" She lifted herself off the bed and limped to the closet. Her foot throbbed where she had rammed it into Avros's face and her arms shook as she pulled on a hotel robe and tied it around her waist, leaving Raji to claw his way back onto the bed on his own.

"You make many good points. I'm not denying it. This got away from me." He laid his head on the pillow and sucked in a breath.

"Now what? The deal isn't even happening! I don't even want the money anymore. If I knew it would put my life in danger, I never would have made the wish!" The panic that had overtaken her moments ago needed a release. She sat on the edge of the bed and rubbed her bruised foot, struggling to fill her lungs.

"Dot. Do you really think I *planned* to take a back-full of bullets?"

"Are you expecting a thank-you or something? You're the reason I was in that situation in the first place!"

"Give me your phone," he said, lifting his head slightly.

She looked over at him. "Why?"

"Just give me your phone. Please."

She spotted the phone on the dresser, hopped over to grab it, and tossed it to him. He caught it and began tapping on the screen.

"Look," he pleaded, holding it out to her.

She lowered herself back onto the edge of the bed and snatched it from him. The screen showed the same Swiss bank account information from earlier, except now the balance said $10,000,000.00.

Her jaw dropped. "How? He said the deal was off!"

"Did he say the words *the deal is off*?"

She thought for a moment. "He said no one will be there when the FBI shows up. That the address was a decoy."

"Yes, that's because right after your romantic beet soup dinner, Avros met the buyers at a completely different location than the one he baited you with. His plan was to meet them right away all along. He had too much riding on the deal to cancel it altogether, or to trust a stranger he met on the internet, no matter how pretty. He's a criminal. He knows better. I should have accounted for that."

Dot pulled her legs onto the bed. "But if the deal was already made, does that mean...?"

Raji struggled to sit up. Every move he made seemed strenuous. "By the time they grabbed you, the wish had been granted. I was no longer keeping track or pulling strings. That's my fault. This is my first time working in the twenty-first century and it got out of hand. I am so sorry."

Her vision blurred. "So you're saying...I really almost died?"

Raji fell back down to the pillow. "Well...yeah."

"And I charged at an armed criminal of my own volition?"

His head popped up in surprise. "Did you?"

"I feel sick." She flopped onto the pillow next to him with a groan. "How could I have done something so stupid?"

"I'm so sorry, Dottie. Are you hurt? Are you okay?"

She felt dizzy, even on her back. Her dazed vision drew patterns on the ceiling. "I can't believe I did that. I really truly actually almost died just now."

"It might not be much of a consolation, but it wasn't all for nothing," he said.

"What do you mean?" she asked, turning her head.

Raji held up his hand. He was holding a remote control, which he pointed at the large TV facing the bed. It blinked on. Dot sat up and leaned forward.

The image was split; one half of the screen showed an interior shot, the other half an exterior, both depicted a lot of commotion. In the exterior shot, she noticed a familiar sharply featured woman. Agent Lydia Daines stood over four men laying handcuffed face-down on the ground.

"Is that Avros and his cronies?" Dot asked.

"It is. Boris, a.k.a. Agent Jones, is one of them. Infinite knowledge isn't mind-reading, even within a wish. I had no idea he was a double agent, and it didn't cross my mind to check him out."

Dot watched Daines kick the big guy in the side, then rest her heel on Avros's back as she spoke to another agent.

"Avros said Boris killed you."

Raji let out a pained laugh. "I got out of that, but by the time I did, you were already getting farther away."

Dot kept her eyes on the screen as he spoke. The interior shot showed the inside of the hangar where she had been moments earlier, which meant the exterior shot covered the outside. San Francisco police officers and FBI agents buzzed around, searching for evidence. One officer sealed the envelope with the ten thousand dollars into a large plastic bag, and another carefully disarmed a small pile of confiscated handguns. They must have shown up seconds after Raji had. But even so, they would have been too late if not for him.

"By the time I got to you, you were already in the hangar. I made sure Daines received an anonymous text with your location, and I found their plane and put a hole in the fuel tank. That's when I heard the first gunshots. I thought I had gotten my best client killed. I should have gotten you out first. I messed up."

When she looked at him, he wasn't watching the screen. Instead, he squinted towards the ceiling, his teeth clenched. Her sickness over the situation wasn't ebbing, and it didn't appear that his pain was either. Maybe she had overreacted. Sure, he couldn't die, but if he could, he would have died several times tonight just to keep her alive.

"It's okay. You got there in time. You *saved* my *life*." Saying the words out loud reignited the dizziness, but it also invoked a burst of the strongest gratitude she'd ever felt. She reached for his hand, which lay limply at his side, and squeezed it, though it seemed like a stupid way to thank someone for something so significant.

"I'm sorry I pushed you off the bed earlier," she said. "Does it still hurt?"

He released another long breath. "I'll be fine. As long as you're okay, that's all that matters."

He closed his eyes. His fingers gently caressed the back of her hand as his breathing steadied.

Slowly, she pulled her hand away. Not because she minded it, but the shock of what she had just been through was enough to process at the moment. She didn't have the emotional capacity to interpret the wave of heat that his touch ignited.

She rubbed her forehead. "I have a headache. And a stomachache. And I never want to see Avros, Boris, or Agent Lydia Daines ever again. I wanna go home."

His eyes blinked open. "Why didn't you say so?"

With a snap of his fingers, the room changed for the second time.

They were suddenly on Dot's bed in her room in Tallahassee. Her luggage was there, too, strewn around the room in the same way it had been in the hotel suite.

She collapsed backwards and happily snuggled her pillows. "Thank you!"

Raji watched, still lying in the space beside her. His expression didn't look any less guilt-ridden.

Fluffing the pillow one more time, she adjusted herself onto her side so that she faced him. "It's okay. Raji. I'm alive. It's over. The wish is granted and we're home."

He turned his head away. "Dottie. You're forgiving me too easily."

She was only trying to comfort him. Now *she* felt guilty. If they were both feeling this poorly after the fallout of her first wish, was it even worth it to make another one?

There were many questions she wanted to ask Raji, but there was one in particular that she was saving for the right moment. Now seemed like the opportune time.

"Don't be mad at me, but I have an idea." She waited for his response.

"I'm listening," he finally said, still facing away.

"Raji." *How do I say this without offending him?* "I have ten million dollars now—sheesh, it feels ridiculous to say that out loud. That's a lot of money, and I don't know that I ever really expected to actually have it. So I'm set. I don't need anything else." She sighed heavily. "Is there a way I can...back out of the contract? It might be better for both of us. If you want, maybe I can...the people in the movies always do it on their last wish, but I can—"

"Don't say it," he said.

Dot frowned. "How do you know what I'm about to say?"

He rolled towards her. Even though he didn't have a scratch on him, somehow he looked like he had lost a fistfight. By a lot. "Okay. Say it. But not as a wish."

"So you know I'm talking about how someone always wishes to...you know. Free the genie."

His expression remained unreadable. "And you would really risk your last two wishes for that?"

She nodded vigorously. "Yeah! Yes, then we can just be...friends. Regular people who are friends. Is that how it works? I mean, I have ten million dollars. I can—what?"

He draped his arm across his eyes. "It isn't possible."

Her heart dropped. "What? Wait. It's because you're not human, isn't it? I knew it. Is your true form something with horns or hooves or wings or—"

His mouth scrunched in confusion. "What? No, Dot. I'm a human."

"Oh. Good...but then, how do you know I can't free you? Did someone try it already?"

Part of her had wondered. But he did talk about his old masters like they were all self-centered imbeciles, so it wasn't hard to assume that no one had thought to try. And here she was thinking she was some pioneer in genie liberation.

He moved his arm. The defeat on his face made her sad. "I can answer your question," he said. "But it requires some backstory. A long backstory. Do you have time?"

A backstory? She sat up. "I mean, I'm still in a damp swimsuit—oh. Thank you." Before she had finished the sentence, Raji had waved his hand, swapping her wet attire with her favorite pajama pants and her Orlando t-shirt, completely dry.

Raji pulled himself up to lean against the headboard and ran a hand through his messy waves. "I can tell you're going to keep asking, so I might as well start giving you answers."

Chapter 17

RAJI & DOT

Do I really want to do this again?

But he felt weak under the intensity of her stare. She weakened him in a lot of ways, and he was getting tired of it. It was time to give in. As only the second master in history to offer to wish him free, and the first to offer it after a single wish and without knowing his origins, she had earned it.

He took a deep breath and began.

I was born in the ancient, pre-Islamic Arabian desert somewhere around twenty-seven hundred years ago. I was born a completely normal healthy human infant, the last of many children that my parents had. I don't remember the exact number of siblings I had—it was well before birth control—and I don't remember what my full given name was. But I remember what my mother and my siblings called me.

They called me Raji.

My father died when I was young. I don't remember how, probably some now-extinct disease, but my older brothers had their own households to run, so I took care of my mother. We were part of a nomadic tribe. We moved around the desert, never staying in one place for long. When I was...as old as I look now, I guess—I know I hadn't hit thirty, but I had passed twenty—my mother got sick. She was getting older, and was probably going to die no matter what, but you have to understand that she was all I had. My best friend. My favorite person. And I stubbornly refused to accept the fact that I would lose her.

Throughout the desert there were cities, one of which was ruled by a well-known sultan rumored to be a very powerful sorcerer, so I decided I would go find him and ask him to use his power to heal my mother. There wasn't medicine back then like there is now, and as absurd as it might sound, the first thing most people turned to in the face of illness and death was magic.

The people and the Gods they revered in those days had a much closer relationship than they do now—that was where the magic came from. In Arabia, rulers weren't always hierarchical. They were chosen by the Gods and imbued with a little bit of their power. The Sultan I went to see had a good reputation among his people. His kingdom was prosperous and his subjects were happy. He had clearly done great things with the power he was given. But what I didn't know before seeking him out was that he wasn't satisfied. Power can do that to a person. I've witnessed it firsthand countless times. But I didn't know that then. I didn't know that at the same time I was saying goodbye to my mother and making the journey to his kingdom, that he was desperately looking for ways to increase his power. But the Gods—the good ones—refused to give him anymore. They know our limits better than we do.

But there were other gods, fallen ones—malevolent spirits, jealous lesser deities, tricksters who got their kicks by messing with mortals—and where I lived, we called them the jinn. They possessed many magical abilities: shapeshifting, healing, creative powers, weather control—but despite all that, they were eternally jealous of the one thing that every single human had and they didn't: a soul.

The jinn were happy to give the Sultan what he wanted, but for a price. They would exchange portions of their power for portions of his soul.

"How could anyone give up their soul? Wouldn't you just die?" Dot asked.

"A soul and a spirit are two different things. Your spirit gives you life, your soul gives you humanity; it connects you to the earth and to everyone else, gives you your desire to love, to nurture, and the ability to feel true joy. Without one, all that's left is jealousy, greed, anger—all the things that cause people to look inward rather than outward. Some people let those things sour their souls, which is a shame, but it's what the jinn like to see. If they can bring a human down to their level of miserable soullessness, they've won."

The Sultan knew the cost of more power and didn't want to pay it—he didn't want to risk his glowing reputation—so he tried to find a loophole. He thought he could make himself an exception to the rule. The idea he came up with was to have some kind of go-between. A middleman. Someone else to pay the price for the power.

He brought his idea to the jinn, and they agreed to go along with it, or so it seemed. They told him that if he brought them a servant, they would give the servant the power to grant whatever wish the Sultan had. But they weren't stupid. They had planned from the beginning to put limits on this servant, so that anyone who got a taste of their power would be hungry for more, and the only way they'd be able to get it was through them.

As you might have guessed, this is the part where I come in. I made it to the palace, and I was waiting to have an audience with the Sultan. I felt good. I believed he would listen to me, and that he would want to help. But once I was called to come before him, I could tell almost immediately that this guy didn't give a flying carpet about a word I had to say. He looked at me like I was the pheasant for his next banquet. When I finished making my request, he turned to one of his guards and said, "He'll do."

I thought he was a good ruler. That's what the people from his kingdom had said. But you have to remember, I was a stranger there, a nomad from one of the desert tribes. No one knew who I was within those city walls. I was a perfect offering for his shady deal.

His guards locked me up. Then that night, they took me out of the city, deep into a nearby cave. The Sultan lashed me to a rock. He fell on his face and summoned the jinn. Then the pain came.

Throughout my existence, I've seen powerful people use pain against the innocent to build themselves up more times than I care to count. I've been forced to serve men who boast about their abuse of the defenseless. Fallen gods are no different. They use pain to convince themselves that they are better than the people they abuse. They made me immortal, but they didn't take away my ability to experience pain—physical and emotional—as their way of showing me that they were in control, and the pain I felt that night was...otherworldly. Mortal men couldn't survive an ounce of it. I felt myself changing, like being broken and put back together. I'll never forget it. I don't think I'm meant to.

At the time, I didn't know that they couldn't actually take my soul. All that pain was a result of them trying, but I've learned a lot about the jinn in the thousands of years I've been their prisoner. They can't take any soul that isn't willingly offered. All they could do to mine was enslave it. I'm glad I didn't know they couldn't take my soul until later, because I might have offered it to them that night in exchange for relief.

"Raji, I...I'm so sorry."

"It's not your fault, Dottie."

"I know that, but it...it isn't...it's *infuriatingly* unfair. It's evil and it's sick. I can't—"

He pursed his lips and nodded in a way that told her she didn't need to go looking for the words. He knew.

When they finished with me, I thought I was dead. I couldn't feel my body. I couldn't feel anything except sorrow and sadness. I thought about my mother. I knew I would never see her again. They poured all this knowledge into my head and I became aware of the purpose they had forced on me. How they would use me to trick the Sultan, and anyone else who thought they could enjoy unlimited power without paying the price. The jinn tease and tantalize greedy people by telling them it can be theirs, but they lie. They'll never fully give away anything they can hold over mortals.

The Sultan didn't allow me time to grieve my fate. He summoned me from my first vessel—a ring—within minutes of my transformation. He also made me aware of my limits pretty quickly. His first wish: to be more powerful than the gods. Couldn't do that. Next, he tried wishing for immortality. Another hard no. Third attempt: the power to kill all his enemies with a single command. You see where this is going, this guy agreed to have me enslaved, thinking he had outsmarted the gods, but they can't be outsmarted. He was the one who looked like a fool.

After I rejected his first six or seven wishes, he settled on a palace made of gold, the power of enhanced persuasion, and for the most beautiful woman in all of Arabia to be his queen. I don't think he gave a single thought to the welfare of his subjects. But for the jinn, the plan worked. He blew through his wishes fast, and even though he got to keep his soul, his increased greediness had corrupted it. A win for the jinn. And through me, unfortunately, they've corrupted a lot of souls.

I was happy to be done with that sultan. But he wore the ring until the day he died. He had become paranoid and jealous, as many of my masters did. He didn't want anyone else to benefit from my power. When he died, the ring was passed from successor to successor until the kingdom was conquered, then my masters became random people from random places, although sorcerers like the Sultan learned about the ring and tried to seek it out.

Eventually, the ring became so well-known and coveted by every sorcerer and ruler from Egypt to China that finally someone enchanted my vessel, turning it into the infamous lamp of legend that only required a rub. But soon *that* became common knowledge, and to keep it out of the hands of enemies—which sorcerers tend to have a lot of—my masters began hiding my lamp after they finished with me. It was a whole thing for a while. Meanwhile, I'm eternally forced to either fulfill the wishes of greedy masters or sit around in a void of nothingness.

Raji leaned against the headboard, staring at the ceiling. "Even when destitute people lucked onto my lamp, it usually only took one wish for them to believe they were better than everyone else. When the lamp thing got out of control, some Merlin type in medieval times changed my lamp into a bottle—your bottle—and it became a lot more complicated to release me. Since then, I've spent most of my time in the void instead of here in the real world, which keeps changing without me."

Dot listened intently. Emotions welled within her; ones she had felt before but were now amplified a million times. Raji had once been a young man trying to live his life, who couldn't get a win despite his best efforts. It was a familiar storyline.

"Raji...I didn't know. I don't know what I thought happened to make you this way, but I didn't expect it to be something so...unfair. What happened to your family? Your mother?"

He shrugged. "I don't know. I haven't seen her since the day I left for the palace."

She wanted to comfort him. Maybe no one ever had. Tentatively, she placed a hand on his shoulder and rubbed it gently. As he turned his head to face her, she instinctively placed her hand against his cheek, her eyes filled with all the sadness and empathy weighing on her soul.

"I am so sorry," she said.

His deep brown eyes penetrated deeply into hers for a long moment. Then he reached up and placed his hand over the top of hers, lifting it and dropping it gently in her lap.

"The story isn't over yet."

Dot nodded, self-consciously tucking both her hands under her legs.

Sometime near the end of the dark ages—about the eleventh century—I was released from my bottle by a man in a small English village by the sea named Rourke. He was the most humble, down-to-earth master I'd ever served. Had a wife and two young sons. They were very poor. Happy, but poor. Like I used to be. He had found my bottle in a fish trap and was smart enough—like you—to figure out how to get it open. When I appeared, bowing like I always do, he bowed *to me*. We were both speechless. We talked, and—also like you—Rourke listened carefully and asked smart, thoughtful questions about the wish process. He didn't want to waste his wishes, either.

We became good friends. Great friends, actually. I told him about my past. Up until then he was the only master interested enough to ask. Before that, I was often a bitter, emotionally distant servant. I didn't care about upsetting my masters. I didn't care about granting their wishes carefully or accurately, because no one cared about me. I think the jinn probably liked that about me. I made a lot of people angry.

But Rourke changed that. Talking to him and telling him my entire story out loud was so healing. He reminded me that I was still a person, not just a slave. We spent a lot of time together before he made any wishes. I would go fishing with him and we'd talk for hours about life and happiness and purpose. By the time he made his first wish, I barely remembered why I was there. I felt so much like my real self.

His first wish was for a bigger house. That's it. Not a palace, not an entire kingdom, not a mansion made of diamonds. Just a more comfortable home for him and his family, close to the seaside so that he didn't have to go far to work.

His second wish was to have some money, but not for himself. For his sons. He wanted to put it away for them so that when they were grown, they'd have a small fortune to start out with so they could go into the world and be whatever they wanted to be.

Then it came time for wish number three...

Raji's words sounded choked. "He...he asked if he could wish for me to be freed. He wanted me to have my own life again. He said I could live with him and his family, like an adopted son."

Dot stared, blinking rapidly. "I don't understand. Don't tell me he went back on his offer."

"No! No, he didn't. That's what I'm trying to tell you, Dot. The answer to your question...he wished for me to be free. And that's when I realized those vile, jealous devils who had given me my power, they intentionally left certain powers out. I couldn't be wished free. Rourke's wish did nothing. It did less than nothing. Dottie. It..." Raji's head dropped, the pain on his face returned.

"What? What happened?"

"It negated his other wishes. The house, the money, they disappeared, and he didn't even get a real third wish. I was around long enough to see his life revert back to poverty and then I was back in the void."

"No!" Dot gasped. "How...? Was that because...?"

He lifted his head enough for her to see the indignation in his eyes. "No warden is going to give a prisoner the power to escape. I'm not just trapped, Dottie. I'm cursed. Cursed to give others everything they wish but unable to have anything for myself. Cursed to say goodbye to every friend I'll ever have. Cursed to feel pain but never die. Cursed to feel love that can't last. Cursed to destroy the lives of anyone who shows me too much compassion."

The words came like a punch to the gut. She understood now.

Wish for what you *want. Don't get attached.*

He was protecting her.

She shot off the bed, she wasn't entirely shocked that Raji's tale had brought tears to her eyes. No wonder he had been so adamant about not influencing her wishes. He believed she could be punished for it.

"Your life is literally a living hell, and I'm complaining about a ten million dollar wish. I feel like such a tool."

Raji shook his head. "No, you have every right to complain. I got carried away tonight. And I did it because...I like having you as a client. Maybe a little too much. I wanted to impress you by granting an amazing wish for someone who deserved it for once. I swear, every time I start to enjoy this job..."

Maybe a little too much?

"I'm glad you told me," she interrupted as she rifled through the drawers of her nightstand for a tissue. "Knowing what made you this way...it wouldn't even be a question that I'd use a wish to get you out of it. And I'm glad not all your masters were d-bags."

"You remind me of Rourke, Dottie. You have a good soul. You were ready to free me on your *second wish*. I am truly stunned by that. But now you know never to even entertain the idea of using any of your wishes on me. Right?"

She held the tissue to her nose, feeling completely helpless and hopeless. Despite the insane aftermath of her wish, she liked Raji. She liked having him around.

Maybe a little too much.

She now knew, regardless of his power, their relationship was doomed to end, as had all the good things in her past.

The clock on the nightstand said that it was nearly three a.m. She was probably on the schedule to work the next day, but she'd call out. The last few days had been a lot. That was to say nothing of the last few hours.

"I need to go to sleep," she said quietly. His story weighed on her. Her kidnapping weighed on her. The general unfairness of life weighed on her. Now, without wish instincts to counteract it all, the urge to hide or sleep or escape was intense.

She threw back her covers and crawled underneath. Raji began to get up.

"You can stay." It surprised her how quickly she said it. The shock on Raji's face told her it surprised him, too. "I mean...I know you don't need sleep, but...you got shot. And the last time I was alone was when..."

"Oh, I'm not leaving you alone," Raji said. He looked down at the bed. "I was gonna recover on the floor...unless...you're really okay if..."

She nodded.

He laid back down—on top of the covers—rolling on his side to face her. "I swear I'm usually a better genie than this. Do you...think you can ever trust me again?" he asked.

"Yeah, I think so," she said, offering him a small smile. "I feel bad for you now."

He returned a smile of his own. "I'm not above pity. It's more than I've ever gotten from most other masters—er, clients."

"Can we just be friends?" she asked. "I think our relationship evolved tonight. Near-death experiences and trauma-dumping have that effect."

"Yes," he responded instantly. "I haven't had a friend in a long time."

Dot yawned. Her eyelids felt heavy.

"I'll get the lights," Raji said. "You dream about what you're going to do with that impressive hunk of cash. I won't let anything else happen to you. I'll tie up all the loose ends. You'll be safe. I promise."

She closed her eyes. Her consciousness fading. Before it went completely, she thought she felt Raji's fingers gently brushing her hair away from her face.

"Thanks for listening, Dottie."

His whisper was the last sound that fell on her ears. A moment later, she was asleep.

Chapter 18

DOT

"What? Do I have milk in my beard?"

Across the unsteady table from Raji, Dot looked away. She hadn't realized until then that she had been staring at him for a solid minute. Though she had slept better than she expected, now awake, her thoughts were a tangled mess with everything there was to digest. Despite all that Raji had revealed, she envied him. All that time in a dark void with no responsibilities and thousands of years to process traumatic events and confusing feelings sounded kind of nice. "No, I just...I'm glad you're enjoying your cereal."

"Best culinary invention since the last time I was out of the bottle." He tipped the bowl and slurped up the milk, then swirled it away into nothingness with a wave of his wrist. "You sure you don't want any?"

She shook her head. The nausea from her near-death experience still hadn't completely left.

"So?" he asked with a smile. "Big plans today with your big money?"

Somehow Raji seemed wholly unaffected this morning, despite everything they had just been through. Perhaps he was shelving it for all that uninterrupted processing time he'd have later.

Dot, however, was not unaffected.

"Something on your mind?" he asked.

Her chair wobbled as she shifted nervously. "Is it okay that we left San Francisco in the middle of aiding an FBI investigation? Will I need to go back?"

"Oh, no. It's all taken care of."

"It is? How?"

"I handled it before my wish power ran out. I planted the idea among the FBI that you were moved to a safe house. You were, it just happens to be your actual house."

She gripped the table, swaying under a wave of familiar dizziness. "Should I be at a *real* safe house? Am I still in danger?"

With a look of remorse, Raji moved out of his chair and kneeled beside her. "Deep breaths, Dottie. It's okay. Trust me, I got it all under control. Before my magic wore off, I made sure Avros's buyers were tracked down, and I erased the evidence that you were ever in that hangar. They won't even need you for questioning. And if any other unforeseen consequences pop up, I will personally take a hundred bullets' worth of pain to make sure that wish never comes back to haunt you."

"Why would you have to take more bullets? Will the Russians come looking for me?" Her heart pounded at the thought of Avros or Boris showing up at her front door.

"No, that's not what I meant. Definitely could have worded that differently." One of his hands flew to her shoulder and began gliding up and down her arm slowly. She closed her eyes and leaned into it, sucking in deep breaths as calmly as she could. "What I meant was...when I attempt to orchestrate events outside of a wish, there's this dumb built-in punishment system. I'm saying I'll take any punishment required to keep Avros, his henchmen, and the FBI from bothering you ever again. There will be no bullets."

Her heart and breathing calmed, and her eyes blinked open as her brain grappled with what he was saying. "What do you mean *punishment*?"

He shrugged, a little more nonchalantly than she thought he should. "Your wish had nothing to do with wanting to help the FBI catch a criminal. By stretching my power to fix everything that went sideways outside the perimeters of the wish, I...I was dealt a healthy dose of supernatural pain. But it's fine. I've learned to deal with small doses over the years."

"So it was a *small* healthy dose?" she asked, slightly relieved.

A guilty smile passed over his lips. "Well...it was enough to make the gunshots not too big of a deal. Silver lining."

"Raji! You said the pain was better before I went to sleep."

"It was! It was much better. Just not gone. But your bed helped."

"Oh my gosh," she groaned, closing her eyes and rubbing her palm across her forehead. His obliviousness was cute, but it still made her cheeks flare. Especially now that she knew they were definitely the same species.

"Beds have drastically improved since the last time I was out. Thank you for so willingly sharing yours."

A loud knock sounded from her front door, saving her from offhandedly answering with the undignified response of "anytime."

But now she worried about who might be knocking.

"I can get that, if you want," Raji offered.

It can't be Avros or the FBI. They're on the other side of the country. There's no way they could get here that fast.

But just to be sure...

"Yes, please," she said.

Raji headed towards the front door while she tip-toed through the living room behind him. He looked through the peephole. "It's your coworker."

Skye? "Uh...get in the kitchen and stay there unless I tell you to come out," she instructed, shooing him away. After taking a second to gather herself, she opened the door, trying her best not to appear like she was still recovering from a minor panic attack.

"Skye! Hey. What are you doing here?"

"Oh my gosh, you're alive," Skye sang, slapping her hand to her chest. Dot's mouth fell open.

How does she know? Was I on the news?

"I thought that possessed bottle sucked you inside or something."

A blanket of relief squelched Dot's paranoia. She reminded herself to check the news later, though.

"You've missed the last two days of work! And you're not answering your phone!"

It took a minute for Dot to remember that the phone she had taken to San Francisco hadn't been her regular one. "I'm so sorry. I've had to...deal with some things. Are you on your way to your shift?"

"I'm off today, that's why I came over. But you're on the schedule. *You* should be on the way to *your* shift."

Dot thought about offering her friend an explanation. She couldn't think of a single past coworker—irritated bosses notwithstanding—who would've ever noticed whether or not she showed up for work. She beckoned Skye inside while she decided what to tell her.

Skye peered around the living room. "Nice place. It's got that minimalistic vibe. I like it."

"Do you want something to drink?" Dot asked. She didn't entertain guests often.

"Oh, this is a full-service visit?" Skye laughed. "No, I'm good. Tell me what's going on."

Dot directed her friend to the saggy sofa and gestured for her to sit, then she sat down to face her. "I'm quitting," Dot said abruptly. "I don't need the job anymore."

"Oh." Skye frowned. "Wait. Is it because of that trashbag of a human who verbally assaulted you the other day? You can't let those people get to you. They're rarer than you think. You just had really bad luck."

It took Dot another second to remember the horrid customer. A lot had happened since then.

"Oh, no. That's not..." She tried to think of a convincing lie, but nothing felt right. Skye was voluntarily being a friend. Maybe telling her *some* of the truth wouldn't scare her away.

"I came into some money, actually. Enough so that working isn't necessary for me anymore."

Skye's eyes widened. "What? That's awesome! Like from a dead grandma or something?"

"Something like that." Dot scratched her head and forced a smile.

"That makes me so happy! You deserve it. I mean that. You're a good person, one of the better ones I've worked with. I wish we could've worked together longer."

With a start, Dot deliberated a response. She hadn't expected such a kind, supportive reaction. "That's...thank you for saying that. You're the only thing I'll miss about it." Which was true.

"Promise you'll say hey if you come by and see me working. And maybe take me out to lunch with your newfound wealth."

Dot hoped she hadn't appeared too taken aback. After working at Target for only a couple of weeks, she had no idea she would leave such an impression. Or any impression. "Yeah. Of course. I promise."

"And, hey, we'll always have that weird bottle incident."

"Oh...yes," Dot laughed nervously. "Yep, we'll always have that."

A thought came to her. A crazy one. Maybe Skye could handle more than some of the truth. Maybe Dot didn't have to be the sole bearer of knowing that genies exist. Besides, it had been Skye's idea to try to get that bottle open in the first place.

"Skye...do you want to see what was *in* the bottle?"

"You got it open?" Her eyebrows drew together. "Is it gross? Is it creepy?"

"It's neither. At least not intentionally."

Skye laughed like Dot had told a joke that she didn't quite get, though she wanted to seem like she did. Then her eyes widened again. "Wait, were you right? Was there money inside?" She gasped. "Is that where your money came from?"

"Just...stay here." Dot stood and hurried into the kitchen, where Raji sat idly on the counter. "Come on," she beckoned.

Raji slid onto his feet. "You sure?" he whispered. "Sometimes when masters show me off, it tends to create a whole jealousy cycle."

"I'm sure." She grabbed his hand and pulled him into the living room.

Skye's eyes narrowed as Dot positioned Raji in front of her. "Hello," she said to him uncertainly, briefly turning her slitted eyes to Dot, who suddenly wanted to shove Raji back in the kitchen.

Raji stuck out his hand. "It's nice to meet a friend of Dot's," he said as they shook.

"It's nice to meet a..."

"Genie," Raji said.

"Genie of—wait. Huh?"

Second thoughts speedily clouded her brain, yet Dot stuck with her original decision; if anyone would believe this, it would be the person who ranked demonic possession over wind interference when it came to jiggling bottles. "There was a genie in the bottle, Skye. Him."

Raji smiled and bowed politely, and Dot felt a surge of gratitude for the speed at which he validated her sanity.

Skye looked at Dot and pointed at Raji. "You say he's a...oh, that's funny. Very funny. Good prank." Dot could tell by Skye's fake smile and worried eyes that she did not find it funny. She found it concerning.

She turned to Raji. "Maybe you can get yourself a bowl of cereal."

"Gladly." Raji reached a hand into the air and swirled his wrist. A bowl of Froot Loops appeared in his palm.

Skye nodded slowly. "Ahh, a magician. Oh hey, if you have a deck of cards I actually know a really cool—" Dot sighed loudly. Skye frowned. "Dot, are you okay?"

"Raji, you'll have to finger-snap."

"Oh, I can only finger-snap you, Dottie, since you're my master—client, I mean."

She scoffed her resignation. "Then *you* think of something convincing to show her."

"Anything of value would require a wish, so unless you want to make one..."

As their exchange went on, Dot noticed Skye slowly rising to her feet out of the corner of her eye, so she moved to block her before she could advance towards the door. Skye already knew too much.

"Wait! Skye, I'm being serious! I came into a lot of money because *he* got me ten million dollars with my first wish."

Skye was looking increasingly uncomfortable. But Dot couldn't let her leave thinking she was crazy.

"Okay, I think there's something I can do," Raji cut in. He swirled the cereal away and waved a hand at Dot.

Suddenly she was wearing a large, poofy gown.

"Holy...!" Dot said, stumbling under the sudden weight.

"Evil!" Skye cried before bolting for the door.

Raji waved his hand again, and the door became a brick wall, stopping a squealing Skye in her tracks. Meanwhile, Dot had regained her balance.

"Skye, this is Raji. He's harmless! I mean...kind of." She and Raji exchanged a look.

In front of the brick wall, Skye clutched the purse strap on her shoulder then she slowly turned to face them. She studied Raji guardedly, then turned her attention to Dot...and snorted a laugh. "You look ridiculous," she said.

A satisfied smile swept across Dot's face. "Okay, Raji. You can change me back."

"You sure? I think you look nice. I always thought you'd make a good princess." But he waved his hand and the gown vanished, thankfully leaving behind Dot's original clothes.

"And the wall," she added.

Another wave and the front door returned to normal. Skye's snickering ceased as she watched everything with an unreadable expression. Finally, she looked at Raji. "You," she said. "You were in the bottle?"

He nodded.

"Um, Dot." Keeping her eyes on Raji, Skye angled her hand in front of her mouth. "He's kind of *fine*."

Raji smirked. Dot struggled not to blush.

"This is a good friend you have, Dottie," Raji said, shooting Dot a quick side wink. "Good call."

Anxious to change the subject, Dot stepped forward. "What do you say we do that lunch date right now, Skye? My treat."

Skye considered, her eyes shifting between them. "Ten million dollars, huh? Yeah, it better be your treat."

"As ridiculous as all of that sounds, I believe every word."

Skye, Dot, and Raji sat together around a table in a trendy restaurant Dot had always wanted to try but previously couldn't imagine ever affording. They had all finished their meals, and Dot had just finished relating the unbelievable events of her first wish. "It's way too insane to make up," Skye went on. "I could be reading you all wrong, Dot, but you've never struck me as an attention seeker."

Dot smiled appreciatively. Though the trauma of everything still lingered, Skye's earnest questions and dramatic reactions allowed her to appreciate the adventure in it, at least the parts that were included in the actual wish. And Raji's hand on her knee had helped her get through the more harrowing details. On her phone, Skye pulled up a press release on a San Francisco news site that corroborated the story, at least to a degree. There was no mention of Dot, Avros, the traitorous agent, or Lydia Daines; it only stated that arrests had been made at San Francisco International Airport and the FBI was involved.

"I'm glad you believe me because I woke up this morning thinking maybe it was all a dream," Dot said. "But then he's always hanging around and I'm so relieved that you can see him." She jabbed a thumb at Raji in the chair next to her, who was wiping the last bit of chocolate sauce off one of the dessert plates with his finger. "I would be lying if I said I didn't wonder if I'd finally gone crazy," she added.

"I'm hurt, Dottie," he said with a playful frown before sucking the sauce from his finger. "Did last night mean nothing to you?"

Across the table, Skye raised her eyebrows, and Dot wondered if she had been too hasty in bringing Raji out in public for his first social engagement.

"Please ignore him, he's still learning twenty-first century tact," she said, forcing a smile.

"So...can I have him next?" Skye asked with the kind of expectancy someone would use to ask for the ketchup to be passed her way.

Dot fidgeted uneasily at the question. She looked at Raji, who kept swirling his finger on the plate as if he hadn't heard. Knowing his past made it feel very wrong to talk about him like something fun for her friend to try out, especially right in front of him.

"Oh my gosh," Skye blurted, looking from Dot to Raji. "That was a dumb thing to say, wasn't it?"

"I mean..." It broke Dot's heart a little to realize that Raji was not going to stand up for himself in this moment. He couldn't. And she felt foolish knowing that she had to do it for him, even though she knew it wasn't his fault.

"He's kind of...no, he *is* a person. Doesn't it feel a little wrong to call dibs on him?"

Even that sounded like she was talking about a small child or a dog.

He does not deserve this.

"Oh, no, it doesn't matter to me." Raji shrugged and smiled, but Dot knew he was only desperate to put Skye at ease. She suddenly understood why he chose to mask his humanity. It probably helped him avoid awkward conversations like this one. "I make wishes come true. It's natural for anyone to want a turn with me."

"Okay, I'm hearing the wrongness now," Skye said with a cringe. "Pretend I didn't say anything."

A heavy silence settled over the table. They needed a change of subject.

"It doesn't even matter," Dot said. "I still have two more wishes to make. Any suggestions?"

Skye tilted her head. "You don't have another one picked out yet?"

"I'm not good at coming up with ideas or making decisions," she said. "It took me forever to come up with the first wish."

"Really?" Skye leaned back. "Just while sitting here, I've come up with a lot more than three things I'd wish for."

Dot looked at Raji, who pressed his lips together in a *see-what-I-mean* smirk. "Like what?" she asked Skye.

"Like money, but you already wished for that. Or a vacation. Something really expensive and luxurious that rich people would throw down millions of dollars on. My boyfriend Winston and I never get to go anywhere together because of our work schedules, not to mention we're always broke, but we fantasize about it all the time."

"See, that's a great idea," Dot said. "I could wish for that and then invite you guys to come, too."

Both Raji and Skye stared at Dot like they were waiting for a punchline.

"Are you serious?" Skye asked, glancing at Raji. "Why would you let me piggyback off your wishes?"

"Dot doesn't seem to know how to be selfish," Raji explained.

"It's not that," Dot quickly defended. "It's just..." But she couldn't finish that sentence out loud unless she seriously wanted to dampen the mood.

It's just that it scares me to make another wish. And it no longer feels right using Raji for my own enjoyment.

Skye waved a hand coolly, saving the conversation before Dot could destroy it. "Hey, nobody at this table is gonna judge you for treating yourself. You don't owe me or anyone else anything with your insane"—she looked at Raji again and took a long breath as she stared him down —"*insane* good luck."

Dot swallowed. She couldn't bring herself to look at Raji for his reaction. He'd already seen her blush so many times he probably suspected she had a skin disease.

"I have to go pick up Winston," Skye said, breaking her stare and gathering her things. "Thanks again for lunch. I hope introducing your genie means you aren't planning on being a stranger. I'd be all about hanging out again, even if you weren't a secret millionaire." Skye smiled warmly at Dot as she stood up. "You completely deserve it. I seriously would have thrown that bottle off a bridge if it were me. It would have been a waste."

Normally, Dot worried people were only friendly to her out of obligation. Now that she had money, she worried people would be friendly to her because she's rich. Skye's unprovoked visit to check on Dot and invitation to hang out after work relieved her worries, at least a little. "We'll definitely do this again," Dot said.

She watched her friend's eyes flit briefly to Raji before she leaned down close to Dot's ear. "You were totally meant to be the one to get the genie," she said quietly. "You make a cute couple." With a little wave to each of them, Skye left.

Then it was only her and Raji at the table. Skye's comment brought a sudden awareness to something Dot had been trying not to think about since Raji had confirmed it the night before. She'd spent almost every minute with Raji for almost five days now, and his company hadn't felt as intrusive as she initially expected. She was finding him easy to talk to and easy to get along with, and he didn't seem the least bit put off by her constant nervousness and social awkwardness. Maybe he was conditioned to be pleasant company, but whether he was or wasn't, one thing was confirmed: Raji wasn't some nonhuman creature. At his core, he was a man. A regular human man. And Dot was a regular human woman. Whose life he had saved. And who stayed beside her all night. To protect her.

He had propped his chin on his fist as he watched her with a patient smile. He had good patience. And a really good smile.

No one's making this weird but you, she reminded herself.

"So..." she began slowly. With no FBI to inform or scam artist to scam or job to rush off to, the next topic would surely be the next wish. She expected him to bring it up at any second.

"Don't feel like you have to make a second wish right now," he said.

Sheesh, can he read my thoughts? But though he brought it up, it wasn't in the way she expected.

"Unless you want to," he hastily added.

Her head shook. "No. I don't want to. I need some...normal time." Images of wrapping up in a blanket and watching TV flashed through her mind. "It was nice talking about that wish in the past tense with someone who claims to believe me, but I'm still a little overwhelmed. Aren't you?"

Though she anticipated a refusal, his slow nod surprisingly relieved Dot. "Can I be honest?" he asked.

"Yeah, of course. Please. Be honest."

"I could use some time to recover from that last wish."

"Yes!" she agreed, leaning towards him. "We're on the same page, then. It was a fun wish, but then it was a lot."

He laughed, and she sensed she wasn't the only one experiencing unexpected relief. "I've never been able to say that to a client before," he remarked. "And if I had, I would never expect total agreement."

A pang of guilt hit her in the chest. Her first reaction was *poor Raji*. But she hated to think about him like that; she certainly hated it when people thought about her that way. But sometimes when she let her guard down and let herself think about herself that way, it could be therapeutic. She guessed that Raji rarely got that opportunity.

"Okay, there's a quick errand I need to take care of now that I have some money," she said. "But after that, I think you and I deserve an afternoon to wallow in our own self-pity. Not each other's, that would be disgusting. Just our own. Sound good?"

"Dot," he replied with a grateful smile. "That's something I've wanted to do for centuries."

Chapter 19

DOT

Dot had only visited her landlords' home to put a check in their mailbox, so she needed time to gather the courage to get out of her car after she parked out front.

"They can't be that bad, can they?" Raji asked from the passenger seat. "Remember the kind of people you were dealing with yesterday?"

"I'm trying not to," she answered, staring at the front door. "Jorge is fine, but Yasmin can be...intimidating." She turned to look at him. "I should have brought them cookies or something. What am I supposed to do with my hands?"

"Will this help?" With his signature wrist swirl, a plate of cookies appeared in Raji's palm. He held it towards her.

She sniffed the air and licked her lips. "Wow, what are those? Snickerdoodles?"

"That's what they tell me. This modern English might have some of the strangest food names I've ever heard. Snickerdoodles, hot dogs, bubble and squeak."

"I don't know what bubble and squeak is and nope"—she lifted a hand to stop him as he opened his mouth to speak—"I don't need you to explain. Not right now, anyway. I want to get this over with first. Wash my hands of debt. Get on good terms with the *lords*."

Raji frowned. "Is that slang? It's not registering with my infinite knowledge."

"No, I made it up because I'm nervous. Don't tell anyone I said that. Ever."

"I can come with you," he offered.

"Nope again. I have no intention of explaining you to anyone besides Skye."

"Okay. Then I'm happy to wait here." He extended the cookies until the plate was in her face. "May the force be with you."

Her eyebrows slanted. "I can't tell if you're being funny or if your super knowledge told you that's a thing people say in these situations."

"Does it not mean 'good luck'?"

She pressed her lips together, then grabbed the plate of cookies. "I'll be right back."

On the front sidewalk, Dot walked past an array of colorful chalk art; rainbows and flowers and a shape that looked vaguely like Spiderman. Two old rocking chairs swayed gently in the breeze on the low cement porch, beside one sat a half-empty plastic bottle of bubble solution, its discarded bubble wand a few feet away.

"I thought Yasmin and Jorge's kids were grown," Dot mumbled. From inside came the happy sound of children laughing.

Maybe this is a bad time.

But I'm already here. I can't give up now.

She hesitated at the door. For a long time. She looked back at Raji, who gave her an exuberant thumbs up through the car window.

Suddenly, the door swung open, and Dot willed herself not to dive into the bushes. Instead, she turned, glancing at the doorbell as she did, noting that it was the fancy kind with a camera. They must have been watching her stand there like an idiot for the past two minutes.

"Heeey, Jorge," she chirped to the tall man in the doorway.

His mustache wrinkled. "Dot. Is something wrong?"

"No. I ...I brought some cookies."

Yasmin appeared behind Jorge, her expression equally baffled, while from behind her, two little heads with large brown eyes and matching tangles of brown hair peeked out curiously.

"Hey, Yasmin," Dot said, a little less chirpy.

"Is something wrong?" Yasmin immediately repeated.

"No, no. Nothing's wrong. I just wanted to bring y'all some cookies and—" The two little heads became two little bodies out in front now, jumping up and down with excitement. "Cookies!" they cried.

"That's very nice of you." Jorge smiled as he took the plate, but Dot detected the slightest touch of suspicion as he glanced at the treats. Before he could say anything, the children snatched the plate and ran off, disappearing back into the house.

"Those are our grandchildren," Jorge explained. "We watch them when their parents are working. Our daughter is a nurse, our son-in-law is a long-haul truck driver. They both work odd hours."

Dot tried to seem interested. Jorge had always liked small talk. Dot didn't. "Oh. That's nice...I hope they like the cookies."

For a small second, the three of them stared awkwardly at one another, but Dot could not let this get away from her. Not today.

She cleared her throat and straightened her stance. "I didn't just come to give you cookies. I owe you guys rent. You've been really generous to me in the past with the breaks when I couldn't pay, but I have some money and I want to settle that now. If that's okay."

Yasmin and Jorge exchanged a puzzled look.

"So you have a job? That's great," Jorge said. "But haven't you been out of work for a while? Don't you need the money? It's nice of you to want to pay us back, but we didn't mean to make you feel pressured."

Dot caught Yasmin making the faintest eye roll. She chose to ignore it.

"No, I want to pay you back because...well, because I want to. I really, really want to. You guys are so patient with me. More than I deserve."

"That's because you're a mess," Yasmin interjected. Jorge forced a smile and placed a hand on his wife's shoulder.

"She's joking," he said, though Yasmin looked quite serious.

"No, she's right," Dot countered. "You're right, Yasmin. I am a mess."

Yasmin crossed her arms triumphantly. "I know. I'm always right."

"I was a mess from day one," Dot stammered on. "I never expected you to rent to me. But you did. And you've put up with my messiness for four years now. I came to tell you that I'm sorry. There aren't many people in my life who have been consistent, but you two have. You deserve some gratitude. And money." She clasped her hands together piously. "Let me pay you what I owe you. Please."

The heavy silence that followed terrified her. Had she made them uncomfortable? Had she overstepped a boundary?

Then a smile appeared on Yasmin's face. Yasmin, of all people. "Come in, *chica*," she said, opening the door wider. "I've been waiting for this visit."

Dot stayed quiet as she began the drive home. Raji hadn't ever been one to press her to speak. He was fine to sit in silence, and she appreciated it, because the visit with Jorge and Yasmin left her stunned and on the verge of emotional chaos. All these years she had only ever seen them as her landlords, but after stepping into their home, she was seeing them in a different light.

Her mind raced back in time to the days after her grandmother had died and Dot had needed a cheap, quick place to live. Because of the pandemic, she had been interviewed by Jorge virtually, an interview through which she had cried a lot as she tried to articulate the stressfulness of her situation. Afterwards, she had been convinced that she'd blown it. These people would never rent to her. But then...they did. It had never occurred to her to question why they would. A person in her situation couldn't afford to question things. She'd just assumed they were as desperate as she was.

"We took you on as a tenant knowing you were experiencing hard times," Jorge had explained as she sat in their living room a half hour earlier. "You said in your interview that your grandmother had passed and you had no family. Your emergency contacts were in nursing homes. Your job was being threatened by the pandemic."

"You were a mess," Yasmin repeated. "We hoped you would have gotten over that by now."

Jorge went on. "We know hard times. We've experienced them ourselves. And we took you on because we felt like you needed it more than the other applicants."

"We always held you accountable, of course, but we never felt like you were trying to take advantage of us," Yasmin added.

"Take advantage of you? No!" Dot affirmed. "Those months I couldn't pay stressed me out. I couldn't sleep until I got a rent check in your hands."

"Exactly," Jorge said. "Because of that, we agreed not to pressure you to pay us back. But we'll take the money. If you really do have it."

Then Dot understood. The signs were there, but she had somehow missed them or refused to see them for what they were. She thought her landlords were attentive because they didn't trust her, but now she realized they had always been discreetly looking out for her.

She remembered how Jorge checked in each time she lost a job and had always been quick to make any repairs (making excruciating small talk each time he did). They gave her a discount on rent for Christmas every year and sent a card on her birthday. They had been weirdly happy for her when she had gotten serious with Howie, and then Yasmin, the ice queen herself, had shown up for her when he dumped her. Why Dot was only recognizing their generosity now, she didn't know. She just never assumed people were being nice to her voluntarily.

And after she settled her debt with them, they invited her to stay for dinner. She had to decline, of course. Not only did she have a genie waiting in the car, but the prospect of sharing a meal with them in the midst of all these sentimental realizations might have triggered some overwhelming emotions and she didn't want to cry all over their food.

"Something on your mind?" Raji asked, yanking her from her thoughts.

She sighed. "Yeah, just how I always seem to think I'm all alone in the world, but now I'm realizing I have people in my life who care about me."

"Boy, if I had a penny for every time one of my clients said that after they wished for a bunch of money."

She laughed. It was a nice reprieve from her heavy thoughts.

At the restaurant, she figured TV and blankets might be the therapy they needed, but the idea felt more like a habitual response the more she thought about it, though she knew Raji probably wouldn't object if she did choose that route. That isn't how she wanted to spend *Raji's* time. If she ever found herself six hundred years in the future, there would be so much more she'd want to experience than the inside of one person's tiny house.

She glanced at Raji. "Hey, do you mind if I take a little detour? We can still have a pity party, just in a different location."

He smiled. "I couldn't mind less."

A little less than an hour later, she turned the Altima onto a quiet, narrow road as the last of the sunlight pooled on the western horizon. The land around them faded into marshes until the road became a bridge, sporadically illuminated by the bright beam of a white lighthouse that loomed taller as the car approached. The road ended in a mostly empty parking lot on a little stretch of island where the lighthouse stood; there Dot stopped the car and the two of them got out.

She led Raji to a lonely bench on the path between the parking lot and the lighthouse and sat down. Raji followed suit, and she immediately turned to him. "What do you think of this place?" she asked, both nervous and curious to get his reaction.

In the dying light, she watched him carefully study the lighthouse, then the dark gulf spread out before them, then the rapidly darkening sky above.

It worried her that he wasn't saying anything. "It's probably underwhelming, right? Considering other places you've been."

His eyes found hers like he needed her to witness his absolute sincerity. "No. Not at all. It's beautiful."

Her body relaxed against the back of the bench as she breathed her relief. "I know it isn't the Rockies or the Scottish Highlands, but to me this is the most beautiful place on earth. My grandma and I used to come to this island for walks or picnics when she needed to get away from her nosy neighbors or when I needed to get away from the mean kids at school. It was our happy place." She paused. "They call this area The Forgotten Coast. It's fitting. We liked coming here to forget about everything else."

Though she faced forward, she could feel his eyes on her as he spoke. "That's really nice, Dot."

She sensed that he had more to say, so she waited.

"But I'm finding this place is making me remember. Good things," he finally said.

"It is?" She shifted sideways on the bench to face him.

"Yeah." He looked out at the water. "The sea and the lighthouse remind me of Rourke and his family. The place they lived looked a lot like this. The lighthouse is a little newer than the one he lived near, but the sound of the waves at night..."

His eyes turned upwards. "And the sand and the stars. They remind me of the desert. When I was with my family."

Dot looked up. She always liked how dark The Forgotten Coast got. The heavens were more vivid here than anywhere she'd ever been. Now that the sun was mostly gone, thousands of pinpricks of light were becoming visible in between the flashes of the lighthouse beam. "I bet the nighttime desert sky was incredible," she said.

"It was spectacular. And I completely took it for granted."

When she turned back to him, he was looking straight at her, and his features softened. "It must be hard to be out here without your grandmother."

She felt a lump form in her throat, but she shrugged. "It is. But how am I supposed to remember her without being sad that she's gone? It comes with the territory, you know?"

"I do know," he said, and it broke her heart. For both of them.

"I used to think when I lost her," Dot went on, "that I lost the only person who ever cared that I exist. I wanted Howie to care more than he did but that never happened. But then today with Skye and Jorge and Yasmin. And you…"

"Howie?" he asked, his gaze unmoving.

"Oh. My ex. We broke up a little while before I found your bottle."

She watched his eyebrows raise slightly, but he didn't say anything else. Howie was the last person she wanted to talk about. But she still hadn't spoken about their break-up out loud. And here was Raji, his attention fixed on her.

She lightened her tone, anxious to downplay it. "He dumped me. I wasn't living up to his expectations. He was always trying to push me out of my comfort zone and I think I resisted more than he liked."

"Sounds like a real prick," Raji said calmly, his pointed expression unchanging.

She laughed. "Wow, um…thanks? No. He really wasn't a bad guy. I was just never gonna be the right person for him. Or maybe I didn't try hard enough. Either way, in hindsight, I know now we weren't meant for each other."

"Well…I already know I don't like him."

Another chuckle escaped her. "You don't even know him."

"Dottie, when he left you, did he hurt you at all?"

She frowned. "Not physically. Only mentally and emotionally."

"Then I don't like him," he said with a shrug.

Dot studied his face for any hint of a joke, but his eyes remained resolute and serious. So serious, she began to cry.

She turned away. "Sorry," she said. "I'm sorry."

"No, I'm sorry. Was that too harsh? Should I not have said that?"

She felt the weight of his hand on the back of her shoulder and she looked up to find him offering her a handkerchief that he likely pulled out of thin air.

"Sorry you're stuck with a client who cries all the time." She grabbed the handkerchief and dabbed at her eyes. "I've been alone a lot lately and only having myself for company makes it hard not to take the blame for everything bad that's ever happened to me. It's...it's a little strange and kind of a relief to have someone take my side when I don't even take my side most of the time."

The beam of the lighthouse passed over them, shedding light on his small smile. "Wow. I know exactly what you mean. It's strange to have so much in common with a client. I mean, a lot of the stuff we have in common is traumatic and depressing, but it's...it's nice at least to relate to someone. As a person."

"We have other things in common. We both like food," she added, wiping away a tear. His laugh made the rest of them dry up quickly. He removed his hand from her back and rested it on the bench behind her.

She had expected it to feel weird bringing him to a place so sacred to her, one she had only visited alone the past four years—not even Howie got the honor of joining her—but it felt right, fitting even, to share this place with Raji. After everything that happened with her first wish, she *did* trust him. More than she had ever trusted anyone. And sharing things about himself with her that no other living person knew made it clear that he trusted her, too, and she didn't want to take that for granted.

"I think I have an idea for my second wish," she said, noting how the corner of his mouth twitched downwards at the revelation. "I want it to be the opposite of the first one."

He tipped his head. "You want someone to scam *you* out of ten million dollars?"

"No," she said with a laugh. "No, I want to give something instead of taking. I like Skye's dream vacation idea. I know you both thought I was lame for suggesting I wish it for her, but she's the nicest coworker I've ever had and why shouldn't I share a wish with her? And Yasmin and Jorge have been keeping an eye on me for longer than I realized. Paying back the rent I owed them anyway doesn't seem like enough of a thank-you."

The lighthouse gave her a glimpse of his awestruck expression. "Your wishes are your wishes, so use them how you see fit," he said. "But...geez, Dottie. How did becoming a millionaire make you *less* selfish?"

"I'm a little corrupted," she countered. "People are always saying revenge won't satisfy you, but I found it incredibly satisfying to steal money from that guy."

"Yeah, but then you promptly used it to treat your friend to a nice lunch and pay off debt."

She scoffed. "Hey, I plan on spending the rest of it on myself. I just need to hire a financial advisor or something. It's a lot of money."

"Yes. You're on a very dark path."

It was weird to laugh with someone so much. A pleasant kind of weird.

"Back to my second wish," she said, trying to appear more serious. "This time, I wanna be a little more involved in the execution. Not because I don't think you can handle it on your own or because I think you'll do it wrong, but because I want this wish to come from *me* to my friends. Does that make sense?"

He nodded. "You want it to have a more personal touch. I get it. We can do that."

"And I feel bad making you do all the work."

"You shouldn't. I'm happy to. But I'm also happy to take more direction from you. That's not uncommon. A lot of people have very specific ideas for their wishes, so I'm used to being micromanaged."

"That's not what I mean. I don't want to be a bossier boss. I want to work together. Be partners. A wish-granting team."

With the sky fully dark now and the lighthouse beam still working its way back to them, she couldn't see his reaction, but she thought she heard something between gratitude and disbelief in his tone when he answered. "Dottie, I would be honored to grant a wish with you."

Though she suspected that agreeing with her was a requirement of being her genie, she trusted that he meant it. "Good. Good. But here's the thing: I need time to figure it out. A few days—or maybe even weeks—of thinking and planning and talking it over until every detail is decided and perfect. And we both said we need time to recover from the last wish, so...we *should* give ourselves time. Sound good?"

She expected him to argue that he could be ready much faster, but there was a knowing twinkle in his eye when the light again passed overhead. "I understand," he said with exaggerated agreement. "Sometimes a good wish needs time to marinate. Very few masters allow them to, but maybe they would have been less disappointed if they did. Like the unicorn bear guy."

He definitely understood what she was doing by asking for time, and she was glad he was on board. It was the only way she could think of to give him some semblance of freedom. And though she didn't think she was totally qualified to be an ambassador to the future for someone from the past, she was up to the task. It would be good for both of them.

She watched Raji stare up at the stars happily, his arm still stretched across the bench behind her. Without thinking, she slid closer to him. Not too close, but enough to feel the edges of his human warmth.

It was the nicest moment she'd had in that place for a long time.

They stayed at the lighthouse longer than Dot intended, talking about wish number two, and then reminiscing about her grandmother and his mother. Raji conjured some tacos and milkshakes as they talked. When they finally left, she wondered if she had ever left that place in such a good mood.

But when they got back to the single-wide, the darkness and loneliness of Dot's bedroom reminded her of life before she got that bottle open, not to mention being blindfolded and tied up by actual criminals the night before. However, she didn't want Raji to feel obligated to watch over her again.

"You can stay out here tonight," she said as indifferently as she could. "I think I'm okay now."

She wasn't.

"Okay," he said without a drop of disappointment, which disappointed *her*. "I'll just watch your TV if you don't mind," he continued. "I'm having a hard time grasping the concept of reality game shows. I'd love to see one for myself."

"Yeah, go for it. There are plenty of them to keep you occupied." She slowly turned towards her bedroom door.

"But Dot," he said. She instantly turned around. His brown eyes gleamed with earnestness. "I *am* here if you need me. For anything at all. All night, I'll be right here on the other side of this wall."

Her disappointment lessened.

That night she dreamed she was back in the cabin in the Rockies wearing a big, poofy ballgown. A lamp like Aladdin's sat on the table before the window. Excitedly, she rushed over to rub it, and when she did, Boris appeared in a plume of black smoke, pointing a gun at her. He pulled the trigger.

"Raji!" she cried, her eyes flying open as she shot up in bed.

In an instant he was kneeling beside her, a dark shape distinguished by the comforting scent of warm sand and spice. "I'm here," he said, pulling one of her hands into his.

She felt stupid all of a sudden. She was a grown woman; sleeping alone in the dark had never been an issue for her.

But being alone hadn't always been a choice, and with Raji here, she didn't have to be alone. Not if she didn't want to.

"Just...go over there." She gestured to the other side of the bed and watched his shadow obey. "Sorry."

"You have nothing to apologize for, Dottie."

Hearing his voice in the darkness caused a rush of heat to come over her, and with a mix of longing and embarrassment, she realized that she wanted him to hold her. She wouldn't ask, though. That would be wrong. Probably.

But once he laid down, she couldn't help scooting towards him a centimeter at a time until his weight on the top of the covers wouldn't allow her to get any closer. When he didn't move away or say anything, she relaxed. The heat of his body through the comforter would have to be enough.

It wasn't, but it would have to be.

"Dot?" he said a moment later.

She swallowed. "Yes?"

"I don't want to make assumptions, but would it help to be...closer?"

She offered a silent prayer of gratitude for the darkness that hid what was surely her deepest blush since meeting him. Regardless, she was becoming more and more aware that he wouldn't be around forever, and before long, she'd be completely alone every night for the foreseeable future.

So if he was willing...

She sat up. "I mean...I would, maybe...but if you don't want to—"

His arm slid around her shoulders and her brain abandoned all thought as she melted against him. A lightheadedness overcame her when he gently guided her back towards the pillow, where she settled, in a state of relieved gratitude, into the crook of his arm.

"How's this?" he asked with an innocence that instantly put her at ease.

"It's good," she said. She closed her eyes, losing her sense of awareness to the soft sound of his heartbeat. "It's really good."

Chapter 20

RAJI

Dot's phone was buzzing. Her real phone. Fortunately, neither of the two people who had the number for the magic phone had called since the wish, so whomever was calling Dot at her regular number would be less of a concern, though calling her at 7:36 a.m. was a terrible lapse in judgment on their part.

Raji watched as Dot sleepily rolled away from him and reached a tired arm towards the nightstand, slapping it around until her hand landed on the vibrating rectangle. She held it in front of her face and cursed softly.

He sat up as she threw off the blankets. Though he had stayed with her during the last five nights, she still avoided eye contact with him every morning until after she had her morning shower, and even then, she never verbally acknowledged their unspoken nightly arrangement. So neither did he. It didn't seem like he should be allowed to get as much contentment as he did from being so close to her, anyway. If she didn't mind and if it wasn't triggering his internal alarm system, then it was best not to question it.

Dot didn't answer the phone. She must have silenced it, because she tossed it onto her dresser and slid back underneath her covers. Raji climbed to his feet and straightened the side of the bed he had occupied.

The buzzing started again.

"Would you like me to answer it?" Raji asked.

"No!" Dot said, pushing the covers off her head. "Don't. It's my mother. I need a solid ten hours of sleep before I talk to her. And then ten more after. But you can silence it for me."

Raji dutifully made his way over to the dresser and silenced the phone again, glancing at the name of the caller as he did. *Diane Mom*.

Raji had learned a lot about Dot over the past several days. Like that she was a slightly obsessive fan of a fictional British wizard boy. And that she knew nothing about the politics of her country but loads about the personal lives of its celebrities. And that she counted any dessert food as breakfast, be it ice cream, cookies, or especially pie.

He had also learned that though she was raised by her grandmother, her mother was still alive, although his knowledge of the situation didn't extend beyond that. In fact, until this very moment, he had no idea that they ever spoke.

The phone began to buzz again.

"Oh, for crying out loud!" Dot threw the covers back and stomped past him, snatching the phone off the dresser. "Hello?" she answered impatiently.

To his utmost gratitude, Dot had been allowing Raji plenty of freedom to be curious about the modern world, but asking about the details of her personal life that she didn't freely offer still felt like crossing a line. So, to give her some space, he made his way to the kitchen.

A few minutes later, Dot entered, still in her pajamas, her mouth and eyelids drooping. Raji was leaning against the sink as he munched on some Lucky Charms. She leaned against the counter next to him.

"You're curious," she said with a yawn. "Don't deny it."

"Deny what?" he responded, feigning ignorance.

She shot him a guilty half-smile. "Come on," she said. "I know you have questions."

She was right. He had questions. He swirled his cereal bowl away with one hand and summoned her a cup of coffee with the other, turning towards her as he offered it. "That was your mother," he stated. She nodded. "I didn't realize you had any kind of relationship with her. Do you ever see her in person?"

She shook her head as she took the cup from his hand. "Not often. She lives in Baltimore right now. She calls, but only when she wants something from me. That's why she was calling this morning. Apparently, a friend of one of her friends saw us having lunch at that expensive restaurant last week and noticed I picked up the check. She's been nagging me to buy her a plane ticket so she can bring her boyfriend here and show him off to all her frenemies and up until now my excuse was that I couldn't afford it. Now she doesn't believe me."

"Well...now you could easily afford it," he pointed out.

She took a sip from her cup. "Yeah, but she doesn't need to know that."

"So you *don't* want her to come visit?"

Dot sighed. "If she was coming to visit *me*, I wouldn't mind. My mother was the one person my grandma had a hard time getting along with, so when she died, I thought that would give my mom and I a chance to get closer, but I see her even less now. I feel like she purposely avoids me."

"I hope I'm not out of line asking you this, but why *did* your grandmother raise you?" It'd been a question he'd wanted to ask for a long time.

She pulled a hand down the side of her face, letting it rest at her jaw. She stared into space as she spoke.

"My mother got pregnant with me young. Seventeen. Obviously, it strained her relationship with her mother. Then the guy that got her pregnant ditched her. According to Grandma, Mom really loved that creep, and it devastated her. Then my grandpa died right around the same time. My mom was closer with him than my grandma, and without him as a buffer, things got worse. Mom ran away when I was about a year old to *find herself* or whatever. And she never came back, except for an occasional visit."

An introspective silence filled the air between them. Raji watched her absently sip her coffee.

"Dottie," he said carefully. "Maybe my understanding is too limited to know whether this is a valid suggestion, but have you thought about involving your mom in your second wish?"

She scoffed, her eyes moving to the kitchen floor. After a moment, she answered. "I don't know. In a perfect world, I think I would love to spend some quality time with her. Ask her some serious questions, even if the answers are hard to hear. But I honestly doubt she would want to come. This might be another case of me blaming myself because no one has ever told me not to, but I think she avoids me because I kind of ruined her life. Any relationship we have feels obligatory, and I've always figured it's because she resents me."

While her gaze remained lowered, he scooted closer, until their shoulders were touching. "Well, I would love to be the first to tell you not to blame yourself," he said softly. "She made the choice to leave you, Dottie. *She* did." He thought about reaching for her. Moving her hair out of her face or gently turning her chin towards him. He thought about that kind of stuff a lot, but in reality, it worried him how much he liked her, how much he thought about her, even when she was standing right in front of him. "Ultimately, you get to decide who you include in your second wish," he went on. "But even though my magic can't force her to be a better mother or to tell you what you want to hear, I *could* create an environment that would give the two of you the space and time to talk."

Her lips rested on the rim of her cup, but she didn't drink.

"All you have to do right now is think about it," he added.

She turned her head, and their eyes met. An understanding passed between them.

Since the night at the lighthouse, he and Dot had discussed her second wish many times, but from him there had been no pressure to make it, and from her there had been no deadline established. It was an agreement Raji should object to—granting wishes was the whole reason he was here, after all. But just like the sleeping arrangements, this unstructured, unlimited time she'd given him since the first wish ended felt too good to intentionally disrupt, especially when there didn't seem to be any adverse consequences.

Clearly, she felt the same way. And it made him appreciate her even more.

"I *will* think about it," she finally said, turning back to sip her coffee. Her gaze shifted to the window behind him. "Right now, there are other things to think about. I'm up early, and it looks like it's gonna be a nice day. We need to take advantage of that."

Raji found it interesting that taking advantage of a nice day in twenty-first century America almost always included a Target trip. Within the past few days they'd visited at least twice amid their leisurely outings to various sites around Tallahassee. Without a job, Dot had become very interested in showing Raji around, and he didn't complain. They had just come from riding bikes around a lake, though having seen plenty of lakes, it was the bike that interested him the most. That and the alligators in the lake that Dot begged him not to touch even after he reminded her he couldn't die.

"Oh, hey!" Skye said brightly as they appeared in her register line. "Dot, I was gonna call you when I clocked out. A guy was here looking for you."

"Oh, no," Dot groaned, placing an armful of cereal boxes on the conveyor belt. "What did he look like? It wasn't a handsome guy in scrubs, was it?"

"No, but I'd like to come back to that," Skye said. "It was like an older, heavier dude, but I only saw him walking away. He asked one of the other customer service girls about you and she immediately came and told me. He left you an envelope. I guess he didn't get the memo that you don't work here anymore."

Dot turned to Raji, her expression panicked.

He immediately understood what she was thinking. "It can't be anyone from the first wish," he whispered, but he too found the news disquieting.

Did I miss something?

Skye flipped off her register light. "If you wait a minute, I'll go get the envelope."

"What if it was someone from Avros's family?" Dot asked once Skye was out of earshot. "Are you sure they can't track me down?"

He shook his head firmly. "No way. It shouldn't have anything to do with that."

A small ache began in his chest, but being honest about sharing her fears wouldn't help the situation. With his wish magic powered down, he had no way of knowing what events had transpired among the Orlov family or the FBI in the past week. He only knew he had tried his best to make Dot's participation seem less than it was to everyone else involved.

She gripped his arm nervously, but he couldn't bring himself to give her anymore false assurance.

Skye returned, carrying an unmarked white envelope. She handed it to Dot and watched curiously as her trembling hands opened it and unfolded the single piece of paper inside.

While Skye peeked over one shoulder, Raji peeked over the other and read it silently.

Dear Dorothy,

My name is Lou Cooper. I am a collector of antiquities and recently made a deal with an acquaintance of mine in Ireland. He agreed I could go through his basement to look for certain collectibles. Unfortunately, before I could, my acquaintance passed and his belongings were dispersed. Some of them went to a family member here in Tallahassee. I tracked her down, but by the time I did, she had already sold many of the items. She did recall a few of her customers, one of which she identified as yourself, and remembering you were wearing a Target uniform, I knew where I could locate you. If you can recall which item she gave you, I would love to examine it and see if it is something I can add to my collection. I will compensate you fairly for it. Please see my attached business card for contact information.

Looking forward to hearing from you,

Lou Cooper

A bright red business card with gold trim stapled to the bottom of the page read *"Cuckoo" Lou Cooper's Chamber of Ill-LOU-sions, Branson, Missouri,* along with a phone number.

Dot turned to Raji, her face screwed up in confusion. He tried to clear the dread from his eyes before she noticed, but he didn't clear it fast enough.

"What? What's wrong?" she demanded. "Who is this guy?"

Before Raji could speak, Skye answered for him. "Dot, this guy knows you have a genie."

"No way. How would he know that?" Dot demanded, looking to Raji even more desperately.

But Skye beat him to a response a second time. "All this detail...why else would he be tracking *you* down specifically? And if the yard sale lady remembered your name and what you were wearing, she definitely would've remembered what she gave you. So what would he want with a basic, ugly old bottle unless he knew it was more than that?" Skye shot Raji an apologetic smile. "No offense, Raji. Your bottle is beautiful to me."

"None taken," he answered quickly, finally looking Dot in the eye.

"Is she right?" she asked.

He inhaled a long breath, searching for a way to explain without causing any further alarm. "There have always been people who believe I exist. Some of them spend their lives looking for my vessel. I've mentioned how sorcerers are always fighting over me. They're the ones most likely to track me down like this."

Her eyes widened. "Is this guy a sorcerer? What would that mean?"

Raji closed his eyes to hide his frustration.

Is this what I get for slacking?

He knew this reprieve Dot was allowing him couldn't last forever, but he was at least hoping for a few more days. Or weeks. Or as much time as Dot wanted. "We can't know for sure if he's a sorcerer," he said, opening his eyes and fixing them on his master. "But if he is, it's not good that he's trying to find you. There isn't a lot my knowledge has to say about sorcerers in the twenty-first century, but if they're anything like the sorcerers I've met, he may stop at nothing to get his hands on my bottle."

Dot chewed on her fingernail. "Okay but, if he takes the bottle now, he can't do anything with it. I'm not done with my wishes. You told me genies can't just be stolen. Nothing can break our contract. Except...oh, gosh..."

He watched the color drain from her face and steadied her as she stumbled against a rack of candy bars. Skye crossed her arms anxiously.

"Hey," he said, gripping Dot's shoulders. "We don't know for sure if this guy is a sorcerer or just some abnormally smart guy who's really into genie folklore—"

"We call those nerds," Skye offered.

"Right. Maybe this is just a harmless nerd," he said with a halfhearted shrug.

Dot didn't look convinced, and he didn't blame her. Her eyes were beginning to moisten and her body remained tense under his grasp. "What do I do, then?" she asked, her voice small. "How do we find out if he's a good guy or a bad guy?"

He didn't want to say it, but Dot was right to be freaked out. There was a sliver of a chance this man posed no threat, but from experience, Raji knew that someone in pursuit of a genie wouldn't give up easily. As close as he was getting, Lou certainly wouldn't.

He hated that he had to suggest what he was about to suggest. "I don't think we should try to find out what this guy's about until all your wishes are made. That's the only way I can guarantee your safety."

Something replaced the fear in her eyes, something Raji recognized instantly, because he felt it, too.

Sickening disappointment.

"I'm not ready," she said quietly, her shoulders slumping between his hands.

He pressed his lips together, feeling as defeated as she looked.

Me neither, he wanted to say. But then what would that imply? That he liked spending non-wish time with her and he wanted more? He did. He really, really did. But this was his wake-up call. He had knowingly strayed from his purpose, but he could never fully escape it. The break Dot had given him was all the freedom he would ever get.

But knowing that didn't make this setback any less aggravating.

"You have a great wish lined up. It will be okay," he assured with forced optimism.

Dot continued to stare for a second, then straightened herself. His hands slipped from her shoulders. "It's why you're here, right?" she stated sadly. "You're supposed to be granting wishes, anyway."

"I don't get it," Skye chimed in. "A sorcerer? What's he gonna do to you, Raji? I thought you were immortal."

"I am," Raji answered.

"But I'm not." Dot's words were resigned and distant, like she was detaching herself from reality.

Skye's intensely confused expression turned to horror. "Genies and now evil sorcerers? What's next? Vampires? Dragons? Winston's stupid D&D characters?"

Raji knew Dot had consulted Skye for permission to use her wish idea days ago, once they had begun planning. "Skye, you and Winston may want to clear your schedules and pack your bags," he said. "If you're okay going ahead with this, Dottie." He and Skye both watched for her response.

"Someone's looking for my genie. I don't see how we can put it off any longer," she answered bleakly, averting her gaze from both of them.

Raji shuddered under a surge of anger. Not at Dot. At Lou. Very few of the masters Raji had served deserved to have their wishes come true, and the person who arguably deserved them most was being forced into making them before she was ready.

It wasn't fair, but her safety was in question. His break was over. By the end of the day, Dot would only have one more wish to go.

The Second Wish

Chapter 21

DOT

Dot's first wish got underway with very little fanfare, but making the second wish proved to be depressingly anti-climactic. Of course, she never intended to be sitting inside her car, parked in her driveway, when it was time to make it.

"I don't know if I'm ready to do this," she said. "For so many reasons. I still don't know if I should invite my mother. And I haven't had a chance to talk to Jorge and Yasmin to gauge their interest like I planned. What if it's only us and Skye?"

"You're thinking like a non-genie," Raji replied. "And I know you can't help it. But as *not* a non-genie, let me assure you that none of that stuff really matters. My magic transcends all those minor details. We've talked about it enough that I'm going into this wish with more understanding than I've ever gone into any wish. I can grant it whenever you're ready."

"Then...should I just say it?"

"Sure."

"Right now?"

"In light of recent events, the sooner the better, I think."

She pressed her forehead against the steering wheel and closed her eyes. Risking death by greedy sorcerer or getting another step closer to sending an innocent man back into an eternity of enslavement were two terrible options to choose from, but very rarely did Dot ever have any good options. The one that didn't include the possibility of being murdered seemed like the obvious pick.

Unfortunately.

It was hard to make sense of the last few days. Apparently, she had to go back thousands of years to find someone who she actually liked being around all the time, and who didn't seem to mind being around her. He laughed at her sarcasm. He challenged her self-criticisms. He was somehow immune to her awkwardness. He made her feel remarkable and interesting and smart and everything she had once been sure she was not. It still embarrassed her to a degree, but it had been years since she slept as well as she did when close to him. It was easy to forget he was a genie in that setting.

But he *was* a genie, and that little detail made it tricky to know which aspects of his behavior were required genie conduct. Maybe that was another reason he didn't talk too much about his past. Knowing he was a human person made it harder to determine if his extra effort was duty or flirting.

All she knew was that the more time she spent with him, the more she wanted *him*. But for her, wanting something basically guaranteed she wouldn't get it.

No sense in fighting it.

"Fine, let's get this moving, then," she grumbled, sitting up. "I wish for a luxurious vacation on a private island for me and the guests of my choosing."

Raji blinked as his eyes flashed purple. "Oh, you meant *now*. Like *right now*. Okay. Yeah, let's jump right in." He cleared his throat and fixed his eyes on hers, taking her hand in his. "Dottie. Your wish is my command."

Like the first wish, nothing seemed any different after she said the words. She remained in the front seat of her car, holding Raji's hand, looking into his eyes as they faded from purple back to brown. But she didn't dare move in case all this was important to the wish. Also, because she didn't want to, and he wasn't making her.

"Does that hurt?" she asked.

Even though he was staring right at her, her voice seemed to jar him out of a trance, which she wasn't sure was wish-related or not. "What, the wish granting? No, but it's a rush."

"What about your eyes?"

"My eyes?"

"Did you know they turn purple when you grant a wish?"

He flinched. "No. I didn't. Are they purple right now?" He raised a hand to his face, as if to feel if they were a different color.

A half smile lifted a corner of her mouth. "No, it's only a flash. But it's…"

"Terrifying?" He frowned.

"No! No. It's nice." She shrugged. "I can't believe no one's ever told you."

"I think people usually have other things on their mind in the moment their wishes come true," he said.

She nodded. "I guess that makes sense. Anyway...sorry. Is something happening right now?"

An excited smile was growing on his face. "Things *are* happening. Incredible things, Dottie. I can't wait to show you."

He squeezed her hand, then released it, and a wave of goosebumps traveled up her arm. "There will be a pilot ready in the morning to take you to your island. That should give me some time to make sure your guests have a clear schedule and no excuse not to come."

She rubbed her arm nervously as the reality of her second wish loomed. Her teeth clicked; her eyes darted to the single-wide, then to the envelope she had tucked on her dashboard. She stared at it for a moment.

"What if he waited around and followed me home?" she asked.

He followed her gaze. "You don't have to spend the night here." Of course he knew exactly what she meant. "Everything you need will be on the island. You don't need to pack a thing."

"What if he breaks in while we're gone and tries to steal your bottle? Could you bring that to the island, too?"

His smile diminished rapidly, and regret filled his eyes. "Dottie, I know I'm the one who suggested that Lou might be dangerous, but I didn't mean to scare you. Truthfully, these guys are at their worst *after* they get their three wishes. Without my magic, they don't really benefit from living outside the law."

"So...you think I shouldn't worry about him?"

He shook his head quickly. "No. That's...not what I said. I'm saying we don't know for sure. He's probably looking for my bottle for the same reason most sorcerers do. He knows real magic exists, but he doesn't want to sacrifice his soul to wield enough power to make his own wishes come true. But it doesn't matter. Your second wish has been made. And now you can make the last wish whenever you want. Even..." He paused. When he looked back at her, his eyes were heavy, and his words sounded flat. "Even while the second one is still in progress. Then you can hand me over and we can all move on. Peacefully."

The suggestion might have depressed her—well, it did—but a sudden wave of intense anger overshadowed the sadness. "What if I don't want this guy to be your master?" she said, struggling to keep her tone even. "What if he's mean to you?"

"Dottie. I can handle it."

"You shouldn't have to handle it. Your life shouldn't have to be back-to-back wish-granting. It isn't fair and it sucks!" She stared at the envelope, willing the anger to subside. Hesitantly, she glanced at Raji. His lips were pressed together firmly, his eyes also on the letter. "I was having a good time hanging out with you," she added softly.

His eyes moved to hers. "Me too," he said just as quietly, but with a resonating firmness that made her heart skip a beat.

"I don't wanna stay here tonight." She turned away. There was a tickle behind her eyes. She needed an immediate change of subject. "I'm parking the car some-where inconspicuous, then you're snapping us to a Hilton or something."

She started up the engine and put the car in reverse. When she turned her head to check behind her, their eyes met again. Within the mutual, heart-wrenching sorrow, something passed between them. Something that caused the beating of her heart to reverberate throughout her entire body.

You've gotta stop pining for this genie, she commanded herself. *You're only setting yourself up for a massive heartbreak.*

She was the first to abandon the moment.

"Still, I want you to bring the bottle with us," she said, looking anywhere but at him. "And this letter. I want to google this guy when I get the chance."

She turned to hyper-focus on backing out of the driveway, kicking herself for missing the opportunity to use her second wish to fling that wizard into the middle of the ocean.

Chapter 22

RAJI

Raji watched as the small airplane touched down and came to a stop. As much as he hated how Dot had been forced into making it, granting her another wish was an exhilarating experience. Normally, his desire to please his masters came out of obligation, but with Dot, it was closer to desperation; his chances to blow her away were more than halfway over now, and he hoped to leave her with some of his finest work. And though the first wish was a masterpiece, it was hard not to let the unplanned finale overshadow the whole thing, which was why wish number two really had to stand out.

He had snapped himself to the island that morning, leaving Dot to travel with her guests under the guise of having won a dream vacation from a local travel agency for six. Well, originally it had been for six, but with the timeline being thrust upon her before she could choose the most suitable week for her potential guests, changes had to be made. Jorge and Yasmin had already agreed to watch their grandchildren this week, so after running it by Dot, the guest list was stretched to add two more child-sized vacationers. Raji didn't care what strings he had to pull in order to deliver on this wish, even if it meant he might have to babysit here and there. Fortunately, he didn't mind kids. They tended to be less annoying than most of the adults he'd encountered.

Once the airplane had come to a stop, Raji approached, waving at Hugo, the pilot he had hired the night before. Hugo had flown the rest of the hastily hired staff to the island that very morning, an easy feat since most of them were from surrounding islands. It was a point of pride for Raji to employ locals when a wish called for it. Once he had given in to his fate, he began looking for ways to remind himself that, though it was forever imprisoned, he still had a soul. So when possible, he arranged opportunities for the people who needed it most. Most of his masters probably assumed their brand-new palaces, cities, ships—and in one case, a camel racing arena—were run by slaves. The truth was that Raji liked to make room in each wish budget for all required employees to receive a modest wage. He was kind of the one paying for it, anyway.

Raji would pose as an employee within this wish, too. Since only Skye knew who he was, he would introduce himself as the trip coordinator sent from the sponsoring travel agency. He had made sure he looked the part, too. He smoothed his linen suit and straightened his aviators as the airplane door opened from the inside and a staircase extended to the tarmac.

First off the plane was Skye, her long floral skirt swishing as she smiled and waved regally at Raji. Behind her came a man who, though Raji had never met, wasn't hard to identify. Tall, athletic, and bald with skin a shade darker than Skye's, was Skye's often talked about boyfriend, Winston. With his mouth hanging open, Winston removed his sunglasses and surveyed the landscape in amazement.

Raji spread his arms out in salutation. "Welcome, honored guests! I'm Raji, your trip coordinator. Please, continue over to the hangar there and help yourself to some island refreshments. Compliments of Wishmasters Travel Agency."

Dot got the credit for the fake name.

"Why, hello Raji. It is great to meet you for the very first time," Skye greeted loudly as Winston helped her down the stairs. "This is all very unexpected, isn't it, Winston?"

"I haven't recovered from the shock, to be honest," he said, still gaping. "Is that where we're staying?" He pointed behind Raji to the palatial building adorning the top of the island's tallest hill.

"Indeed, it is!" Raji replied. "Once all the guests have deplaned, I'll take you on a tour."

As Winston moved to catch up to Skye, who was already bolting towards the hangar, two dark-haired children scampered down the stairs as an older man and woman emerged behind them. Jorge and Yasmin. Yasmin yelled in Spanish, and the children stopped in their tracks near Raji.

"You must be Ava and Anthony," he said to them. "You two aren't twins, are you?"

"They're seventeen months apart, actually," Jorge answered as he and Yasmin came up behind them.

"I'm ten, she's nine," Anthony said proudly, gesturing to his sister. "I'm older."

Raji shook each of their small hands as he introduced himself.

"Thank you for making it possible for us to bring the kids," Jorge added. "It's unbelievable how things worked out in such a short time. It had to be fate! I'm sure Dot's tired of all our gratitude. We've thanked her about a thousand times already."

"I've always assumed she had more friends than she let on. Lucky for us, she doesn't," Yasmin said dryly.

Jorge laughed loudly, poking Yasmin in the ribs with his elbow. She glowered at him in return.

"Well, the pleasure is mine," Raji replied. But before he could direct the family towards the snack spread, another guest appeared at the top of the stairs. *The* guest. Dot. Even in gray leggings and a T-shirt that read *Welcome to Miami* above a sunset-colored palm tree, she was lovely. The tropical setting suited her.

It had only been a little more than half a day since he had left her, but the relief that loosened every muscle in his body when her eye caught his made him realize he had missed her. That was an unsettling revelation, knowing eventually he'd never see her again.

As she worked her way down the stairs, she glanced at Jorge and Yasmin, who still stood within earshot as they tried to corral their grandchildren who raced across the tarmac. She smiled politely when she got to Raji. "You must be..."

"Raji, your trip coordinator. We've spoken..."

"On the phone. Yes." Dot extended her hand, which he took and held for maybe a little longer than necessary for two people who were supposed to be meeting for the first time. They shared a sneaky grin.

He released her hand once Yasmin and Jorge were able to direct the kids' attention to the food.

"You look good," Dot said softly, leaning in close enough that the scent of citrus hung in the air around him. "Very beachy."

"She's right, you do clean up nice," Skye said, stepping up beside her with a plate of cheese and fruit.

Raji moved his sunglasses onto his head. "You think so? There are so many fashion choices these days, I never know if the infinite knowledge is feeding me a good idea or not."

"Your infinite knowledge has very good taste," Skye affirmed.

He looked down to examine himself. "It seems counterintuitive to keep so many buttons *un*buttoned on these kinds of shirts. Should I fasten a few more of them?"

"No," both women said at the same time.

Dot turned to her friend. "Are you just gonna leave Winston to fend for himself over there?"

"He's fine." Skye stabbed her plastic fork into a pineapple chunk. "If there's food, he's occupied. Besides, I wanna see Raji meet your mom."

Dot groaned and rubbed her fingers across her forehead while Skye slapped a hand on Raji's shoulder. "I already met her. She's very interesting. You're gonna love her."

Maybe he was imagining it, but the delight in Skye's voice seemed to carry a slightly sadistic undertone.

Dot's eyes darted towards the plane. "Listen, Raji. She saw you through the window and suddenly she needed to fix her makeup. Do me a favor and ignore what she decided to wear. Being the center of attention is a competitive sport to her."

Before he could agree, the final guest appeared at the top of the stairs.

A middle-aged woman—a curvier, blonder, older version of Dot—placed one hand on her head dramatically, securing her giant floppy beach hat, and placed the other hand on the rail, revealing her sheer, white dress that made the pink bikini underneath clearly visible. Had Dot not already made their relationship known, the word "mother" would have been the last word to come to his mind.

Dot impatiently waved her forward. "Hurry up, Mom. We're all waiting on you."

Diane removed her large sunglasses and looked straight at Raji with a pouty smirk. "Hello," she said.

With a small nod of reassurance to his master, Raji stepped up and took Diane's hand, leading her gently to the ground. "Welcome, Ms. Dudley. I'm Raji, your trip coordinator."

"The pleasure is mine," Diane said in a sultry voice that drew a pronounced eye roll from Dot. "Dot told me this trip would have everything, but I'm seeing now that she undersold it."

Raji kept an eye on Dot, whose jaw muscles went rigid. Behind her, Skye's eyes shone with morbid curiosity as she looked from mother to daughter.

Being flirted with by vain women (and men, on occasion) wasn't new to Raji. But this was the first time he found himself genuinely eager to reassure a master that he valued her attention over anyone else's.

"Ladies, I'd love to give you a tour, but first enjoy something from our complimentary snack table." His hand dropped Diane's and moved to Dot's back. He felt some of her tenseness melt away in the moment of contact. "You haven't said anything about the island," he whispered into her ear.

Dot slowed her pace until Diane and Skye were out of earshot. "I'm sorry," she said. "Being stuck on a plane with my mom and a bunch of people who have never met her was stressful, to say the least. She spent most of the flight passively berating me for not letting her invite her boyfriend. I'm giving her a free vacation! Is it stupid of me to expect a little gratitude?"

Suddenly, she stopped in her tracks, and he noticed a familiar fear in her eyes as she stared ahead to where her guests were chatting around the food-laden table inside the hangar.

"Is something wrong?" he asked, trying to pinpoint what she was looking at. When it hit him, he silently kicked himself. The wish had barely begun and he'd already made a glaring error. "Oh. It's the hangar, isn't it?"

"I...don't really have great memories of being in those things."

Raji didn't either, but he could say that about a lot of places. "Stay here. I'll bring you some food and then I'll take everyone up to the house. I promise, once you see your wish in the flesh, airplane hangar trauma and passive aggressive mothers will be the last things on your mind."

"What about wizards who want my genie?"

He grinned. "Aw. You're getting possessive of me." When she didn't react he moved his hand to her arm, then tentatively slid it down her wrist until he was holding her hand. Her eyes shifted towards it, then to the guests in the hangar. Raji followed her gaze to where Diane stared at them curiously. He dropped her hand and went on. "Dottie, this island is uncharted to everyone except me and the pilot. I did that on purpose. No one can follow you here. This is the safest place on earth for us right now."

She nodded, giving him a small smile before her eyes finally panned over the backdrop. He awarded himself the tiniest fist pump when they lit up. "Oh my gosh. Raji. You didn't do all of this, did you? This island was already here, right?"

"The thing about being well past the age of exploration is that all the suitable islands were taken. So...no. I had to yank this chunk of rock out of the sea. I may have a lot of rules but I think I can still do some pretty incredible things."

"You just broke my brain," she breathed. "This is amazing."

Another surge of satisfaction lengthened his smile. "I'm glad we got the brain breaking out of the way early because, Dottie. You ain't seen nothin' yet."

Chapter 23

RAJI

Having given a lot of tours in his many lifetimes, often for critical, hard to impress masters, it was refreshing to have high expectations about one for once. Not even showing off the customized palace to the pretty girl that his master had been trying to force into matrimony had been as enjoyable, and Raji considered that a high point in his career. Every gasp, ooh, and ahh from Dot and her guests stoked the flicker of his hungry little ego. It wasn't good genie practice to gloat over his wish-granting—he had learned that the hard way during the days when corporeal punishment was very much in fashion—but he couldn't hold back the pleased grin that pulled at his lips every time he pointed out something that left his master speechless. Things like the expansive, intricate hedge maze, a huge infinity pool complete with water slides and pool bar, and even a hidden swimming hole in the jungle fed by a crystalline waterfall.

"All plants are indigenous to the climate," Raji explained as they trudged a sandy, wildflower lined path up to the main house. "And there's a garden south of the house where most of the ingredients for the meals will come from."

"I have a question," Diane said, and he pressed his lips together tightly. While most of the guests showed no restraint in expressing their amazement, Diane's reactions had remained mildly amused at best. Raji chalked it up to what Dot said about competing for attention. Clearly, she didn't want to give anyone else too much credit. "What's the retail price of this kind of trip? Out of pure curiosity."

"Not relevant," Raji answered with a smile. "Dot *won* our giveaway. No one here needs to worry about cost."

"Well, what if one of us wanted to use your travel agency in the future? Not me, I prefer privately owned rentals, but it's poor marketing not to let us know the package price."

It was nice that the killjoy in the group wasn't his master for once.

The tour moved inside, through a set of large wooden doors that opened into the foyer, an airy room with high ceilings, tall windows, and several cozy places to sit. Though the house was massive, Raji kept the layout intuitive and easy to navigate. Through the back of the foyer lay a sizable courtyard, furnished with a few small tables and chairs positioned on an open stone floor lined with vivid greenery.

The rest of the house branched off from that central location. Through a door to one side, Raji showed them the spacious indoor dining room and adjacent professional kitchen. On the other side of the courtyard, he led them through a theater room, a library, and a few quiet lounges. Off the back of the courtyard lay a long, enclosed porch that ran the length of the house, adorned with wicker furniture and paneless windows that looked out to a veranda overlooking the pool deck.

"Now I'll take you all upstairs to your rooms, which have already been furnished according to information Dot provided."

"Did I provide information for furnishing?" Dot asked him privately as the rest of the group headed up a grand, embellished staircase in the foyer. "I remember suggesting the theater room and the pool and stuff, but room furnishings?"

"Don't worry about it," he whispered so closely that his nose lightly brushed her ear, sending a surprising ripple of heat down his neck. "I added a fun little feature to give your guests a personalized experience. Their rooms will adjust to each guests' personal preferences as soon as their hands touch the doorknobs. *I* don't even know what they'll look like inside."

A long hallway, lit by an array of skylights, lay before them at the top of the stairs where the guests waited for him.

"Each suite includes a personal bathroom and balcony," Raji informed them. "Skye, Winston—why don't you take this first room? The Jiminez family gets the second, then Diane, yours is that third door. Your luggage should be waiting for you inside, so feel free to get settled. You'll be notified when dinner's ready."

Raji watched the guests spread out and open their rooms to a beautiful chorus of wonder and shock, which seemed to fall on Dot's ears with equal delight.

"Can we go see everyone's rooms?" she asked.

He held out his arm. "First, don't you wanna see *your* room? You get the master suite, since you're the...you know."

"Hold on, I'm not the *you know* in this wish. I'm your genie apprentice, remember?" She laced her arm through his. "But yes. I wanna see. Show me."

He led her to the corner room at a bend in the hallway. Being on an island, every room had a good view, but this room had the best one.

She shot him an anxious grin—the good kind of anxious—then turned the knob and pushed the door open.

He followed her in and leaned against the wall near the entrance, curious to lay eyes on everything she had manifested for herself.

The windows and balcony doors were open, letting in the breezy, late afternoon air and the soothing sound of distant, crashing waves. Each outer wall had an entrance to the balcony that wrapped around the side of the building, giving them a glimpse of an entire half of the island and a one-eighty view of the ocean surrounding it. A huge canopy bed sat centered against another wall, and nearby a bookcase held a library of Harry Potter books, games, and reference guides. In one corner, a cozy blanket lay draped over a chaise lounge with a basket of yarn and crochet hooks nearby.

The most interesting details to Raji, however, were the floral wallpaper that lined the top of the walls, the worn oriental rug, and the collection of cat knick-knacks on the top shelf of the bookcase.

"Oh my gosh," Dot said slowly, her back to him as she looked around.

She stepped over to the nightstand which held his bottle and Lou's letter, but also a magically produced duplicate of the framed photo he had noticed on her dresser on his first night as her genie. She picked it up and smiled.

He didn't know exactly why, but clearly his magic had come through. The distinct dimples on her face confirmed it.

She gestured behind her. "Do you know what this is? What am I talking about? Of course you don't." She shook her head, but her face-splitting smile remained. "This is my grandma's house. *My* house. From when I was a kid! Or parts of it. The wallpaper, the knick-knacks, the bedspread, the rug—this is even the same basket I kept my yarn in! This is insane!" Her eyes flitted around the room. "We had to sell that house. My room there had been my sanctuary my entire life until then. And now it's here on an island in the middle of the ocean that didn't even exist yesterday!"

"I'm glad you like it," he remarked modestly, though inwardly the satisfaction of seeing her joy was almost beyond his ability to process.

She stopped and stared at him. "Hold on! What about *your* room?"

The question caught him off guard. What a strange thing to ask. He scoffed lightly. "Dot, I don't need a room. If you're afraid I'm going to hang out in here, don't be. There are plenty of places for me to go when I'm not needed."

Her hands flew to her hips. "Okay, I don't agree with you. We are partners this time. If I get a room, you get a room. Come on. When's the last time you had your own space filled with things that make *you* happy?"

He bristled. Her reasoning resembled Rourke's justification for wishing Raji free. Granted, it wasn't an entire wish that Dot was offering him, but using any wish magic for his own benefit gave him an uneasy feeling.

"I don't think that's a good idea."

"You're one of my guests," she argued.

"No, I'm not here as a guest. I'm here as a servant," he reminded her, ignoring her impatient huff. "The staff quarters are further down the hall. I'll stay there if you insist I have a room. They aren't magically tailored, but believe me, they're a million times nicer than any room I've ever had."

Dot frowned and stalked across the floor to where he stood, stopping an inch in front of him. She looked him in the eye and poked him in the chest.

"You're making me do this, huh? Fine. As your master, I *command* you to take one of the guest rooms for yourself."

"Fine." Raji shrugged.

She blinked. "You're not going to fight me on it?"

"You gave me a direct command. I have to obey."

"Maybe I should boss you around more often," she said with a triumphant smirk.

"That's what you're supposed to be doing," he pointed out.

His eyes drifted down to the inch of space between them and the urge to close it disoriented him. Serving someone like Dot was so fantastic and so frustrating.

She had more control over him than any master ever had, and he both loved and hated it.

But in his daze, she moved past him, pulling him with her into the hall. She stopped at the door next to hers.

"Alright, get in there." She looked as giddy as he felt when she had been standing at her door. He gave her one last apprehensive glance, and she nodded firmly towards the room.

Relentless.

Like a good servant, he placed his hand on the doorknob, and like a seasoned genie, he kept his expectations low. Then he drew in a deep breath, pushed the door open, and stepped inside. Dot followed so closely she bumped into him.

His heart contracted in his chest.

"Okay, for me, it's giving Turkish bazaar," Dot said beside him. "I would say it's *Aladdin-esque*, but I know how you feel about that guy."

"Turkish bazaar isn't far off," he replied in a stupor.

Everything was so familiar, in a distant sort of way. The rich colors of the fabric draping the walls, the overlapping carpets covering the floor, the scattered pillows and cushions, the tassels on the heavy curtains—it felt like stepping inside the tent of an ancient desert tribe. Maybe it emulated one he had lived in once, but in his memories, those details had become fuzzy with the passage of time.

There were modern touches, too. Like a kitchenette on one side of the room, separated from the rest of the space by a butcher block island. He had always wanted to learn to cook without magic, but he had buried that idea long ago. Apparently, it still existed somewhere in his subconscious.

His eyes landed on the pictures at the same time that Dot's did. "Is that...?" She gasped and slapped a hand over her mouth.

An unfamiliar lump formed in his throat as he walked towards a wall—an entire side of the room—covered in framed photos. At first, the photos didn't make sense to him. Then, in a flash of glorious realization, they did.

These weren't photos. These were framed *moments*. Moments taken straight from his memory.

Dozens of ragged but happy faces with his same sandy skin, brown eyes, and dark hair looked back at him. Faces he thought he had forgotten, but that his magic must have pulled from the recesses of his mind. The largest frame in the center featured a frail, kind-eyed woman in a weathered headscarf, crouched next to a fire, stirring something in a ceramic pot.

His mother.

Raji's hand moved from frame to frame, his voice quivering as names rolled off his tongue. He thought he had forgotten them, but each face reminded him who they were. They had been real. He had known them. In the void they seemed more like imaginary friends than a family he had once been a part of, but seeing them again with physical eyes gave his faded memories new life.

His eyes burned, and a tear rolled down his cheek. He quickly wiped it away, moving his gaze from the wall to the moisture on his fingers. "I'm crying! I haven't cried since...since the night I realized I'd never see these people again."

He pulled Dot to the frames, eager to introduce his family to someone for the first time in twenty-seven hundred years. Brothers, sisters, nieces, nephews, and of course, his mother. When he got to her picture, he lifted the frame off the wall and kissed it gently.

"What was her name?" Dot asked.

He wiped his face on his sleeve. "Her name was Sameen."

"Sameen," she repeated. "She's beautiful, Raji."

His eyes drifted to his master. His friend. A woman who exuded more joy in this moment than she had while making either of her two wishes so far.

He reverently replaced his mother's frame on the wall, and before any doubts could stop him, he pulled Dot into a tight embrace. He closed his eyes; his hands moved up her back and pressed her closer. To feel a person this way—to feel *Dot* this way—felt criminal to him, but she made it feel right to want things, deserve things, feel things, find joy in things. Like in the way she relaxed against him as if to eliminate any unfilled space between them, or the way she turned her head so that he could feel her breath on his neck.

How had he ever let himself dismiss the fact that he was human?

A small stab of pain began to grow in his chest.

His eyes snapped open; he pushed her away reflexively. but gently, keeping his hands on her waist.

"How do you feel?" he asked quickly, feigning composure.

"How do *I* feel? Why are you asking me? How do *you* feel?" She studied his face anxiously.

He forced a smile and shrugged stiffly. "I'm fine. I'm...I'm only worried this is putting you at risk somehow."

She wrinkled her forehead. "I don't see how it would. *I* told you to take the room. You were following *my* command, doing something *I* wanted. It isn't like I made a wish on your behalf or anything. It's still *my* wish."

"And I'm...not upsetting you?" he asked tentatively.

She lifted a hand to his cheek. "Raji. No. Why would I be upset?" Her blue eyes stared into his in a way he had often dreamed about. In a way he should *only* be dreaming about. "Are you sure you're okay?"

Her response invoked both joy and heartbreak. If the steadily growing cosmic pain he felt wasn't triggered by overstepping *her* boundaries, then it came from overstepping the boundaries of his purpose. He was letting himself believe that he could have things that he couldn't.

It was the last thing he wanted to do, but he pushed her a little further away, hoping she could see the apology in his eyes as his hands fell away from her waist.

She quickly dropped her head, and his body began to ache, but he could no longer tell what pain inside him was being caused by what.

"Spend all the time in here you can," she said with her eyes on the ground. "I don't know if there's anything better I can give you, even though there's so much more I want to."

She turned towards the door. "I'll go...check in on everyone."

He didn't want her to go, but he had to stop kidding himself. The fantasies were not meant to become reality.

When the door closed, he placed his hand on his face where hers had been and turned back to the picture frames, comforted by the fact that he could reacquaint himself with the only people he had ever been allowed to love.

Maybe the only people he ever would.

Chapter 24

DOT

"What just happened?" Dot muttered to herself, leaning against the outside of Raji's door. She placed her hand on over her wildly pounding heart. "I did something wrong."

But everything was going so right. Wasn't it? Well, with Raji, at least.

It had been a loaded day from the beginning. Her thoughts returned to that morning when she had met her mother at Miami International Airport, the connection point for Dot and her Tallahassee companions' private plane to paradise. Diane had flown in from Baltimore.

It had probably been a year or more since Diane had last been in Tallahassee. But even then, her mother had spent most of her time with friends and had left town without saying goodbye. Though Dot couldn't think of a reason to be surprised, it still hurt more than she wanted to admit.

So when she saw Diane coming towards her on the tarmac as they headed to board the smaller aircraft, she wondered if the last-second decision to add her mother to the guest list was the worst one she'd ever made.

Diane had smiled and waved as if they were old pals. Her first words weren't even a greeting.

"How did *you*, of all people, win a vacation like this? It's ridiculous and unfair." Her mother's teasing smirk gave the illusion that she was joking, but Dot knew joking was Diane's way of passing judgement in an acceptable sounding way.

"I invited you to come, didn't I?" Dot said.

"Well, you had to. If you hadn't and I found out about it, I would've disowned you." Again came the teasing smirk.

On the plane, Diane quickly became the least popular passenger, thanks to her need to dominate every conversation and challenge every piece of information. More than once, Dot had noticed Yasmin shooting Diane an irritated glare. Thankfully, Diane was too much in her own world to notice, but it made Dot worry about what might happen when she did. Diane practically *looked* for opportunities to be confrontational, and Yasmin wasn't one to back down. How had Dot not thought about compatibility before putting two of the most strong-willed women she knew on an island together for a week?

Oh, right. She'd run out of time.

On the plus side, Skye and Jorge were excellent tension breakers; Skye could turn anything into a joke and Jorge consistently countered Diane's subtle criticisms with praise, which gave Dot hope that maybe her mix of guests might balance out after all.

Diane's top complaint was that her boyfriend, Brendan, hadn't been invited. It got worse when she heard that Ava and Anthony weren't even on the original guest list. She brought it up so often that by the time they landed, Dot wondered what it would take for Raji to get Brendan there just so Diane would be quiet about it. Then the second her mother got a glimpse of Raji, suddenly it was a good thing for her and Brendan to have some time apart since absence makes the heart grow fonder or whatever.

Then Dot wondered what it would take for Raji to revoke her mother's invitation altogether and send her back to Baltimore.

On top of that, Cuckoo Lou's letter continued to haunt her. It was harder than she expected letting Raji out of her sight to prep for their arrival. He assured her he would feel a tug on his invisible leash-thing if she was in danger, which could stretch as far as needed if a wish called for it, apparently. But all Raji's reassuring still couldn't erase the fact that his ultimate departure was imminent, which made the interaction between them just now in his room confusing and painful.

"It's my fault," she rebuked herself quietly. "I always make things harder. There are men all over the place. Why do I have to like the one in the most complicated situation that's ever existed?"

She closed her eyes and leaned her head against his door.

Ugh, I like him so much.

She thought he liked her, too. She thought that was implied by the way *he* pulled *her* into his arms. If she had initiated it and he had gone along with it, she would have certainly doubted whether or not he wanted it. But he started it. He acted, for lack of a better word, selfishly. Thinking about it made her knees weak. Raji had turned selfish for her.

At least that's what it seemed like until he pushed her away. And looked into her eyes *sadly*.

But was it sad like, "I'm sad I can't be with you", or sad like, "I'm sad for you because I just wanted a hug and now you're embarrassing yourself"?

To distract herself, Dot made her way to Skye and Winston's room for a peek at their personal paradise. Skye squealed with joy as she showed her a freezer full of Ben & Jerry's and a menagerie of video game consoles for Winston. They also happily pointed out the flat screen TV mounted on the balcony, allowing an easy view of it from their private jacuzzi.

Next she moved to Jorge and Yasmin's room, which came with an enormous, beautiful painting of the Virgin of Guadalupe, a detail that Yasmin seemed especially pleased with, and a corner stocked with an easel, a stack of canvases, and a cabinet of art supplies, which Jorge was excited about. But the best part was watching Anthony and Ava scream with unhinged glee as they played on their mini, indoor jungle gym, complete with a twirly slide and built-in bunk beds.

When she came to Diane's room, Dot wasn't sure she wanted to see the woman's idea of a personal paradise, but she knocked nonetheless.

"Oh, good, I was about to come find you," Diane said as she cracked the door wearing a silky pink robe, which, coincidentally, was the most modest thing she had worn all day.

I've got to stop being so critical of her. I don't want to hate that she's here with me.

"Is...there a problem?" Dot asked.

"You tell me," Diane answered cryptically, pulling the door wider and waving her inside.

Dot struggled to keep from squinting. The walls were a blinding shade of pink. In fact, most things were: pink bedding, pink curtains, soft pink carpeting, even the alarm clock on her nightstand was a strong shade of magenta. A huge vanity took up almost an entire wall, stocked with more beauty products than Dot thought one person could use in a lifetime. The comically large flat screen television was playing an episode of some reality show featuring fancy catty women tossing drinks at each other.

"How in the world did they do this so fast?" Diane asked. "I had to scramble to get ready after you called last night. You must have told them I was coming before *I* knew I was coming."

"This travel agency is top-of-the-line," Dot improvised. "They can...do stuff fast."

"Apparently."

They faced each other awkwardly; the silence broken up with the occasional sound of bleeping coming from the TV.

"Listen, I'm sorry I didn't invite Brendan," Dot finally said. "I know you're mad about it, but I didn't want him to come because...well, because I wanted to spend time with just you."

Diane's eyes widened. "Are you dying?"

"What? No."

"Okay...is there some other catch, then?"

"Yes," Dot answered flatly. "The catch is that I want us to spend some quality time together."

Diane crossed her arms and cocked her head. "Yes, but *why?*"

The urge to roll her eyes and walk out was strong, but her mother's skepticism was justified. It was the same skepticism Dot met her with each time they spoke, developed over a lifetime of not being a priority to her own family. Maybe starting this week out with a little bit of honesty wouldn't be a bad idea.

She still rolled her eyes, just in a more *I didn't want to say this but you're making me* kind of way. "Since Grandma died, it feels like you're avoiding me. I know we've never had a super close relationship, but you're my mom. I...I've really needed you."

She expected Diane to immediately turn defensive, but instead she shrugged, nonplussed. "You're an adult, Dot. You shouldn't need someone to tell you what to do anymore."

This was a mistake.

But she didn't want it to be a mistake. She wanted it to be an opportunity. So she stood her ground.

"I'm not looking for you to tell me what to do. I'm only hoping we can take a minute to get to know each other. Does that...appeal to you at all?"

Diane looked away. After a second, she turned back to Dot, her arms still folded cagily across her chest. "You know what? If that's really all you want, then fine. I should be grateful, I guess. I...I honestly wouldn't have expected you to invite me on a trip like this, so...it's the least I could do."

It wasn't the heart-to-heart Dot had envisioned, but it would have to do for now.

"Of course. Thank you. I...I'll let you change or whatever you were doing. Was there an actual problem with your room?"

"Dot, my room is almost too perfect. And here you are saying we don't know each other. Obviously, one of us does." She muttered the last few words, but Dot heard. She hadn't expected the personalized room feature to backfire.

As she left her mother's room, she silently cursed Cuckoo Lou for the ninety-seventh time since reading his letter. Because of it, she had been thrown into this wish before she was ready and now had to contend with a skeptical parent, a looming goodbye with the genie she was developing feelings for, and a fancy house full of people she wasn't even sure she knew well enough to present with such a huge gesture.

They were probably all very weirded out right now.

But it was too late to change all that. The wish was in full swing, and for her sake and Raji's, the last thing she wanted to do was waste it.

At breakfast the next morning, Raji presented everyone with a colorful brochure of available activities on the island, while Dot tried to make it clear (as she had at dinner the night before) that her guests were under no obligation to hang out with her just because she invited them. Seeing all these people around one table made her doubt she had chosen the right wish, but the first thing Raji pointed out that morning was how happy and excited everyone looked. He didn't seem to be dwelling so much on whatever had happened in his room. In fact, neither of them had mentioned it since. Although, it was partially Dot's fault, since after dinner she had mumbled something to him about being tired and went straight to her room, insisting strongly that she would be fine by herself.

And she was. That didn't mean she slept very well, though.

After breakfast, Yasmin, Jorge, and the kids opted to hit the beach while Skye and Winston went to check out the pool. Dot left it up to Diane to decide if she wanted to do one or the other or something entirely different.

"The pool sounds nice. Less sand," Diane said, her eyes darting to Raji. "And Raji can come, too."

He complied when Dot gave him the smallest nod. Some backup on her first day hanging out with her mother might be nice.

An hour later, Dot arrived at the pool wearing a long t-shirt over her swimsuit, her hair pulled back into a high ponytail. Skye and Winston were already in the water, and Raji sat in a pool chair, looking even more like a vacationer than the day before in his tropical print shirt, swim trunks, and sunglasses. The way his dark, wavy hair tousled in the breeze was a nice touch.

How is it that a guy from ancient times knows how to style himself better than I do?

"How are you feeling about the first day so far?" he asked as she approached.

She settled in the chair next to him. "A little more optimistic than yesterday, I think."

"Good! You're really doing a great job."

She scoffed. "Are you kidding? I'm barely doing anything."

"I don't think you give yourself enough credit. You're making sure your guests are enjoying themselves while I handle the logistics. It's a perfect partnership. And it's only day one. Aren't you pumped to be granting a wish?"

She feigned annoyance, though he did get a small smile out of her. "I am *cautiously* pumped."

"I'll take it!" He rubbed a hand on her shoulder encouragingly and her mind flashed back to being pulled into his arms the day before.

Don't read into it.

She cleared her throat. "So. How was your first night in your own room?"

The gratitude in his expression was obvious even through the shades. "Dottie, it was amazing. I felt so much like myself in there. Oh, and guess what!" He reached over the opposite side of his chair and lifted a basket stacked with flat, roundish bread and eagerly held it out to her. "I made pita bread without magic, like my mom used to. I brought you some."

A rush of pure, honest joy wiped out her biting anxiety. "You *made* this?" she said, taking a pita from the top of the stack. "Raji! Look at you, doing something for yourself!"

"It's my pleasure to please you." He offered a humble smile as he watched her take a nibble.

"Wow. Raji, this is amazing! You should totally—"

"Yoo-hoo!"

Dot turned to see her mother coming down the path from the house and immediately cringed. Even though Diane was young—still in her early forties—and relatively fit, it still made Dot uncomfortable seeing her mother in a string bikini. Dot herself was barely comfortable in a one-piece. Even with a T-shirt over it.

"I get that times have changed since my last job, but I'm still processing how little clothing is acceptable in this century," Raji said quietly, lowering his basket of bread.

"'Acceptable' is a relative term," Dot replied. In the pool, she watched Skye shoot Winston a scandalized look after laying eyes on Diane.

"Hey there!" Diane said, plopping her large bag in the chair on the other side of Raji. She reached inside and pulled out some suntan lotion, handing it to him. "Do you mind?" she asked sweetly, turning and sitting on the edge of his chair with her back towards him.

Dot bolted out of her seat. "I got that, Mom."

Raji didn't hesitate in passing her the lotion. "I'm going to make the rounds," he said, standing and ushering Dot into his place. "See if everyone is doing okay."

"All work and no play," Diane pouted. "Promise you'll come back when you're done."

Raji looked at Dot questioningly. "Take as long as you need. We'll be fine," she told him.

"You're no fun," Diane said as Raji disappeared up the path.

"Mom, you're being inappropriate. He's our host, not the pool boy!"

"I just feel like the more, the merrier, that's all."

Dot continued slathering lotion all over her mother's mostly bare back until Diane snatched the bottle back and did the rest by herself. Dot settled back onto her chair and continued nibbling her pita bread. "Is this all you want to do today? Or is there something else you had in mind?"

Diane glanced over at her daughter. "You're still set on this mother-daughter quality time, aren't you?"

"Uh...yeah. I am. So what sounds fun to you?"

Diane closed the lotion and tossed it into her bag, settling onto her own chair. "What would you recommend?"

"What about horseback riding?" Dot asked.

Diane laughed. "I don't think I've ever been on a horse."

"Then let's do it! No better time to learn, and no better place to learn it."

"Sure. After lunch."

An awkward silence blossomed as they watched Winston chase Skye around the pool. She squealed as she halfheartedly splashed away, but he easily overtook her and pulled both of them under the water. After a second, they came up laughing. Diane stared dreamily.

"So...how has life been for you lately? What have you been up to?" Dot asked.

"Oh, you know. The same old stuff."

"I don't know what the same old stuff is, Mom. Are you working anywhere? How are things with Brendan? I don't know anything about him. How did you meet? What does he do? There's a lot we could talk about."

Diane perked up. "You know, I *am* selling beauty products—in fact, you could sell them too. I could get you on my team and if you sell a certain amount every month, you could make a lot of money. You know, after a year or two."

Dot frowned. This wasn't the first time her mother had tried to suck her into whatever multi-level marketing scheme she was into at the moment. She had sucked Grandma into a ton and Dot had to cancel her out of them when Avros stole all their money. Diane had not been happy about that.

"Thanks, but you know how I feel about those companies."

"Oh, I know. But you asked."

Dot knew she had to work harder if she wanted to reap any kind of benefit from having Diane here. "How about you show me the catalogue and I'll buy some products from you?"

Diane scoffed. "They're pricey. If you hosted a party, though..."

"No. No party. I'll just buy some things. If that helps."

"Depends on how much you buy."

"I'll buy as much as you want me to."

Her mother didn't respond. They watched Skye and Winston in the pool, holding each other and looking at the view as they spoke in low voices.

Diane sighed. "I hope they make it."

"You don't even know them," Dot pointed out. "Why do you care?"

"Because I've been looking for someone to hold me like that since he-who-must-not-be-named."

"You mean my father?" Dot said.

"Don't be ridiculous. He was no father."

That was a statement Dot could agree with. She knew next to nothing about the man. "Have you...heard from him?"

"Not a word. If he ever contacted me, he'd have to acknowledge that I had given birth to his child and he would die before he did that."

Dot frowned, wondering if this was a safe topic to pursue. "Grandma always said you two were hot and heavy and not much else,"

Another scoff. "Maybe for him. I was in love. Like them." She nodded towards the pool. "When I realized he was losing interest, I panicked. I didn't want to lose the feelings he made me feel. I guess you could say it impeded my maternal judgment. So...you can blame him for that."

"Is that why you're always dating a different guy?"

Her mother's hands flew into the air, and Dot suspected she was rolling her eyes behind her sunglasses. "What is this, therapy?"

Diane abruptly stood and walked towards the pool bar.

Despite the dramatic exit, Dot smiled to herself as she ripped off another chunk of pita with her teeth. However brief, she had just had a personal conversation with her mom. The first in years, and maybe the deepest one ever.

That would have to count as a win. And if not a win, it was at least progress.

Chapter 25

DOT

Dot announced her and Diane's afternoon plans during lunch and recruited Skye and Yasmin to join them at the stables. The others headed off to do some deep-sea fishing. Dot figured it would be less distracting for her mother (and maybe for her) if Raji stuck with the fishing crowd; without him around she had managed to squeeze a drop of interaction out of Diane and she was ready to see if she could do it again.

As Yasmin was the only one of them who had ridden a horse before, their afternoon started with a short riding lesson from the island's riding guide, Gina.

"Watch out for the water," Gina explained once they all were feeling confident enough to begin. "It can make you or your animal dizzy, and I don't want anyone—animal or human—fainting. There are also plenty of things that can spook your animal, like seaweed or driftwood. Look ahead and steer away from any of that. As the lead horse, I'll try to point them out to you."

"This doesn't sound safe," Diane said. She wore large sunglasses and a head-scarf, looking more ready for a ride in a sixty's convertible than an afternoon on the back of a horse.

"It'll be fine," Dot assured her.

"Let's go, then!" Yasmin said. Dot wondered how she seemed so comfortable on her horse. The landlady was full of surprises.

The little herd set off. Slowly. Diane struggled to get her horse to move at all.

"Mine is broken!" she yelled.

Gina rode up beside her and began giving her tips, but Dot suspected a horse, like any animal, could tell when their human companion was scared or apprehensive. For a split-second, Dot wondered if she should let her mother off the hook, but Skye and Yasmin were already a good distance ahead, not even noticing the others weren't moving yet.

Eventually, Diane's horse trotted up towards the others, and Gina rode to catch up to Yasmin and Skye. Dot stopped her horse to hang back until Diane's caught up.

"You're doing great, Mom." She smiled, impressing herself with the patience she had shown with her mother so far. "Relax. It'll help your horse relax, too."

"My horse hates me," Diane said. "I can see it in her beady eyes. No animal has ever liked me. I tried to get a little chihuahua once and it wouldn't stop pooping in my shoes."

Dot stifled a laugh. "Maybe they can sense how uptight you are around them."

"I'm not uptight, I'm cautious."

Cautious. Maybe Dot wasn't as different from her mother as she thought.

They rode in silence for a few minutes, and Dot found herself caught up in the beauty of the island. To her left spread the lush, colorful jungle, her wish palace visible on the hill over the trees. To her right, an endless crystal-clear ocean gleamed. Directly before her, the shimmer of the water and the vibrance of the jungle were joined by the fine, white sand of the beach. Gina and Skye rode on either side of Yasmin, who talked animatedly, even invoking laughter, strangely. The combination of all these lovely sights hit her with a wave of *I don't belong here*, which was quickly followed by thoughts of Raji. He had a way of neutralizing those kinds of thoughts. It had to have something to do with his magic. Though she was starting to seriously wonder if magic had nothing to do with it.

For a moment she lost herself in thought about the genie and forgot about Diane. When she remembered, she turned her head to find that her mother's horse had come to a standstill about a dozen yards back. Dot followed Gina's instructions for turning around, smiling proudly to herself when her horse promptly responded.

"You need to relax," Dot said as she approached her mother's stalled animal.

"How am I supposed to relax? I'm sitting on top of a wild animal!"

"She isn't a wild animal. She's very tame. Now come on, tell her to keep going."

Diane snapped the reins and knocked her feet against the animal's sides, alternating between making a loud clicking noise and shouting "Heeyah!"

The horse shifted slightly.

"Don't command her, ask her nicely."

Diane grumbled under her breath and tried again, a little more softly. The horse began walking.

"See!" Dot said with unexpected pride. "I knew you could do it!"

Diane gave a small smile.

"Okay, let's talk to distract you from the fact that you're riding an animal."

Diane sat stiffly in her saddle, her knuckles white where she gripped the reins. Dot tried to think of something to say that wouldn't make her mother shut down again. "I'm sorry if I was out of line earlier. If I ask a question you don't want to answer, just tell me. I'm not trying to force you into talking about things that make you uncomfortable. I'm trying to get to know you."

"Okay." Her mother's shoulders relaxed ever so slightly.

"You didn't tell me about Brendan," she said.

"There isn't much to tell," Diane answered. "He's gorgeous. Trying to get into modeling. In the meantime, he works as a barista."

"Oh. That's...nice."

"He's probably cheating on me."

Dot blinked. "Why would you think that?"

"Because even if I don't look it, I'm an old woman. He's young, probably younger than you. I've been paying for his headshots and letting him live with me. I'm ninety-nine percent sure he has another girlfriend and he's just using me. That's why I wanted to bring him. I don't trust him enough to leave him alone for too long."

The information made Dot want to roll her eyes and point out that her mother's suspicions were almost certainly true. But then she saw Diane's crestfallen expression. "I'm sorry, Mom. That really sucks."

"Whatever. I know you're judging me right now. I can always tell when you're judging me."

A guilty feeling formed in Dot's stomach. "No. I'm...sad...to see you making the same mistakes. The guys you date never stick around. There are a lot of nice guys your age, you know."

Diane scoffed. "My age? If I date someone my age, it'll make me feel old."

Dot wondered how to respond to that in a non-offensive way.

"Well, I know what it's like to get dumped. Do you remember Howie?"

"Vaguely. Who is he again?"

Dot pursed her lips until the irritation passed. "He's the guy I've been dating for the past couple of years."

"Oh, yes. So why did he dump you?"

Do I want to answer this? But how else was she going to get Diane to open up if she was unwilling to? She decided to take the risk and plow on. "Honestly, he probably should have dumped me sooner. I've always felt so out of his league. He's successful, attractive, well-liked, assertive—basically my exact opposite."

Diane perked up. "Wait, is this the guy who would sometimes answer your phone when I called and tell me to get a life?"

"Oh...yeah."

"Good riddance, then."

The horses were at a steady trot now. Dot almost pointed out to Diane how her relaxing had calmed her horse, but figured that might restart the cycle. Instead, she kept talking to keep Diane from noticing.

"Anyway, I think he knew I was out of his league, so he tried to, like...empower me. Bring me up to his level. I tried. For a while. But I think he dumped me because I kind of stopped trying so hard. Being like him was too exhausting. And...I still feel bad about that."

"Don't. He sounds like a jerk. You're perfectly fine the way you are."

Was that a compliment?

Dot steadied herself against an unexpected surge of emotions. "Oh. Thank you for...saying that."

Diane's mouth opened, then closed into a frown. She seemed surprised. Dot wasn't sure if it came from inadvertently complimenting her daughter or receiving gratitude from her. Both surprised Dot.

"Listen, honey. Men are the absolute worst. We crave their attention so much that we basically throw ourselves at them, then they break our hearts when they're tired of giving it to us. Stop believing any of them are decent people."

"That...sounds similar to some of Raji's opinions."

"Oh, so he's gay? I knew there had to be a catch."

"No, he isn't gay." Dot laughed. "But he's had to deal with some douchey people in his line of work. He literally lives to help people, give them everything they want, but they always take advantage of him. They don't treat him like a person. They treat him like a tool. A means to an end."

"Unfortunately for him, when you're in hospitality, that's what people do."

Dot shook her head. "But I disagree. Yes, there are terrible people out there, but sometimes we're so fixated on the terrible ones that we forget about the good ones right under our noses." Dot watched the three women ahead crane their necks to see how far back Dot and Diane were. They waved. Dot smiled and returned the greeting.

"That's very deep and profound and everything, but I think it's easier to assume the worst about people. You get your expectations too high, there's a bigger chance you'll get let down."

Another pang of guilt. Dot looked at her mother. She was so hard to read. The sunglasses didn't help. "I...I don't want you to think about me that way," Dot said, watching Diane's mouth turn down. "I know I haven't been perfect, but I want to be there for you when you need me. And you know what? I changed my mind about buying you a ticket back home. But if I do, I...I think it should be one way."

Extending the invitation surprised even Dot, but it felt right. They both had terrible worldviews—different, but terrible. If they could be a real family and rely on each other, they would each benefit.

Diane stared ahead without responding. The silence was too heavy for Dot.

"At least consider it. I'll pay for the move. Just say the word. When you're ready."

I said the wrong thing, Dot thought. *I freaked her out.*

Then her mother's shoulders drooped. "Dot, how—"

A large gust of wind pulled the scarf off Diane's head and lifted it straight up into the air. She yelped and let go of the reins to grab for it.

"Mom! The reins!"

The wind receded, and the scarf floated down, settling right over the eyes of Diane's horse.

That's not good.

The horse reared up, nearly sending Diane to the ground. Fortunately, she chose that moment to regain the reins. Unfortunately, the horse took off, bolting forward with Diane screaming and bobbing wildly on its back.

Without thinking (at least not to the point of overthinking), Dot jammed her heels against her own horse's shanks and took off towards her mother. Ahead, Yasmin and Gina had noticed and were already going into action mode, positioning themselves to stop the runaway horse once it ran past.

But it never happened. Diane's horse switched directions and headed towards the water.

Dot watched with awe as Yasmin expertly handled her horse and beat them all to Diane's side. Both their horses were now several yards into the waves, which seemed to spook the already-nervous horse, or maybe it was just the bloodcurdling screams Diane was sending directly into its ear.

Dot stopped her horse at the surf to watch as Gina and Skye pulled up beside her. Yasmin was now reaching across, rubbing the neck of Diane's horse, grabbing for the reins. The steed calmed—and so did Diane—as Yasmin shushed both of them.

But when it looked like all parties had come to their senses, a large wave crashed right at their horses' feet. "Oh no!" Skye screamed as they watched Diane's horse rear up once more. This time Diane didn't have the reins to grab onto, but she did have Yasmin.

It happened in an instant, but it felt like slow motion. Dot watched her mother grab onto the landlady's arm while slipping off the opposite side of her animal. Diane's hands clawed and gripped their way up Yasmin's arm until she was clinging to the other woman's neck, bringing them both from their saddles and into the ocean. In a flash, Gina was off her horse, running into the water.

Dot scanned the waves until she saw the two women resurface—Diane still clung to Yasmin, who struggled to free herself from the other woman's clutches—only to be hit with another wave. Gina had reached the horses and began guiding them to shore, while feet from Dot and Skye, an entanglement of two waterlogged women washed up on the sand. They quickly dismounted and ran to help.

When they came upon Diane and Yasmin, the women were laying side-by-side in the surf, gasping for air.

"Are you hurt? Are you okay?" Dot yelled.

Diane seemed in a stupor. Yasmin spit out a mouthful of ocean water, looking just as stunned.

Then her mouth gradually broke into a wide grin.

She began to giggle as the other women stared. Then the giggles became great peals of laughter.

Diane sat up, her expression twisting into offended confusion. Then a smile flickered across her lips, a deep laughter began in her throat and her shoulders began to bob, until finally she threw her head back and her laughter joined Yasmin's.

Next, Skye joined in, unable to withhold her own giggles any longer. And when Dot watched Yasmin sit up only to double over again, she couldn't stop herself. The laughter escaped her body almost involuntarily, like a gunshot, fueled by the guffaws of the other three women. Even Gina was chuckling as she checked over the horses a few yards further up the beach.

When the laughter finally died down, Diane stood up to compose herself—only to be immediately knocked back down by a rogue wave. Then it all started up again.

Diane retorted by kicking Dot's legs out from underneath her, forcing Dot to fall with a splash into the shallow water. Within seconds, the women were chasing each other in and out of the waves, laughing and tripping one another until they were all soaked and exhausted.

Gina had taken the horses over to the jungle's edge and was overseeing their grazing. Dot wondered what it looked like from her vantage point, watching four grown women emerge from the sea on their hands and knees like sea turtles coming ashore. They collapsed just beyond the tide, drying off in the sun, basking in the warm aftermath of their mirthful moment.

"I haven't had that much fun since I was a teenager," Yasmin said with a smile. "I always have to be the boss, you know? The mom, the grandma. The *landlord*." She looked at Dot. "It's nice to play around."

"Just because we're adults doesn't mean we can't act like children," Skye said. "It takes too much self-control to act like an adult."

Diane snorted. "Facts."

They mounted their steeds for the ride back to the stable, the mood much more relaxed than it was when they set off. Yasmin and Diane reminisced about their childhoods, with Skye drawing comparisons to her own. As they chatted, it made Dot think of how Raji talked so fondly about his childhood, too. The thought prompted Dot to bring up some funny memories she had of her elderly neighbors, and she found that the memories didn't make her as sad as they once did. It was odd. She had always convinced herself that her childhood was more terrible in hindsight than it seemed at the time.

As the conversation went on, Dot was surprised to find that none of them had easy childhoods, yet they could all recall happy moments amid the hardships. Good among the bad. Fortune within misfortune. She wondered if she had never been able to see it that way before now or if some part of her had simply chosen not to.

They headed to their rooms to get ready for dinner when they got back to the house. Before she reached her door, Dot felt a hand on her arm. She turned to find her mother, looking more her age now that the ocean had washed away the layers of makeup and dampened her perfectly coifed hair. She was pretty. The sunny smile on her lips helped.

"I just wanted to say...today was fun. Thank you for inviting me. And...I'll consider the offer you made."

Dot's mouth fell open. She closed it quickly.

"I said *consider*," Diane reiterated.

"I know. I get it. That's cool. I'm cool with that."

Diane gave a little nod and disappeared into her room, leaving Dot standing alone in the hallway, too stunned to remember which direction her room was.

Because despite the genie and the magic and the wishes, that was the most unbelievable thing she had ever witnessed.

Chapter 26

RAJI

The end of the first full day came fast, but Raji was ready for it. He hoped his magic had worked a few miracles on Dot's behalf after how preoccupied she had seemed on arrival the day before. Besides that, he was just excited to talk to her. He was always excited to talk to her.

She arrived at their alfresco dinner on the veranda in a flowy, yellow dress that buttoned up the front, the breeze picking up her long hair as she walked. He was relieved to see her smiling and laughing with the other women. Things must have gone well.

During dinner, Skye gave a great dramatic retelling of their horseback riding adventure, then Anthony and Ava captured the table's full attention as they told of the shark they reeled in on their fishing trip and how Winston had let out an impressively shrill shriek at the sight of it.

Raji found himself glancing at Dot frequently, eager to catch her reactions. To his delight, she never stopped smiling.

After dessert, Jorge suggested dancing. They pushed the furniture on the veranda aside while he turned on some Salsa music. Ava gave lessons—the kid had moves—but Dot insisted on sitting out. Diane wasted no time in urging Raji to pair up with her, much to his disappointment. To keep up his role as fake trip coordinator, he obliged, shrugging at the apologetic look from Dot. Diane gripped him a little more tightly than she probably needed to, and her hand "accidentally" brushed his butt a few times, but in this instance it was necessary that he take one for the team. Easy enough to do when the team had pretty blue eyes.

Winston and Skye were the first to say goodnight, while Jorge turned on some slower music and held Yasmin close for one more dance. The kids recruited Dot for a game of Uno, and as desperate as Raji was to join, Diane was still hanging from his arm.

"Come on, one more dance," Diane said uncomfortably close to his ear.

It would feel fantastic to tell someone like her *no*.

"It's been fun, Diane, but I'm beat. I think I'm done."

"At least walk me to my room."

Groaning inwardly, Raji smiled politely. "I need to check on the other guests. I'll see you at breakfast."

He walked away before she had the chance to argue or pout, his eyes fixed on the table where Dot and the kids were playing.

"Who's winning?" he said, sliding into the chair next to Dot and scooting it closer to hers.

"Ava's killing us with her stash of Draw-4s." The way Dot leaned close to him as she spoke made him wish he had insisted on at least one dance with her, but it wasn't his place to ask.

"When we're done, can we make the same cookies you brought to our house?" Anthony asked Dot.

"Oh, I didn't actually make those," she said as she tossed a card on the pile, glancing sidelong at Raji. "But he might be able to hook you up."

"It's getting late," Raji pointed out, clocking Ava's massive yawn. "But I'll have a big plate of cookies for you tomorrow, I promise."

"Uno!" Anthony cried, waving his final card. Dot scowled and threw down another card from her hand, then Ava laid a Draw-2 on Anthony, and Anthony placed another Draw-2 on top.

"Aw, come on!" Dot slapped her cards on the table as the children laughed. Dot turned to Raji. "For some reason, they think my competitiveness is funny."

"Niños, time for bed!" Yasmin called. Reluctantly, the kids hurried off to follow their grandparents inside.

"I should go to bed, too," Dot said with a stretch. "I was not kidding when I said I need a solid ten hours before I have to talk to my mom."

"And now I think I understand why."

She frowned and placed her hand on his where it lay on the table. He forced himself not to look down at it. Maybe she didn't realize what she was doing. Or maybe she knew exactly what she was doing. "I'm really sorry about her being all over you. It's what she does when she's around younger, really attractive guys."

"I'm actually much older," he said, though he instantly took note of the *really* tacked onto her *attractive*.

"Yeah, well, she will never know that. Can you imagine if she was your client?"

"Oh, I can imagine it," he said. "Clients like her are a dime a dozen. It'd be harder imagining a client like you. You're like the unicorn of clients."

She breathed out a laugh. "Says the genie."

A glorious tension flooded the air between them. He let it build, rationalizing that it was a safe substitute for the closeness he craved but couldn't risk. It bewildered him that she could so effortlessly revive centuries of dormant human emotions in his immortalized body. Clearly, she wasn't as ordinary as he initially thought. Not to him. And though it felt indulgent to sit here admiring her, wishing things were different in a secret part of his soul, he didn't see how it could be against the rules.

Yet, deep in his chest, a distant ache began, and he knew it was because his feelings for her were deepening in a way his creators did not preapprove.

He turned away and slid his hand out from under hers as the ache increased. "You should get a jump on those ten hours of sleep."

He stood up, and she followed, though he couldn't bring himself to look at her just yet.

"Yeah. You're right. Do you wanna...walk up together?" she asked.

"Of course." He lifted his hand to place it on her back, then quickly balled his fist and pulled it away. He had reached the point where it was taking conscious effort not to touch her.

And the powers that be were now telling him in no uncertain terms: he had to stop.

"Today I'd like to check out the spa treatments," Diane said at breakfast.

"Sounds like a great idea," Dot replied, spreading cream cheese on a bagel. Raji sat between them, eating a bowl of cereal, trying not to let his elbows touch either of them for different reasons.

"Raji, you could probably use a spa day, too," Diane added. "You spent all day yesterday running around and making sure everyone was okay. What about you? Who makes sure you're okay?"

In his peripheral vision, Dot rolled her eyes. He shook his head. "I don't want to distract from Dot's time with her guests. I'm more than happy to stay out of the way and ensure your trip is running smoothly."

"I wouldn't mind if you came along," Dot said quickly.

"Me neither," Diane agreed. He could sense that she was trying to get his attention. When he turned to look at her, she licked her spoon and stared him dead in the eyes. He shuddered.

Dot and Diane would never get quality time with him hanging around. And as much as he would like to spend every possible minute with his master, it would be wiser for Dot to invest her time in Diane.

"Just come for a little while. You don't have to stay the whole day," Dot said from his other side, placing her hand on his arm. He sighed. He couldn't skip out if Dot specifically requested it.

"Alright, but don't forget. I'm not a guest. I'm the trip coordinator. I *co-ordinate* trips. And this trip isn't going to coordinate itself. I've got a lot of responsibilities."

He tentatively glanced at Dot, who hit him with some heavy side-eye.

"Raji, you would know," Jorge said loudly from down the table where he and Winston were talking. "Will this tropical storm be a problem?"

"Tropical storm?" he and Dot asked at the same time.

"Yeah. The one that's supposed to hit tonight."

He and Dot shared a look. His infinite knowledge didn't cover ever-changing weather forecasts, but that didn't mean that he hadn't prepared for something like this. His genie brain *did* include knowledge of typical weather patterns in every climate.

"The house will be perfectly safe," he assured the guests. "We can weather the storm inside when it hits. This place is built to withstand the worst mother nature can throw at it. I guarantee you won't miss being outdoors."

His answer seemed to placate everyone. Except Dot. She pulled him aside as the others filtered out of the dining room.

"Can't you change the course of the storm or something?" she asked.

"I would, but that's God-level power. If it wasn't included in the original wish, I can't do anything. Unless you want to wish for it to change course. Separately."

Her eyes darkened at the suggestion. "I'm not doing that."

"You don't have to. This place was designed for the climate. It'll be great. You and your mom will be trapped inside together all day. That's prime bonding time."

She didn't look convinced. "Sometimes I feel like you really have to stretch to find that bright side."

"It takes stretching to find a downside, too. I'm just picking a direction."

She opened her mouth to say something, then closed it and nodded. "You're right. It'll be fine."

"That's the spirit! Now go get ready for your spa day."

The spa goers collectively decided to start in the sauna, which was in a separate building that also housed the island's state-of-the-art gym. The ability to reduce his clothing to only a towel (as his knowledge informed him was customary) with a wave of his hand made Raji the first one inside.

He sat in a corner for a few long minutes and waited, still unsure if it was wise for him to be there, when Dot walked in, also wrapped in a towel. She paused at the entrance when she saw him. Steam dampened the dark blonde tendrils around her ears that had slipped out of her ponytail and Raji had to remind himself that how soft her skin looked was irrelevant to his wish-granting.

But it did look incredibly soft.

She seemed unsure about what to do; her eyes flitted from him to the many available empty spaces on the bench as her mouth formed into a compressed smile.

"I've never...sauna'd before. What do we do? Just sit around?"

"I haven't either," Raji said, hoping to put her at ease. "But it's been known to reduce stress, improve circulation, and a bunch of other things. And yes, you just sit."

She steadied her eyes on him as he spoke. "Sounds...beneficial. And easy," she said. "Maybe I should buy one for home."

"You can buy whatever you want." He smiled, forcing his eyes to stay on hers. For another moment, she remained frozen in the doorway, that cloud of tension reforming.

I should leave, he thought.

Just when she finally took a step forward, Diane-in-a-towel entered, breezing past Dot and settling right next to Raji, briefly catching his eye and smiling playfully.

I should have left.

Dot sat on the other side of him, to his relief, but a little further away. When Skye and Winston entered soon after, chatting and laughing, Diane slid closer to Raji even though there was plenty of room for them to sit. He looked back at Dot to watch for her usual eye roll, and his pulse quickened when he noticed her gaze slowly moving up his abdomen.

His thoughts became frantic—what to think, what not to think, respond or ignore, good or bad. Their eyes met in his mental chaos. He swallowed. She drew in a breath.

The inside of his head was just as foggy as the sauna. He couldn't think clearly.

So, ignoring Diane's protests and Dot's eyes, he excused himself and left.

Raji usually found it refreshing to focus on wish-related tasks—in this case, checking in with the staff and making sure the island was prepared for the oncoming storm—but today all he could think about was Dot. It felt wasteful not to be spending time with her, considering that in the context of thousands of years, this would all be over in a heartbeat. But he knew it was stupid to consider himself her friend or guest, when he was neither, no matter what she insisted. No matter how he felt. He didn't have a claim on any of her wish time.

So he found Yasmin, Jorge, and the kids at the beach and whiled away the afternoon building elaborate sandcastles with sand magically engineered to be the perfect consistency for such undertakings. He listened as Jorge and Yasmin talked about their twenty-first century lives and then imagined what his life might look like if he had been born in a time when mysticism and magic were lost arts and sorcerers didn't call on dark forces to enslave innocent souls for their own pleasure.

The thought gave him pause. He bid the little family farewell and walked a ways down the beach before settling on a quiet stretch of sand. With a swirl of his wrist, he summoned a smartphone, the one he had provided Dot for her first wish. Dot had mentioned googling, and it didn't seem like a bad idea to use modern means to learn things his not-as-infinite-as-he-once-thought knowledge couldn't fill him in on.

He typed 'Cuckoo Lou's Chamber of Ill-LOU-sions' into the search engine.

The only result matching the full name was a link to a Facebook page featuring a grainy photo of a worn brick building on a dirty street. Seventeen followers and two reviews. He scrolled to the first one. It had four stars.

If you are sick of all the other fluff in Branson, check out Lou's place. It isn't just magic tricks. This was real. Met Lou. Nice guy. No bathrooms.

He scrolled to the second. This one gave two stars.

We had to sign an NDA before we went in so I can't say much except I still can't figure out how this guy does the things he does. It didn't sit right. Nice owner but wouldn't explain much or answer our questions. Could find a better location. Also didn't have a bathroom.

It wasn't much, but it was enough to confirm Raji's suspicions.

This guy was no mere nerd.

Yet, he didn't completely know what that meant. The world had changed so much since the last sorcerer he served. People had changed. Besides popular fiction and some wacky beliefs about herbs and crystals, people these days didn't pay much heed to things that known science couldn't define. What would a sorcerer be like in a society where they were regarded as a magician at best or a devil worshipper at worst?

He would find out soon enough.

The prospect stirred up a series of emotions, none of them positive. He fell backwards into the sand and closed his eyes. For centuries he had accepted that his situation would never change. He had learned to roll with it, and even found comfort in knowing that he wouldn't have to serve any one master for long. Even his near-freedom experience with Rourke had led to a firmer acceptance of his circumstances. But before that, in the early days, he had mourned his fate often. It was the only way he could rebel when he still had the energy to.

He still accepted his fate. He knew nothing could change it. But he never expected to find a place he wanted to belong, and a person he could belong with.

And as a *human being*, he had every right to complain.

Beneath the cloudy sky, he leaped to his feet. A mighty yell ripped from his throat as he pulled his arm back and chucked the phone a mile into the ocean. Then he summoned his bottle and threw that into the ocean with an even angrier bellow, then he summoned it again, and threw it again and again and again, wailing his frustration each time.

But he had learned long ago that rage isn't as sustaining as one might assume, and after a few minutes of angry throwing, his emotions were spent. Outbursts like this never got him anywhere. They didn't make him feel better. They only left him exhausted and frustrated. He halfheartedly threw the bottle a final time, then fell back into the sand. He summoned the bottle once more and held it in front of his face.

I could go back in. Wait out the rest of this job alone in the darkness.

But he couldn't bring himself to do it, because no matter how accustomed he became to it, he didn't belong in there. He belonged out here. He wouldn't let the unfairness of it all stop him from living his life to the fullest while he could.

Even though there were plenty of reminders that, for him, living just meant pretending.

He turned the bottle in his hands. "I wish I was done being a genie," he said to it. "I wish I could stay here. With Dot."

Nothing happened.

He sent the bottle back to its place in his master's room and dropped his arm into the sand.

In the gray sky above, darker clouds were rolling in.

Chapter 27

DOT

A mud bath had never been at the top of Dot's bucket list, but she also never expected to have the opportunity to try one. Until now, she honestly thought they were made-up.

These mud baths were side by side *in* the jungle. She and Diane had to walk down a narrow path to a little clearing, where they found two tubs of what Dot's brain immediately identified as sludge. The location was quite genius, it turned out; the shade, the thick greenery, and the sound of the tropical birds made the idea of a mud bath bearable. Diane didn't seem disgusted at all, and Dot wondered if her mother had a lot of spa experience. If she didn't, she seemed to adapt to luxury naturally. There was clearly a lot they still had to learn about each other.

"Isn't this amazing?" Diane said, relaxing in the dark liquid. They both had small pillows to rest their heads on. Diane utilized hers, but Dot was too tense. Maybe it was the mud, or maybe it was because of the topic she was about to bring up.

"Hey, quick question: could you leave Raji alone?"

"I don't know what you mean," Diane said without a reaction.

"You know exactly what I mean. You've been hitting on him like crazy."

Diane laughed. "It's not like I'm pursuing a long-term relationship. I'm just flirting."

"You're making him uncomfortable."

Diane raised her eyebrows. "Did he tell you that?"

"In so many words, yes."

"What's that supposed to mean? Did he say I make him uncomfortable or not?"

"He implied it."

"And you think because you won this trip, you're his boss?"

Dot didn't respond. She had to pinch her mouth shut before she impulsively shouted that yes, actually, she *was* his boss.

"Didn't think so. Don't worry about it, it's between him and me. Or is it he and I?"

Her flippant attitude earned a scowl from Dot, even though Diane didn't see it. Maybe it was better that she missed it.

"Unless...*you* like him," Diane suddenly said.

"That has nothing to do with it." Dot slid further into the mud as thoughts of him filled her mind. In reality, that had a lot to do with it. "Is there something else we can talk about?"

"I have something," Diane said, her eyes popping open.

"Good. What is it?"

Her mother squared her mud-covered shoulders and turned her head to face Dot. "Don't judge me, but last night I was talking to Brendan."

"Great," Dot mumbled.

"I know I need to leave him, but I feel bad about kicking him out right away. The poor guy has nowhere else to live."

"Can't you let his side-chicks worry about that?" Dot said, throwing her hands up and accidentally flicking mud all over her face.

"Oh, please. He doesn't have any *side-chicks*. I said that because I was angry at him. We had an argument before I left. But he apologized last night."

Dot wiped the mud off her face, despite knowing she was probably only smearing it. The haughtiness in her mother's voice made her wonder if she was embarrassed by yesterday's vulnerability and was trying to downplay it. It was a response Dot had been guilty of, too. "So...you *don't* want to leave him?"

"No, I do. He's not going to stay once he gets famous. I just want to help him get started."

The conversation was getting confusing. Dot sat up, the mud sticking to her skin like a suit. "I thought you were considering coming back to Tallahassee?"

Diane sat up too. "Are you listening to a word I'm saying? I just think it would be nice to...leave Brendan better than I found him. I'd say it's the right thing to do."

"I don't think that's—"

"If you could contribute a little something, it would speed up the process. With all this talk about buying my products and paying for my move, you're obviously holding out on me."

Dot frowned. It felt shady—not to mention unnecessary—to fund her mother's boyfriend's modeling career. Yet...this could be an opportunity to establish trust. "I'll think about it," Dot said. "I mean, I would need to know you aren't gonna ghost me again. Grandma used to give you money, hoping it would help mend some fences, but it never did."

Diane didn't respond, and Dot worried she had again gone too far.

"You know, you're right," Diane said after a moment. At first, the words didn't process. They were words Dot never expected to hear from her mother's mouth. Grandma had waited fruitlessly for years to hear them.

"Huh? About what?"

Her mother sighed. "I don't want my relationship with you to be an extension of the one I had with her. And...I'm probably the one making it that way."

Dot looked around, hoping someone else was witnessing this.

Diane threw a hand up, flicking more mud across Dot's face. "Change is hard. And it would probably be easier if I didn't think too much about it. Just...tell me what you want me to do."

There was a lot of uncertainty in Diane's voice.

She's asking me *to tell her what to do? Me?*

She could not blow this.

Instinctively, Dot straightened and reached a mud-covered hand towards her mom. Diane stared at it in surprise, then took it in hers.

"Change *is* hard. But it's easier if we take it one step at a time. Don't make a decision right now. But know that I really mean it when I say I want us to work on this. There are no ulterior motives. I...I *do* miss you. And I do want you to come home."

Her mother's expression softened in a way that Dot knew couldn't be faked.

"You do?"

Dot nodded, conveying as much sincerity as she could muster. It was more than she expected.

Then another miracle. Her mother's eyes unmistakably began to glisten. "I miss you, too."

The ridiculousness of sharing a moment with her mother that she had longed for while they both sat naked in pools of mud wasn't lost on her. Life was weird sometimes. But this was a good weird. Scary, but good.

"If you really mean that," Dot said. "Then come home."

Something happened in those mud baths. Something big. Diane had changed. She became nice. No sarcastic comments. No cutting remarks. Part of Dot struggled to accept it. Was it a calculated change, or a genuine change? At some point during their spa day, which included massages on the beach, mimosas in the jacuzzi, and facials on the veranda, she stopped questioning it and enjoyed each moment with her mother. A wall had fallen, and Dot didn't know if it would stay down for long.

The dialogue between them began to flow easier. Diane talked about her life since she left. Dot shared a few details about major milestones her mother had missed. Every conversation both hurt and healed.

It almost got to the point—almost—of Dot asking her mother why she had never come back to take over raising her own daughter, but she decided it would be better to keep the vibes positive and safe. The harder conversations could come once the relationship grew out of infancy, after the getaway was over.

As the day progressed, Dot became more convinced that her mother *would* be coming back to Tallahassee to stay, and the possibility left her with a reserved optimism. In the past few weeks, she had discovered that she had real friends. Maybe she would soon have a real mom, too. And with Raji's departure inevitable, she knew it would help to have that to fall back on.

"I haven't tried that one yet, but I've heard good things," Diane said, pointing to a photo of hand lotion on Dot's phone screen.

"Okay," Dot responded, scrolling to the next item.

Side-by-side in beach chairs near the base of the jungle waterfall, they relaxed in the evening breeze. The whole group had picnicked there for dinner, to enjoy the outdoors before they became shut-ins for a day with the tropical storm scheduled to hit. Skye and Winston were on a romantic stroll along the beach, the kids were exploring a network of caves below the waterfall with Raji, and Jorge stood a little ways off, painting the scenery while Yasmin napped on another beach chair nearby.

"Okay, I love this shampoo, but I can't say the same about the conditioner," Diane said as she peered over Dot's shoulder.

Dot sighed and put the phone down.

"Hey!" Diane cried. "We hadn't even gotten to the lip color yet!"

"Listen," Dot said. "If you really want me to buy something, I will. But I could also be a little more straightforward."

Though the sun hadn't set completely, the accumulating cloud cover dimmed the available light. The day would be ending soon, and right now, the atmosphere of general contentment was putting Dot in a generous mood that, for once, she could afford to be in.

She took her mother's hand. Diane tensed, then relaxed and returned the squeeze. They shared a soft smile. "Let me just give you some money," Dot said. "Enough for you to get Brendan settled somewhere else, since you're so insistent on being a good Samaritan, and to get you moved back to Tallahassee. I'll find you an apartment and have it ready for you."

Diane frowned. "Dot, how on earth would you be able to do all that?"

Dot paused as she tried to think of a way to explain, then reminded herself she didn't have to. "You're right. I've been holding out on you. I have money now. Enough to help you out. I've had a really good day, and I want it to be the first of many. I'm ready to be a family. I'm ready for more of *this*." She gestured towards their entwined hands.

Her mother's frown deepened. "I am too, believe it or not. I always wished that I had been a better mother. I just didn't know how. I still don't."

Hearing those words brought a sting to Dot's eyes. Even knowing a wish like that was outside Raji's power, it was still a beautiful thing to wish for. "I can tell you're trying now. I'm not perfect, either."

"Well, then I shouldn't let my insecurities get in the way." Diane let go of Dot's hand and wrapped the arm around her daughter's shoulders. To Dot's surprise, she welcomed it.

She leaned her head against her mother's. "It's never too late to get better at something."

"Wise words. You were always smarter than me."

Dot sat up and grabbed her phone off her lap. "I'm going to send some money over." She looked Diane sternly in the eye. "But it's conditional. You *have* to come back home. You don't have to see me every day—you don't even have to live on the same side of the city—but we won't get better at this until you're close enough that we can show up for each other."

"I understand," Diane said, and Dot felt her sincerity.

"Okay," she breathed.

The first real test begins.

A few taps later, Dot lowered her phone as Diane's dinged with a notification in the bag beside her. Diane smiled graciously before digging it out. She glanced at the screen, then did a double take.

"Dot! Where did you get this kind of money?" she gaped. "Is this drug money? Are you selling drugs?"

While a lot of the money probably did come from drugs, Dot smiled and shook her head. "No, I'm not selling drugs. Is that enough, though? Will that cover your needs?"

Diane's eyes glistened. "Ten thousand dollars is more—a *lot* more—than I expected. I...I don't know what to say." Suddenly, her mother's arms were around her neck, for probably the first time in her entire life.

A tear fell down Dot's cheek. Happily and hopefully, she returned her mother's embrace. This was really happening. Things were changing for the better. And all it took was a genie in a bottle.

Thunder echoed in the distance.

Diane was shaking when she pulled away, glancing at her phone one more time with disbelief before putting it away. "You know, honey. It's been a long day—a great one—but this—you, your generosity, which I really don't deserve—it's a little…emotionally overwhelming. I'm gonna turn in, if that's alright."

The hurried exit stung a little, but Dot could relate to being emotionally overwhelmed. Besides, they had already spent more time together today than they had spent cumulatively over the past ten years. Time apart to process might be helpful for both of them. She nodded and watched her mother disappear up the path.

I hope I did the right thing.

"I take it you had a good day."

Dot turned to find Raji standing in front of her in his swim trunks. Soaking wet, water shimmering as it dripped down his chest. It brought back memories of the sauna that morning that made her face burn.

Ava and Anthony scampered up behind him, searching for their towels.

"It was a really good day," Dot answered, consciously training her eyes directly on his, hoping he didn't notice them flicking down once or twice.

"Let's end it on a high note," Raji suggested. "I just talked to Jorge and offered to take the kids up to the house for a bedtime snack while he finishes up his painting. Care to join us?"

"Yes! Come with us!" Ava chimed.

Dot didn't need time to decide. She had been waiting all day to see Raji. "A bedtime snack sounds amazing."

After everyone dried off and Raji put a shirt back on—although she didn't mind it being off—the little group headed up to the kitchen where a plate of cookies awaited them. They gathered at one end of the long table in the empty dining room with glasses of milk while Raji took it upon himself to correct some falsehoods from one of the kids' (to his obvious annoyance) favorite movies.

"No, listen," Raji said, waving a cookie in the air. "Aladdin—the real Aladdin—wasn't handsome or wholesome or a good singer. He was arrogant."

"What's arrogant?" Anthony asked, crumbs spraying from his lips.

"That means he thought he knew more than me—er, the genie. Even though genies know everything." With a glower, Raji crammed his cookie into his mouth.

"What about the real Jasmine?" Ava asked, eyes enlarged.

"Jasmine wasn't her real name," Raji said, grabbing another cookie. "But the princess that Aladdin pursued, she was fine. More of a victim in real life than she was in the movies."

"What's a victim?" Ava asked.

Dot shook her head. "You're gonna traumatize the poor kids."

"They need to hear the facts," he insisted.

"What about the genie?" Anthony asked. "Was he actually funny?"

Raji's eyes widened solemnly. "*Was he funny*? Anthony, he was *hilarious*. As well as handsome, smart, skilled in every skill you could imagine—"

"Humble..." Dot quipped.

"Could he do flips?" Ava asked excitedly.

"Ava." Raji laughed ostentatiously as he pushed the plate of cookies out of the way. He leaned towards her, staring with intense seriousness. "Do you want to see the kind of flips the genie could do?"

Ava nodded.

"*Show-off*," Dot coughed into her fist. "Oh," she said with a smirk when Raji narrowed his eyes at her. "You may not have heard me. I was calling you a show-off."

Dot reveled in his little smirk as he leaped onto the long table and casually executed a perfect backflip. The kids gasped as Raji coolly brushed off his shoulder. But when he turned to step off the table, he slipped and tumbled to the floor, toppling a couple of chairs on the way. Both kids burst into fits of laughter as Raji clambered to his feet and brushed himself off again, composing himself quickly as he walked back to sit beside Dot.

He leaned towards her as he sat. "A *hilarious* show-off," he whispered under the sound of the continued giggles.

"What's going on in here?" Jorge's voice boomed playfully from the doorway.

"Hide!" shouted Ava. She, Anthony, and Raji quickly slipped under the table. Before she could react, Dot felt their hands grab her legs to pull her under, too.

She found herself body to body with Raji, straddling his knees. His hands fell around her waist; in the tight space, hers had nowhere to go but stretched over his shoulders.

Staring into his eyes at such close range made her dizzy, but they held one another's equally stunned gaze without blinking. "We...we have to hide," he explained.

His breath hit her lips, and she lost awareness of everything but him.

Her hands found his shoulders, and impulsively, she pulled him closer. His grip tightened around her middle and his eyes moved to her lips so slowly it had to be deliberate. She wondered if he could feel how fast her heart was beating.

"Ew, are you guys gonna *kiss*?" Anthony asked with great disgust.

Raji immediately pushed himself backwards, pulling his legs out from underneath her and hitting his head on the underside of the table in the process, sending the kids into another fit of giggles.

Then, with a yelp, Anthony suddenly slid away through a gap in the chairs. Ava screamed and threw her arms around Dot's neck while Raji continued to rub his skull. "Dot, save me! Abuelo's gonna get me next!"

The moment played out so surreally—giggles and happiness and a child in her lap—she almost balked at the influx of positive emotions, but the day had been so good that she overrode the uncertainty and played along, wrapping her arms around the little girl. "I won't let you go," she assured her.

A pair of hands grabbed Ava's ankles and pulled. Dot tightened her grip and began to slide with her. Raji's arms wrapped around both of them from behind and Dot pressed herself back against his chest as the three of them giggled and screamed.

"I think we've got her, Anthony!" Jorge shouted.

"I can't...hold...on!" Raji said with exaggerated stress, and Dot and Ava slipped out of his grasp and popped out of their hiding place.

"Two for the price of one!" Jorge laughed as Dot and Ava slid out onto the floor. Ava's adorable, infectious laughter filled the room as Raji crawled out and helped them both to their feet.

"Fun's over, time for bed," Jorge said, leading the children from the dining room.

"Good night, *niños*!" Raji waved

"Good night!" Both kids waved back.

"Good night, Dot!" Ava smiled, and Dot's heart melted. She never imagined herself as kid-approved, but she was humbled to find that wasn't the case. She waved back until they were no longer in view.

Then she was alone. With Raji. In a silent, semi-dark room. The mood was upbeat; the ambiance was romantic. The day's success still pulsed through her veins, alerting her to the realization that despite the growing ache of his impending leave, he was right here right now. In the flesh. And so was she.

She couldn't have wished for a better moment to punctuate the day.

"So," he said softly. "Tell me about your good day."

After all the commotion and laughter, the sound of his voice in the empty space felt intimate in a way that made her knees tremble.

When she turned, he was already facing her. She tracked his eyes as they searched her face. "I...I think I convinced my mom to come back to Tallahassee."

His eyes lit up. "That's great! Isn't it?"

"Yeah," she said. "I hope it will be."

As soon as her words faded into silence, she forgot what she was talking about. The way he was looking at her—was she imagining it? There was an intensity coming from him that she could physically feel; it filled her with longing and drained her of breath, in the best way.

Unconsciously, she took a step towards him.

His jaw tightened and his smile straightened, but he didn't look away.

"I had a good day, but...I missed you," she said. The urge to place a hand on his face or step into his arms overwhelmed her. It was the last thing she needed to make this day perfect. But she hadn't forgotten their encounter in his room.

As if to remind her, his Adam's apple dipped, and the smile in his eyes disappeared.

"I'm sorry," he said in almost a whisper. The words sounded pained. He took two steps backwards and averted his eyes.

The heat of embarrassment flared up her neck. "Did I do something wrong?" she asked.

"No, of course not." His voice trembled as he spoke. "I'm the servant"—she cringed as he said it—"if there's anything wrong, it's my fault."

"So there *is* something wrong?"

"That's not what I meant—"

"I read the situation wrong, didn't I?"

"You didn't do anything wrong, Dottie—"

"Do you not have feelings for me?" she blurted.

The few steps he had put between them suddenly felt a mile long. He drew in a shuddered breath and pressed his lips together.

A sickening self-loathing clamped around her stomach as she moved her eyes to the floor. "I made it awkward, didn't I?" She wiped her hand across her forehead, sliding away the sweat forming there. "Ugh, this is so typical! How do things like that just come out of my mouth?"

She wanted to run and hide. And she was going to, but she glanced at Raji before she could.

Even though she had humiliated herself in record time, even though the pain hadn't left his eyes, he still somehow made her want to stay.

"It's my fault," he said with such force that she flinched. "I...I never expected I'd be in this kind of situation." He ran a hand through his hair as he turned away. "Thousands of years, you'd think I've experienced it all."

Her shoulders slumped. "What are you talking about? What situation?"

With a sigh, he closed his eyes. "I'm not supposed to fall in love with you."

She reeled backwards, her eyes wide, her lungs suddenly devoid of oxygen. "Wait. What?"

He winced. "I should *not* have said that."

She didn't know how to respond. This kind of confession should result in her running into his arms, kissing him and clinging to him while they both smiled like idiots. But he was acting like he had accidentally thrown an egregious insult.

"No, it's okay, it's nice to hear." She cringed at every word as she took a step towards him.

But again he stepped back, his head bowed. "No, I've been letting my imagination get away from me. I'm sorry. I've led you to believe that it's okay for me to behave in a way contrary to my purpose. Any other wish you have, I can make it come true. But it can't be *my* wish. Even if it's your wish, too, I can't risk it. I told you, Dottie. I'm cursed."

Dot scoffed, shaking her head, her brow knitted in confusion. "You're seriously reverting into submissive servant mode after telling me you're in love with me? Using the *I can't be with you for your own protection* excuse? That's a dumb excuse!"

"It's a legitimate excuse!" He looked up at her briefly. There was clear frustration on his face before he turned back to the floor. "I'm sorry. I shouldn't speak to you like that. I should never have allowed you to treat me like your equal. That's my fault. We're not equals, Dot. We're not friends, we're not...love interests. That's not how this is supposed to work."

None of this made sense to her. "So what you're saying is...it's wrong for me to treat you like a human being? It's wrong for me to want to give some of your life back to you? It's wrong for us to care about each other?"

"I'll take the blame. You're doing nothing wrong."

"No, obviously I'm doing *something* wrong," she retorted. In its final few minutes, her day was crashing and burning before her eyes and she was now desperate to let it die. "I let myself develop feelings for you, too, knowing I can't free you or be with you for very long. I even put off this wish to get more time with you."

"Dottie—"

"I know. That was stupid of me. Very, very stupid. And now I'll probably spend the rest of my life feeling stupid about it. But that's my life. Even with a freaking genie, I can't get a win."

Without giving him a chance to respond, she was out the door, headed towards the stairs while holding back the tears forming in her eyes.

Outside, the thunder grew louder.

She knew she hadn't been completely honest. She had experienced an unwarranted amount of wins lately, but none of them would have ever come about without Raji. He hadn't just granted her wishes, he had opened her eyes. Without judgement, without pressure, and without guilt.

All she wanted was to be something good for him, too. But it sounded like all she did was fill him with regret.

When she reached her room, the tears had broken free, but for once she didn't want to numb herself to them. She needed them to fuel her. She'd given up easily on a lot of things, but this was different. Raji was different. And after everything that had happened with Diane today, the taste of victory still lingered on her tongue.

Her eyes fell on the bottle and the letter on her nightstand.

She didn't know exactly how to fight for Raji, but she would never forgive herself if she didn't try.

Chapter 28

RAJI

The storm grew louder and stronger throughout the night, but Raji hardly noticed. At first he could do nothing but lie on the floor, wallowing in the intense mixture of emotional and cosmic pain that paralyzed him. He fixed his eyes on his mother's picture for strength, forcing himself not to think about the woman he couldn't stop thinking about, the woman he had hurt, and trying to come up with ways he could rush the job so that this could all be done and he didn't have to be around her all the time.

But then he wouldn't get to be around her all the time.

Eventually the pain ebbed enough for him to get on his feet and distract himself with cooking, but it only resulted in burned chicken and watery hummus, so he gave up and spent the rest of the night propped against the wall, under a weighted blanket, surrounded by pillows. His appreciation for the modern age increased as he discovered the many ways people had come up with to comfort themselves when they didn't have a real person to comfort them.

By the time morning dawned somewhere behind the heavy clouds, the pain was mostly gone and he was dead inside, which he perceived as a good thing. He was now nothing more than an empty, wish-granting robot.

Exactly like he was supposed to be.

He found Dot in the foyer coming down the stairs after most of the guests had already eaten breakfast. He stopped himself before he could analyze her ragged exterior: the dark circles under her eyes, the crumpled pajamas, the unkempt hair.

A servant never judges a master for their appearance.

When she noticed him, a mix of emotions played out on her face, like she couldn't decide how to look at him. She settled on staring at her feet as she continued down the stairs.

Enforcing his emotional barriers, he focused on her the way he would on any master: with anticipation of how he might be of service.

"Good morning," he said with excessive submissiveness as she stopped in front of him. "May I prepare you some breakfast?"

"Later. I'm looking for my mom. Have you seen her?" Her tone seemed to aim for apathetic, but as with her expression, he picked up an array of possible emotions, though he wasn't entirely sure which ones she was trying to hide.

But it didn't matter.

"I haven't seen her come down yet. Is there something *I* can help you with?"

Dot shook her head. "I knocked on her door for five minutes."

"The wind's been loud all night. That level of white noise can make people sleep harder than usual."

"Raji. I knocked. She's not there."

He nodded acceptingly. The last thing he wanted to do was annoy her. "She must be around here somewhere," he assured her. "I've seen everyone else, but maybe she came down before I did. I'll help you look."

Though her head swayed impatiently, her eyes remained directed at her feet. "I just wanted to see what she wants to do today." She sighed, lifting her head, but still refusing to meet his eyes. "I'm worried...I'm worried that yesterday was too much for her. I'm afraid she's avoiding me again, so I don't want to, like, pressure her. Maybe you can find her for me and let her know it's cool if she needs some space today."

"Absolutely," he answered eagerly. Her tired eyes filled him with guilt; his selfish confessions last night only added to the weight of things she was already dealing with.

It was useless. There was no way he could ignore how much he cared about her. "I'll double check her room. Then I'll check the downstairs."

"Thank you. I'm hoping she didn't answer because she knew it was me."

Don't do this to yourself, he wanted to say. *If Diane's avoiding you, it's only because she feels guilty about how unnecessarily kind you're being to her.*

But that wasn't assurance he'd ever give any other master, so he kept it to himself.

Upstairs, Raji knocked on Diane's door for a few minutes before justifying that, as the "host" of the trip, he would have access to every room. Tentatively, he turned the doorknob and pushed the door open. It might have been locked for anyone else, but anyone else didn't pull this entire house out of the folds of space with their own metaphorical two hands.

"Rise and shine, Diane...well, there is no shine, but—oh. Oh, no."

His face fell. The inside of the room, though spacious, appeared completely generic. No personal adornment of any kind.

Because no one was staying there anymore.

He swore as he hurried down the stairs. Where did she go? How did she leave? The answer only occurred to him as he burst into the theater room, led there instinctively by his master-servant bond.

He halted as soon as he entered. On the giant screen, MarioKart was paused mid-game. Ava, Anthony, Winston, and Jorge held the controllers in their hands, Yasmin was standing in the middle row holding a book, and Dot and Skye stood near the door. They all turned to Raji when he entered.

"Was she upstairs?" Skye asked hopefully.

"Um...no." He looked at Dot, unsure how to begin his explanation.

"I'll call her," Dot said before he could try. "I just need to get my phone. I left it in my room."

Behind his back, he quietly summoned her phone, then held it out to her. "Actually, I have it. You left it in the foyer."

She stepped forward to reach for it, but he knew he needed to warn her before she discovered the devastating news for herself. "Dottie, I need to tell you...some of the staff that live on surrounding islands wanted to go home to their families before the storm hit..."

She plucked her phone from his hand but met him with a curious look.

"...and Hugo wanted to get his plane somewhere more secure. I said it was fine. He said he would leave last night. Before the weather got too bad and after everyone was done for the day, so he could take anyone who wanted to..."

He trailed off as her expression turned to subtle panic. She was piecing it together.

Now all eyes in the room were on Dot. She lifted the phone to her face.

The pain in her eyes confirmed it. Immediately, she shoved the phone back into Raji's hand. He glanced at the message on the screen. A message sent by *Diane Mom* at 10:43 the night before.

Only four words.

> Please don't judge me.

"Did she seriously leave?" Skye demanded, picking up on the silence. Dot swallowed as her eyes turned glassy. She looked at Skye and nodded curtly.

Skye slapped her hand over her eyes and groaned. Yasmin let out a string of angry Spanish. Even Winston slumped defeatedly in his seat.

"What? What happened!" Ava cried. Jorge leaned down and whispered something in her ear. "Oh no! That's so sad," she said quietly.

Raji's shoulders dropped. Dot caught his eye, and he did his best to convey the immense, agonizing hurt he felt for her. "Free will," he said.

"I'm actually fine," Dot said, looking around at the concerned faces. He knew she wasn't. But he also knew she hated this attention and was desperately looking for an escape route. "It's really a miracle she came in the first place, so...I'm fine. I'm just gonna go...and..." She pointed towards the door.

Raji took a step towards her, hesitating. He was a genie, and a genie didn't comfort. A genie allowed their master space. "Please let me know if I can do anything," he said, bowing his head. And for the first time, the gesture felt unnatural.

But she didn't seem to care. Without another word, she hurried out of the room.

He sat in the back of the theater for longer than he wanted to. The master/servant bond made him painfully aware that she was still hurting, but even with all his power, he was helpless. He couldn't force Diane to come back, he couldn't turn back time, and the thing that killed him the most was that he couldn't be the one to wipe Dot's tears away.

Around him, the others mourned for Dot and lambasted Diane, but eventually the game of MarioKart resumed and Yasmin went back to her book. Skye came and sat next to Raji.

"Is there a reason you're not up there offering her your shoulder?" she asked quietly.

"Yes. A lot of reasons." He didn't want to get into it. He felt sick enough that it was his own suffering keeping him from helping Dot through hers.

"Okay, well, you had your chance," she said, slapping his knee as she got up to leave. "Maybe you'll get another one in another few thousand years."

If she was trying to make him feel even more terrible, it worked. Now all he could think about was a life with Dot he could never have.

I'll have memories, he assured himself. *That's all I can hope to take from this.*

And there are plenty of good ones. The way she shined throughout that first wish. The way she listened to me blab about myself, even after I almost got her killed. Those few rejuvenating days of freedom, talking about what she wanted her paradise to be like.

How I sat around knowing she was alone and depressed and did nothing.

He closed his eyes and exhaled deeply, then slowly rose to his feet.

Skye caught his eye and gave him an approving smile, bobbing her head toward the hall. He nodded and let Dot's pain pull him to her door.

After knocking for almost a minute without any response, he thought about walking away, then a deflated voice came through the door.

"Just come in."

Darkness greeted him when he entered, backed by the sounds of the intense wind and heavy rain outside.

"Do you mind if I turn on a light?" he asked.

"Whatever," she answered from the bed.

He found and pulled the chain of a lamp near the door. His eyes landed on the lump under the bedsheets.

"Skye suggested that I come check on you," he said.

"As the trip coordinator or my indentured servant?"

She's hurting, he reminded himself as he rubbed his chest at the sudden sting of pain.

The covers flipped back, and he watched as she slid out from under them and worked her way to a sitting position on the edge of the bed, dropping her head. There were still wet streaks on her face. "I'm sorry," her voice shook. "It's not you I'm mad at."

Seeing her this way filled him with pain that had nothing to do with being a genie.

"Raji, I gave her ten thousand dollars last night. She took the money and ran. Did all of this mean nothing to her? Do *I* mean nothing to her?" Her reddened eyes searched him for an answer. But though he'd had countless experiences with materialistic and narcissistic masters, none of them had been his own mother.

"You don't have to try to understand her motives," he said. "I'm sorry I can't fix this one, but I can stay here with you. If you want me to."

She regarded him with an intoxicating intensity. It pulled him a step towards her.

A fresh tear formed in the corner of her eye and trailed down her cheek. "I want you to."

Screw it, he thought.

In an instant, he crossed the room and pulled her into his arms. It only took her a second to get over the initial shock and relax against him, and a second longer for each of them to catch their breath. Her tears soaked his shoulder. If there had to be tears, that's exactly where he wanted them to be.

She nestled her face in his neck and gripped the back of his tropical-printed shirt, pressing herself into him. Without restraint, he reciprocated, pressing his arms into her back, sliding his hands into her hair. He held her as close as physics would allow, but it didn't feel close enough.

A sigh escaped her when he kissed her head.

"I'm sorry, Dottie," he whispered.

"Don't talk," she murmured against his neck. "This is good."

He kissed her head again. "Yeah," he agreed. "This is good."

It was a level of bliss he had never experienced, and one that he would probably never experience again. Because at that moment, a crippling burst of pain exploded in his chest.

Chapter 29

DOT

She didn't know it was possible to be held the way that Raji held her.

This should be my third wish. That I just stay here forever.

Then a sudden tremor shook his body. At the same time, a knock sounded on the door frame, and Raji practically jumped out of the embrace. They both turned to find Jorge standing at the open door with worried eyes. "Sorry to interrupt," he said. "And Dot, I'm so sorry about your mother."

She nodded self-consciously. "Thanks. Is everything okay?"

"Did Ava follow you up here? Is she with you?" he asked.

Raji looked at Dot. She shook her head.

"No, we haven't seen her. Is she missing?"

"We've checked the whole house. We've got everyone looking, but no one's found her." Jorge's eyes landed on Raji. "Yasmin's worried she went out in the storm."

Dot moved to the closet and rummaged around until she found a rain jacket. She quickly pulled it on. "Do you have any idea why she would go outside right now?" Raji asked Jorge.

"She's been upset since I told her about Diane leaving. She really likes you, Dot."

Dot's heart instantly dropped. She had already caused enough of this wish to fall apart. If she had unknowingly triggered a strike three...

She hurried to Raji's side. "I like her, too, Jorge," she said. "Let's go find her."

Downstairs, the group agreed that Winston and Jorge would check the beach where they had been playing the past couple of days, while Dot and Raji would check around the pool and the swimming hole. Everyone else would continue to check the house. Raji handed out rain jackets and boots to the search team,

retrieving them from a closet in the foyer Dot knew for a fact hadn't been there a
second ago.

"If this is my fault, and if something happened to her, I'll never forgive myself,"
Dot said to Raji as they zipped up their jackets. His only answer was a sad but
comforting smile.

Despite the ominous, dark clouds, there was still enough dim daylight for the
search party to see a few feet in front of them, but the slanted rain made it difficult
for Dot to keep her eyes open, and the wind made it hard to maintain her balance.
After Jorge and Winston broke off, Raji waved his hand. An invisible protective
bubble encased Dot, shielding her from the wind and rain.

His forethought touched her. "What is this? Some kind of invisible umbrella
shell?" Dot asked loudly and gratefully, projecting her voice over the wind as she
pulled off her hood.

He nodded. "Let's check the pool first."

At the pool, the water roiled and splashed over the edges. Another wave of his
hand, and the entire thing drained in seconds. He and Dot shared a look of relief
to find nothing and no one at the bottom.

He raised a hand to snap them to the waterfall, but Dot grabbed his arm as a
possibility occurred to her. "Take us to the airstrip," she said.

With a nod, he snapped his fingers.

They arrived in the middle of the tarmac. Dot scanned the runway as carefully
as she could, praying to see a child-sized shape through the rainy haze.

"The hangar?" Raji pointed.

"I hate airplane hangars," she reminded him with an anxious frown.

"Me too," he shouted. Then he slipped his wet hand into her dry one, lacing
their fingers tightly. "But this time we're going in together."

Did something change? she wondered as she searched his face. He gave her hand
a squeeze, and she knew he was asking her not to worry about it. Not now, anyway.
"Okay." She nodded.

The large outer door was up, leaving one entire side of the hangar open to the
storm. The closer they got, the emptier the inside appeared. Dot closed her eyes,
stiffening as they crossed the threshold. Once inside, her eyes opened, but her
muscles remained tight.

She looked around, trying to ignore the sick feeling in her stomach. A distant corner caught her eye, triggering a vivid flashback of her near-death experience in a similar spot not long ago. But the warmth of Raji's hand in hers tugged her focus back to the mission at hand.

The place looked empty—until her eyes fell on a pile of sopping wet beach towels in a corner just inside the door. It was trembling.

Dot let go of Raji's hand and ran to it. It wasn't a pile of beach towels. There was only one towel, which Dot pulled away to reveal a wet, shivering little girl beneath it.

"Ava!" Dot cried, kneeling next to her.

"D-Dot!" the girl chattered. "I w-wanted to tell your m-mom to stay, but I-I think she left already."

Dot teetered as a wave of equal parts sickening guilt and tremendous relief came over her. She glanced at Raji whose mouth curved in deep concern, concern that she suspected wasn't completely directed at Ava.

"I b-brought a towel to keep me d-dry but it didn't work," Ava added disappointedly.

Raji took the towel and snapped it like a whip. Right before their eyes, it went from soaking wet to warm and fluffy. He kneeled next to Dot, draping it over Ava's shoulders.

"H-how did you d-do that?" She beamed, pulling the towel tightly around her as Dot rubbed her back.

"I know some tricks." He winked. He picked up one end and rubbed it on her head. When he took it away, her hair was no longer wet. "Don't tell anyone. I'm shy about my magic," he said, shooting Dot a knowing smile.

It was a solid effort to lighten the mood. It worked on Ava, who touched her dry hair in wonder, but Dot was past feeling at the moment.

"Come on. Let's get you inside," she said.

Despite the wind and rain and thunder, all it took was a magically amplified yell towards the beach to let Winston and Jorge know they had found her. Then Raji carried Ava back up to the house wrapped in her now rain-proof towel. Dot walked beside them in her umbrella shell, feeling queasy and downcast the whole way.

Once Ava was back inside, dry and safe, she explained her reasoning to the crowd of guests and staff who had gathered to breathe a collective sigh of relief.

"Everyone was talking about how mad and sad they were that Dot's mom was leaving, so I wanted to stop her," Ava explained plainly. "I didn't know she was already gone."

After a chorus of charmed praise and a few soft words of correction, all eyes were on Dot.

She didn't want the attention. She hadn't wanted it that morning, either. That attention had led Ava to put herself in danger. Feeling sorry for herself was no one's obligation but her own; Dot didn't need or want that from her friends. Not right now. "Thank you, Ava, for thinking of me. But next time you're feeling sad for me, it's enough to just feel sad for me, okay? I guess you take after your *abuela*. You're more of a doer, huh?"

Thankfully, the focus of the room quickly shifted back to Ava. Seeing her chance, Dot apologized profusely to Jorge and Yasmin and slipped out of the room before they could respond.

The hiding reflex was strong today, but she didn't want to go to the obvious place—her room—where people would know where to find her, so she made for the enclosed porch along the back of the house. Because of the storm, the others would avoid this area today, but no one else knew the architect like she did. Just because the windows had no panes didn't mean they wouldn't keep the rain and wind out.

Her premonition proved correct. Though she could see the now dying storm through the windows, the air on the porch hung calm and quiet, and the floors remained dry. Even so, the weather kept the normally bright space dim and shadowy, creating the perfect environment to wallow in self-pity, be racked with guilt, and stew in anger all at the same time.

She leaned against a stretch of wall between wicker chairs and slid to the floor, dropping her head into her hands, letting her hair form a protective curtain around her face. A makeshift hiding place.

Then she cried. Again.

I'm so pathetic.

"Hey," Raji's voice said.

She lifted her head. He stood in front of a window, but slowly lowered himself until he sat on the floor across from her, his back against the stucco wall behind him. The shadows made it hard for her to see his face.

"Is it okay for you to be here?" she asked. "You don't feel like you're putting me at risk?"

"I don't know if I am or not. There's a lot I don't know, I'm realizing. But I told you I would stay with you. You're still in pain, Dottie."

"What about you?"

His silhouette shrugged. "I'm alright."

She didn't know whether or not to believe him. Maybe he had learned how to compartmentalize his feelings. Maybe he could give her some tips.

Pressing her head against the wall, she stared at the ceiling. "Why does everything I touch fall apart?" she lamented. "Why does every decision I make blow up in my face, even when I'm trying to do the right thing?"

After a minute, his voice came from the shadows. "Did I ever tell you about the master who wished that she was always right?"

"No. But where was that suggestion when you were helping me come up with wish ideas?" she asked, wiping her eyes with her sleeve.

"Because—spoiler alert—it does not go well."

Already her tears were slowing. His voice had undeniable soothing power. "So it's a story to teach me a lesson. Like the tiger guy."

"As your genie, I would never dream of trying to teach you a lesson. It's just a fun little anecdote."

She snorted an amused snort. It was all she could muster. "Okay. Go for it."

He cleared his throat. "This was one of my other female masters. A pharaoh's wife in one of the many ancient Egyptian kingdoms. People back then already believed their rulers were literal gods, but this woman didn't want to cause any doubt. So she wished she would never be wrong. And before you think this was a moral decision, it wasn't. It was a power move. She wanted to become this pillar of wisdom that people from all over would come to consult with. Consequently, she did make many wise decisions and developed a confidence that left her immune to guilt and shame."

"That doesn't sound so bad."

He chuckled. "She also became insufferable and completely out of touch with her subjects. She refused to listen to anyone else, and she was loud and annoying at parties. Fortunately for her, that kind of attitude was expected from people in her position. None of that made her wrong. So in that regard, she got exactly what she wanted.

"But that wasn't always the case. Her insight was solid, yes; when she advised the Pharaoh to make their younger son the heir, that was definitely the right call. He was way more level-headed than their older son. But that didn't stop the older son from murdering his little brother."

Dot flinched. "Yikes."

"And she couldn't have chosen a more perfect plot of land for her subjects to grow their crops. The soil was unbelievable. The wheat it produced was high quality. So much so that it frequently attracted the attention of thieves and locusts. And good soil doesn't exempt a hearty crop of wheat from shriveling up and dying when the droughts came."

Dot was starting to see the lesson here, whether or not Raji would admit that there was one.

"She was more than a little frustrated with me," Raji went on. "Because from her perspective, always doing the right things should mean nothing could go wrong. But those are two entirely different problems. Things will always go wrong. Even when you make the wisest decisions, other people will make bad ones and nature will continue to function unpredictably, like it always has. Life is a mixed bag for everyone, even the people who make all the best decisions. No one is immune."

"Huh." She took a deep breath. "That's a depressing moral."

The sound of the rain had softened, and the clouds were thinning enough that she could see Raji's face in the increasing light. He watched her carefully, in a way that made her heavy emotions seem lighter.

"I wasn't trying to make you not depressed," he said. "It is a depressing truth. Dottie, you're an exceptional human being. You make smart choices. Your instincts are solid. And it depresses me too that you get the short end of the stick more than you deserve. So...I'm here to be depressed about that with you. Joining the pity party, so to speak."

She willed her chin not to tremble as she forced a sad smile. "Being depressed together sounds nice."

A short laugh drifted out of the shadows. "The being together part does."

A tense, uncomfortable silence filled the space. "Raji, I'm so confused...did something change?" she asked nervously, finding his eyes in the shadows.

"Not the things I wish could change." He paused as his eyes began to glisten and his chest heaved. Dot leaned forward, but he spoke before she could say anything. "Everything I said last night was irredeemably thoughtless. That was Raji the genie speaking. He's an idiot. Now I'm just Raji. And...I would really like to kiss you."

She blinked. "Oh. Okay," she whispered stupidly.

Then he was on his feet, holding his hand out towards her. Without hesitation, she placed her hand in his, immediately forgetting how to breathe as he pulled her into his arms for the second time that day. His deep brown eyes fixed on her with solid determination and a hunger that extinguished any inclination to question what was happening or whether it should happen.

"Last night I said what I said because I thought I was saving both of us from having any regrets." He pressed his forehead to hers. "But having to live forever knowing that I passed up the opportunity to kiss you...I can't imagine anything I would regret more."

She swallowed as their lips drew closer. "Me neither," she murmured.

There were certain kisses that Dot was sure could only ever exist in movies between two exceptionally attractive trained actors. In her experience, those perfect, passionate, explosive kisses couldn't possibly happen naturally in the wild. Her first awkward kiss with a neighbor's visiting grandson behind the clubhouse when she was fourteen felt like pressing her lips against a wet sponge. Howie had been better, but the feeling she got from kissing him wasn't any different from the feeling she got when stumbling upon an unexpected mall sale.

Kissing Raji was a different experience entirely. As soon as their lips met, she understood how people could compare kisses to fireworks. As her arms curled around his neck and her toes curled in her rain boots, explosions fired off in every nerve ending in her body, like her own personal Independence Day.

She pulled him closer, gripped him tighter, assuring herself of his reality with all of her senses. She could taste him, smell him, twist her fingers in his hair, be pushed against the wall under the soft guidance of his hands on her hips and still gaslight herself into thinking that this idyllic moment had to exist only within her own head.

No. This is real.

But as he pressed her harder into the wall, she realized something wasn't right. He was using her for support. She slid her hands down to his chest and wrapped them around his middle, gripping his trembling body. Whatever was happening wasn't enough to make him want to stop, and if he didn't want to, she didn't want to even more.

But when he began rapidly sucking in air through his nose, she reluctantly called it.

"Raji," she said against his lips as she opened her eyes. "Are you okay?"

"Mmmhmm," he said it like a shrug, but the moans coming from him were not the good kind. She moved her hands to grab the front of his shirt and pushed him back as gently as she could.

"Raji." She looked into his eyes firmly. She had never seen them so alive.

His eyes drifted across her face as a smile spread across his. "Worth it," he said. Then he collapsed to the floor.

"Raji!" She fell to her knees beside him. He winced harshly, and her heart dropped. "Are you being punished for this?"

Through labored breaths, he choked out a response. "I don't think I'm supposed to feel as good as that made me feel." His eyes blinked open. When they fell on her, the smile returned to his face. "And I was not thinking very servant-y thoughts."

"Geez, Raji. After one kiss?"

"I've kissed you a lot more in my mind."

She blinked back the sudden sting behind her eyes. "That's not very fair to the version of me that actually exists." She placed a hand against his cheek. "So I can't kiss you without hurting you?"

"It's just pain," he said, leaning into her touch. "As long as I let myself love you, it will always be there to some degree. But I only have *you* for a little while longer."

His eyes twinkled. If he wasn't a couple of shades paler than normal, lying flat on his back, she might say she'd never seen him so happy. It was a beautiful glimpse into the person he was. Dot had a knack for letting her pain overshadow her joy, but Raji was proving it could be done the other way around.

She drew in a deep breath as she slipped her hand into his. "There's something I should have told you the moment I saw you this morning," she said. "But so many things distracted me, so I'll tell you now. You...you might be mad."

"At you? Never," he answered. "But...what is it?"

She swallowed. "Listen, I know by telling that story, you're saying that there are things I have no control over. Things like a narcissistic mother or a tropical storm. And maybe you were implying we can't do anything about your situation, either. Except...what if we could?"

The twinkle faded from his eyes, replaced with trepidation. "No," he said as a plea rather than an answer. "If you think you've found a loophole...it'll fail and I'll be gone. And you won't get a third wish. You may lose *all* your wishes."

"I'm not talking about using a wish. I already know you don't have the power to free yourself." In her hand, she felt his fingers tense. "But what if someone else does?" She clutched his hand with both of hers. "I was feeling a lot of emotions last night. It was risky and stupid, but I was desperate."

He rolled his head to the side. "Tell me you're not saying what I think you're saying."

"Raji, you don't deserve the life that you have. You don't deserve this pain. What kind of person would I be if I didn't at least try to get you out of it?"

He rolled his head back, and she could see in his eyes that he knew exactly what she was implying.

She pulled his hand to her lips and kissed it to reaffirm her actions. In the loneliness of the stormy night, she had scolded herself heavily for this decision, and by dawn she had decided to pretend it never happened. But the storm clouds were parting. Raji had kissed her regrets into oblivion, and now she was sure that she had no other option. Fighting meant taking risks, and she had taken a huge one.

"You may have picked up on this," she said. "But I'm falling in love with you, too. Which is why I did something I have avoided doing my entire life."

"What's that?" he asked cautiously.

"I initiated a phone call." She smiled stiffly. "Raji, I called Lou."

The Final Wish

Chapter 30

DOT

The road from the Kansas City airport to Branson, Missouri, was a far cry from the paradise Dot had woken up in that morning. But despite the fast-food signs and sun-bleached billboards and cell phone towers crowding the skyline, there was nowhere else she'd rather be. Besides in the future, after the only sorcerer she knew of had freed the genie currently sitting in the passenger seat.

"It's a little under an hour away now," she said, glancing at the GPS on the dash of the rental car. "Are you nervous?"

"Are you?" Raji gave her hand a gentle squeeze.

His aversion to the question didn't come as a surprise. Since the day of the storm, the worry had been written all over his face. But she couldn't blame him; the last time he had sought out the help of a sorcerer, it had upended his entire life, and not in a good way.

She'd known that going into the phone call but stubbornly ignored it. She was desperate. There had to be a way to get him out of his prison, and if he couldn't be wished free, it made sense that if a sorcerer had been key in making Raji a genie, then a sorcerer could undo it. The soundness of that logic overrode all her fears about picking up the phone.

And the call hadn't been unpleasant. Lou had been surprisingly patient and inquisitive. Right off the bat, she admitted she had a genie and she knew he was looking for it. He didn't even attempt to deny it. It had been strange to have a serious conversation with a stranger about freeing a genie, but it hadn't been disheartening. Once she told Lou Raji's story, they both agreed that the right thing to do would be to set him free, and he offered to give it a try.

But she didn't want to make a deal until she spoke to Raji about it, and she was still too hurt to bring it up when she had seen him the next morning.

Then they found out that Diane had left, and she forgot all about it. Dot hadn't spoken to her mother since the night she handed over the money, and Diane hadn't said a word to her beyond the text message she sent after dipping out. Then Ava had run off, and all Dot could think about was how the minute she believed her relationships were better than ever, they all exploded in her face.

Until Raji kissed her. When her inner turmoil was at its worst, he chose to love her, even though he would suffer for it. If she had known it would hurt him, she would never have let him do it, and as much as she wanted him to kiss her again, she hadn't let him since. He seemed willing, but the guilt of causing him pain was too much for her to take.

Once he was free, she'd make up for it.

She smiled. "I'm always nervous, but I feel okay about this."

"That's encouraging." He paused. "But when are we going to talk about what happens if it doesn't work?"

"Raji—"

"Hey. Believe me. I know it's more fun to fantasize about the good possibilities. I've spent these last few days imagining that our time together will never end. And I wasn't about to ruin that by bringing this up. But it needs to be addressed."

She understood exactly what he meant.

They made an agreement the day of the storm. Raji would willingly go see Lou, but Dot had to enjoy the rest of her second wish to the fullest. He wanted her to have a good time with the people who didn't abandon her.

So she did.

Swimming, zip-lining, snorkeling, eating amazing food, and doing it all with people she could now say were her closest friends—it was the perfect suggestion. And on the final night, as they stood on her balcony, Raji presented her with the deed to the island. "This place didn't exist last week," he'd explained. "It's up for grabs. And I needed a good finale for the last wish I ever grant."

She couldn't argue with him. That was a pretty good finale.

And though she'd prefer to avoid acknowledging the harsh realities and possibilities that could result from this hastily thrown-together plan, she'd be delusional for doing so.

"You have more experience with sorcerers than I do," she said. "What do you think could happen?"

Out of the corner of her eye, she saw something like dread flash across his face. "Let's not list the specific possibilities," he said. "Just be aware that I won't have a lot of power now that the second wish is over. But I *can* snap you away if Lou turns out to be as cuckoo as he implies."

"Snap me where? Back to Tallahassee? He probably knows where I live, Raji."

"Then maybe you'll have to lie low somewhere else. Or make your third wish."

She drove in silence for a moment as she digested that bitter slice of information.

That's not going to happen, she promised herself.

"There *is* something you can do for a little insurance, if the opportunity presents itself."

"Okay. Tell me."

"Sorcerers come in all shapes and sizes. But there is one thing they all have in common."

"Let me guess: A slick goatee? A magic wand? An evil laugh?"

"You were getting warmer with the wand."

She scrunched her eyebrows. "They carry wands? I always thought the wands were the most pointless part of wizard culture."

"Not wands. Staves."

"Staves? Like the tall sticks elderly wizards carry around?"

"Yeah. Those. But they aren't always sticks. That's just what the earliest sorcerers carried."

She shot him a blank stare. "So all sorcerers carry staves, but not necessarily? Not sure I'm following."

"Let me explain." He released her hand and shifted to face her. "A sorcerer's magic isn't a part of them, so it needs something to be carried in. A vessel, like how I have a vessel because I *am* magic, their magic also needs a vessel to contain it until they need to use it. Traditionally they all carried staves. But staves are obvious, and they can be seized and destroyed easily by anyone with a pure enough soul.

"Over time, sorcerers got wise and began disguising their staves. Amulets are a popular choice, but I've also seen them as gems, turbans, armbands, a belly ring—but regardless of what it is, a sorcerer can't do sorcery without one. It doesn't necessarily need to always be on a sorcerer's person, only when they're using magic, but the sorcerers I've known have all been too paranoid to leave it lying around somewhere."

Dot nodded slowly. "Okay, so presumably, Lou will have one of these, and if things go sideways, we can steal it before we peace out."

"No, we don't just steal it," he answered. "We destroy it. *You* destroy it."

"But couldn't I use it to free you myself?"

"No!" He yelled it so suddenly that she swerved a little, earning a honk from the car in the next lane. "Sorry," he said more evenly. "No, any magic contained in his personal staff is toxic. It won't work for you. It may even harm you."

"Sheesh. Okay. Destroy the staff. Understood."

"*You*," he corrected. "*You* destroy the staff. It can be easily destroyed by anyone with a good, strong soul."

"Why wouldn't that include you?"

"My soul is imprisoned. Destroying a sorcerer's staff is too significant for me to do unless you wished for it."

"Right. That makes sense," she affirmed. "I guess I'll keep my eyes open for his staff, just in case. What else should I know?"

He didn't answer right away, but even without him in her direct eyeline, she could feel the air in the car become heavier.

"I've been reluctant to bring this up," he finally said. "Because it makes me sick to think about, but as nice as Lou sounded on the phone, we don't know him, and we don't know what he'd be willing to do if he...if he was absolutely set on getting his hands on a genie."

A chill ran down her spine. She didn't like to think about it either, although talking to Lou had eased her fears significantly. "You don't have to say it. I remember. Only one way to steal a genie that's already in use."

She felt his gaze on her. "You need to know what you're risking."

"I'm risking nothing that I'm not willing to." She turned her head to briefly meet his eyes, wanting him to know she was serious.

Just because they hadn't spoken about the risks didn't mean she hadn't thought about them. She'd thought about them in great detail before she ever picked up the phone. And when she had, it was because she had concluded that she would be okay, because she had something she didn't normally have. Something Raji didn't have when he'd gone in to see that first sorcerer.

She wouldn't be going in alone, and neither would he. They had each other. She'd experienced firsthand what a difference that made every day since the night Raji popped out of his bottle. There was no reason to think it wouldn't make a difference this time, too.

He released a long breath of what she hoped was acceptance. "But you said he sounds okay," he stated like he was convincing himself.

"Yes. On the phone he listened very patiently as I blubbered about you. And then when he said he'd be willing to help, I could tell that he wanted to. He said he resents the evil sorcerer stereotype. He was raised a good Missouri boy and that's always been the core of who he is or whatever. I can't remember exactly how he put it."

"Alright. But I've never met anyone raised in Missouri so that doesn't really mean anything to me."

"I had some neighbors once who were from Missouri," she said to put herself at ease as much as him. "They were super friendly and patriotic, always dropping off casseroles because they said that's what good neighbors did where they were from."

He rubbed his beard. "I guess I've never known a truly evil sorcerer to drop off casseroles to anyone."

The GPS had directed them off the interstate and Dot now navigated them through city streets. Her heart began to pound, and a pit formed in her stomach as the arrow on the screen got closer to the destination pin. She placed her hand on Raji's knee. "I'm not gonna pretend to know how this is gonna go," she said, her eyes darting from the road to his still worried expression. "But I have to try. I *have* to."

"I know," he answered. "And I'm not trying to talk you out of it. Just...be careful. I feel like I've had to hold myself back from wanting this, for your protection, but the truth is...I want this so bad, it hurts."

"Me too," she said, pulling her hand to the wheel to make their final turn.

It was the wanting that worried her more than anything else.

Chapter 31

RAJI

Raji's infinite knowledge painted Branson as a vibrant city full of entertainment, museums, and an abundance of tourist traps, but from the part of town where he stood, he never would have guessed that on his own. Discarded trash rolled down the sidewalks like tumbleweeds, and he couldn't quite tell whether other businesses existed in any of the decrepit surrounding buildings, or if they were all merely abandoned. Even Cuckoo Lou's looked like it had been out of business for years. The only thing that signified its existence was a large, tattered banner that hung lifelessly above a grimy glass door flanked by two dark, equally grimy windows.

Dot had parked across the narrow street and now they stood side-by-side outside the car, staring uncertainly at the building.

"It's actually a good omen," he said hopefully. "A really corrupt sorcerer would be running a casino or something."

"It doesn't look like anyone's here." She pulled her phone out of her jacket pocket and glanced at the screen. "I texted him to tell him our ETA before we left the airport. We're on time."

"Let's knock," he suggested. But when he began walking towards the front door, Dot didn't follow.

The absence of her usual anxiety up to this point had not only surprised him, it had encouraged him. So seeing her suddenly uneasy made him suddenly uneasy.

"What's wrong?" he asked, stepping in front of her to disrupt her line of sight. She dropped her head, shaking it vehemently.

"Nothing. I mean, I don't know. This place looks exactly like the photo on his Facebook page, but being here in person..." She looked up to meet his eyes. "It feels a little...off."

"Off, like...we shouldn't be here?" he asked tentatively.

She shook her head again. "No, we should definitely be here. We *have* to be here. It's more like a...like an absence of feeling. Like walking into the unknown. Like..."

"Like a deadness inside?"

"That's a disturbing way to put it, but...yeah."

"Then this is the right place."

"What does that mean?"

"Dottie, I've told you before." He took her hands in his. "You have a good soul. A strong soul. No matter where Lou is on the sorcerer spectrum, he's already made some kind of trade with the jinn. If he's given them a piece of his soul, then they'll be lurking nearby, badgering him for another. Your soul can sense them. As their long-term prisoner, it doesn't affect me as much anymore, but I know the feeling you're talking about. A soul can detect when there's something hunting it."

"Geez, Raji." She shuddered. "Do you wanna say that again so I can play some creepy organ music and really set the—"

Something behind him made her freeze. He turned to follow her stare.

The lights inside the building were now on, and behind the dirty glass of the front door stood a man, watching them. One not nearly as menacing as Raji expected. Stocky build, round stomach, with a bushy brown mustache obscuring his mouth. A Kansas City Chiefs trucker hat cast a shadow over his eyes. He raised one hand and waved.

"The timing on that," she muttered beside him, taking a deep breath and composing herself. "Okay. I promise I'm good. Let's go meet the wizard."

"Hope you weren't out there long. I was in the back working on some things. Come on in," Lou said as he pushed the door open. Raji ushered Dot in and stopped to look around as the door closed behind him.

They had entered a lobby of sorts; the low buzz of the fluorescent lighting, the chipped and dirty linoleum floor, and the outdated wood paneling gave the space a vacant chilliness. A long, high counter stretched across the back wall, with a heavy metal door off to the side. A large red sign with black lettering hung above it.

ENTER HERE!

Behind the counter, plastered against the wall, was a mass of redundant admission information and a few signs loudly declaring specific rules.

No video recording or photographs!

No refunds!

No backpacks!

No strollers!

No smoking!

No public bathrooms!

One other narrow door almost blended into another wall behind a bulky brochure rack. Raji could make out a restroom symbol beside it that had been scratched out.

"We just barely got here," Dot answered as Lou shook her hand warmly. "I'm Dot. This is—"

"The genie. Wow." Lou turned to Raji, but he didn't reach out for a handshake. Instead, he placed his hands on his hips and stepped back, appraising Raji with wide eyes and an even wider grin.

Here we go.

"He doesn't look like I expected," Lou observed with a finger on his chin.

Raji looked down at his jeans, button-down shirt, and light jacket. It was a fair point. Most people expected a genie to have a larger-than-life presence, complete with a surly attitude, a bodybuilder's physique, and a booming voice. No doubt those rumors had been spread by past masters who thought it would impress others that they got to boss someone like that around. Though the surly attitude rumor probably stemmed from how sulky Raji had been in those early days.

"Well, that's because really, he's just a human," Dot explained. "And his name is Raji."

Lou nodded slowly. "Yes, I see why you would feel inclined to free him. In this form, you wouldn't ever suspect him to be a genie. He looks like an average Joe, just with an unnaturally perfect jawline."

"Exactly." Dot agreed.

Raji crossed his arms and scoffed quietly. Undergoing a humiliating physical evaluation was the most genie-like he'd been treated since he got here. His learned instinct was to take it and keep his mouth shut until called upon, but considering he was here to break free of that kind of existence, this treatment felt especially unnecessary.

Lou rubbed his hands together and turned to Dot. "Do you mind having him do some magic? Just so I can confirm it with my own eyes."

Dot blinked a few times. "Uh..." She glanced at Raji. "What do you want him to do?"

But Raji couldn't stand by and let Dot potentially lose the upper hand until they better understood who they were dealing with.

"No, thanks," Raji said, staring straight at Lou. "Take her word for it. You have no reason not to trust her. But she has plenty of reasons not to trust you. I think *you* need to prove to her that you can and will do what she's asking. She doesn't owe you a thing until then."

Lou crinkled his mustache and glanced from Raji to Dot, who looked slightly mortified.

Lou raised his eyebrows. "We still good on the price, Miss Dot?"

Raji frowned as Dot quickly answered. "Yes. A little under ten million dollars. It's yours as soon as Raji's free."

Lou smiled approvingly. Raji's jaw dropped.

"It's just money," Dot said to him quietly, placing her hand on his arm. "You're more important."

A stab of overwhelming gratitude hit Raji square in his ever-beating heart. Gratitude, and an affection for her so powerful, he faltered from the ensuing pain. He grabbed onto her to steady himself.

"Why didn't you tell me?" he whispered as Lou watched them through slitted eyes.

"We'll talk about it when this is over," she whispered back. She linked her arm into his and turned back to Lou. "The terms haven't changed. But I agree with Raji. I'd be more comfortable knowing that you have the power to free him."

"Well, the only way I can prove that is to try it," Lou replied. "It isn't like I've freed a lot of genies. But I can show you my magic, assure you that I'm not just one of those wannabes from downtown." He bobbed his head towards the ENTER HERE door.

"Is that some kind of funhouse or something?" she asked. She took a wide scan of the outdated lobby. "Or did it used to be?"

Lou laughed. "Oh, it's not a funhouse. It's much more than that. And it's still in business." He slapped a palm on the counter and a tiny cloud of dust encircled his hand. "It's not as fancy as some of the local shows, but I'm a humble man. I do it for the smiles, not the money. I enjoy showing people things they've never seen before, but I also can't be drawing too much attention to myself, for obvious reasons. I'd be happy to give you a turn in the chamber."

Raji and Dot shared a look, and Raji thought he noticed a distinct shiver move through her shoulders. Her soul must be incredibly alluring to the invisible entities surely following Lou around like hungry sharks. He wanted to get her out of here as fast as he could, but they needed to get a better picture of what this guy was capable of, for more reasons than one. And despite the shiver, it was clear from Dot's willing expression that she agreed.

She faced Lou. "Okay. We'll check out the chamber."

"Perfect!" Lou clapped his hands and turned to reach over the counter. The sound of rustling papers filled the room. "Now normally I would have you fill out a questionnaire so I could make the experience a little more personal for you. But I think for now I'll just give you a teaser. I'll still need you to sign these, however."

He came up with two slightly wrinkled sheets of paper, handing them to Dot. Raji read them over her shoulder.

"Just some boring legal stuff." Lou waved his hand and rolled his eyes.

"A non-disclosure agreement and liability waiver?" Dot asked suspiciously.

"I can't be letting people blab my secrets all over town," Lou explained. "And the liability waiver is standard with any attraction like mine. Well, there is no attraction like mine, but you'll understand once you see it."

Dot shuffled the papers in her hands. "Shouldn't Raji sign these, too? I'm not going in there alone."

"I can't get hurt and I can't tell anyone without your permission," Raji interjected before Lou could respond.

Dot squinted, her brow lowering. "Yeah, except soon I'm not gonna be your master and you won't have to do anything I say."

Raji looked at Lou, who nodded and dug around until he came up with an extra NDA and two pens. "You are so right, Miss Dot. That's my oversight."

Lou stood by patiently as they signed, grinning giddily when they handed back the documents.

"Thank you kindly. Now give me two shakes of a lamb's tail and I'll have the chamber ready for you."

They watched him disappear through the large door. As soon as he was gone, Dot grabbed Raji and turned him towards her. "Are you okay?"

"I'm okay. Are you okay? How's that deadness feeling?"

"Still there, but not an issue. Are we still feeling good about this?" she asked.

"I wanna keep going." The words flew out of his mouth before he could think them. There were a lot of odd things about Lou, but there would be with any sorcerer. "He seems...fine. I still can't get a good read on him. There are certainly risks, but—"

"This could work!" she finished, her eyes lighting up. It forced an excited—but still cautious—smile to form on his lips. He was thinking the same thing.

"I think it's a good sign that he had you sign an NDA. He wouldn't make you sign one if he didn't really plan on setting you free," she pointed out.

His expression dropped slightly. "Well, he *is* getting ten million dollars out of it."

"Yeah," she said with a cringe. "Listen, I know you worked hard to grant me that wish. I just...thought of something I'd rather have more."

A tiny sting pierced his chest. He raised his hand to her face, sweeping it down her cheek and letting it stop at her chin. Since the moment they kissed—a moment that he replayed in his head about every five minutes—the pain in his body had never fully gone away. The leisure island lifestyle had helped him cope and adjust to it over the past few days, but moments like this, when she made him fall a little more in love with her, the base pain increased by a few brutal degrees.

But he refused to ignore his feelings for her. They were his feelings, and he could do what he wanted with them.

The funny thing was that though the pain was intended to redirect him from feeling everything he felt for Dot, the way she loved him back sustained him through it. And it only made him love her more. It was a sick, magnificent cycle.

He leaned in and kissed her softly, because he could, and he wanted to. And the fervency with which she responded gave him a rush strong enough to forget about feeling anything else for an entire worthwhile second.

But when he stifled a groan, she pushed him back and whacked him gently on the shoulder. "Raji! I told you not to do that!"

"I cannot wait until I don't have to listen to you anymore," he said through a strained smirk.

The heavy metal door creaked open and Lou reappeared with a grin underscoring his mustache. "The chamber is ready. Right this way."

Raji and Dot exchanged a look of solidarity, and Raji gestured towards the door. "After you."

He kept a curious eye on Lou as he followed behind her. Raji knew better than to trust him completely, and the only reason he hadn't protested to Dot being lured into a dark room by a sorcerer was because he knew he could instantly snap her out of danger if it came to that. Lou didn't know he could do that, nor did he need to.

"My specialty is illusions," Lou noted as Dot stepped past him. "Nothing you're about to see can hurt you, but be aware that your brain may not understand that right away."

Dot stopped to look at Raji over her shoulder, and he saw a trace of discomfort in her eye. Lou placed his hand on her back to urge her on.

Raji did not like that.

If his staff was on him, it could feasibly take only a single touch to harm, curse, or cast some kind of spell on her. So with one hand, Raji swiftly grabbed Lou's wrist and forced it back while pulling Dot behind him with his other.

For a long beat, Raji held Lou firmly by the arm. Lou met his stare and a patient smile formed. "It's alright," he said cheerfully. "I'm a good man. Not trying to pull any funny business."

Raji still wasn't convinced, but when he felt Dot's hand on his shoulder, he let go.

Lou stepped back and adjusted his hat, seemingly unaffected.

"Come on," she whispered, slipping her arm through his. She led him into the chamber, but Raji didn't take his eyes off the sorcerer until he disappeared behind the closing door.

Chapter 32

DOT

As the door closed behind them, Dot caught a glimpse of the chamber, a cavernous and bleak room with concrete floors and no windows. But when the door shut completely, there was only pitch blackness.

"Why does it have to be so dark?" she asked, clinging to Raji's arm.

"I'll snap us away if anything happens."

"What do you think is gonna happen?"

"I guess we'll find out."

She didn't love that answer.

Then, slowly, the darkness began to fade from the ground beneath them. A vivid green spot on the floor grew and spread; she expected it to start climbing up the walls, but somehow it spread further. More colors appeared and a scene took shape. Dot's eyes widened as her brain deduced what her eyes were seeing.

"Is this a football stadium?"

Beside her, she could see Raji clearly now. He peered around guardedly.

"Yes. Arrowhead Stadium, from the looks of it. Where the Chiefs play. But it's all an illusion. We're not really there."

His voice disappeared into the air, as though they were standing in a wide-open space; it didn't echo like it should have in a room like the one they entered.

"This is weird," she muttered. They stood on the fifty-yard line, giving Dot a panoramic view of the enormous empty arena.

The loudspeaker system crackled.

"Thought I'd give you folks a tour of my home state," Lou's voice announced. "I'm a born and raised Missourian and proud of it. Go Chiefs!"

Crowds materialized in the seats, increasing the volume gradually until every seat was filled and cheers and chants flooded the air. With the two of them being the only ones on the field, it felt like the fans were cheering for *them*. The uneasiness was lifting, and Dot felt...important. An apprehensive grin began to form on her lips as she loosened her grasp on Raji.

Then, from one corner of the stadium, a throng of gigantic football players in red and gold uniforms burst onto the field, increasing the already deafening sound of the crowds. They didn't slow down, though. They picked up speed.

"Raji, those guys are running right at us," she pointed out.

"They're not real," he assured.

But they were getting closer, and they kept multiplying. Even though she couldn't make out any faces, they seemed angry. They slapped their helmets with a chorus of growls and snarls as they ran full speed towards the center of the field. If they didn't slow down, she and Raji would be trampled.

"Raji..." she squeaked, moving behind him.

He put his arm out to shield her.

"Shouldn't we run?" she asked.

"You'll only run into a wall. This isn't real."

The cheering and chanting from the crowd and angry yelling from the players became almost frantic. The players didn't, or couldn't, see her and Raji, and they were only yards away now. There were dozens upon dozens of them, way more than a standard football team.

"Raji."

He stepped backwards, pushing her with his body. She squeezed her eyes shut, bracing for impact.

Then the stadium sounds abruptly stopped, as if sucked into a vacuum, and she stumbled at the force of a strong wind pushing her sideways, whipping her hair wildly around her face. She opened her eyes and screamed.

They were hundreds of feet in the air above a wide, rushing river. Was she falling? No. She was teetering. She grabbed Raji, who waved his arms as he tried to steady himself.

Beneath their feet was a floating stone platform. No, not floating. When she noticed the platform slope out of view in either direction, she understood. They were on top of the famous Gateway Arch in St. Louis. She had only ever seen it in pictures, but never from this angle. Very few people probably had.

She bent her knees a little, attempting to keep her center of gravity low in case the wind knocked her off balance and sent her plummeting to the river below.

"It's okay," Raji shouted, taking her hands in his.

"Then why are you crouching, too? Afraid you're gonna fall?" She had to yell so the wind didn't whisk her words away before they reached his ears.

"It's not real, but it looks and feels real enough to trick our natural reflexes." His hair rippled with another gust of wind. "I'll show you."

He dangled one foot over the edge.

"Raji!" He was right. She reacted before she could remind herself that he was still on the solid concrete floor of the chamber. Even so, when he leaned forward, she grabbed at him, which only meant when he started to fall, he took her with him.

Again, she held her eyes shut as she felt herself being pulled after Raji, who was dropping like a dead weight.

She tumbled on top of him. A solid floor had broken his fall instantly, and *he* had broken hers. She opened her eyes, but it didn't help much. They were in a large shadowy room similar to the chamber—but it wasn't the chamber. The ceiling was too tall, the room too wide, and on either side of it...

"What *is* this?"

Instead of walls, two stories of prison cells with rusted iron bars lined the room. Some were open, some closed. At one end of the room, the bottom of a metal staircase emerged from the shadows of the second floor platform.

"A cell block at Missouri State Penitentiary, I think." Raji pushed himself up off the floor and helped Dot to her feet.

"What's so special about this place?"

Raji walked towards the nearest open cell and grabbed the bars. "These illusions are incredible. Some of the best I've ever seen." He pivoted back towards her. "This penitentiary was once known as the bloodiest forty-seven acres in America. There was a lot of death. And now they say it's haunted."

Dot shuddered. "Great. Do I need to add ghosts to the list of Made-Up Things That Are Turning Out To Be Real?"

"Don't be ridiculous. Ghosts aren't real. And any we run into here will be even less so."

He seemed to really enjoy assuring her that nothing was real. She wondered if he was assuring himself, too.

Going from two loud outdoor illusions to a deadly silent indoor one added an extra sense of creepiness to the scene. A creepiness that Dot didn't feel was necessary.

"I think we get it!" Dot yelled as Raji looked around. "You're really good at illusions!"

Her words echoed into the pressing silence. "And maybe also more of a psychopath than I thought," she added softly.

But the illusion remained.

"I don't like this one," she said to Raji. "The other two were clearly meant to amaze us, but this one…"

"Yeah, it *is* a little—"

Before he could finish, like some strong, invisible force had punched him in the gut, he flew backwards into the cell behind him. When he cleared the door, it slid closed with a hard metal *clank*. Dot ran towards it and began pulling at the bars, but the door wouldn't budge.

"It's okay! I'm okay." Through the bars she saw Raji climb to his feet, half hidden in shadow, brushing himself off.

"What was that?" Dot continued pulling at the rusted cell door, fighting the panic creeping into her chest. "These aren't supposed to be real. How come the door won't open?"

"He's showing off." Raji grabbed the bars from the other side and pushed, to no effect. "It's what people like him do," he added between grunts.

Clang!

A loud metallic sound sliced through the air.

"What was that? What did you do?" Dot asked frantically.

"That didn't come from in here."

Clang!

Their faces swung towards the noise. It came from the top of the rickety metal staircase. The shadowy part.

Clang!

Someone was coming down the stairs.

Dot faltered. Something was not right in her head. Whispering, hissing voices flooded her mind, manipulating her fear until it surpassed the level of being in a dark room with a strange noise. There was a pressing hopelessness weighing on her, an unrelenting feeling of powerlessness. She was shrinking beneath it, sliding towards the floor.

Raji reached through the bars and turned her head to face him. "Whoa, hey. Remember, this isn't real."

Clang!

She forced her attention back to the stairs, unwilling to be taken by surprise. Something was moving in the darkness halfway down. Whatever was coming towards them, it was causing the strange wave of foreboding. It connected itself to her from those shadows.

She reached to grab Raji's hands through the bars. "I don't want to do this anymore," she said. "Something's wrong."

"Okay, we're done now!" Raji yelled into the air. Again, no answer.

Clang!

She decided she didn't want to look after all. She lowered her head and closed her eyes.

I'm going to black out. Her eyes began to roll into her head as she slid further down the bars, slipping out of Raji's urgently reaching fingers.

Then the cell door between them evaporated, and she fell into his arms.

Relief replaced the terror as she buried her head in his chest. When the strange heaviness lifted, she tentatively cracked an eye open and directed it towards where the stairs had been.

Cuckoo Lou stood in front of the big metal door where they had first entered. She looked around. The chamber of illusions was now illusionless, back to the dark warehouse room it had been minutes before. A bright floodlight over the door framed Lou.

"Miss Dot. Are you alright?"

It took all her depleted strength to nod.

Raji held her head between his hands. He stroked her hair back into place as he searched her face. "Are you sure?"

"Yeah, it was just a weird panic attack or something. I'm okay."

By the time Raji helped her up, Lou was standing near them. "I'm so sorry about that. Did I frighten you? That illusion is my most popular around Halloween, so I thought I'd throw it in, but I really dialed back on the scares. Clearly not enough, though."

She wasn't sure how to answer. The illusion had been creepy, but she wasn't completely sure it's what triggered the panic attack. Raji's warning about the jinn made her wonder if it was just evil spirits.

Just *evil spirits. What world am I living in?*

"I have anxiety issues," she explained. "It was probably just a little too real for my brain to process. Like you said." From the corner of her eye, she caught Raji's skeptical frown and ignored it. "Those illusions were incredible. Are you sure you weren't teleporting us around the state?"

Lou's cheeks rounded as he beamed proudly. "No, I don't teleport. That's very high-level magic. Maybe one day, though. No, ma'am, what you just witnessed was one hundred percent not real. I am what I say I am. You're a kind woman, Miss Dot, and I really respect that. So I want to prove to you that I am the salt-of-the-earth honest man that I claim to be."

He reached to put a hand on Dot's shoulder, then glanced at Raji and lowered it back to his side. "I see I accidentally put you through the ringer tonight, and I do feel bad about that. Why don't you go get yourself a nice dinner, maybe take in a show, and I'll get things ready here. You can meet back here at, oh...midnight. Then we can set your genie free."

Her heart leaped. "You're gonna free him tonight?"

"I think it would be best to do it sooner rather than later. Don't you?"

She turned to Raji, who appeared equally stunned.

A few minutes later, they were getting back in the rental car as Lou waved to them from the other side of the dirty windows of his lobby. Night had fallen and Dot sat quietly in the darkness once she closed the door. But she didn't start the car.

"I can't believe he's willing to do this," Raji said.

She shifted to face him, no longer able to hold back her smile. "You're gonna be free."

But his expression didn't reflect her relief. "Dottie, something happened to you in there," he said somberly. "The jinn are there, inside that building. Maybe we can trust Cuckoo Lou, but we can't trust the spirits he's consorting with. They can sense when someone wants something so bad they'll do anything for it. They're trying to get your attention."

"You think I would sell my soul for your freedom? Wow, you are giving yourself a lot of credit," she teased.

But he didn't laugh.

The thing was, she *would* do anything to free him. But it didn't matter. Lou was taking care of it and Dot would ignore the jinn. They had nothing to offer her.

Besides, she couldn't let herself worry about things that were outside her control. She and Lou made a deal, and now the ball was in his court. They would just have to wait and see and pray that Lou was as reliable as he insisted he was.

She reached to start the car, but Raji grabbed her hand.

"We can come back to Branson anytime," he said. "Let me take you somewhere else."

Chapter 33

DOT

The time was almost at hand. Raji was keeping track of that, though. Dot's brain had no idea how to figure out the time difference between Branson and Saudi Arabia. All she knew was that here, it was already morning. The most beautiful morning she had ever seen.

They sat close together atop a golden sand dune, staring out at the infinite desert before them. The freshly risen sun cast large black shadows in the valleys, so dark they looked like holes in the sand. She used to think deserts like this only existed in the movies, or in Raji's original lifespan. But the proof was undeniable that she was wrong on both counts.

"I can't believe you used to live out here," she said.

"It's so strange to think about."

"It's always strange to be in a place where you existed as a different person once. You've lived a hundred lifetimes since the last time you were here."

"No," Raji objected. "I've barely lived at all since the last time I was here. Every moment I was out of that bottle, I was a plot device in someone else's story, with a few exceptions." He slid his hand up her arm, pulling her attention away from the view. "The past few weeks might be a microscopic amount of time in the big picture of my existence, but it's the most I've lived since my mortality."

A tingly warmth rippled across her skin from where his hand rested. "Is that why you're so immature for your age?" she asked.

His hand moved to her back, where his fingers played with her hair. "This morning, I tried Raisin Bran, so I'd say I've matured quite a bit."

The lighter mood was nice, but it didn't remove the tightness in Dot's stomach.

"Raji..." she said, looking for the familiar comfort in the brown eyes. "I'm completely committed to freeing you. I have been since I told you I called Lou."

"That was a good day." He smiled, but with reservation as he waited for her to continue.

"But I'm still me and..."

His expression softened and his smile relaxed. "You think because you're you, things won't happen the way you want them to?" He shook his head. "Dot, that is the least of my worries."

"I screwed up my other two wishes."

"How did you screw up your other wishes? Overall, they both went very well, I thought."

"Um...remember when I wandered off alone and got myself kidnapped in the first wish? And how I stupidly gave my mother ten thousand excuses to ditch me in the second one? And let's not forget how that also led to a little girl taking a stroll during a tropical storm."

"Dottie," he said, turning so they faced one another cross-legged on the dune. "Do you remember how with your first wish I gave you an enhanced set of instincts?"

"Yes. Why? Can you give me some more?"

"No," he laughed softly. "But I should tell you, I never gave you anything you didn't already have. The magic only gave you the confidence to act on your own instincts, maybe sharpened them a little, but it was *you* making the decisions. Have some trust in yourself."

"That's...a hard thing to do. And a hard thing to believe. That wish happened because I asked you to make it happen, but every other time I've found myself in a tough situation, my instincts are what led me there."

"Good instincts aren't the same as clairvoyance. There's too much about the future that doesn't depend on you. Tough situations happen, and when they do, your instincts will help you know the right things to do to get through them. Whether things work out perfectly in the end has little to do with it. It's a gamble."

She stared at him thoughtfully. "Your pep talks always end on a bummer, you know that?"

"You're not focusing on the point. Dottie, not many people could go through the things you've gone through and remain a good person. Your soul is solid, so you've obviously been listening to the right instincts your entire life. When we get back to Lou's, just keep doing that."

She watched the bright desert sun illuminate his face. She really liked his face, but no longer just for the absurd physical appeal. The honesty in his eyes, the humility in his smile, the way he looked at her like he couldn't believe *she* existed, captivated her.

She was still afraid to trust herself, but she had no qualms about trusting him.

"Okay," she said. "But you're saying it'll still be a gamble."

"You don't have to risk it," he blurted. The words rang in her ears as they stared at one another, and she knew what he meant was *it's okay if you bail*.

She turned and scooted until she was snuggled beside him, turning her neck to see his face. His arm wrapped around her shoulders and he pulled her in, pressing his forehead against hers.

"The only way I'm guaranteed to lose you is if I don't try," she whispered.

"So you're doing this for selfish reasons."

"You implied I'd get greedy. And I did."

He squeezed his eyes closed. "Thank you."

A thousand reasons to thank him back raced through her brain, but there wasn't enough time to get through them all. Besides, the more words she used, the farther she got from the point she was trying to convey. So she gently cupped his face and pulled it down until her lips met his forehead, and she held them there for a long second.

Then she lowered her head and laid it on his shoulder, and though she could feel the tenseness of his muscles and the trembling of his arm, he pulled her closer, and they stayed that way as they watched the last few minutes of the desert sunrise.

By the time this morning reaches the other side of the world, she thought. *Raji will be free.*

They were still shaking sand out of their clothes when they crossed the street to the old brick building. In the desert, the air had been hot and dry, but here it was chilly and rainy. Dot pulled her jacket around herself as they approached the shop, watching Lou smile and wave from the window. His smile seemed much creepier than before, but she chalked that up to the darkness and the rain. She wouldn't let herself get in her head about this. Not now.

Lou held the door open for them.

"Good to see ya!" he greeted. "I have good news! I think I've figured out exactly how to do this. It shouldn't take more than a few minutes."

Raji and Dot hurried into the lobby area, removing their jacket hoods as Dot watched Lou lock the front door from the inside via a small metal knob. The simple turn of a bolt was the only thing keeping them in. That was reassuring.

When she turned away, she caught Lou's eye. He straightened his hat and winked at her, and she prayed that it was a *I have this in the bag so don't you worry* wink.

The sorcerer pressed the tips of his fingers together and brought them to his mustache. "Now, there is one caveat."

"Which is?" she asked.

Lou clasped his hands together. "I will need the genie's vessel. Do you happen to have it with you?"

She looked at Raji and nodded, but he hesitated. "Are you *sure* you need it?" he asked Lou.

"It's your prison, isn't it? I can't let you out of a prison if I'm hundreds of miles away from it, now, can I?"

The answer seemed to be enough for Raji. He lifted his hand in the air and the bottle appeared in his palm. He handed it to Dot, and she tossed the bottle to Lou.

"Fantastic!" He turned it in his hands, studying it intently. "Look at this thing. Who would ever think there would be a genie in this hunk of junk? No wonder people kept missing it. I might've missed it myself." He tucked the bottle under his arm. "Okay, if you two will accompany me into the chamber—"

"Why would Dot need to go in?" Raji asked.

She watched for Lou's reaction. He paused.

"Well, if you want me to break your bond..."

"It isn't my bond with her that's the issue. It's whatever is binding me to that bottle that we want broken."

Lou tapped his chin, looking from Raji to Dot, then back to Raji.

"She can wait out here, if that makes you feel better."

"No!" she protested, turning to Raji. "What if it's painful? What if you need my support?"

Raji leaned towards her ear. "I think you should stay here, near the exit," he said softly enough that Lou couldn't hear. "I didn't see another way out in there last night."

"*You're* my way out," she whispered back.

"I'm more than happy to have you in the chamber," Lou interrupted with an inviting smile.

She frowned. She wanted to stay together, but for some reason her gut agreed with Raji. It felt smarter to stay near the door, where she could see the car.

"Fine." She flinched when she thought she saw Lou's brow furrow slightly under the rim of his hat, but when she looked again, his expression was as friendly as ever.

Everything is fine.

"Have a seat, then." He pointed behind her to a metal framed chair with blue padding that hadn't been there earlier. "Make yourself comfortable. Not sure how long this will take; I've never done it before."

Lou chuckled as he pointed towards the chamber door, but before Raji moved towards it, he pressed his lips to Dot's temple for a long second. A lump formed in her throat.

"I'll see you soon," he whispered.

Then her body began to shake. The anxiety she had been holding back for days flooded her nerves.

"I promise the chair is not an illusion," Lou said with a laugh. "Seriously, make yourself at home."

Then both men disappeared through the metal door. She jumped when it slammed hard behind them.

She barely gave the chair a second look; she needed to pace to release the tension. If only she could see what was happening, maybe that would help calm the queasiness in her stomach.

A thought occurred to her. Earlier, when she and Raji were in the chamber, the illusions changed at the most precise moments, like Lou could see them. Was that his magic, or could he really *see* them?

She tiptoed behind the long wooden counter. On the other side she discovered a desk littered with papers and empty soda cans. After a quick glance towards the door, she began moving papers around, a lot of which, she noticed, had the official seal of the IRS. After studying a few of the letters, it was clear that Cuckoo Lou owed a lot of back taxes. Apparently, there were some situations even sorcerers couldn't magic their way out of.

But the actual countertop still wasn't visible, so risking the noise, she scooped an armful of paper and soda cans to the side. Her eyes lit up.

Oh, thank goodness.

Installed on the face of the counter were two small monitors. On one screen, there was an image of the quiet street out front. On the other, Lou and Raji were standing in the middle of the chamber, empty of illusions and brightly lit. She pushed aside more junk, looking for a knob or button for sound. She found a switch above the monitors, below a small, inlaid speaker.

She clicked it.

"...I'll just place the bottle here for now."

She watched as Lou adjusted his hat, then bent and placed the bottle on the floor. Raji watched silently, arms crossed, glancing at the door every few seconds. He seemed impatient. She could relate.

"And I'll need you to sit there."

In a blink, a chair identical to the one Lou had conjured in the waiting room appeared behind Raji. He sat.

"Say, genie," Lou said. "I've done a ton of research on your kind, and I've come across some weird ideas about what you can and can't do, but since I got you here, maybe I can get some facts straight from the horse's mouth. You've already proven that you're not some legless, incorporeal, turban-wearing jokester. What else have we humans gotten wrong?"

"What does any of that matter?" Raji asked.

"You're right," Lou said. "It shouldn't matter. It really shouldn't."

But for an awkwardly long second, Lou didn't move. He stood with his hands on his hips, facing Raji. Dot wished she could see his face, but his back was to the camera.

The silence stretched on. Despite the graininess of the picture, she could see Raji's eyebrows gradually lowering as the two men stared at each other.

Then Lou turned around and walked towards the bottle on the floor. He picked it up and rolled it in his hands. He seemed mesmerized by it. Dangerously mesmerized.

His countenance darkened.

Oh no. Please, no.

"I...I really am a good man," Lou said, barely loud enough for Dot to make out through the speaker. "I wanted to help. But three wishes...three *free* wishes."

Raji started to rise from the chair. Then he started again. Then he began to struggle to stand. The chair seemed to stick fast to the ground, and Raji was stuck fast to the chair.

Her heart dropped. Her head began to spin.

"DOT!" Raji yelled. "Dot, *run!*"

She watched him snap his fingers over and over, but nothing happened. She slapped her hand over her mouth and looked towards the front door, towards the car beyond it.

If I get far enough away, Raji will bounce back to me.

An unfamiliar laugh echoed from the speaker, pulling her attention back to the monitor. It wasn't Raji's laugh, but it didn't sound like Lou's either. At least not the Lou she had been talking to.

"She can't hear you."

But it *was* Lou, his voice now low and arrogant.

"This room is soundproof," Lou went on. "She could be pressing her ear against the door and not hear a peep."

Raji struggled harder. "DOT!"

She bolted from behind the counter and headed for the front door. But a wave of nausea nearly sent her sprawling when she saw something completely different from what she had seen moments ago. At least five padlocks, locked from the inside, each requiring their own key, sealed the front door.

She yanked at them as Lou kept talking. "Unfortunately, I doubt she's got an ear to the door. She's got a chair just like yours. She's not going anywhere. She's probably realized that by now, but you wouldn't be able to hear her screams, either."

Ready to grab the chair to try to break the window, she halted when she heard Lou's words and stumbled backwards. She wasn't touching that chair.

"These traps are useless," Raji's voice said as Dot pitifully began ramming the glass door with her shoulder. "Sorcerers have tried tricks like this on me before. You can't steal a genie. And this isn't gonna hold me once Dot—"

"Oh, I know. I'm not trying to steal you. I just need you to stay out of it while I have a conversation with your master. I see now that you've managed to seduce her for your own selfish purposes. You *are* tricky. Lucky for that poor girl, I'm a good man."

The locks weren't budging. The windows weren't breaking. Dot had nowhere to go. She frantically scanned the room until her eyes landed on the brochure rack, moving to the scratched-out bathroom symbol on the wall behind it. If she couldn't escape, maybe she could hide.

Raji continued yelling her name.

"Could you calm down before I open the door?" Lou asked. "I don't want to scare her. Poor thing is probably frightened enough."

Dot struggled with the heavy brochure rack as she listened, praying that the door behind it wasn't locked. Finally, the rack fell, sending tourist information spilling across the grimy floor. She grabbed the knob to the hidden door and pulled. It swung open.

But it wasn't a bathroom.

It was a staircase leading into complete darkness.

Behind her, she heard the heavy latch of the chamber door lift.

Time had run out.

Chapter 34

DOT

I had to try. I had to.

As Dot stood alone in the lobby, the heavy chamber door began to open, and her world seemed to crumble for what felt like the millionth time in twenty-five years of life. All of this could have been avoided. Easily. But she loved Raji too hard. She wanted his freedom too much. She had gambled and lost.

The tinny sound of Raji's voice yelling her name shook her from her stupor. With less than a second to spare, Dot dove behind the counter, cramming herself in a corner underneath as Lou's heavy footsteps entered the lobby.

She held her breath and listened.

"What in the...you've got to be kidding me!" Lou exclaimed. "And she found my secret lair!"

His footsteps moved across the floor. Brochures flew past her as he kicked his way through them.

"What kind of maniac doesn't sit in the only chair in the entire room?"

The footsteps grew faint as they disappeared down the staircase. Dot didn't waste any time.

She hustled into the chamber and kneeled at Raji's feet, holding a shaking finger over her lips before laying her hands on his knees.

"Dot!" Raji breathed with relief. He smoothed her hair away from her face, then held her head in his hands. "Of course you didn't sit, you beautiful, smart, anxiety-ridden woman!"

"I don't know how much time we have. He went down a staircase in the bathroom and the front door is very, very locked. How do I get you out of this?"

"The bottle," he said. "You've got to command me to go back inside and then summon me again."

"What?" A wave of panic seized her. "But you can't unless I make another wish, which I am *not* doing."

"You won't have to make a wish." His hands dropped from her face and he lowered his eyes. "Dottie, I lied to you. I told you I can't be put back in the bottle while I'm in your service, but I can. I didn't want you to put me away when we first met. I had been in there for so long. I'm so sorry. I should've told you."

Her mouth fell open. She had never been so happy to have been lied to.

How can I be mad at that? And at a moment like this? "It's okay. I see why you did it. Maybe if I had learned that at the beginning I'd be annoyed, but it turned out pretty good for us, I'd say. Well, for the most part."

He smiled at her, but there was defeat in his eyes. It killed her to see it. Back in the lobby, watching it all fall apart, for a second she had felt defeated, too. Defeated and alone. But here with Raji, she had a clearer picture of what she was fighting for. He was worth it.

"Raji." She lifted his chin. "We *had* to try this. And now we know. Lou was trying to track me down, anyway. We would've had to face him, eventually. And now that we've met him, there is no way I'm going to let him be your next master."

The resignation in his eyes wavered, but it didn't completely go away.

She needed to make it go away, because she needed him on her team. Which meant she had to get that bottle.

But coming up with a decent plan on the spot wasn't a skill she possessed. "I'll follow him downstairs and I'll...I'll jump him or something..." she trailed off, biting her lip.

"You'll figure it out as you go," Raji said. "I trust you. Take it minute by minute. If you can just get the bottle and summon me, I can snap us out of here."

She placed a hand on his face. "I'm sorry," she whispered.

"One more thing," he said. "He's an illusionist. This room is airtight, that's why his illusions work so well in here. But anywhere that has doors or windows or cracks, you'll see where the illusion is leaking through, and that's how you'll know where it ends."

She nodded, holding back a reflexive whimper. She hadn't thought about the illusions.

"Okay," he urged. "Tell me to go back to my bottle."

The empty lobby was so littered with brochures that Dot had to step carefully to avoid slipping on the glossy paper as she repeated her piecemeal plan in her head.

Get the bottle, summon Raji, teleport to Timbuktu.

She kept to the side of the room, out of sight of the open bathroom/basement door in case Lou was working his way back up. She contemplated waiting for him at the top, so she could jump him and take the bottle there, but she knew she wasn't strong by any means. On the other hand, Lou certainly wasn't the kind of guy that knew what a leg day was, either. The only thing he had on her was mass. And there was a downside to mass. Mass slowed you down.

I'll just be faster.

Her plans sounded so easy in theory.

She flattened herself against the wall beside the open door, listening for the sound of footsteps, or the creak of a stair, anything to indicate he was still down there.

"I really needed you to *take a seat*!"

At the sound of Lou's voice, she dove to the floor. A heavy blast of air whipped over her head, ruffling her hair in its wake. She looked up to see the booby-trapped chair slide several inches. Scrambling to her feet, she launched herself through the open bathroom door, turning her head to catch a glimpse of Lou scowling on the other side of the counter before she tripped and tumbled down the stairs into the darkness.

A stomach-churning crack and a sharp pain shooting up her left arm greeted her at the bottom, where she landed in an unnatural heap on a solid floor. Above her, the light from the lobby trickled down the stairs for a brief second before it went dark. She struggled to her feet. Everything hurt, but nothing as much as her wrist, which she cradled gingerly against her chest. She clenched her teeth to keep from crying out from the pain, then reached a hand into the darkness to feel her surroundings.

The solid walls on either side of her indicated that she was in a hallway. Holding her good arm out in front of her, she felt her way forward, going from one wall back to the other in search of a door, a window, or anywhere to hide.

Then a dim light appeared at her feet. A dark green spot formed on the ground and began to spread.

But she kept moving, feeling, trying to keep the tears of pain on the backside of her eyes. The space brightened slightly, and though she knew she was still in the hallway, it did not look like one.

In every direction, rolling hills covered in mossy, crumbling tombstones dominated her vision.

"This guy *is* a psycho," she moaned. A headstone appeared directly in front of her, stopping her in her tracks. Like the iron bars in the fake penitentiary, it was sturdy and immovable, but she was able to climb over it, fighting to ignore the pain screaming at her from her injured limb.

"Oh, Dot," Lou's voice echoed sweetly from somewhere behind her. "I need to talk to you. I'm not going to hurt you. I only want to reassess our original agreement. That genie is not to be trusted. He's using you."

Be faster.

On the other side of the tombstone, she pushed herself, darting around more graveyard obstacles and keeping her eyes to the ground. A few times she slammed into a block of solid air—what she deduced to be a camouflaged wall—until finally she found what she was looking for: an unnatural blurring near her feet. The illusion was leaking under a door, like Raji had said.

She pitched herself forward until she slammed into the hidden exit. Frantically, she felt for the knob and turned it, tumbling inwards and turning her head to check behind her as she did. Lou was getting closer. He was only a few yards behind, the tombstones in his path disappearing before he reached them.

"You don't want to go in there!" he yelled. "It's a dead end!"

Eager to disregard him, she slammed the door shut, feeling the wall on either side for a light switch.

A delirious giggle escaped her when she found one, flicked it, and the lights actually worked. A series of yellowy sconces lit up around the room.

Immediately, she locked and bolted the heavy wooden door. Next to it, she found a large shelf and pushed on it until it toppled over, blocking the entrance.

The handle jiggled. She scanned the wall for more furniture, and her eyes landed on a nearby cabinet that she figured she could knock over and add to her blockade.

She hurried to it and yanked it from the wall with all her strength, screaming in agony at the pain in her wrist. The cabinet came down and the sound of shattering wood and glass filled the room. Broken glass spilled from the drawers and cupboards, and she had to jump back to keep from taking too much shrapnel. Using her shoulders, she pushed the piece of furniture against the other.

Lou pounded on the door, shouting hysterically. "What are you doing in there? What is happening?"

Dot paused a second to really look around the room, suddenly realizing where she was.

Lou hadn't been kidding. This was a bona fide secret lair.

Runes, crystals, vials, spellbooks—even a couple of cauldrons—covered every inch of surface space. Strange symbols adorned the walls, and weird odors filled the air. Using her shoe, she swept aside some of the broken glass, shuddering at the sight of the giant pentagram painted on the floor.

"This just got very dark."

Aside from all the empty soda cans scattered throughout the room, this place looked like Voldemort's home office.

Lou's pleading became desperate. "Don't touch anything! Please! That's my life's work in there! Let me in *now*! Let me in and I won't *kill you*!"

A solid wooden table against the far wall caught Dot's attention. Several overlapping tomes lay open on it. With the blockage holding firm, she took a moment to catch her breath and cry out loudly as she repositioned her arm, before making her way to the table.

A few of the books looked like they could be as ancient as Raji, while more of them looked like they had been recent purchases from some obscure section of a Barnes & Noble. Judging from the numerous sketches of middle-eastern lamps and solemn-faced, absolutely shredded genies scattered across the open pages, all of them had something to do with Lou's interest in Raji.

Despite the tremors of fear that ripped through her body with every crazed thump on the door, she took her phone out of her pocket and began snapping pictures. There were languages and words and symbols she didn't understand, but she could google them later.

"*Please!*" Lou shrieked. "I don't want to do this, but you're making me!"

She moved a book out of the way and her eyes fell upon a legal pad. She recognized the messy penmanship from Lou's letter.

But this was no letter. This was a list. Of about ten or twelve names. And the words at the top filled her with a dread so heavy the edges of her vision began to darken.

Other Magi Who Know About the Genie.

She leaned against the table for support, startling as the pounding on the door turned into sudden, erratic blasts. Whatever he was using to hammer with that much force had to be magic. The furniture blockade shifted slightly with every impact.

Her arm shook as she lifted her phone to take a picture of the list. As she did, the device vibrated in her hand.

The screen read, *Diane Mom*. Even amid the tense situation, it provoked a dramatic groan.

"How does she always know how to call at the worst possible time?"

A sharp *crack* grabbed her attention. She turned to find the blockade had collapsed and the door behind it had split down the center. Jamming the phone in her pocket, she hurried across the room to ram her shoulder against the cabinet to reinforce what remained of the struggling barricade.

Her phone vibrated in her pocket again.

"Heeeeere's Johnny!" Lou cried through the crack in the door, chuckling menacingly. "I've always wanted to do that."

"Go! Away!" Dot pressed against the blockade with all her strength, but she could feel it waning. The adrenaline helped, but it wouldn't be enough. Especially if—

A final mighty blast of air ripped through the door, sending wood, glass, and empty soda cans flying in every direction. Dot was thrown against a shelf full of crystals on the far wall.

She felt the air leave her lungs, but she still managed to pull herself up to sit. She couldn't turn her back on Lou.

The angry scowl on his face made him look like an entirely different person than the friendly man they had met hours before. He stepped over the chaos, stopping directly in front of her before kneeling down.

"You messed up my room," he growled. "It took me a lifetime and pieces of my very soul to acquire all of this!" She flinched as he violently drove his fist into the shelf beside her head, splintering the wood. "Why couldn't you just *sit down*?"

A pressing darkness filled the room; the lights flickered, the walls seemed to bleed, and Dot began to wilt. It was the penitentiary illusion times ten.

The jinn were here. They had come with Lou.

"You're just as treacherous as that genie! Did you just come to toy with me?"

The room returned to normal, lights on, walls free of blood, but before she could take a breath of relief, Lou lifted her by the neck and pinned her against the shelf behind her. "Here's our new deal. Make your last wish, and you get to live."

"Were you...were you ever gonna help us?" she gasped.

For the shortest second, he looked almost offended. "Yes," he said calmly. "Yes. But then I realized your genie is using you, and you've clearly fallen prey to his deceptions. The only way I can help you now is if you hand him over to me."

"I have a whole island now," she pleaded. "You can have it. Just...do what you said you were going to do. Please. You're not seeing things clearly. Why would we come to toy with you? We need your help. These soul suckers are the ones toying with you!"

His eyes darkened, and he gritted his teeth. "*I* am in control here! I am a *good* man who only desires the power to do *good* things!" Any self-control in his voice had gone. Now there was only rage. His hand tightened around her neck. Her vision began to fade.

Death by sorcerer. Not on my list of ways I thought I'd die.

Then his grip loosened. He blinked and his gaze shifted to his hand, which he quickly tore away from her neck. She slumped against the broken shelf, gasping for breath.

His eyebrows remained slanted as he cleared his throat. "Your last wish will have to be quick and easy. Something straightforward, so we can get on with this changing of hands. But no tricks! No wishing for the building to collapse. No wishing for lightning to strike me down. If you try any of that, I'll kill you before you finish your sentence, out of self-defense. Because I really, really don't want to kill you. I'm a good man, Miss Dot."

He reached behind his back. When he brought his hand forward, he held the bottle. The beautiful, ugly little bottle that changed her life. The one she needed to summon Raji. So close, but still maddeningly out of reach.

She felt a soft buzz in her back pocket. The beginning of an outrageously risky idea was beginning to form in her mind.

"Okay, I'll make a wish!" Dot blurted loudly to cover the sound.

"Smart woman," Lou said.

Her plan relied almost entirely on luck, that stupid human construct that normally left her high and dry. Maybe just this once, it would come through for her.

Lou didn't know Raji's complete rules, or else why would he ask about them? Her only chance was to wish for something Lou didn't realize was ungrantable.

Slowly, Dot reached into her pocket and pulled out her phone. Lou watched her guardedly as she placed it on the ground between them. "I wish," she began. "For my mother to call me and apologize. She knows what for."

Lou's beady eyes widened; an excited grin extended across his face.

"Ha! That's a good one! I mean, it's a terrible waste of a wish, but it should be over quickly." He looked down at the unmoving phone. Nothing happened. The excitement began to fade from his expression.

"Is this a trick?" His voice boomed and the lights flickered.

Dot stared at the phone, too, willing her mother to do what she always did and not take a hint.

The phone buzzed.

The relief almost made her finally pass out, but she fought to stay focused. Her life depended on it.

Lou looked at the name on the screen suspiciously. "Answer it. Make sure it's her. Put it on speaker."

Dot lifted herself to her knees and used her good hand to accept the call and switch it to speaker mode.

"Mom!" she cried. Her voice quivered with emotion. Diane had actually come through for her. She couldn't believe it.

Her mother's surprised voice echoed through the room. "Oh. Dot. I wasn't expecting you to pick up this late. And then after...well, you know. Listen, I wanted to call sooner but...I didn't know what to say."

Lou pulled the phone towards him.

"Is this Dot's mother?" he demanded.

"Who's this? What happened to Dot?"

"Dot's fine. Answer the question."

"Put me back on with my daughter, please!"

Lou nodded to Dot.

"I'm here, Mom," she said. "That was Lou. A...guy I know." She sneered at the sorcerer as she spoke.

"My gosh, Dot, and you accuse me of burning through boyfriends."

"Ugh, no! He's not—"

"Is there a reason for this call?" Lou demanded impatiently.

"I owe my daughter an apology, not that that's any of your business, *Lou*. Dot, could you take me off speaker, please? We really need to talk. Privately."

Dot wanted to throw her arms around Diane and give her another ten thousand dollars. Lou was buying it! A triumphant smile overtook his pudgy face.

"She'll call you back." Lou ended the call. Then he stood up, dropped the phone on the floor, and crushed it under his foot.

"Hey!" Dot protested.

"You got your wish. Now it's time for me to get mine!"

Her brain struggled to figure out her next move as Lou held Raji's bottle before him, greed gleaming in his eyes. Dramatically, he lifted his other hand and slowly rubbed the bottle.

He rubbed it harder. Then faster. Then he rubbed it in different places. "How the hell does this work?"

"It's complicated. It took me a week to figure it out," she said.

"Show me or I'll kill you."

And like his head on a platter, he presented the bottle to her. She could have cried. But instead, she retained her downtrodden demeanor, suddenly grateful for the acting practice she got from her dinner with Avros.

"Kill me then," she spat.

Lou yelled angrily, and his eyes flashed red. "Show me, *now*!" he demanded.

Dot took the bottle by the neck, struggling to downplay the joy she felt from holding it in her hands. "There's an incantation etched on the glass. I think I remember it. Um...here, put your hand on the bottle and repeat after me."

Lou gripped the bottle below her hand and gestured for her to get on with it.

"I command you to open..." Dot started.

One line at a time, Dot spoke the words and Lou repeated them, though Dot wasn't paying much attention to him. She just wanted Raji.

Dot's heart pounded in her chest. What if this didn't work? Could her mother have called as a result of Dot's false wish? It directly involved someone else's free will, but maybe she misunderstood what that meant. These things didn't always go according to plan. In Dot's case, they never did. It was hard to take all this at face value.

Then a plume of golden smoke filled the room, and Lou leaped to his feet and whooped loudly, dropping his hold on the bottle, which Dot quickly shoved inside her jacket. Still hurting and weak, she fell limply against the shelf as Raji appeared in the middle of the room between herself and the sorcerer, facing her, wearing those ridiculous puffy purple pants again.

Resummoning must be like a hard reset.

He fist pumped the air. "Dottie! You did it!—Dottie?" His excitement dissipated at the sight of her, heaped against the shelf, surrounded by glass and wood, covered in probably a million nicks and scratches.

"Nope, eyes over here!"

Dot nodded weakly towards Lou. Raji's jaw tightened, and he turned.

"Forget about her. You belong to *me* now," Lou sang.

She held her breath, hoping he'd know to play along.

Raji hesitated, then lowered himself into a bow.

"Your wish is my command," he said.

"Ha! Yes! I can't wait to rub this in everyone else's dumb faces! Genie, for my first wish, I wish to be the richest man in the world!"

Lou fell quiet as Raji straightened and took a step forward, lifting a hand into the air, balling it into a fist.

"Granted!" Raji said.

"Wow! Are you seri—"

As quickly as the giddy smile appeared beneath Lou's mustache, it disappeared as Raji's fist connected loudly with his face, sending him flying through the broken door and into the hallway.

Okay. Dot's throbbing body seemed to say. *You can pass out now.*

So she did.

Chapter 35

RAJI & DOT

Raji ran to the hole in the door to put eyes on the sorcerer's unconscious body. Satisfied that Lou was sufficiently incapacitated, he rushed to Dot's side.

She was out cold. He checked her pulse, even though he knew he'd be sucked back into the void if anything fatal had happened to her, which it wouldn't.

"Dottie." He took her face in his hands and shook it gently.

She groaned.

He ran his hands through his hair and exhaled a deep breath. Things were a mess. He'd always known this was a major possibility, but Dot made it difficult not to hope. He wouldn't be free tonight, or probably ever. Morning would come and things would be no different. And though his shattered hopes made his insides feel like how Dot's outsides looked, he loved her more than ever for trying.

Which also meant that he was hurting more than ever. The different forms of pain kept piling on.

He kneeled beside his master and took her into his arms, then through a kiss on the forehead, he gave her the magic equivalent of an adrenaline shot.

Her eyes shot open. "Where is he?" she gasped.

"He's out, but he won't be for long. Are you okay?"

"I feel weird," she said between rapid breaths. She scrambled out of his arms and sprang to her feet. "We have to get the staff."

Raji remained on his knees, the reality weighing him down. Dot still believed there was something she could do when it was so obvious that there wasn't. What a cruel, genius plan the jinn had conceived. The only people who had the power to free him were the ones who wanted his wishes the most.

Then Dot was kneeling in front of him. "What? What is it? We've got to move. We can search him for his staff while he's unconscious!"

Raji shook his head, his shoulders hunched as a different sting burned his eyes. The last time he had shed tears they had been joyous. The ones forming now were the exact opposite. "He's never gonna give up, Dottie." He lifted his head to meet her wild blue eyes. This would be a difficult suggestion to make, but he saw no other way. "You need to make your third wish."

She pursed her lips impatiently. "No. Come on, we've gotta go! Let's get the staff and it'll buy us some time!"

"Dot," he said firmly. "Destroying his staff is only going to give him more fuel to track you down and *kill* you. He's under their power. They've got him. These sorcerers think my wishes are free, but that's a joke. People corrupt themselves just to get their hands on me." His body throbbed. Every limb weighed a thousand pounds. But he lifted his hand to her chin. "Dottie," he breathed. "It might not be a bad idea to use a wish to erase all of this from your memory. Then you can pick up from where you left off before you met me, just much better off than you were; than you are now."

But it wasn't registering. Her expression remained unfazed as she stared at him for a long second. Then her eyes widened.

"It's his hat!" she exclaimed. "It's got to be. He's always touching it before he does anything skeevy."

"Did you hear anything I said?" he asked. "It doesn't matter! This isn't gonna work out! Not the way we want it to."

She sprang to her feet. "No!" she said, grabbing him by the arms and pulling him to his feet to meet her eyes. She grabbed his shoulders to steady him. "It *does* matter. Maybe eventually I'll have to let you go. Maybe you won't ever be anything other than a genie. But that is not what we should be worrying about right now. I'm not done fighting. I'm going to destroy that dumb Chiefs hat and spend every single second I can with you while I have the chance! It's the closest thing to free you're gonna get."

The room fell silent as they faced off. Her chest heaved. His body trembled. Then he looked over to where her hand gripped his bicep.

Everything hurt so badly. The intense pain circulating his system made every-thing foggy and bleak. But the points where she touched him felt different. Underneath her hands there was warmth. Comfort. Hope.

And it wasn't coming from him.

He put his hands around her waist and drew her into him.

The warmth spread to every corner of his body, neutralizing every ounce of his pain. He squeezed her tighter, burying his face in her hair, inhaling her soothing scent, pressing his lips to her head. "You're relentless," he whispered.

"Not usually." One of her hands slid up and down his bare back slowly, leaving relief in its wake. She laid a soft kiss on his neck. "But I could tell you really needed a pep talk. A good one."

Reluctantly, he let her go.

"Are you alright?" she asked, concern pulling at her mouth.

"I'm okay," he answered. With a half smile and a satisfied nod, she pulled him towards the hallway.

But when they looked out the hole in the door, they both groaned.

The shadowy bulk of Lou's unconscious body was nowhere to be seen.

"He's gone!" Raji rammed his fist into the door. This was his fault. He had stalled them.

"Okay, new plan," Dot said. "You look for him upstairs and I'll look down here. If you find him, get his hat and bring it back to me. If I find him, I'll destroy it on the spot."

He shook his head. "I'm not leaving you."

"Yes, you are," Dot stated. "Because I told you to."

With a frustrated grunt, he gave his assent.

She gestured to his genie pants. "You doing this in your legacy pants?"

Halfheartedly, he waved his hand and the outfit that Lou had found so under-whelming replaced his purple pants.

"Now get upstairs. And fight him if you have to. You're freaking immortal!"

He nodded, taking her in one more time, then snapped his fingers.

Once Raji was gone, Dot let her knees buckle under a wave of debilitating dizziness, leaning against an archaic stone lectern to steady herself.

They had entered damage control mode now. She, and now Raji, had come to grips with what they had lost as much as they could, and now she was grasping at parts of a plan in a desperate attempt to get out of here alive and still cosmically bound to Raji.

A shiver suddenly shot up her spine. The air wasn't chilly, but a coldness settled in her core. She looked around the room. Though not a single object moved, there was an odd vibration in the air. Like the shadows were breathing.

The jinn had gotten to Lou, and now they were trying to get to her. But she would be careful. She didn't want anything from them.

Or did she?

She shook her and turned towards the hole in the door, but the thought clung to her, and in a moment of morbid curiosity, she stopped.

There were voices in her head, but not voices. Thoughts that weren't her own were appearing like raindrops in a puddle, making ripples that echoed across her mind.

We're the ones with the power, they said. *Not the chubby man.*

And we can give it to you.

It won't cost much, and there's no other way.

There's no other way.

An image materialized in her mind. An image of her...*crushing* Raji's bottle in her fist right before his eyes. A hero. A fighter. Someone who *took* the things she deserved instead of watching them slip through her fingers.

We can help you get what you want.

Her own thoughts were becoming murky, blending with the voices. She winced and squeezed a clump of sweaty hair with her good hand as her balance faltered.

"Shut up!" she yelled.

And they did.

Thank you. She didn't need that confusion right now. Her priority was to defeat the evil sorcerer so she and her genie could teleport far away from all these demons.

Her reality had certainly changed a lot in the past month.

With a deep breath and rush of courage, she crawled over the broken furniture and through the hole in the door. She emerged into the dark hallway, only to find it wasn't a dark hallway. And it wasn't a cemetery either.

It was a freaking hall of mirrors.

The lobby loomed dark and still. A dull, blinking light from a glitchy streetlight outside dribbled in through the foggy glass. Raji surveyed the room, scowling as his eyes passed over the lone chair in the corner. Dot could argue all day that she had defective instincts, but for someone who liked to be comfortable, it was no coincidence that she chose not to take a load off the one time doing so would come with dire consequences.

His body still tingled from her touch, and though the warmth was fading back into perpetual pain, the renewed determination that came with it remained. And as someone with an excessive amount of firsthand knowledge about human souls, he thought he understood why.

His soul had broken, and hers had healed it.

Their souls responded to one another in profound ways, he already knew that. But that kind of connection was something he never thought he would experience, or could. It was power stronger than anything he could replicate, and something that the jinn couldn't smother.

In a sense, he and Dot's cosmic bond had just leveled up to something far beyond a servant and a master.

A shuffling noise coming from the chamber tore him from his thoughts. The door stood wide open, but there was only blackness beyond it. He didn't want to go in there. He wanted to go back to Dot. But if Lou was lurking around up here, at least that meant he wasn't lurking around downstairs.

He snapped his fingers again and faced the open chamber door from the opposite side, now seeing the dull light of the lobby from the darkness he had been peering into the second before.

Then the door closed.

"Nice try," he mumbled. He held his hand up to snap back to the lobby.

"Is there a reason she sent *you* after me, genie?" Lou's voice said quietly near his ear. "Doesn't she realize you can't harm me?"

Got him, Raji thought.

With a wave of his hand, he turned on the lights, ready to snatch the hat off the sorcerer's head.

But when he could see clearly, he realized he'd have to come up with a different strategy. Because he was standing in the middle of a sea—a sea of identical metal framed chairs with blue padded seats. And standing atop one a few feet in front of him, with an unstable look in his eye, was Lou.

"Don't worry," Lou trilled. "Not all of these are traps. Only one or two. I know what you're after, genie," he adjusted his hat. "But I have a better proposition."

"I *really* hate sorcerers," Raji complained.

Lou began leaping from one chair to the next. "If you want to be free so badly, tell the girl to make her last wish, let me be your master, then I'll free you after I get my wishes. I'm a good man! I really can help you."

"Yeah, you have a solid track record of helping people you promised to help." Raji watched Lou carefully, waiting until he was positioned to leap to the next chair. Then he waved his hand.

A brick wall appeared in Lou's path. The Missourian hit it like a bug on a windshield and collapsed into a mess of toppled chairs.

With his master's instructions fixed in his mind, Raji kicked chair after chair out of his way, clearing a trail through the sea until he reached the spot where Lou was staggering to his feet.

"That was cheap! It isn't fair that she gets her wishes. I deserve mine, too!" Lou stumbled backwards as Raji arrived where he stood.

"You're talking to the wrong guy about fairness," Raji said. He leaped at the sorcerer.

He had the large man pinned immediately, but as he placed his hands on the cap, Lou vanished and Raji came away with fistfuls of air.

"I don't want to kill your girlfriend," Lou yelled, standing on a chair fifty feet away. "I've never killed anyone! I'm a good guy!"

"I thought you couldn't teleport!" Raji shouted. With another wave of his hand, a single brick appeared in his fist. He flung it at Lou, who vanished before it struck.

"Who says I'm teleporting?" Lou yelled, now a distance behind Raji. "I'm an illusionist. You shouldn't trust everything you're seeing."

As if on cue, the sorcerer's sinister giggle began to multiply as Cuckoo Lou decoys appeared on every chair, their smiles giving credence to the sorcerer's nickname.

Raji turned around slowly, looking carefully for the one out of sync with the others. When his eyes landed on the only non-laughing Lou, he took the risk. He snapped himself onto the chair next to that Lou, knocking the decoy who had been standing there into another until an entire row of them began toppling like dominoes. Raji grabbed Lou's hat with both hands, yanking with all his might. It stuck tight. "Why won't your stupid hat come off!" he yelled.

Lou kicked Raji in the knee, making him momentarily lose his balance. Then Lou's fist connected with Raji's stomach.

Ouch. Definitely the real Lou.

He fell through a crack between chairs and hit the concrete floor.

But living the past few days in a constant state of pain had increased his tolerance for it, and he got to his feet quickly. Just in time for a blast of rock solid air to lift him, propelling him through the chamber, sending up waves of blue chairs and laughing Lou's in its wake until his back met the wall. Hard.

If not for his immortality, his spine would have cracked. It didn't, but he still got to experience what it would feel like. Around the room, the laughing Lou's melted away, followed by all the blue chairs but two. The lights flickered. With his hands thrust forward, the real Lou held Raji against the wall with his magic, stepping towards him with an infuriated sneer and flames in his eyes.

"You can't fight me, genie. I know you're not allowed to kill anyone, and you're only powerful when you're working for someone. You can't do anything to me. Now, your girlfriend will be up here in a minute. Convince her to make her last wish. If you don't, I'll kill her. And it'll be your fault, because I really didn't plan on killing anyone. I'm the nicest man you'll ever meet."

The lights went out and the force holding Raji to the wall disappeared. He fell to the ground and, just for a moment, let himself disappear into his pain.

"This place has now ruined carnivals, cemeteries, and the state of Missouri for me," Dot muttered under her breath. "I guess this is what I get for calling it a funhouse."

Her frightening reflection, multiplied a dozen times, stared at her from every angle. She cringed, and they all cringed back. She took off her jacket to examine her hurt arm, which was swelling gruesomely at the wrist. After fashioning a sling, she took a closer look at herself.

"It's been a night."

A smattering of tiny, bloody cuts covered her legs and there were dozens of little rips in her clothes. She touched the side of her brow, where she found an ugly blood-matted scrape she didn't even know she had, probably thanks to the fall down the staircase.

She looked a mess. Yet, a smile formed on her lips. Because she also looked strong. Fierce. Alive. Her eyes glowed with brazen determination, something she hadn't ever seen them do before now.

She trusted the woman in the mirror. She was tough.

"I'm coming for you, Lou," she growled.

She placed her hand on the reflection directly in front of her and pushed. The mirror was solid, but so had been the tombstone and the bars of the prison cell, even though they weren't real. Maybe her brain was tricking her into thinking it was solid and she needed to figure out how to prove to herself that it wasn't.

She kicked the mirror hard. The bang echoed, but the mirror didn't crack. She kicked the mirror to her left with mostly the same result, with one difference. Her foot throbbed with pain, even though she had kicked the other mirror just as hard with no such reaction. This truly felt like kicking a cement wall.

"If it's not real, it can't hurt me," she reasoned.

She kicked the first mirror harder. The glass began to splinter until it finally shattered. She kicked the remaining shards away and stepped through.

Still more mirrors, this time on more sides. She experimented with a few more kicks and punches until she found another false reflection.

This is taking too long.

"Lou, I'm right here! Come get me!"

No answer.

Her resolve was weakening. Her reflection was starting to look exhausted.

"I don't know what to do," she moaned, resting her head against the glass. She closed her eyes.

How can I still feel this fake mirror when I'm not even looking at it? she wondered. Without opening her eyes, she imagined the hallway.

And her body fell forward.

She shrieked with triumph, but when she opened her eyes, there was still a wall of mirrors before her.

"So, what? I have to close my eyes and picture where I really am instead of looking at it and getting tricked?"

She closed her eyes. When she put her arm out, she felt cold glass. Then she imagined a hallway...and propelled herself forward.

After a few painful bumps into the wall, she tripped against the narrow staircase sooner than she expected. When she opened her eyes and looked behind her, all she saw was a dark, empty corridor.

"Argh!" she screamed with clenched fists. "So pointless!" She floundered up the stairs as fast as she could and emerged into the lobby—right into Raji's arms.

"Raji!" she cried, burying her face in his neck. "If you're an illusion, I swear I will punch you in the throat."

"It's me," he said, pulling her close, and she knew it was the truth. He smelled like the desert and his arms felt like home. Lou could never reproduce that.

She looked up at him. Just like the infamous night after the airplane hangar, he didn't have a scratch on him, but he looked rough. "Did you get it?" she asked with the last bit of hope she had left.

He shook his head, and her heart dropped. "I don't know where he went," he said, his voice weak. He gestured towards the window. "But I think we should go while we can. He has the advantage as long as we're on his turf. All these enclosed spaces for illusions and the jinn getting in his head make it hard to know what's real."

"So you think it would be easier to get his staff if we lured him away?"

In unison, they turned their heads towards the grimy window, to the car beyond. Dot shifted her eyes to the front door. The assortment of locks that had been there earlier were gone. The turn of a metal bolt was the only thing standing between them and the outside.

She looked at Raji, and he looked at her.

Then they were on the move. Raji turned the bolt, and they were out on the street.

"Do you have the phone I used for the first wish?"

"You need it now?" he asked.

"Yes, while I'm thinking about it." She glanced back at the building, still shadowy and silent.

With a swirl of his wrist, the phone appeared, and he tossed it to her before running around the car to the passenger side.

Dot quickly brought up the contacts. There were only two. *Prince Scumbag* and *Agent Lydia Daines*. She tapped on the FBI agent's phone number and typed out a text message before she opened the car door. If Raji couldn't defeat Lou by magic, maybe she could nab the FBI another criminal. It was worth a shot.

"Dot!"

Across the roof of the car, Raji pointed past her.

A few yards away, on the other side of the street, stood Cuckoo Lou. Arms folded, a stupid grin plastered across his two-timing face.

Perfect. Just in time for the chase.

Then something caught her attention. The nearby streetlight lit up the spot where Lou stood, and there was an unnatural fuzziness near his feet, like a blur between the ground and air.

And even though it had been raining, the ground wasn't wet. And the glitchy streetlight wasn't glitching.

Dot dropped the phone on the ground.

She turned. "Raji! Don't get in the car!"

It was too late. He was in the car, which melted away around them, leaving nothing but two metal-framed, blue padded chairs in a large, windowless, warehouse-like room. One of which, Raji was now stuck to.

They were back in the chamber.

Chapter 36

DOT

Lou stepped across the threshold of the chamber's entrance and pushed the heavy door closed behind him.

"What do you have against *sitting down*?" he yelled at Dot.

They were back where they started. Nothing gained. Everything about to be lost.

"This is SO STUPID!" Dot shouted through clenched teeth.

Lou raised his arms, and she knew she had mere seconds before he hit her with a blast powerful enough to knock her into the trap. Then there'd be nothing to stop him from killing her while Raji watched helplessly.

If I have to fail, do I really have to fail this *miserably?*

"You've lost the chance for any more wishes," Lou roared. "You're forcing me to make my first kill and that makes me *really upset*!"

The lights flickered. He drew his arms back.

"You know what? No," she said. "Dot freaking Dudley does not fight for nothing."

Her face hardened. Her pulse quickened. Her nostrils flared. She zeroed in on the Chiefs hat, letting the fear and frustration bleed into her veins to fuel her.

Then she snapped. Screaming like a rabid banshee, she ran straight at Lou.

The horror in his eyes filled her with grotesque delight as she threw all her weight against him, tackling him to the ground. With her injured arm, she elbowed him in the face while yanking at his hat. But the thing seemed to be glued to his bulbous head.

She screamed as he grabbed her injured arm and twisted it away from his face. In her moment of weakness, she fell to the side, giving Lou time to get to his feet, bolting for the chamber door.

But she wasn't done. She flew after him, slamming her body into his as he tried to push the door open. He fumbled forward, and she launched herself onto his back, wrapping her good arm tightly around his neck and yanking at his hat with her injured one, even pulling at the hat with her teeth to relieve some of the stress on her aching appendage.

In the meantime, Lou fumbled with the door while trying to shake her. He got it open and staggered into the lobby, haphazardly slamming her against the walls and the counter, but she wouldn't let go, no matter how much it hurt.

The room melted into a muggy rainforest. It melted again and again, at hyper speed. It was a snowy Christmas village, then they were in an old country store, then at a rodeo, then on a rollercoaster platform. Lou rotated through illusions faster and more chaotically, all the while Dot clung to his back, pulling on the hat.

Her strength began to wane, and the pain pulsing through her body almost forced her to give up, when suddenly, Lou slipped on something and they both went skating across the room.

She looked up, seeing a sight that once made her shudder, but now gave her hope. As each scene around them rapidly melted into another, the lobby remained in the mix, and Lou, slipping and sliding on brochures, was heading straight for the only chair in the entire room. Like a rider on a runaway horse, she did her best to steer him true.

He hit the chair and Dot swung herself away, using the last bit of her pull to ensure he stayed on target. And when he did, with a cartoonish *pop!* the Chiefs hat came off his head into her hand.

The illusions ceased. Lou struggled and strained in the chair, then in desperation, his hands flew to his bald head. A cry of unbridled horror ripped through the air. A victory chorus to Dot's ears as she lay on the ground behind him, her exhausted lungs heaving.

Huh. She thought deliriously. *I got the thing I wanted to get.*

Holding the hat close to her chest, she crawled towards the chamber, giving Lou a wide berth. He grabbed at her, on the verge of tears; it took great restraint not to approach him and add her fist imprint to his face next to Raji's.

At the chamber door, she pulled herself to her feet.

"You got it?" Raji cried when he saw her.

Still wheezing, she held up the hat and dangled it in the air with a triumphant smile.

"Yes! I knew you could do it!" He pumped his fist in the air.

A spell of dizziness overtook her, and she slumped against the door frame.

"Dottie, hey. I know you've been through a lot, but you've got to destroy that thing. Right now. Don't wait."

She brought the hat in front of her and examined it. It looked like a regular old hat.

Then something nagged at her consciousness...

"Raji," she said, her eyes fixed on the hat. "If I put this on, maybe *I* can free you."

Raji lurched forward, but the chair held him firmly in place. "No. No, no, no," he pleaded. "I told you. It's not your power. It wasn't paid for with your soul. Don't let them bait you with it!"

Still, it held her attention, like it wanted her to try it on. Get a preview of what this kind of power felt like. Lou got to know, and so did Raji, in a way. The hat in her hands told her she deserved to know, too.

She popped it onto her head.

"Dot, don't do that!" Raji yelled.

Gradually at first, and then in a rush, she felt it. *Power*. Real power. Power to bend space and time to her will, power to take anything that she wanted, power to crush her enemies. Power to pound Raji's bottle into dust.

She looked over her shoulder at Lou. He looked more like neighborly-Missourian Lou again, but with a terrified expression. No more smug grin on that face.

As the otherworldly power preview pumped through her body, the pain from her injuries calmed, and so did her mind. Straightening herself, she focused on Raji.

"What if this is the only way?"

"Dot, you've got to take that off and destroy it. I've seen the effects this kind of magic can have on even the best people. It's all lies. It won't help you. It will ruin you."

"But it will *free* you," she replied. "Tell me if you really think there's another way."

His face fell. It didn't seem like he thought there was another way.

But something made her pause, something deep inside her. A voice that she had always been hesitant to trust until Raji had come along. Maybe this was a good time to see what it had to say.

She closed her eyes.

And she dug deep.

First, she pushed aside her anxiety, her uncertainty, her fear, and her doubt. They were all pretty dense, like digging through wet cement, and it took her a minute.

Then, she shoved aside the shadows that were gathering on her soul like moths on a lightbulb. Interestingly enough, those were easier to move out of the way.

Then she opened her proverbial eyes and stared straight at the proverbial light within herself.

What do you *think?* she asked. Proverbially.

I think you're being an idiot.

Her instincts were rude.

Think about it. What's the illusion here and what's the truth?

The truth? The truth was that there were things she didn't have control over. Things that Raji didn't have control over. Things that no one, human or otherwise, had control over, no matter how much they tried to convince her that they did. But that didn't mean she didn't have control over anything.

When her eyes blinked open, they fell directly on Raji, who seemed to be holding his breath as he watched her. But when their eyes met, he flashed her a sad but encouraging smile.

She felt all tingly with his brown eyes on her like that.

Tears filled her eyes, and she quickly brushed them away. He made her feel so much like herself. She was beginning to really like who she was. If she was going to give a piece of herself to anyone, she wanted to give it to someone who liked who she was, too.

She lifted the hat from her head and dropped it on the floor. A few yards away, Raji doubled over to heave a sigh of relief.

"Now, please," he said. "Destroy that hat."

Her eyes fell upon the unassuming cap at her feet, and then, she stomped on it. It exploded into dust.

A scuffling noise arose from the lobby behind her. Dot turned to see Lou, freed from his chair now that the magic holding him there had been destroyed. Without looking back, he disappeared out the front door.

Dot started to chase him, but as she passed the counter, flashing blue and red lights lit up the front of the building. Police vehicles were pulling up on the once dead street, and she watched with sweet gratification through the foggy glass as a powerless Lou was tackled, handcuffed, and placed under arrest.

Raji appeared beside her, sliding his arm around her waist and squeezing her gently. "You texted the police? I didn't know that was possible."

"No." She turned to face him, placing her uninjured hand on his chest. "I texted our old pal Lydia Daines. Said I found her another criminal and to send help. But I never got around to sending her the address, so I guess she just tracked the signal. She's good."

"Why would the FBI care about Lou, though?" he asked.

Dot nodded towards the counter. "Lou has an impressive pile of federal warnings and subpoenas over there. They might care about that."

She faced him, studying him intently. "Are you okay?" she asked. "Are you in a lot of pain?"

"Eh, I'm used to it. I'm much more worried about you. Are *you* in pain?"

"Oh, yes. Very much. Pain *and* shock, in fact—"

She whirled around and doubled over to vomit on the floor, sullying a pile of brochures for a pirate-themed dinner theater as Raji held her hair back. She turned to him as she wiped her mouth on her sleeve. "Maybe we should have them call me an ambulance," she said.

Raji turned to the window. "Yeah. But since no wish is in play, I might raise some unnecessary questions. Should I...should I wait in the bottle?"

"No way. Can you do like you did at my work and hang around somewhere where no one will see you?"

He nodded weakly. "I would help if I could."

"I can handle it." She straightened herself. "I just defeated an evil wizard. I think I can answer a few questions by myself."

He brushed his fingers down her cheek, pushing some matted hair behind her ear, then with a reluctant frown, he snapped his fingers, vanishing into thin air.

Once outside, she asked an officer to call an ambulance, then sat on the curb and waved at Lou as he was driven away, his head pressed forlornly against the back window of a cop car. Dot couldn't help it. She pulled Raji's bottle out of her jacket and waved it in the air with a smirk until the car was out of sight, tucking it away just as the lead investigator approached her to introduce himself.

"So you're the one who alerted my colleague," he stated as they shook hands. "Thanks. We've been trying to nail this guy for years. He's committed every sort of fraud you can imagine across several states under various aliases. He's slippery."

"I don't think you'll have an issue with that anymore," Dot said. "As long as you keep him away from his demon worship dungeon downstairs."

The agent cringed. "Fantastic. Thanks for the heads up."

She answered his questions as honestly as she could, leaning into Lou's obsession with getting her bottle, stating he believed it housed a genie. Dot even let the agent see the bottle and give it a rub. By the time the ambulance arrived, no one was questioning Lou's cuckoo-ness.

After spending the rest of the night in the hospital getting her arm fitted for a cast, she was left to take a long nap. When she woke up, Raji was sitting beside her bed, eating a bowl of cereal, a *visitor* sticker stuck to his shirt.

"They said you're ready to be discharged," he said, swirling his cereal away. "And I told them I'm your ride."

It was already dark in Florida by the time Raji snapped them back to the single-wide. Dot figured she'd be happy to be home. But the instant they were alone, the emotional dam within her that had miraculously held steady for the better part of the last twenty-four hours gave way. Her body shook and tears filled her eyes.

She dropped her head, unable to look at Raji, and took her keys out of her pocket, throwing them on the coffee table a little harder than she needed to.

Raji stepped towards her and pulled her to his chest. She wrapped her arms around him—even the one in the cast as much as she could—and leaned into him as her body shuddered with sobs.

"It'll be okay," he soothed. "As long as you don't make a third wish, I can stay."

"But you won't be free. And there are more sorcerers looking for you. I found a list in Lou's lair."

"Of course you did." He sighed. "Have I mentioned that I hate sorcerers?"

"I'm sorry. I wanted you to have your own life and make your own choices."

"Hey." He eased her back enough so he could study her face, and her body calmed under his gaze. Her lungs found their rhythm when he leaned in to kiss away the tears on her cheeks. "It's not ideal, I know," he said. "But you did get me some freedom. Any time with you *is* freedom."

In vain, he attempted to stifle a wince.

"You're in pain, though," she argued. "You're not really free."

His eyes buried themselves in hers. "It is *nothing* compared to the agony I would be in without you."

Dot blinked back more tears. She didn't see herself as the kind of person who should be on the receiving end of love like that. Though her first impulse was to balk at it, she stopped herself and let the words sink into her soul. Like they were pieces of his.

"You're probably required to say that to all your clients," she said.

He laughed, pulling her close to him again. She closed her eyes and nuzzled her face into his neck. It wasn't permanent, but at least they were together, for now. And there was no way she would be taking that for granted.

Chapter 37

DOT

To make things less weird, they decided that going forward, Raji should live as normally as possible: he would eat regular meals, sleep during the night, and have a wardrobe of store-bought clothing. Dot even began teaching him to drive her car.

Meanwhile, with a chunk of her millions, Dot bought a modest farmhouse outside Tallahassee. It had a big kitchen for Raji to practice cooking in, and no neighbors for miles as a bonus for Dot. Breaking her rental contract with Yasmin and Jorge wasn't fun, but to make up for it, she got them a new tenant. Shortly after Raji and Dot returned to Tallahassee, so did Diane, penniless, boyfriendless, and unsure if she would be wanted. After a few difficult conversations and a pledge from Diane to find a job and take self-reliance classes, Diane moved into the single-wide. It was the least she could do for the woman who unknowingly saved her life, and having Yasmin as a landlady would hopefully give her mother a lesson in humility. There was still a lot of healing and forgiving to do, but Dot always knew those things would take time.

For Raji, part of living a normal life meant dating Dot like a modern gentleman, and with his finger-snapping still enabled, he could take her out all over the world. They ate paella by the ocean in Spain, took walks on the Great Wall of China, and went ice-skating in Norway. Dot's favorite place, however, remained her island. With all the staff dismissed after the wish had ended, it was only the two of them when they visited, and she preferred it when people weren't around. Raji excluded.

But though Raji was happy to pretend he was a normal(ish) person, there were still plenty of reminders that he was still a prisoner.

First and foremost was the constant pain. It ebbed and flowed, but never fully stopped. He swore that being near Dot helped to ease it, but it still broke her heart every time she caught him struggling to hide a wince or stifle a moan.

Three months after the Cuckoo Lou showdown, Dot really began to worry about him.

His bottle lived on the mantle in the living room. One day, she walked in on him holding it in his hands, staring at it.

"What are you up to?" she asked in a forced casual tone.

He quickly placed the bottle back on the shelf. "I'm okay. I'm just...having a day," he said.

"Tell me about it."

She could tell he didn't want to, but she had inadvertently commanded it. He took a deep breath. "There's a constant pressure inside me, Dottie. To fulfill my purpose. The power I hold demands to be used as it was intended, and by ignoring it I'm fighting against it, and it...it can be exhausting, to say the least."

Dot struggled to keep her composure as she moved her eyes to the bottle in his hands.

"You can go back in there for a little while, if you want. Will that help?"

"No! No. I'm trying to live like a regular person. If I go back in...it will only remind me that I'm not."

She didn't know what to say to that, so she didn't respond.

"I'm sorry," he finally said. "Please forget I mentioned it. I don't feel this way all the time. Sometimes there are just days, you know?"

But she didn't know, and she couldn't forget. And Raji knew she couldn't. She pretended to sleep at night, but she knew that their cosmic bond told him when she was awake and alert, yet he pretended to sleep, too. When night came, it only found them both staring at the wall in different directions, secretly worrying about one another.

More concerning to her was Raji's relapse into servant mode not long after the bottle incident. He took over all the housework, prepared all the meals, and waited on Dot hand and foot. He insisted on sleeping in a separate room. He kissed her less when she only wanted him more. It was all very disconcerting, but she didn't say anything for fear it was the only way he could alleviate his pain and his purposelessness.

It afforded Dot a lot of reflection. In a room of her house that she hadn't found a use for yet, she set up her laptop. With the help of the internet, she attempted to decipher the pages she had taken photos of in Lou's lair, hoping to come across some alternate method to free him. But the more she learned, the more she realized Lou probably knew all along he couldn't free Raji without asking the jinn for help. They really had not made it easy.

She looked at the list of other sorcerers frequently, wondering if any of them would have some advice. They were thoughts she quickly shut down. There would be no seeking them out this time. Anything with the potential to put a cap on Raji's stay was not an option.

But she knew it was only a matter of time before they had another one on their tail, and she was growing more disheartened by the day.

She confided in Skye when she came over for lunch one day, a lunch that Raji prepared, served, and cleaned up, leaving them alone to sit in the sunroom with their iced tea.

"I'm worried about Raji," Dot admitted.

Skye cocked her head. "Do you think he's unhappy?"

Dot thought for a second. "I think he wants to be happy, but the powers that be didn't include that in his blueprint. So he wanders around acting like my butler to keep from falling into a deep depression. On top of that, he can barely touch me without experiencing a cosmic heart attack. I want his life to be his; I don't want him to just exist under my direction. It's not fair."

Skye placed a hand on Dot's shoulder. "You know, there was a time when I was a teensy bit jealous that you got a genie. Just a teensy bit. I kind of wanted him, but, obviously not to the point where I would murder you or anything."

"Your point?"

"Now I can see that you two belong together. You love each other. Hard. Keep him as long as you can, but if you need to test different wishes out to free him, use your third one, then give him to me and use all of mine. Whatever you think will help."

"That's really nice, but it's already been proven he can't free himself. But maybe—I don't know. Maybe granting a wish will refresh him? I honestly have no idea what to do." Dot couldn't help it. She began to cry.

Skye rubbed her arm sympathetically. "I know, it's completely messed up. If I could meet the wizard douchebag who did this to him, I would—"

"Dottie, are you okay?" Raji poked his head in the door.

Skye waved him away. "She's fine, she's on her period."

Five months had passed since Lou.

Five months? Is that really all I get?

It was a Friday night, and at her wit's end, Dot had finally talked herself into at least discussing with Raji the idea of letting him move on. She was terrified that he'd say yes too quickly, or that he'd say no out of obligation. And she wasn't sure which would hurt worse.

Even though he had already seen them all, she suggested to Raji a Harry Potter movie marathon. They were her comfort movies, after all, and she suspected she was going to need some comfort.

They watched the first movie in its entirety while they ate dinner. Raji had made Dot's favorite: Tikka Masala. He made it at least once a week.

"Chamber of Secrets?" Raji asked as the credits rolled.

She forced a smile. "Start it up."

The knot in her stomach was still too tight to start the dreaded conversation. She needed a little more Hogwarts exposure to loosen it up.

But then the second movie was almost over. Throughout it, Raji had tried to engage her by making silly observations and asking questions he already knew the answers to, but he clearly noticed her minimal responses. For the past thirty minutes, he had been stealing concerned glances at her. The time was at hand. She was going to do it. She was finally going to say something.

"Dot, what's wrong?" He beat her to it. "And if you say nothing, I will turn off this movie. Unless...you don't want me to."

They were sitting on Dot's new, not-saggy sofa; she leaned against the arm with her feet resting in Raji's lap. He rubbed them gently as he spoke.

"Why would you think something's wrong?" she refuted ambivalently.

"Since the day you found me staring at the bottle, you've been different. I shouldn't have said anything. I'm fine."

But she didn't believe him. "So...you don't miss having the breaks from being a slave?"

"Those were hardly breaks. And I'm not a slave. That's not the dynamic here."

She threw her hands up. "But it *is* the dynamic. There is no other dynamic. And it will always be the dynamic. And when you're not granting wishes—"

"I want to stay," he said simply.

"I know you *want* to stay, but you'll always be a little bit miserable."

"Of course I will," he retorted. "But I have no choice. You're right. I will always be *someone's* servant. If that's my fate and I can't escape it, I want to be yours as long as possible."

Dot huffed and turned back to the television. Anger rippled through her body. Not entirely at Raji, but at the hopelessness of the situation. Despite all the power at their disposal, there was nothing either of them could do.

On the screen, Lucious Malfoy was handing Dobby a book.

"Unless...this isn't working for *you*," Raji said, his voice so soft it was almost a whisper. "Then I would understand if you're ready to make your last wish."

She couldn't look at him. She closed her eyes, fighting back tears. Hearing him say it out loud filled her with guilt.

In the heavy silence that ensued, the house-elf on the screen cried out in disbelief. "*Master has presented Dobby with clothes. Dobby is* free!"

Dot had seen this scene a hundred times, but tonight, it hit different.

Her eyes snapped open.

Master.

A lightbulb turned on. Her chest tightened.

It was so simple, she'd feel like such an idiot if it worked, but *if it worked...*

Her heart pounded at the possibility. The wonderful possibility.

She sat upright and looked at Raji to see if he caught it, too. But he was staring off dejectedly.

"Raji!" she said. "Raji, I think...don't laugh at me, but I'm gonna try something."

He watched her as she crawled onto his lap and straddled him, pressing her forehead against his.

His hands slid up her sides. "What is it you're gonna try?"

She wasn't sure if there were exact words she needed to say, or how she would go about finding that out, so she decided to make something up.

She blew out a little breath. "Raji. I am no longer in need of your services."

He laughed. "Dottie, what—"

"As your *master*, I release you from your bond, er, our bond. I don't want you to serve me anymore. I don't want a genie. I'm done making wishes. Stop being my servant. Please."

He frowned and stroked her hair. "Dot...if only that was all it took—" He froze. "Your eyes...just...turned gold."

They both whipped their heads towards the mantle. His bottle began to vibrate.

So did Dot.

They watched it, eyes wide, mouths agape, as it trembled faster and faster and then—

POP!

It exploded into green dust that glittered and faded as it fell to the ground.

Raji's breaths became rapid. He wriggled out from under her and ran to the kitchen. She followed, shaking so much she could barely stand up straight.

"Raji. *Raji!*"

"I need something to—aha!"

He yanked a knife out of the block on the counter.

"Wait, what're you—Raji!"

He wrapped his other hand around the blade and pulled.

She watched in stunned silence as he slowly opened his hand towards himself. A wild grin formed on his lips. He turned his hand around for her to see.

She slapped both palms over her gaping mouth. Bright red blood began to seep from his wound, like ink spreading on paper.

"You're...you're..."

"I'm *bleeding!*" He stared at the blood dripping from his hand like it was his newborn baby, awe and exultation pouring from his eyes. "Dottie. How did you...?"

She pressed her hands against her forehead as words spilled erratically from her mouth. "I saw in the movie, the master had to release the servant and I'm the master—so I just started saying stuff, but I didn't think it would...and now..."

"And now I'm bleeding!" He shouted it with such glee that Dot began to laugh, then he began to laugh, waving his hand around, splattering blood onto the floor and counters.

"Raji, *you're bleeding*! A lot!" She ran to a drawer and found a dish towel, which she hurriedly pressed to his hand. "We've got to get you to a hospital!"

In the car, the joyful disbelief continued.

"Wish for something!" Raji demanded from the passenger seat.

"No! What if—"

"I gotta know for sure. Please."

"Okay, um...I wish for a unicorn bear!" She braced herself on the steering wheel, but nothing happened.

"They're just words!" he laughed. "They mean nothing to me! Lucky for you. Why would that be your test wish?"

At the emergency room, the excitement had still not ebbed. On the contrary, it had heightened some.

"What seems to be the problem?" the tired intake nurse asked.

"He cut his hand!" Dot bragged.

"How did the injury happen?"

"I wanted to see if I would bleed, and I did!" Raji cried, drawing attention from the other patrons. He proudly held up his hand, wrapped in the blood-soaked dish towel for everyone to see.

Dot accompanied him back to be stitched up after a nurse temporarily bandaged his wound. Then they were left alone in a room to wait for the doctor.

"Finally, we're alone," Raji said, sitting on the edge of the tissue-paper lined table. He grabbed Dot by the hand and pulled her between his legs, pressing his uninjured hand into the small of her back. Her breath hitched at his touch.

"I love you," he whispered. They were so close that his lips brushed hers lightly as he spoke. Electricity danced across her skin. "And if I had been thinking clearly, I would've done this before I sliced my hand open."

He pressed his lips to her. The charge heightened. She slid her hands into his hair, anchoring herself as he wrapped his good arm around her waist and drew her closer. Her nerves exploded with heat like the first time he had kissed her on the island, but this time the sensation lasted much, much longer.

Eventually, they broke to catch their breath. "Did that hurt?" she asked, still struggling to get her respiratory issues under control.

He gently tilted her head back with his bandaged hand, trailing kisses down her neck. "I've never felt better," he whispered against her skin.

She contemplated locking the door, but then the doctor came in before she had a chance.

It was past midnight by the time they stepped out of the hospital with Raji's hand stitched up and rebandaged. They stopped outside the door to share one more look of unbridled disbelief. Then Raji smiled and kissed her quickly before running out into a patch of grass near the parking lot, whooping and cheering into the night like a hyena.

She stopped at the edge of the grass and watched, amazed and humbled at what she was witnessing: Raji. *Free.*

"I'm FREE!" he cried.

"Shut up!" someone yelled from the parking lot. "You won't be hollerin' like that when you see the bill!"

"I assure you I will, sir!"

Dot turned to watch an old man on crutches shoot Raji a disgusted look.

"Raji, you've got to calm down," she said with a laugh. "People think you're insane."

He pointed at her with a sly grin. "I don't have to listen to you."

Apparently, he felt the need to prove his point. He ran at her and tackled her to the ground.

Pulling her on top of him, he settled his arms around her body. "I can't believe I never thought of it. *Of course* the servant can't release himself. I belong to *you.* All the power to release me lies with *you*...or it did, anyway."

"Well, I'm miffed," Dot complained. "Those jinn idiots lied to me. I had the power inside of me all along? Are you kidding? I feel so lame."

"This is not lame. *You* are not lame."

For a moment, he stared into her eyes. But though she couldn't stop smiling, her heart suddenly felt heavy.

She wanted this for him so badly, and now that he had it, wouldn't she just be holding him back? Wouldn't he still be a prisoner of sorts if she asked him to stay with her?

She brushed her fingers through his beard. Annoyingly but expectedly, more tears flooded her eyes.

"I don't want this to make you feel obligated to stay," she struggled to say. "You can be your own person now. And you should."

Raji's grin faded, but his eyes continued to sparkle.

"You're no longer my master," he said. "That's true. But I'm not leaving. I've been in and out of centuries and I finally found the time I want to stay in and the person I want to stay with. Dottie, none of this would have happened if I didn't want to be with *you*."

"Don't be ridiculous." The tears blurred her vision. "You've granted my wishes. You don't owe me anything else. You should live your own life. Make your own choices."

He lifted his injured hand and wiped a tear from her eye.

"I'm making a choice right now. I'm choosing you."

They were the words she hoped he'd say. It was exactly what she wanted, but she wasn't supposed to get what she wanted.

Of course, she realized now that she hadn't ever known what she wanted—what she really, *truly* wanted—until he came along and forced her to think about it. Now she knew without a doubt.

"You're my first wish. And my second. And my third," he whispered. "I'm attached."

His lips intercepted her massive sigh of relief.

They didn't leave that patch of grass until the sun started to rise, revealing the new day they had looked forward to months ago on the sand dunes. And they only went home because Raji was exhausted and starving, and he had to pee, all things they both got weirdly excited about.

At home, Dot watched over him as he slept, too anxious to sleep herself. With her track record, she worried he might age rapidly and explode into dust or that his ancient organs would suddenly fail. But his chest rose and fell rhythmically, and he remained as he was: a mortal man with a beautiful, free soul, taking his first real nap in twenty-seven hundred years.

Everything she could ever wish for.

Surprisingly high-pitched snoring notwithstanding.

Acknowledgements

Guys, writing a book is the easy part. Getting it to press takes a village. As much as I like to fantasize about being a reclusive writer in a cabin in the woods, I could never do this without the team of talented, supportive people who helped give my story life. If you have supported me in any capacity, this section is for you, even if you aren't mentioned by name.

First, it's the obvious one but also the most important. I believe in a God who loves all of us and wants to be involved in our lives, and I saw ample evidence that I was not doing this without His help. He was with me at every step. And it certainly required heavenly aid to keep me from tripping over my pile of insecurities.

The hardest first step for me had to be sending my early manuscript to my beta team (or alpha team, to be technical, which makes me imagine them busting into a space station with helmets and laser guns): Becky, Angela C., Angela G., Sydney, and Katey. The only reason why I hadn't attempted to publish in the thirty years I've been writing was because my crippling self-doubt made it so hard to share my work, but you ladies treated my baby with respect and care while being honest and direct. Thank you! Your input was paramount and your excitement urged me forward! I seriously love you guys so much.

Each member of my crack team of indie-author supporting pros was a complete godsend. Kourtney and Jessica, you are the editors of my dreams! You both took an unsure, nervous newbie and made me feel like I can do anything. I can't thank you enough. Sarah, I was so worried about being the boss when it came to deciding what my book should look like, but you are so talented and easy to work with I immediately felt like we were old friends. Now I get emotional every time I look at our cover!

I never would have taken the leap to publish if it wasn't for the authors and bookstagrammars who influenced me and offered me support. Breyanna Evans, Samantha Rose, Rachel Parker, and every author I met at the 2025 Charlotte Book Fair to name a few. And even though we haven't directly connected, Allie Lewis, author of *American Gauntlet*, had a single line in her bio that finally pushed me into action. I cannot *not* thank you.

Ginormous thanks to my adorably supportive husband and best friend for life, Harry, for comparing me to Brandon Sanderson un-ironically and inflating my ego enough to keep me moving forward (I sure do love you, man); our kids, Molly, George, Ruby, and Charlie who allowed me time to work, miraculously; my parents who cheered me on from Japan; my siblings and in-laws and cousins and aunts and uncles and Grandma who shared the general response of "it's about time!" instead of "really?" when they found out I was publishing a book, and that meant the world to me, actually.

The entire English department at Southern Virginia University from 2005-2008 definitely gets a shout-out. My writing improved significantly under the tutelage of these people who challenged me and inspired me and mentored me: Cluff, Dransfield, Card, and my creative writing professor, the GOAT, Karen Hufford. You told me I was good at this, and that I should keep doing it, and because I revere you so much, I did.

There are so many others I want to name but then I would bore you and you would skip the acknowledgements in my next novel which I would hate because these people deserve to have their names on this book as much as I do, if not more.

So finally, to my readers: thank you for taking a chance on me. I can't wait to give you another fun story to read!

About the author

Sara George has been writing since she could read and reading since before her long-term memory developed. She only attended one year of public school, and then became a weird, homeschooled kid, blissfully unaware of her weirdness until she got to college, though by then it was too late. She received her BA in English with a minor in Creative Writing from Southern Virginia University. People are her favorite, and she loves hearing personal stories from anyone who will offer them. She loves her home state of North Carolina where she lives with her husband Harry, their four kids, and their three cats.

Sign up for her newsletter!

Bonus content

Wish Wrecked: The Soundtrack

Apple

Spotify

www.ingramcontent.com/pod-product-compliance
Lightning Source LLC
Chambersburg PA
CBHW050011120726
47903CB00006B/1721